RED STAR RISING

ALSO IN **BRIAN FREEMANTLE'S
CHARLIE MUFFIN SERIES**

BRIAN FREEMANTLE

RED STAR RISING

THOMAS DUNNE BOOKS
ST. MARTIN'S PRESS ✵ NEW YORK

FIC
Freemant

This is a work of fiction. All of the characters, organizations, and events portrayed in this novel are either products of the author's imagination or are used fictitiously.

THOMAS DUNNE BOOKS.
An imprint of St. Martin's Press.

www.thomasdunnebooks.com
www.stmartins.com

Library of Congress Cataloging-in-Publication Data

Freemantle, Brian.
    Red star rising / Brian Freemantle.—1st ed.
            p. cm.
    ISBN 978-0-312-31553-5 (alk. paper)
   1. Muffin, Charlie (Fictitious character)—Fiction.   2. Intelligence
service—Fiction.   3. British—Russia—Fiction.   4. Moscow (Russia)—
Fiction.   I. Title.
    PR6056.R43R43 2010
    823'.914—dc22

                                                                    2009047573

First Edition: August 2010

10   9   8   7   6   5   4   3   2   1

For the real Paula-Jane.

And for DV, for whom there was
no named part but in thanks for his generosity
to Naomi House Children's Hospice.

You cannot have people assassinated on British soil and then discover that we wish to arrest someone who is in another country and not be in a position to do so.

> —British Prime Minister Gordon Brown, commenting on July 23, 2007, upon the refusal of then Russian Federation President Vladimir Putin to extradite former KGB agent, Andrei Lugovoy, for trial for the murder in London by radioactive polonium-210 poisoning of former KGB colleague, Alexander Litvinenko, November 23, 2006

★

They [Britain] are making proposals to change our constitution that are insulting for our nation and our people. It's their brains, not our constitution, which needs to be changed . . . they forget that Britain is no longer a colonial power and that Russia was never their colony.

> —Then Russian Federation President Vladimir Putin's rejection of the British extradition request for Andrei Lugovoy, July 25, 2007

★

The cynical murder of my son was a calculated act of intimidation. I have no doubt that he was killed by the FSB [successor to the KGB] and that the orders came from the former KGB spy, President Vladimir Putin. He was the only person who could have given that order. I haven't a shadow of doubt that this was done by Putin's men.

> —Walter Litvinenko, December 16, 2006

★

I will not rest until justice has been done.

> —Marina Litvinenko, widow of Alexander Litvinenko, May 23, 2007

RED STAR RISING

1

CHARLIE MUFFIN DECIDED IT WAS A TOSS-UP BETWEEN THE British embassy's third secretary or the Russian Foreign Ministry official who'd be the first to throw up or simply faint. Or messily do both, not necessarily in any order. Charlie didn't feel that good himself. It had been a busy, largely sleepless forty-eight hours since his emergency London assigning, and he'd never liked mortuaries anyway. The unease wasn't helped by a mortuary assistant four autopsy tables away, munching a meat-overflowing sandwich. The grayness of the sandwich filling matched the color of the surrounding corpses, including that of the man around whom they were grouped.

From the size of the entry wound in the base of the skull, Charlie calculated the bullet was from a Russian-manufactured 9mm Makarov, its tip cut into a dum-dum cross to flatten on initial impact in order to take away on exit the entire face, including both jawbones. The fingertips on the right hand had individually been burned away, either by acid or heat. The pathologist, a fat, dough-faced man who hadn't been introduced by name, declared the amputation of the left arm to have been a surgical operation, carried out several years earlier. "But not particularly well," he added, professionally critical. "A hurried job."

"It's obviously a gangland execution," announced the only Russian whose name Charlie knew so far. Sergei Romanovich Pavel had been identified as a senior investigator from Moscow's Organized Crime Bureau.

Charlie looked around the group, waiting for the question. When no one asked he said, "Why's it obvious?"

"It's a trademark killing, the way they always do it. Bullet in the back of the head, after the torture punishment for whatever he did wrong," lectured Pavel. "You are. . . . ?"

"London-based embassy security," said Charlie, wondering which of the men facing him across the metal slab was from the *Federal'naya Sluzhba Bezopasnosti,* or FSB, which replaced the internal directorate of the former KGB. The presence of the internal intelligence agency was inevitable after the finding of a murdered man in the garden of the British embassy; Charlie guessed it to be the thin, balding man holding back from any part in the stilted discussion.

The bespectacled, sparse-haired Pavel smiled, patronizingly. "There is, regrettably, a lot of organized crime in the city. We've come to recognize their methodology."

"He was very obviously tortured," endorsed the pudgy pathologist, pointing toward the murdered man's clothes bundled into a see-through plastic sack. "The jacket and shirt are clotted with blood. The bullet would have smashed most of the teeth, making an identification difficult from dental records. But I'd guess most of the teeth were pulled out while he was still alive, to cause that degree of blood loss. Probably a lot more was done to him, as well. They usually take the eyes out . . ." He went back to the body. "See the ligature bruising on the wrist, as well as his ankles and across the chest? That's where he would have thrashed in agony against whatever they restrained him with . . ."

It was the Russian Foreign Ministry man whose stomach erupted. The man managed to reach a deep-basined sink before being violently and repeatedly sick, groaning as he retched. Jeremy Dawkins, the embassy diplomat, looked determinedly away, his lips tightly clamped.

Charlie said: "Didn't you tell us at the beginning that all the labels and makers' marks have been removed from the clothes?"

"That's why they're bagged up. They're clearly Russian and I thought they'd be needed for forensic examination."

Turning back to Pavel, Charlie said, "Is that another gangland trademark? Removing all manufacturers' details from the clothing, as well as taking away the face and burning off the finger ends to prevent any identification?"

"They don't usually do that," conceded the Russian detective.

Going back to the medical examiner, Charlie said, "How do you think the fingertips were destroyed?"

"Forced over a flame or a hot plate," suggested the man. "Acid, possibly."

"Are any of the fingers broken?" persisted Charlie.

The pathologist frowned, needing to go back to his notes. "No, they weren't."

"So, we've got a body bruised by his binding from the thrashing agony of what was being done to him, but without the fingers being broken where he tried to keep his hand away from a flame or hot plate?" said Charlie. "Which would, by the way, have burned the torturers trying to hold the fingers over the heat."

"Yes," allowed the doctor.

"I don't think his fingers were held over anything hot," argued Charlie. "I think the tips were burned off by an acidlike agent; that's why the wrist is so marked, more deeply than anywhere else."

"Are you going to tell us the point of this cross-examination?" demanded Pavel.

"Looks to me as if a very determined effort was made to conceal who the man was," said Charlie.

"Which we will do our utmost to discover," promised the man whom Charlie guessed to be from the FSB.

"The body was found in the grounds of the British embassy," reminded Charlie. "Technically, the embassy and the grounds in which it is built is British, not Russian territory. This is a murder committed on British soil."

"I don't think we need to become distracted by diplomatic technicalities," broke in Dawkins.

"But if we are being technical, I am not entirely satisfied that the murder was committed *on* British soil," challenged the pathologist. "From my preliminary examination at the murder scene, I'd say the body was dumped in the grounds *after* the man was shot: there wasn't sufficient blood or physical debris around him. And if he were killed elsewhere it is a Russian investigation."

"Surely, until it actually becomes an investigation, it should be a joint operation?" pressed Charlie.

The ashen-faced ministry official came back into the group. He said, "I'm sorry . . . I've never been in a place like this before." To Charlie he said, "Every cooperation will be extended. It's a very unpleasant business. Your country's need to be involved is most regrettable."

Not regretted by me, thought Charlie. He smiled at the Russian detective. "I look forward to our working together. I presume you're based at Ulitsa Petrovka?"

Pavel frowned. "You know Moscow that well?"

Charlie felt a spurt of annoyance at his smart-assed mention of the location of the organized crime bureau headquarters. It gave them a pointer they didn't need to have and which he hadn't intended to give them. But if the thin-faced, balding man was FSB, then a background intelligence check was automatic. With no alternative, Charlie said, "I've served a posting here before."

"Which explains your excellent Russian," said the man, smilingly, whom Charlie suspected was FSB.

It didn't necessarily, but Charlie was anxious not to stray any further. "And why I was seconded here specifically to inquire into this murder," he said. He looked between Pavel and the medical examiner. "I'd welcome a full copy of your pathology report, including a skin residue analysis to establish if the fingers were burned by acid. And any forensic findings from the examination of the clothes. There'll be toxicology and stomach contents analyses, too, won't there?"

"Of course," said Pavel, tightly.

The pathologist nodded, but didn't speak.

★

"I don't think you handled that very well back there," complained Dawkins, in the car ride back to the embassy. He was a very tall, angularly featured man who found it difficult to keep his fair hair from flopping forward over his forehead. The public school accent was sharp enough to cut glass.

"How's that?" Charlie sighed. How was it he always seemed to get under people's noses, like a bad smell?

"Our government doesn't want the bodies of murdered Russians strewn around its embassy grounds."

"I didn't leave it there."

"Don't be fatuous!" protested the man, whom Charlie estimated to be at least twenty years his junior. "What I mean is that it would have been better to have gone along with what the man Pavel suggested: that it's a Russian murder of a Russian national and better left to their people to handle, distancing ourselves as quickly as possible."

"No it wouldn't," rejected Charlie, curtly. "I've been specifically seconded here to ensure the British government isn't sucked into an as-yet-unknown embarrassment or difficulty. And I'm not going to succeed in doing that by sitting on my ass, waiting for other people to tell me only what they want me to hear."

"What sort of difficulty could there possibly be, apart from his being found where he was?" demanded the younger man.

"You're assuming he's Russian because the clothes are Russian. What if he turns out to be British?"

"*What!*" Dawkins turned across the car in his alarm, swerving it out of the lane.

"Easy!" said Charlie, calmly. "I'm just floating a 'what if.' Trying to suggest why we've got to be involved from the inside, not kept outside."

"You certainly worked hard to ensure that," criticized the diplomat.

"How the hell could I talk to people without knowing their names and where, hopefully, to get hold of them?" asked Charlie, impatiently. He'd ended the mortuary encounter by insisting upon the identity and contact number of every Russian in the room, even the Foreign Ministry official. "You don't ask, you don't get—one of the truisms of life."

"I need to be kept fully informed of everything you do, everyone with whom you get involved," demanded Dawkins. "I want to be told everything you have in mind, well *before* you take any action. Those are the ambassador's orders: I'm your channel to him, at all times."

Bollocks, thought Charlie. "I know the rules."

"Why didn't you tell me you'd served here before?"

"I've scarcely had time to tell anyone anything. It was a long time ago." Five years wasn't that long, Charlie mentally corrected himself. Sasha would be eight now. Upon reflection he didn't have too much to worry about whatever checks Mikhail Guzov, the correctly guessed FSB officer, made about him through their internal intelligence records. He knew Natalia had sanitized both their files. It was even possible that his records wouldn't have been kept by the FSB. Hers would still exist because Natalia had been retained after the KGB changeover and was still a serving officer, although he didn't know in what division. They'd never talked about their separate intelligence functions, apart from their initial, professional encounter.

"How long were you here?"

"About four years," said Charlie, intentionally vague.

"A difficult time?"

"You know I can't give you any indication of my work. But I can tell you we certainly didn't find any dead bodies in the grounds."

"Sorry. I shouldn't have asked you." Dawkins retreated, embarrassed at showing his inexperience. "The current contingent, MI6 as well as MI5, want to meet you. I think they were surprised you didn't come to the embassy before going to the mortuary."

"My coming here specifically for this investigation was to distance them and the embassy," reminded Charlie. Which had been his accustomed and all-too-frequent role in a very varied espionage career, sparing others with more delicate hands the distaste of getting them dirtied.

"I don't think they appreciated that, any more than I did," said the diplomat. "And the housing officer also wants to see you."

"I'm sure he does," accepted Charlie, who had anticipated the confrontation. Dawkins had taken the long way round to reach the British embassy, driving now parallel to the Moskva River along Smolenskaya Naberezhnaya. Charlie gazed nostalgically out at the familiar, once happy surroundings. Before the building of the new embassy, he and Natalia had pushed Sasha along this bordering river embankment, after he'd managed the Moscow posting to return to marry her. They'd talked—perhaps fantasized was a better word—during those walks about their future together. Need it to have been such a fantasy? Not really, not even in those newly thawed days at the supposed end of the Cold War. All it would have needed was Natalia's acceptance that she'd have to leave Moscow and her beloved Russia, a compromise she'd never been able to make. Nor could he make the matching compromise himself. He'd believed his inevitable discovery as a British intelligence officer—even a *former* intelligence officer if he'd resigned, which he had been prepared to do—would have made his remaining there impossible. Certainly, Natalia would not have been allowed to continue in the KGB or its succeeding FSB.

"I don't think he's happy."

The louder-voiced repetition broke into Charlie's reverie. They were talking about the housing officer, he remembered. "I'll talk to him," he promised, welcoming the appearance of the four-towered embassy, although not the inevitable irritating confrontations. Bollocks to those, too.

"You've got all my numbers, including my home and mobile," said Dawkins, as they entered the building with its modern-art etchings dominating the reception area. "Don't forget what I told you about wanting to know everything you do *before* you do it."

"Indelibly engraved in my mind," assured Charlie, emptily.

★

The reception-desk security officer closely examined Charlie's ID, up to and including camera confirmation of his facial and eye characteristics, and insisted upon accompanying Charlie to the embassy intelligence section offices, despite Charlie's assurance that he knew the way.

"Everything's been tightened up," explained the guard.

"Bit late now, isn't it?" remarked Charlie.

"I've just got back from home leave," the man said, quickly evading the question. "I can't believe he climbed over the walls or the railings without setting off the sensors."

It always paid to pass the time of day with the lowest of the gossiping staff, reflected Charlie. "Neither can I, with or without sensors. He only had one arm."

"Ah!" exclaimed the man, with the intensity with which Charlie imagined St. Paul greeted the revelation on the road to Damascus. "It has to be the gates then, doesn't it? Makes sense now."

"How does it make sense now?" encouraged Charlie.

"The closed circuit television cameras have been playing up."

"What about gate guards?"

Again, with the military spontaneity of someone trained always to avoid any responsibility, the man said, "I'm internal, not external. Don't know anything about that. Or them."

And he already knew more than enough, Charlie accepted, as they reached the door to the intelligence *rezidentura*, for him to be passed on to another uniformed guard. Charlie went again through the ID ritual, including facial measurement and retina recognition before finally entering the inner sanctum.

"I've been waiting!" impatiently complained the woman on the other side of the door.

★

Paula-Jane Venables was a slight-bodied though full-busted woman, who wore her auburn hair short and who knew she looked good in designer clothes. The dress was blue, knee-length, and had the logo-identifying matching shoes. Charlie guessed there would be an ensemble-completing handbag somewhere in the river-fronting office into which she led him, but if there were, it was hidden away to maintain the dust-free neatness of the uncluttered office.

Charlie took what he recognized to be the victim's chair and sat back for the obviously intended inquisition. He crossed one leg over the other, to make it easier to lift the pressure on his left heel. The Hush Puppies were new, not yet broken in, and they pinched. She frowned at his doing it. It was too early to tell but she looked capable of pulling out fingernails, which prompted an immediate question. Had those on the right hand of the man back in the mortuary been intact? He'd forgotten to ask, and certainly to look, and he felt a surge of annoyance at the oversight that might have gone further to confirm the extent of any torture to which the man had been subjected.

"We need to get to know each other," Paula-Jane announced. "I want to get things straight between us from the start."

"That's always best," agreed Charlie, noting the peremptory tone.

There was an imperceptible tightening to her mouth at his close-to-mocking response. "There was clearly a change in your travel plans?"

Charlie frowned. "You've lost me already."

"London's alert was that you were arriving yesterday. I'm guessing that, instead, you flew in this morning and went straight to the mortuary, without having time to make contact with me here."

"No. I got here yesterday."

"But didn't bother to call or make personal contact before seeing the body?"

"Didn't London tell you in their message *why* I have been sent in?" asked Charlie, patiently.

"To minimize as much as possible any direct connection with the embassy," acknowledged the woman. "I'm the MI5 resident here: it's my territory. You can front it all, but I want to know everything that goes on. Understood?"

Charlie sighed. Instead of bothering to answer, he said, "Why don't you tell me what you know? Like where and how the body was found. By whom. And how you think it got there."

Paula-Jane hesitated, clearly undecided whether to dismiss his questions or to demand an answer to her own. Eventually she said, "It was found by one of the grounds staff—"

"A Russian?" Charlie interrupted at once, knowing the diplomatic agreement—and counterespionage nightmare—requiring local nationals to be employed as domestic support staff.

"Yes," answered Paula-Jane, shortly.

"Name?"

"Personnel will have it."

"So you haven't questioned him?"

"I was making arrangements to do so when London told me you were being assigned."

"Making arrangements!"

"The protocol is that in any criminal investigation involving a Russian national employed at the embassy, a Russian Foreign Ministry official has to be present."

"Did you go to the scene?"

"Yes."

"While the groundsman who found the body was still there?"

"Yes." Her face was beginning to redden with anger.

"And you didn't ask him anything!"

"I told you . . ."

". . . about the unbreachable protocol," finished Charlie, angry himself and intentionally mocking.

"I was told to obey the rules."

What was the benefit of pissing into the wind? Charlie asked himself, resigned. "You saw the scene?"

"Yes."

"Was he on his back or his front?"

"His front."

The answer was vital to keeping him on the investigation, and she wasn't sure, Charlie guessed. If the Russians found a half unarguable reason or excuse to shoulder him aside—or if he fucked up—the personal repercussions in London would be far more serious than here in Moscow. Charlie knew he was on the weaker side of the power struggle being waged between Aubrey Smith, the ascetic, quiet-voiced man who had championed him since his unexpected appointment from Cambridge University don to Director-General and his passed-over and resentful deputy, Jeffrey Smale. Who hated his guts, like so many in a department in which for far too long—apart from rare respites like that which he'd initially enjoyed under Smith—Charlie had clung by his fingertips. Which would be destroyed like those of this murder victim, if he screwed this assignment up.

"I don't think we're getting off to a particularly good start and I know you think the same," Charlie said. "So let's, as you suggested at the beginning, understand each other. I'm going to work this job entirely alone, keeping you well away from any involvement and any possible risk to the career you've just begun. But here, with just the two of us in the room, I want everything you can give me. Which is why this question is very important. Are you absolutely sure that the murdered man was lying face down on his front? I know he didn't have a face . . . not much of a head left at all . . . but front's very different from back. So which was it?"

"He was definitely lying on his front," said Paula-Jane, formally.

"Whereabouts, precisely, in the grounds?"

"Quite close to the conference hall. There's a grassed verge, with flower beds beyond. The body was mostly on the grass, with what was left of the head and his shoulders protruding over onto the flower bed."

"How closely did you look?"

"It was disgusting!"

Charlie sighed again. "So you can't tell me how much blood loss or facial debris there was?"

"Why's it so important to know that?" she demanded, truculently.

"If there was a lot of blood and skin and bone debris, it would indicate he was shot where he was found. If there wasn't, it indicates he was shot elsewhere and dumped. If he was dumped, the Russians have a reason to keep me at arm's length or to exclude me altogether."

"My recollection is that there was a lot of blood around." The belligerence was receding.

"Did you stay for the forensic and medical examinations at the scene?"

"Most of it."

Charlie avoided another sigh of frustration. "Tell me about it. In as much detail as possible."

Paula-Jane hesitated, assembling her recollections. "External security was there first, obviously. When I got there, summoned as an afterthought I think, I was told the Moscow authorities had already been called and were on their way—"

"Which authorities?" broke in Charlie.

"I wasn't told. You'll have to ask Reg Stout. He's in charge of both internal and external security. There were a lot of people around—"

"How close to the body?"

"Stout's people were very close, like right next to it. Stout told the rest of us to stay back. When the Russians arrived, they told Stout and his men to move back. A man I assumed to be the forensic pathologist spent about twenty minutes examining the body before it was put into a body bag and then into an ambulance. The police—I assumed they were police, although not all of them wore uniforms—looked around, spoke to Dawkins, and then left."

"Why Dawkins?" asked Charlie. And why hadn't the bloody man told him about being at the scene on their way back from the mortuary?

"He's responsible for embassy administration."

"What about the ambassador? Wasn't he in any way involved?"

"He came out when the Russians first arrived and spoke to Dawkins. He left as the body was being removed."

"Did he talk to any of the Russians?"

"Not that I saw. And I'm sure I was there all the time that the ambassador was."

"Did the Russians take soil samples from where the head and shoulders lay?"

There was another hesitation. "I'm not sure. I think so."

Shit, thought Charlie, concerned about the amount of blood residue. "What about photographs?"

"They certainly took photographs. A lot, it seemed to me. I . . ." she started, but stopped as the phone rang. She answered it. "He's here with me," she said, offering the receiver to Charlie. "It's Howard Barrett, the housing and facilities officer."

"I've been waiting since you came back from the mortuary to arrange your accommodation." It was another glass-cutting accent.

"I'm staying at the Savoy."

"I am responsible for the housing of embassy personnel. Which makes me also responsible for the applicable budget. The Savoy is not on the permitted list of outside accommodation. If you insist on living outside, we must consult that list and rehouse you."

"Howard, you will not be required to pay whatever bills I incur at the Savoy so your budget is not endangered. We're not going to consult any list or have any sort of discussion about anything."

"I have not received any authorization from London, which is necessary under the regulations."

Just as there was a regulation forbidding the questioning of the man who found the body of a murder victim, thought Charlie. "You want London's approval, you go ahead and ask for it."

"You go out of your way to upset people?" asked Paula-Jane, when Charlie put down the receiver.

"Always seems to happen, no matter how hard I try to avoid it." He'd been out of the field for too long and had forgotten the bureaucratic madrigal of embassy existence, Charlie recognized. It wasn't going to help him.

2

CHARLIE MUFFIN HAD TAKEN HIS TIME, AS HE ALWAYS DID, checking the intruder trap in his hotel room—ensuring that the drawers he'd left slightly protruding hadn't been pushed closed after a search and that their specially arranged contents were as he'd left them and that flaps pushed into pockets hadn't been correctly replaced outside—satisfied after almost an hour that no one had entered. Now he sat hunched at the corner stool of the bar, his back instinctively protected by its abutting wall, wishing that the vodka glass into which he was gazing was a crystal ball to tell him the last time an assignment had begun as badly as this one. He certainly couldn't remember. Which made it a wise move to have concluded the encounter with Paula-Jane with so many initial questions unanswered and leave the embassy, needing to clear his head and to calculate just how many mistakes had already been made. Or had been allowed to be made. He really had forgotten the head-in-the-sand mentality of embassy life.

Had too much already been avoided or ignored for him to pick up all the dropped pieces? Charlie wondered. He couldn't allow there to be, came the immediate determination. The poor faceless, one-armed bastard hadn't survived but Charlie had to, as he'd always survived. But this time could be difficult. He'd never known the department so positively divided as it had been by Aubrey Smith's promotion over Jeffrey Smale, nor for that division to be so marked by Smith's consistent operational failures against the litany of successes controlled by his deputy. What Charlie did know was that on this assignment he was very definitely between two warring men, with Aubrey Smith seeing it as his positive last chance and Jeffrey Smale regarding it as the potential coup de grâce in the fight to the promotional death. Which was why, with bizarre irony, both men had for the first time ever been in perfect accord that he got the Moscow assignment. Which, even more bizarrely, Charlie welcomed despite its close-to-overwhelming risks. Now that he didn't have Natalia or Sasha any longer, the job was all he had left and to keep it, he'd do anything just short of dipping someone else's fingers into any available acid bath.

How did that crush-anyone-in-any-way determination square with the placid acceptance that he didn't have Natalia and Sasha anymore? Charlie asked himself. They weren't together anymore, as a family anymore, because he hadn't sufficiently persuaded Natalia. And hadn't been in Moscow to be able to. But now he *was* in Moscow. Could he contemplate that distraction from a job so professionally vital and try to convince Natalia that they could still have a life together? Of course he could. It would be ridiculous, his being in the same city as her and their daughter, for him *not* to make contact and for him to try, yet again, to convince her how perfect everything could be if only she'd come to live in London.

The simple way to do it was to prioritize, Charlie reasoned. The job first then. Which meant going back to the mortuary and pathologist Vladimir Ivanov, to resolve the uncertainties that had occurred to him since this morning. And to the embassy, to finish the conversation with Paula-Jane Venables and get from Jeremy Dawkins his comparable account of the murder scene. Reg Stout's, too, to find out the problem with the embassy gates' CCTV, as well as the identity of—and hopefully to interview—the so-far unnamed Russian groundsman who'd discovered the body. Which Charlie supposed would now have to be in the restrictive presence of the diplomatically required Russian Foreign Ministry official. And then there was Sergei Romanovich Pavel. It wasn't going to be easy to establish a working relationship with the organized crime detective who'd worn the resentment of Charlie's involvement like a lapel badge. He had to do his best to build bridges there, because Pavel represented either the pathway or the barrier between him and any official forensic findings. Which left Mikhail Guzov, the watchful FSB observer, about whom Charlie had the greatest uncertainty.

A lot of people, none of whom appeared either friendly or helpful. He'd left off his priorities list the most important participant of all so far, Charlie abruptly reminded himself: a faceless, one-armed man. How difficult was it going to be to learn the story he wasn't able to tell?

"I'd hoped I'd find you here," said a voice, in English.

★

David Halliday was an overweight, soft-bodied man whose gray-flecked hair was greased so tightly to his head it appeared to have been painted on rather than combed. The tie was vaguely regimental and didn't really go with the sort of single-breasted blue suit mass-produced for door-to-door salesmen the world over. He even carried an order-taking pen in his breast pocket. Charlie admired the determined anonymity, and wondered what else the man might do to establish his professionalism.

"You want a drink?" invited Charlie, to illustrate his own professionalism, by knowing at once who the man was from the photographs of embassy personnel, although it officially listed Halliday as a financial officer, not the MI6 resident.

"Better stay with what I'm already on," accepted the man, nodding unnecessarily behind the bar to the whiskey that Charlie had already detected upon the man's breath. "It isn't really Famous Grouse but it's not a bad fake." The head movement turned to one of approval at Charlie's bar command that got his vodka replenished at the same time as the counterfeit scotch was poured. Halliday said: "Thought you were a whiskey man, too?"

"Only when it's real." The mental arm wrestling was beginning.

"Islay single malt, isn't it?"

"You've done your homework."

"It's still logged as a special order in the embassy's commissary book from the time of your permanent posting here."

That really was professional, Charlie acknowledged, knowing the man would have trawled London records, too. "I dropped by today, but you weren't there."

"What do you think of our P-J?"

"What?" asked Charlie, frowning.

"Paula-Jane. That's how she's known at the embassy. She told me you'd tried to make contact. Feisty little thing, isn't she?"

"Why does she insist on that double-barreled name?" said Charlie, avoiding a personality discussion this early, but content for the other man to gossip about whatever or whoever he wanted, eager for all the inside help he could get about the embassy.

"Father was American; met her mother when he worked in the same trade at the U.S. embassy in London."

An offering of sorts, accepted Charlie. "FBI or CIA?"

"CIA."

"What's Paula-Jane doing working for us if she's American?"

"She isn't," corrected Halliday. "Had the choice between American or British nationality when she reached eighteen. Took her mother's side in the divorce to be British but compensated by taking Dad's profession. Ambitious as hell. Wants to follow the already established precedents and put that cute little ass in the Director-General's chair at Thames House."

The opening lit up like a beacon. "Didn't get the impression she did so well with my one-armed man."

Halliday gestured hopefully to the bartender, grateful at the response that kept him level with Charlie. "Difficult one for her. If you want to climb the slippery pole, you go by the book and don't get involved in anything attracting the publicity that this episode is getting."

"What book do you go by?" asked Charlie.

"Self-preservation," replied the other man, at once. "I've got ten years to go and certainly don't intend fucking up an unblemished, pension-assured record by getting caught up in the sort of shit *you've* got to wade through. You're welcome, old boy, with my deepest sympathy."

"Did you see the body?"

"For as long as it took me to decide I didn't want to know what was happening. I suddenly remembered an important meeting with a contact that took precedence."

Seizing the opportunity, Charlie encapsulated Paula-Jane's recollections, which Halliday considered before saying, "That's about it."

Marking Halliday as a useful insider to cultivate while not forgetting the man was in turn doing his best to cultivate him, Charlie said, "What's the problem with the gate security?"

"Reg Stout's the problem. All mouth and trousers, and Dawkins let's himself be bullied. The CCTV has been playing up for days, weeks even, and hasn't been fixed properly."

His priorities for the following day began to arrange themselves in Charlie's mind. "I won't involve you, of course, but I'd appreciate a sounding board to bounce things off, as they come up."

"I know a few quiet bars," accepted Halliday.

"It's quite a while since I was here," further enticed Charlie. "I'd also appreciate a steer if you think I might be going in the wrong direction."

"Guaranteed," assured the other man. "And that's official. You heard of our director, Gerald Monsford?"

"Not a lot."

"Wants to rule the world, which is fine if you're one of his soldiers. He's told me to offer you all the help you might need. If your dead man hadn't been found inside the embassy grounds, British territory, it would be an MI6 case."

"I'll remember that," promised Charlie, politely. "At the moment it'll stay MI5."

Unexpectedly, Halliday said, "Aha! Here's your first steer!" and gestured toward the mute television picture in the corner behind the bar.

The sequence, which Charlie guessed to be the lead item on the main evening news, showed a smiling, immaculately dressed man of about forty-five. A stunningly attractive, couture-clad woman was at his side, both arms aloft in acceptance of an obviously rapturous reception from a rally audience.

"Stepan Grigorevich Lvov, with his totem wife, Marina," identified Halliday. "The next president of Russia, the only subject of conversation at the embassy before your body was found. And one they're anxious to get back to as soon as possible."

"Already getting newspaper space back in England," recognized Charlie. "With a woman like that beside him I'm surprised there haven't been pictures as well."

"There'll be a lot when he gets elected," predicted Halliday. "Interesting similarities between him and Vladimir Putin, but without the baggage Putin's accumulated. Former KGB, like Putin, until he quit, once attached to the same divisional headquarters as Putin in St. Petersburg."

"Caused you some work, I guess?" anticipated Charlie, happy for the conversation to drift after gaining as much as he had.

"Haven't managed much of a file, for all the obvious reasons," admitted Halliday. "But there's a contrast between the two. Putin's taking Russia back into the dark ages, with KGB-style assassinations and using the gas and oil supply as a weapon against Europe. Lvov's promising to free everything up again, which makes him flavor-of-the-month in the EU as well as in the U.S. of A."

"There was also a lot of speculation that Putin got the presidency with dirty money and heavy criminal, as well as ex-KGB personnel, support. How's that match with Lvov?"

Halliday shook his head. "The word is that our new boy is squeaky clean. . . ." He smiled. "Or as squeaky clean as a politician can be."

★

Reg Stout's office overlooked the river and was about three times the size of the temporary accommodation allocated to Charlie. Stout wasn't wearing the ribbon-bedecked uniform that Charlie had half expected but the tie was that of the Royal Engineers; the office was virtually wallpapered with military photographs of parades and regimental dinners and reunions—all of which prominently featured Stout, usually in the front befitting his rank of major. He was a loud-voiced, florid-faced, burly man who frowned in dismay at Charlie's haystack dishevelment. It was obviously difficult for the man, whose pinstriped suit was razor creased, to address Charlie as "sir," but he did.

"I'm looking to you for a lot of help," opened Charlie. Which so far he very definitely wasn't getting and about which he was thoroughly pissed off. The rabbit hutch that had been allocated to him that morning was obviously the housing officer's idea of revenge, compounded by the waiting message from Jeremy Dawkins on the card-table desk to make contact before attempting any meetings with embassy staff.

"Sir!" barked the man.

"I'd like, firstly, the full report you'll have obviously prepared."

"It's with Mr. Dawkins, sir."

"You don't have a copy?" Charlie sighed.

"It's my understanding it has to come through Mr. Dawkins, sir."

"Reg," set out Charlie. "I've been sent, specially, all the way from London to investigate a murder that is probably the biggest security situation you're ever going to become involved in. I know embassies are governed by rules and that you've got to conform to them. But I just told you I need your help, and I'm sure you don't want my having to complain to the third secretary or to London that I'm being obstructed in what I've come here to sort out. So here's what we'll do. I'll tell you what I want, and you decide whether we're going to communicate like adults or whether you've got to communicate all the time through Dawkins. I want your report. I want to see the photographs I'm confident you took, before the Russians arrived. I want to know why you summoned the Russians as quickly as you did. I want you to tell me why you let your people trample all over the scene, probably destroying forensic evidence, and why you let whoever did it fill in the hole that was left after the Russians apparently dug out all the earth into which the blood and facial debris soaked, from where the body lay. I want to talk to you in the minutest possible detail, irrespective of whatever's in your report, about everything that you did before the arrival of the Russian investigators. I want to know the name of the Russian groundsman who found the body and, in the most specific detail, hear everything—and I really mean *everything*—that he told you, before I talk to him myself. I want to know what went so consistently wrong with the CCTV security cameras—and why it continued going wrong—up to and including the night the body got where it was found. And why and how a man, with his intended killers, got into embassy grounds that you and your staff are supposed to keep clear of any unauthorized intrusion. And when I've got all that, I'll probably want to do it all over again because the first time I won't get half, even a quarter, of what I want. And in passing, it's not necessary for you to call me sir. Charlie's fine. You keeping up with me so far, Reg . . . ?"

There was no immediate reply and Charlie thought he could almost see reflected in the transfixed eyes the slow-moving cogs in the man's brain. Finally Stout managed, "I thought Mr. Dawkins was handling it all?"

"He isn't," corrected Charlie. "I am."

"I think I should talk to Mr. Dawkins."

"We'll both talk to Mr. Dawkins," insisted the exasperated Charlie. And it was still only just after ten thirty.

3

CHARLIE DIDN'T BELIEVE THAT RAINBOWS ALWAYS FOL-
lowed rain or that every cloud that brought the downpour had
a silver lining, so his satisfaction at London's insistence on un-
fettered, unimpeded assistance within the embassy was muted.
Appealing both to Aubrey Smith and the Foreign Office had been
the very last resort he'd had no alternative but to take against
Dawkins's obdurate determination to be the hands-on controller
of every move Charlie made. Sure that the housing officer would
have already complained as well, his demand for a liaison ruling
racked up two petty but officially recorded disputes in the space of
twenty-four hours and Charlie feared Smith's irritable reaction—
"What about the real problem you're there to sort out?"—was a
reaction to the internal pressure in London and not a belief that
he needed a bigger boy's hand to hold, which was the very last
impression Charlie either needed or wanted. There was something else he didn't need or want, either: the foot-aching twinge
Charlie never ignored as a warning, that even at this early stage
there was something he'd missed or hadn't realized, which for
once he hoped was not its usual talisman but merely the tightness of new Hush Puppies.

"Having wasted the entire morning, are we finally ready to
begin?" Charlie asked the head of security.

"Sir!" replied Stout, the parade-ground loudness less belligerent than before. From a desk drawer, the man extracted a file and said, "My report, sir!"

As he accepted the dossier Charlie said, "For Christ's sake, cut out the 'sir' crap, will you? What time were you told about the body?"

"Eight thirty-three exactly, as I say in my report. . . ." He just stopped himself.

"I want to hear your account, as well as read it. Who told you?"

"The man in charge of the gardening detail. He called me, here in the office."

"A Russian?"

"Yes. He told me one of his workers had found a body; that it didn't have a face."

"What's the name of the man who actually found it?"

"Maksimov. Boris Maksimov."

Charlie nodded to the telephone on Stout's desk. "Can you arrange for me to speak to Maksimov, as well as the Russian in charge?"

"I'm afraid you can't. Not speak to either of them, I mean."

"What's the problem now?" demanded Charlie, the exasperation returning.

"Neither is here, at the embassy. One of the Russians who came when I raised the alarm told me to put both of them on extended leave, to help the organized crime bureau."

"Colonel Pavel told you to do that?"

"I don't know his name."

Charlie had to swallow hard before he could continue. "You've got their home addresses?"

"The Russian staffs are supplied by the Foreign Ministry."

To which they were supplied by the FSB, as they had been before the renaming of the KGB and before that by the MVD-MGB and before that by the NKGB-NKVD, Charlie knew. Nothing had changed except the titles. And everyone in the West imagining that espionage had been swept away in the flood of the Cold War thaw, worried instead about Islamic terrorism. "You spoke to Maksimov?"

"Briefly. He spoke hardly any English, I speak hardly any Russian."

Charlie knew—every intelligence professional knew—that local Russian support staff spoke more than adequate English, which was why they were there, to listen and read everything they could. "Don't leave out a single word, tell me everything you saw and talked about and heard."

"It really was very brief. He'd started work at eight that morning, he told me. His job was to weed the flower beds around the conference hall. He said he saw the body the moment he finished the first bed and came around the corner to continue on the next section. He thought it was someone asleep or drunk until he got close enough to see what it really was, that it was a dead man. He ran to get his supervisor. He said he hadn't done it."

"He said what?"

" 'I didn't do it. He was like that when I found him.' That was the last thing Maksimov said to me."

"Who was there ahead of you at the scene?"

"Demin, the Russian team leader, and Maksimov."

"None of your security people?"

"No."

"Had the two Russians touched anything?"

"They told me they hadn't; that they were too scared."

From the hesitation before the reply, Charlie guessed Stout hadn't asked either Russian about touching the body. "Tell me, in every detail, what you found."

The hesitation now was for recall, and the account was punctuated by pauses when the man finally began to speak. Charlie, who was well aware of the psychological peculiarity that few witnesses to dramatic events had the same recollection, was caught by the similarity in Stout's account to that of Paula-Jane Venables.

"Did you touch the body?" picked up Charlie.

"No!" insisted the man, at once. "I didn't go through any of his pockets."

"That wasn't the question," persisted Charlie. "Did you touch it? If the clothes were wet, it would give us an indication of how long it had been there, before or after dew might have fallen."

"I didn't touch it," repeated the man. "His jacket looked as if it might be damp."

"How much blood was there?"

"A lot, from what I could see."

"Soaked into the ground?"

"Yes."

Charlie thought that Stout was telling him what the man imagined he wanted to hear. "After the body was removed, the Russians—a forensic examiner—dug up the soil where what remained of the head had been, didn't he?"

"Yes."

"How big, wide as well as deep, was the hole?"

"I don't know." Stout frowned. "Why's that important?"

"The size might have given an indication of how much blood there was, which in turn might have told us whether he was shot there or somewhere else. How deep it was might have suggested whether the bullet was found."

"There was no sign of a bullet being found. It was a deep hole, maybe two foot round."

Again what the man thought he wanted to hear, decided Charlie. "The forensic people took photographs?"

"I think so," said Stout, immediately correcting himself. "Yes, yes, of course they did."

"Didn't you take photographs?"

"By then Mr. Dawkins had arrived. He told me it was a Russian investigation and that we should leave everything to them."

Now it was Charlie who hesitated, unsure if there was anything to be gained from questioning any further. He wouldn't know unless he tried, he reminded himself. "Tell me about nighttime security."

"The gatehouse is staffed. Two men."

"What about ground patrols?"

Stout shifted, uncomfortably. "No."

"There used to be," Charlie remembered.

"There hasn't been, not for a long time."

"London's decision? Or local?"

"I was told by Mr. Dawkins." As if in sudden recollection, Stout added, "There are ground sensors now! And CCTV."

"Which, according to what I've heard, don't work?"

Stout's face clouded at Charlie's awareness. "There have been some technical problems recently."

"Like what?"

"Some of the cameras have blanked out."

Could it possibly be? wondered Charlie. It should have been inconceivable. "These cameras that blanked out? Would they have covered the area where the body was found?"

There was a pause before Stout's reply. "Not all of them."

"Reg! Stop fucking about and answer the question!"

The man swallowed, a sheen of perspiration pricking out on his face. "Two of them do."

"The two covering where the body was found? And the area between there and the gatehouse?" easily predicted Charlie.

The man nodded but didn't speak.

"Were they out the night the body got to where it was found?"

"Yes. But it was happening for several days before the body was found."

Of course it was, thought Charlie, although with the mentality here it hadn't really been necessary to make it appear accidental. "Why weren't they fixed?"

"They were. Electricians were called in and the cameras were okay for a day. Then they crashed again."

"Technical electricians from London?"

"They're due in the next day or two," said the man.

Charlie's pause this time was one of total, incredulous disbelief. Spacing his words when he did speak, he said: "Who was brought in to do the repairs that failed?"

"It wasn't considered a difficult job, technically."

"Answer the question," insisted Charlie, his voice still hollowed in despair.

"A Russian contractor, recommended by the Foreign Ministry," finally admitted the security manager.

"Were there two men on duty in the gatehouse the night the body got into the grounds?"

"Yes."

"British?" The answer should have been obvious but Charlie had given up on anything being as it should have been.

"Yes. Hoskins and Jameson."

Charlie nodded toward the desk telephone again. "I want to see them"—he looked at his watch—"in half an hour's time. You got a spare room?" There wasn't space for more than one other person in his contemptuously allocated office.

"No."

"Here then."

While Stout telephoned around the embassy to locate the two men, who were that week on day duty, Charlie sat, head bowed, anger burning through him. This was an out-and-out, all-time fucking nightmare of incompetence and ineptitude on an unimaginable scale demanding an internal investigation quite separate from that to which he had been assigned. But not yet, came the immediate halt, for several reasons, the least of which was escalating any hand-holding impressions in London. Feeling again the warning twinge in his left foot, Charlie reminded himself that nothing that had already occurred could be undone or rectified. Better to leave everything as it was but use it to his benefit.

"They'll be here at a quarter to," promised Stout, replacing the telephone.

"What was the duty period of these two men, Hoskins and Jameson?" resumed Charlie.

"Twenty-two hundred to six hundred."

"No break?"

"One spells the other for half an hour, working it out between them. Not a lot to do except be there at that time of night."

"What was in their log for that night?"

"I don't remember."

"You don't remember the log of the night a murdered man was found in the embassy grounds, the security of which you're responsible!"

"It's *because* of that I don't remember anything else!"

"What about noise?"

"Noise?"

"A gunshot sufficient to blow off a man's face would have made quite a noise, wouldn't you think?"

"I wasn't told about any unusual noise," insisted the man. He finally took out a handkerchief to wipe his sweat-shined face.

"You still have the log?"

"We should have."

"Should have!"

"There's a loose-paged filing system. It'll be there."

"While I'm talking to your two night-duty men, I'd like you to find that particular log reference. And all the others in which the faulty CCTVs are recorded and individually identified. They *are* individually identified, aren't they?"

"Yes."

Uncertainty echoed in the man's voice and Charlie decided that when he did blow the whistle, he'd recommend the sweating Reg Stout undergo interrogation to determine whether the man might have been suborned and actually *be* a security risk. The contradiction against his being so was that Stout was blatantly too stupid. The caveat to that dismissal came just as quickly. Unless, that is, Stout was the eminently qualified buffoon to conceal the person reducing the embassy to a security farce. That led inevitably to the question overhanging all others: What the fuck was going on?

★

Both William Hoskins and Paul Jameson wore campaign ribbons. Both had the backbones of career soldiers and Charlie abandoned any resistance to the word "sir" as verbal punctuation. They told him that because of their blank CCTV screens they'd taken turns to make short patrol walks, although not as far as where the body was found. For just two men to maintain any sort of proper security was virtually impossible without closed circuit television, particularly when the majority of the embassy's outside illumination went off at midnight. There were no automatically triggered movement or body-heat activated burglar lights. Ground sensors sounded an audible alarm by tread or passing movement, with no visual screen display. There had been nothing on the night of the body discovery that sounded like a pistol or automatic weapon report.

"Which we would certainly have recognized," offered Hoskins, the plumper of the two ex-soldiers.

"Even below the rest of the noise that there was that night," added the mustached Jameson.

"Below what noise that night?" quoted back Charlie.

Hoskins shrugged, dismissively. "There was a lot of noise around midnight. An altercation among a birthday party group, something like that, farther along the embankment."

Charlie let the despairing frustration pass. "How much farther along the embankment?"

There was another dismissive shrug. "A hundred, hundred and fifty yards. Quite close to the pontoon. A bunch of guys trying to throw someone in the river."

"How do you know it was something like a birthday party and that someone was being threatened with being thrown into the river?" asked Charlie, sure he already knew the answer.

The two men looked at each other. "We went along to check it out; make sure it wasn't going to be a problem that might involve the embassy," said Jameson. "That's our job, making sure the embassy doesn't get caught up in any trouble."

"Yes." Charlie sighed, as Stout reentered the room. "That's what your job is."

"I don't understand it," complained Stout, intruding into the meeting.

"Let me guess," offered Charlie, wearily. "The log for the night of the murder isn't in the file where it should be?"

Stout nodded, in agreement. "There are some other days that are missing, too."

"Nights and days when the CCTV didn't work?" suggested Charlie.

"How did you know?"

"It's a knack I have," said Charlie.

His meeting with the two nighttime guards over, Charlie insisted on being taken to the electrical control box governing the embassy's CCTV cameras, his stomach lurching at the immediate discovery of at least twenty other control terminals forming part of the same bank.

"The Russian electricians had access to this box?"

"Of course. They had to have."

"For how long?"

"An hour. Maybe a little longer."

"Who was here, monitoring them?"

"I was," replied Stout, his voice lifting at being able at last to respond positively.

"Here, all the time?"

Stout gave another of his now familiar hesitations. "Apart from the times I went with the other Russian to check the CCTV screens, to confirm that they were operating normally again."

"Leaving the other man working on the terminals here all by himself?"

"I couldn't split myself in half to be in two places at the same time, could I?"

"No, I don't suppose you could," agreed Charlie.

4

CHARLIE'S ESCAPE FROM HIS SCOURGING FRUSTRATION AT the embassy security debacle was to immerse himself and his every thought on Natalia and Sasha. And the more he did, the more his confidence grew that his return to Moscow presented him with an opportunity to salvage a relationship he'd never imagined possible to save. And that there was no reason why he shouldn't make every attempt and effort to do just that. Their relationship hadn't collapsed. At its worse assessment, it had been interrupted. They certainly weren't enemies. If anything, on his part at least, his feelings for Natalia had grown from their being apart. They corresponded regularly, sometimes more than once a month. Natalia kept up a steady supply of photographs of their daughter, and when he'd eventually, although reluctantly, accepted that Natalia wouldn't join him in London, he'd put all the necessary bank arrangements in place to provide monthly maintenance, never missing a payment although occasionally leaving himself strapped for money. At the beginning of their odd separation there had been telephone calls, but they had gradually lessened; the last had to be four months earlier and on that occasion Charlie had imagined—and hoped it had only been imagination—that there was a coolness from Natalia. Never, in any of the letters or any of the telephone conversations, had there been any mention of divorce.

He had to plan the approach very carefully, though: warn her he was here, in Moscow, and leave any actual meeting to be on her terms and at her convenience. A phone call would be too abrupt and unexpected, even though Natalia would understand the short notice with which he'd been dispatched, despite their never discussing their respective intelligence work.

A brief letter then, dismissing the reason for his being here as business, giving the hotel as his contact address. He'd leave it to Natalia to decide if Sasha should be included in the initial meeting: paramount in both their thinking had always been to minimize as much as possible any disruptive effect upon Sasha by their living apart. Charlie hoped the stories he had heard about some Russian stores and shops bringing themselves up to European quality and choice were true, although he didn't have the remotest idea what a child of eight would appreciate as a fitting present from a suddenly appearing father. He should buy a gift for Natalia, as well. Something else that wouldn't be easy. Natalia always protested he was too extravagant in his present-buying for both of them.

His decision made, Charlie missed breakfast to write his note on hotel letter-head paper, scrapping two attempts before he was satisfied, in no hurry to get to Smolenskaya Naberezhaya, unsure whether to go to the embassy at all until after contact was established with Sergei Pavel and pathologist Vladimir Ivanov. The decision was made for him when there was no response from Pavel's Petrovka phone.

Halliday was at the embassy when Charlie arrived. Paula-Jane wasn't. Nodding to her office, Charlie said, "She seems a very busy girl."

Halliday grinned. "And a very popular one, particularly with our American cousins. I've got the most recent newspapers, including the British. The speculation about your murder ranges from the Russian preference for the man being the victim of a gangland contract killing, through to the elimination by pursuing Russian police or intelligence agents of an intended traitor at his moment of defection, finally to the man being an Islamic suicide bomber shot by British security officers seconds before detonating his explosives. Three London newspapers appeared to have flown reporters specifically to Moscow to cover the story."

"Thanks for keeping them. I'll read them later."

"And the world media have finally discovered the about-to-be new First Lady," continued Halliday. "The beautiful Marina Lvov is all over the newspapers."

"I'll stick with the murder coverage."

"On the subject of which, you going to fill me in now or wait for P-J?"

"What?" Charlie frowned.

"The press conference." Halliday frowned back. "I didn't know there was going to be one until I bumped into Dawkins first thing this morning."

"And I still don't know anything about it," said Charlie.

"You're not involved?"

"No," said Charlie.

"And here comes P-J," said Halliday, looking farther down the corridor along which the woman was hurrying toward them, raising her hand in greeting as she got close to Halliday's open office door.

"When I couldn't reach you by telephone, I went to the Savoy to find you; messages never get through," she announced, breathlessly. "You all set?"

"I think I'm close to being set *up*," qualified Charlie. "Who asked you to find me . . . bring me here?"

"Dawkins," replied Paula-Jane. "The embassy's being overwhelmed by media approaches. The ambassador has decided upon a press conference, so you've got to be there. It's scheduled for eleven."

It was ten forty, Charlie saw. "There's obviously an internal e-mail direct to the ambassador, from the communications room?"

Paula-Jane gave an uncertain laugh. "What's happening here?"

"Nonsense is what's happening here," replied Charlie. "If Dawkins gets in touch with you again, tell him the press conference is canceled, and that I want to see him one hour from now."

It was the same communications officer in charge as the

previous day, so there was no identification delay. Charlie began his e-mail to the ambassador, insisting a press conference would further sensationalize an already oversensationalized media situation. For it to have been held would unquestionably destroy any possibility of a successful investigation and, for that reason, he was advising the third secretary that it should be canceled. He, certainly, had no intention of taking part. There had already been procedural difficulties upon which London had adjudicated, putting him in charge of the murder investigation and he took full responsibility for the cancellation. It was inevitable that it would inflame the media, which was unfortunate and would not have occurred if there had been proper consultation, which there should have been from the third secretary, knowing of the previous day's London ruling.

Charlie copied the message to Dawkins, Stout, and the two resident intelligence officers to coincide with his sending it to the ambassador, and chose the commissary office to confirm his Islay single malt order in which to lose himself for fifteen minutes beyond the time the press conference had been scheduled to begin.

Paula-Jane was waiting for him when Charlie returned to the *rezidentura* level. She said: "All hell's broken loose."

"I'd have been disappointed if it hadn't," said Charlie.

★

The moment he entered the ambassador's suite, Charlie recognized Sir Thomas Sotley as the quintessential career diplomat, from the top of his gray-tinged head, past the old Etonian tie, the Savile Row suit, and the family-crested signet ring, to the tip of his hand-tooled Lobb shoes. Jeremy Dawkins, a younger clone apart from the tumbling-forward blond hair and already fury-flushed face, was to the right of the ambassador's antique, green leather inset desk. Behind them was almost an aerial view of the Moskva River.

"What's the meaning of this?" immediately demanded the ambassador, waving the printout of Charlie's e-mail like a penalty flag. There was no invitation for Charlie to sit.

"I'd hoped it was self-explanatory," said Charlie.

"It is self-serving, unforgivable impertinence for which I demand an explanation," spluttered the outraged man.

"There was no intended impertinence."

"The third secretary is responsible for the general administration of this embassy and got the approval of the deputy Director-General for the conference, to discount some of the most preposterous media fantasies. By refusing to appear, causing the conference to be canceled, you've assured those fantasies will be exacerbated."

Doubly trapped before he'd virtually started, Charlie recognized he was making an immediate enemy of the ambassador. "You were aware of my being seconded here?"

The ambassador frowned again. "Of course I am aware of your being seconded here! Mr. Dawkins has kept me fully informed."

"Seconded for what specific purpose?"

There was a hesitation before the diplomat said: "Do you imagine that you can interrogate *me*!"

"No, Your Excellency," said Charlie, belatedly deciding that he should show the expected respect. "I am trying to prevent any further misunderstandings. Are you also aware of yesterday's exchanges between this embassy and London concerning my role here?"

Instead of answering, Sotley looked inquiringly at Dawkins. The flush-faced man said, "There were some working arrangements that needed to be clarified. I decided—"

"Excellency," broke in Charlie, talking directly to the ambassador. "I would respectfully suggest that this meeting is suspended to give you the opportunity to read for yourself the exchanges being referred to here, and perhaps discuss them more fully and in private with Mr. Dawkins. I will, of course, be available if you decide there is any reason to discuss the situation further."

As he made his way back to the *rezidentura*, Charlie guessed that Dawkins probably wouldn't have shown him the same mercy, but there was nothing to be gained impaling Dawkins's head on a spike. Far more important—and worrying—was the revelation that Jeffrey Smale was involving himself in such a hands-on way and that embassy officers were unquestioningly accepting the deputy director's authority. Maybe, Charlie thought, he was going soft in his advancing years. Then again, perhaps he wasn't—just impatient with all the interruptions and anxious to get on with the job. Which looked like being further delayed by another wasted day. Then he saw Reg Stout talking animatedly with three men in the corridor along which he was walking, directly in front of the open-doored control box containing the faulty CCTV terminals. All three had cameras around their necks and open work boxes packed with electronic equipment. One of the three was a man named Harry Fish, an MI5 electronics sweeper who'd been in the counterespionage business almost as long as Charlie. The recognition between them was immediate. Fish raised his eyes to heaven at the same time as shaking his head, which Charlie knew wasn't in denial at God living up there but at the shambles down here on the ground.

★

Charlie hadn't expected to be back in the ambassador's presence so quickly, although on this occasion he was not in the man's office but in a larger, adjoining conference room. Assembled around the table with Charlie and the three sweepers was the ambassador, Dawkins, Stout, and both the MI5 and MI6 officers. The object of everyone's attention, in the very center of the table and laid on a white handkerchief to make them more visible, were four black objects the size of pinheads.

"State of the art," declared Fish, the team leader. "Any electronic or verbal communication conducted through the four terminals in which we found them would have been received with crystal clarity by the FSB or the external directorate, the *Sluzhba Vneshney Razvedki* in their Lubyanka headquarters. I am going to have to bring a much larger team from London to sweep this embassy from top to bottom..." The balding man looked between Stout and the two intelligence officers before continuing on to the two diplomats. "There will obviously be a complete and extremely full internal inquiry, which I would expect London to send independent people to conduct. In preparation for that it will be necessary for all of you to go back to every communication that was sent on equipment through these terminals—equipment which my team and I will identify—from the date the Russian electricians were allowed on to the premises supposedly to repair the faulty CCTV cameras. Their being allowed within the embassy is a breach of every security guidance and instruction with which every British embassy, particularly this one, is issued. The inquiry will need to see all the documentation, between whomever was involved and consulted, authorizing the Russian entry—"

"I had authorization for everything I allowed to happen," burst in a stuttering Reg Stout.

Fish raised a hand against the outburst. "The involvement in any inquiry of my team and me will be strictly technical, fully identifying the extent of the penetration." He nodded to the pinhead bugs. "From this moment, this embassy has to conduct itself in the belief that not one piece of electronic equipment is safe, and that includes private telephones in the apartments within this building, as well as all those in every office, and extends to all mobile and cell phones, the radio masts for whose transmission are on the top of this building. It is inevitable that other listening or monitoring devices will be detected. . . ." For the first time Fish included Charlie as he looked around the table. "The embassy is already under the sort of scrutiny the Foreign Office would do its utmost to have avoided. For this penetration to become public, on top of a murder in its grounds, would be a total catastrophe. It is only known about by those of us in this room. It must not, under any circumstance, go beyond."

"It's already a disaster," said Sir Thomas Sotley, more to himself than to others in the room.

"Yes, sir," agreed Fish, unsympathetically. "It is a complete and absolute disaster."

★

The only totally guaranteed bug-free apparatus was now in the embassy's basement communications room, and Charlie stopped Harry Fish as he was about to enter the descending elevator.

"I'm on my way down there, too," announced Charlie, unsure if their long association, which had never developed into a friendship, would be sufficient for what he was going to ask. "But first I need a favor."

"We do very different jobs," said the man, cautiously, letting the elevator doors close against him.

"The Russians are trying to push me aside from the investigation," declared Charlie. "I've got to prevent that happening, particularly after what you've just discovered."

"How?" asked Fish, holding back from any additional questions as he listened to what Charlie told him, shaking his head at the finish. "It'll never work."

"I can make it work."

"I won't swear any formal statements . . . let my name be used."

"Just be there, with me," urged Charlie. "You won't be identified."

"Twenty minutes," insisted Fish. "I've already given London a contact schedule."

"Twenty minutes," agreed Charlie. Nodding to the camera still slung around the other man's neck, Charlie said, "Can I have the images of what I want?"

"I hope to Christ I'm not going to regret this."

"You won't," promised Charlie, wishing he could be sure.

It took them five minutes of Fish's stipulated schedule to collect buckets, a spade, trowels, and plastic sheeting from the gardeners' shed Reg Stout had earlier identified to Charlie, which ensured they got the necessary attention of the Russian grounds staff. Three stood watching when they got to where the body had been found, the newly turned soil filling the Russian-dug hole visibly different from that which surrounded it. Charlie demanded from one of them that their overseer be summoned and ordered the man to keep all the Russians not just away but out of sight of what he and Fish were about to do. Charlie, reluctantly, did the digging, gouging a mark in the conference-hall wall with the spade edge, grateful for the effort Fish put into the apparent selection of dirt heaped onto the plastic sheeting.

"You get into any shit over this, you're on your own," warned the man, as they walked back to the embassy, their soil samples on the plastic sheet slung between them.

"I owe you," thanked Charlie, accepting the offered digital camera images from Fish's camera.

Fish waited while Charlie transferred all the soil onto a fresh piece of sheeting, locked his cubbyhole office, and returned the tools to the gardeners' shed. In the elevator finally taking them to the communications room, Charlie said, "How bad is this?"

"For a lot of people here, up to and including the ambassador, I'd guess it will be terminal. As it deserves to be."

"How were the CCTV cameras sabotaged to make them work intermittently as they did?"

"With what's called breakers, cutting the power on and off, to give the impression of a power interruption. The bugs work on a time system, so that the power goes off completely at whatever specific moment you want the screens to go blank."

"Does the power actually go *off*? Or is it their operation that's interrupted?"

Fish stopped as they emerged into the basement facility. "What's your point?"

"Stuff that's wiped off computer screens can be recovered from a hard drive by specialists, can't it?"

"With CCTV, you're talking continuous film that revolves for a certain period and then reverses to record again: that's why it's called a loop. Computers are electric: even if something is saved and then erased, it's possible to recover the ghost from a hard drive."

"The old loops that were affected? What's going to happen to them?"

"They get destroyed. We've installed new ones."

"Can I have the old ones?"

"I'm glad I do what I do, not what you do," said Fish.

"Most of the time I don't like it much myself," said Charlie.

It took Charlie almost as long to pack up for dispatch to London the discarded loops, what he considered sufficient soil samples, and to list the significance of Fish's digital camera images already transmitted to London as it did to send his requests to London. After what he considered a usefully spent day, he was disappointed that his feet still throbbed in tandem at the continuing feeling that he was missing something.

5

THE POSTAL SYSTEM OF MOSCOW IS AS HAPHAZARD AS ITS swirling winter blizzards, even in the topsy-turvy summer in which the city was now embalmed. In little more than a twenty-four-hour period it would have been impossible for Natalia to have given a written response to Charlie's note. Despite which, in the unlikely event of her having received it and decided instead to telephone the Savoy, Charlie still waited until long after any delivery before at last calling the number Sergei Pavel had given him for the organized crime bureau at Ulitsa Petrovka. Charlie had forgotten the Russian system of individually assigned numbers, expecting a general switchboard, and was momentarily surprised when the militia colonel personally answered.

"I'd expected contact before now," said the man, when Charlie identified himself. The voice was bland, practically monotone, without any criticism at the delay.

"There've been some unforeseen developments at the embassy."

There was the hesitation that Charlie hoped to engender and the tone of Pavel's voice changed. "What unforeseen developments?"

"Things we need to talk about," generalized Charlie. "Thought I'd give a couple of days, too, for all the other things we discussed at the mortuary to come together . . . fuller pathology details, photographs of the scene, further forensic findings, stuff like that."

"There are a few things, not all," begrudged the Russian, cautiously.

"I'd hoped we could get together some time today, take it all forward?"

"We're certain that the murder wasn't committed anywhere near where the body was found, which makes it a Russian investigation," declared Pavel, as if he were reading from a prompt card.

Altogether too soon, too quick, judged Charlie: he could afford to bluff more. "That's intriguing."

"Why?' demanded Pavel, the curiosity very evident in the no longer neutral voice.

"It's not quite either the indication or the impression I've been getting from those who've come across from London to go through everything at the embassy," lured Charlie, knowing the arrival of Harry Fish and his team—and their digging expedition the previous afternoon—would have been recorded by the diligent FSB gardener informers, even if Pavel himself was at the moment unaware. "We really do need to meet. Exactly how many of the reports have you managed to assemble?"

"Some photographs . . . the preliminary medical report," stumbled the other man, confronted with something different from what he'd expected.

Charlie doubted that whatever Pavel was minimally offering was actually assembled yet. To give the Russian time to go through the pretense of collation—and doubtless speak to others about the unexpected approach—he said, "Why don't I come around this afternoon, for us to get started? Three o'clock's good for me."

There was another hesitation. "I should have everything together by then, although I can't guarantee it."

If the Russian wasn't sure he could get his own bullshit together in five hours, nothing at all had yet been assembled. Not believing that possible, Charlie said, "It'll be a start."

Which wasn't any way the object of Charlie's exercise. It was to bluff Pavel, and through him the inevitable monitoring FSB and Foreign Ministry, that there was a lot they'd missed in their comparatively short forensic examination at the scene inside the

British embassy grounds. The FSB bugging of the embassy electronics worked more to his benefit than theirs in taking advantage of the security stupidity presented to them on a shiny silver platter. They'd believe him because he would be telling them what they already knew. Or imagined they knew. He was going to have a dream hand for his poker game. The expertise was going to come in his not overplaying it.

The scurrying activity at the embassy reminded Charlie of an anthill. There were at least a dozen photographers and journalists grouped outside the firmly closed gates and there was uniformed security forming an admission cordon around the pedestrian entrance adjoining the gatehouse. Inside the gatehouse, the now properly working CCTV cameras displayed in sharp panoramic detail the entire front of the building. Charlie endured the ritual of ID checks and descended into the communications room. Waiting there for him was a warning from the head of the technical and scientific services division that, until the arrival of the discarded CCTV loops, they could not guarantee his detailed overnight request was possible—their more normal function was to detect counterfeit and deceiving enhancement, not create it—but that what Charlie wanted was certainly scientifically and technically feasible: It might help, after they'd received the recording material, for Charlie to talk directly by telephone, as well as in more detailed messages answering their specific questions. Charlie detected a note of tetchy irritation in the assurance that they had samples of 9mm Makarov ammunition. There was also a personal acknowledgement from Director-General Aubrey Smith, insisting that Charlie continue working not just totally independently from everyone at the embassy—especially those most likely to have been compromised—but also from the incoming internal inquiry team. All communication had to be personal, between the two of them, which left Charlie undecided between the advantages compared to the disadvantages of such close contact with the man who for several months had appeared the loser in the power struggle with his deputy. Smith was a university professor of Middle Eastern studies and an acknowledged expert on the revolutionary movements of the region, who had been pitchforked from academia into intelligence in a knee-jerk reaction to Islamic fanaticism. Smith's way was ingrained from that academic background to consider and judge events from every perspective. It had seemed to chime with Charlie's independent way of working and he enjoyed having Smith's confidence, which in matching measure had alienated him from Jeffrey Smale. And, survival savvy as he was, Charlie was well aware that his job security depended upon Smith emerging the victor in the current department power struggle.

For once Paula-Jane Venables and David Halliday were in their offices, both doors closed with NOT TO BE DISTURBED signs in their occupancy slots, which Charlie ignored, still with time to fill before his appointment with the embassy lawyer. The woman jerked up irritably at his unannounced entry, relaxing when she saw who it was.

"This is proving to be an absolute fucking nightmare!" she announced, unasked.

"How bad could it be, bottom line?" asked Charlie. His being forbidden to share anything upon which he was engaged was no obstacle to his learning as much as he could about everything else in the embassy.

"God only knows. I'm going to have to admit gaps in the telephone log I'm supposed to have kept but haven't."

"Don't admit anything," advised Charlie, the survival expert. "Wait until you're asked, answer one question at a time, and don't volunteer anything."

"At the moment, I'm guessing the bastards could have listened to something in the region of a hundred, maybe a hundred and fifty, incoming and outgoing calls."

"What about written stuff?"

"Luckier there. I do have a full log of the sensitive e-mail material and it's all gone through the communications room, which your friend Harry Fish tells me isn't compromised."

"You're not supposed to rely upon luck," reminded Charlie.

"You've been seconded to the internal inquiry team as well!" she challenged.

"No," said Charlie, mildly. "But if I were, that would have been the wrong response. You didn't open the doors to let the bad guys in. As far as I am aware, it was Reg Stout, under Dawkins's authority, condoned by an ineffectual ambassador. You haven't got any reason to be defensive. All you've got to do is warn the guys who are coming from London of anything the FSB might have learned."

"I just told you, my telephone logs—the logs they are going to want to examine and question me about—aren't complete."

"How much—how many—can you remember of what you haven't logged?"

"Most of it, I'm pretty sure."

"So verbally include from memory whatever's missing from the log when you're questioned in detail about your telephone records."

"Considering the way I greeted you when you arrived, you're being very kind," said Paula-Jane, smiling.

"Who told you I was anything otherwise?"

"You wouldn't believe me if I told you," said the woman, her initial uptightness easing. "I want to make amends!"

"I'm not sure you've got any amends to make," coaxed Charlie, curious to know who'd been digging the mantraps ahead of him.

"I am," she insisted. "I've been invited to a dinner party tonight by the current CIA guy at the American embassy. And I don't have a partner. Would you have a problem filling the vacancy?"

Charlie found an immediate response difficult, the uncertainty of Natalia's reaction to his letter in the forefront of his mind. If she missed him on her first call, she'd phone again, came the quick reassurance. It was unlikely there'd be any professional benefit socializing with the Americans, but there was always the possibility of the unexpected. Which was all Charlie ever asked for, a simple possibility. "That could be fun."

"Let's try to make sure it is."

★

"Don't tell me it's a nightmare: I've been told that already."

Halliday gestured Charlie farther into the unexpectedly lit-tered MI6 *rezidentura*, files, dossiers, and newspapers—English language as well as Russian—overflowing from benches and side desks onto a floor shadowed by unclosed cabinets and open desk drawers. Halliday said, "Not as bad as it looks."

"Which looks bad enough," commiserated Charlie, needing to move some of the records to take the offered seat. The headline in that day's unfiled *Moscow News* on top of the heap read: MYSTERY DEEPENS IN BRITISH EMBASSY MURDER.

Halliday shook his head, smiling. "On open, possibly inter-cepted transmission, little more than embarrassment. A lot of analyses about Stepan Lvov's presidential chances, which is occu-pying every Western embassy in Moscow and shouldn't surprise anyone in the FSB. My judgement is that Lvov's a shoo-in, so if I'm right, it's not even embarrassing that we've been monitoring him. If he loses, I'm a bad analyst they don't have to worry about keeping too close an eye on."

"Very pragmatic," complimented Charlie. "I've never seen so many worried people running around so many corridors. Or quite so many journalists, cameramen, and TV crews outside this em-bassy."

"The inquisitors are due any time, thumbscrews and all. There's bound to be a lot of other transgressions swept up in the spring cleaning. And Reg Stout, who's rightly shitting himself, says he's called the militia to clear the media away."

"He told me he hardly speaks Russian."

Halliday shrugged. "He's always talking through the hole in his ass."

"How worried are you about the internal inquiry?"

Halliday smiled again. "I certainly didn't let the FSB bug-masters in."

"You must have recognized how fucked up the security was here, before the shit hit the fan?"

Halliday patted the closest folder to him on his desk. "I did, long before the shit hit any fan. And here's the log, with attached copies of every warning message I've sent to London over the last six months. London's going to have a lot of self-explaining to do, as well as the idiots here . . ." The man patted his special folder again. "With this already on my record, I'm going to come out of this inquiry smelling like a rose."

"Always better than smelling of shit," agreed Charlie.

"I told Monsford, my director, you'd declined my offer of help, by the way. He said he might take it up with your boss. Thought you should know in advance."

"I appreciate your telling me that," said Charlie, deciding at that moment that although admiring Halliday's apparent professionalism, he didn't personally like the man. But then, Charlie asked himself, when had liking someone have anything to do with anything?

Charlie had wondered if in five years the official interior design preponderance of desk and countertop Bakelite with matching linoleum floor covering would have disappeared but, of course, it hadn't—it just became more scratched and scuffed. The insolent, blank-faced disinterest of the counter clerk at Ulitsa Petrovka was the same as Charlie remembered, too: Charlie's guess at four minutes before the man would bother to look up from the curled-edged, unturned page of what he was reading was short by an additional full minute.

"Important to keep up to date with all the regulations," sympathized Charlie, sure the man was looking at the latest office-circulating porn magazine: the clerk was two pages short of the photographic offerings.

There was grunted surprise at Charlie's mockery being in Russian. "You the Englishman to see Sergei Romanovich Pavel?"

"That's me," agreed Charlie, equally surprised at the expectation.

"It's the top floor, second door on the right when you get there," dismissed the man, nodding toward the linoleum-clad stairs as he went back to his magazine.

Charlie took his time and was glad he did. The top floor was six flights up, and by the time he got there his feet were burning and he was panting, even though he'd paced himself. He'd passed seven people on the way up two of them women, and been ignored by them all, despite being an unauthorized, foreign stranger. It wasn't casual security, Charlie decided, but stage management to indicate his unimportance. Charlie waited until he'd fully recovered his breath before knocking on the identified door. He had to knock twice more before there was an unintelligible shout beyond, which he took to be an invitation to enter. The outside office was empty, but Pavel was visible through the open door of the next room, behind a cluttered desk. The man's jacket was looped around the back of his chair, crushed by his leaning back against it. Pavel's tie was loosened and his shirt collar open. The shirt and tie, as well as the suit, were what the man had worn at the mortuary: at least, Charlie thought, he'd changed his own shirt. And socks. It reminded him he needed to get some laundry done at the hotel. He supposed he'd have to change again, into the better of his two suits, for that evening's dinner with Paula-Jane's American friends.

"At last!" greeted Pavel.

"There's been time for things to develop."

"I'm looking forward to hearing what they are," encouraged Pavel.

"As I am from you," parried Charlie, anxious to get the exchange on his terms.

Pavel pushed two folders through an already cleared space on his desk. "The photographs and the pathology findings of Dr. Ivanov."

The meeting was obviously being recorded, Charlie accepted, disbelieving the apparent casualness with which he had been allowed to walk unescorted around the building. He couldn't isolate a lens but he had to assume the encounter was being filmed, too, so he had to be careful even with facial reactions. There were twelve images in the album, which Charlie instantly decided were inadequate without needing any closer examination. The only two pictures of the flower-bed hole, dug to retrieve blood samples and perhaps the bullet, gave no indication of its depth from which to assess the amount of soil removed. Charlie merely flicked through the pathologist's report, without trying to read anything, judging it equally inadequate simply from its thinness, allowing the frown for the benefit of the undetected camera. He said; "This is only a preliminary medical report, of course? And I'm disappointed there aren't more photographs."

"I understood from Dr. Ivanov that it was complete," equivocated Pavel, giving himself an escape from the challenge.

"It'll obviously be necessary to talk it all through with the pathologist after I've read it in detail," said Charlie. "Might have to send it to London, to be checked through there."

"You said there had been developments?" pressed the Russian.

"Most of which I don't fully understand and others of which are very awkward," said Charlie. "I'm particularly concerned that our working relations and arrangements could be affected."

"I need you to explain precisely what you're telling me," protested Pavel. There was no longer any bland condescension.

"I'll set out everything as clearly as I can," said Charlie, without the slightest intention of doing anything of the sort. "On the phone, you said you were certain that the man wasn't murdered in the embassy grounds?"

Pavel shifted at the onus being put upon him. "We recovered a lot of earth, where the shattered head lay. There was remarkably little blood residue, scarcely more than a liter. Very little bone or skin debris, either. And most certainly no bullet, which there obviously would have been if he'd been shot where and how he was found."

Far, far too complacent and far too obviously rehearsed, recognized Charlie: if it hadn't been so overwhelmingly to his own benefit he might even have been offended at the contemptuous dismissal. "*If* he had been already lying face down," agreed Charlie. "Not if he'd been standing up . . ." He let the pause in, enjoying his own performance. "Or kneeling, to be executed, which is what our forensic pathologist believes to have been the position in which he was shot and which there is some evidence to support.

There's a substantial grooved mark close to the base of the wall of the conference hall, and a lot of blood and possibly debris at least half a yard from where the body fell and was found."

"I didn't see anything like that," broke in Pavel, forward in his chair now, no longer lounged back, creasing his jacket.

"From what I've been told everything was rushed, confused," said Charlie. "We've obviously collected a lot of the other blood-soaked earth quite a way away from where you dug. . . ." He lifted what the Russians had bothered to include in the photographic selection. "Very much more than your scientist appears to have done. It's being sifted as well as electronically searched, to find the bullet. The forensic scientist calculated the most likely trajectory from the mark on the wall."

"Where is it, all this other forensic material?" demanded the Russian.

Charlie hesitated, as if discomfited by a too difficult question. "In London. It's all been shipped back for further and more detailed examination." He knew the size of the untouchable diplomatic shipment, including everything Harry Fish had helped him assemble, would have been logged by the FSB staff at Sheremetyevo Airport as a matter of course.

"There are more than adequate forensic facilities here," said Pavel, tightly.

Charlie remained silent for several moments, looking down as if either in contemplation or unwillingness even to look directly at Sergei Pavel. Eventually he said, "There is a problem. I know—accept—that it is not of your creation: that you don't know anything about it. It has nothing whatsoever to do with what you and I have been assigned to do, but it has obviously affected the thinking in London."

The bewilderment was mirrored on Pavel's face. "Something else I don't understand?"

"What I am going to tell you, I do as an indication of how much I value our further and continued cooperation," said Charlie. "I ask you, at the same time, to treat it in the strictest confidence. I do not yet know what my government intends publicly to do about it but I certainly don't wish either of us to be accused of initiating a diplomatic incident."

"What's going on? What's happened?"

Charlie's assessment of Pavel's reaction was that the Russian had no knowledge of the embassy bugging. "I have your assurance that what I am going to tell you remains strictly between the two of us?"

"Upon the honor of my mother," pledged the man.

Who must have been a 50-kopeck whore if Pavel were to be believed, gauged Charlie. "The embassy sought the help of local electricians—recommended by your Foreign Ministry—to rectify some faults in its security system, particularly the CCTV cameras. Some spying apparatus was installed while Russian electricians were within the embassy."

Pavel shook his head. "I did not know . . ."

"I am not accusing you. I've given you my confidence for you to understand the attitude of people to whom I am responsible: why they ordered whatever their forensic people retrieved to be examined and tested in London, instead of here, by your people."

"How can we be expected to continue with such a barrier between us?" Pavel asked, desperately. "It's been made impossible."

Charlie hadn't anticipated that capitulation and the alarm swept through him. "It's only impossible if we allow it to become so. We have to cut ourselves off from it, entirely. But if we are going to continue with total openness between each other, there is something further I must tell you, because it affects our investigation."

"What more can there be?"

"The CCTV cameras kept failing, intermittently, finally failing altogether. But there are some images upon them: images of what could be our murder victim and those who killed him."

The Russian's complete silence, the man's inability momentarily even to speak, further convinced Charlie of Pavel's ignorance of the spying intrusion. At last, Pavel haltingly managed: "The films, the recordings, whatever they are? Where are they?"

"Back in London, being enhanced, with all the other recovered material."

"Is it possible that you will get identifiable pictures?"

"That is what our scientists are trying to achieve."

Sergei Pavel personally escorted Charlie down to the ground-floor reception area, animatedly assuring daily contact. Charlie felt a satisfying warmth at how Pavel's attitude—from dismissal to reliance—had changed. Charlie's estimate of how long it would take Sergei Pavel to contact the FSB's Mikhail Guzov at the Lubyanka coincided with his reaching a pavement newsstand, at which he was brought to a halt by the *Moscow News* billboard. There was no other story on its front page apart from the bugging of the British embassy, with a sidebar speculation of it plunging diplomatic relations between Russia and Britain back to the frostbitten era of the Cold War. His revelation to Pavel was far too recent for the Russian detective to be the source. So which of the others at yesterday's confrontation in Sir Thomas Sotley's suite hadn't been able to keep their undertaking of secrecy?

6

THE MEDIA POSSE HAD GROWN BY THE TIME CHARLIE RE-
turned to pick up Paula-Jane Venables from her embassy compound
apartment. Some uniformed Russian militia officers had arrived
to supplement the British security cordon, keeping the pedestrian
door clear. They weren't doing anything, though, to prevent the
television cameramen and photographers from taking pictures,
and Charlie told his taxi driver to continue on to a telephone kiosk
farther along the embankment and wait while he made a call.

"Ashamed to be seen with me?" Paula-Jane asked, flirtingly,
when Charlie warned of the likely ambush.

"You don't need to be identified with me by the FSB and I
don't want to be linked with you by them."

"Don't you think they already know who we're from: you'll be
on file, for Christ's sake!"

"Why advertise it?"

"There's caution for you!" she mocked.

"Pity there hadn't been a lot more of it in the last few weeks,"
said Charlie, heavily.

"You had a bad day?"

"Not at all," denied Charlie, hoping he wasn't showing his
disappointment at not finding a telephone message from Natalia
when he'd gone back to the hotel to change. "I've got a cab. I'll pick
you up at the Kalininskaya Bridge, okay?"

"Okay," she said, her lightness gone.

It took her twenty minutes, arriving uncomfortably on elevated high heels, the shoes coordinating with the clasp bag. The cleavage was so deep, the single rope of pearls looked like a suspension bridge between two peaks. Settling gratefully into the back of the cab, she said, "Television didn't really show the extent of the scrum. I guess you were right."

"Where are we going?" asked Charlie, as the cab moved off.

"Where else but the American Café, just off the ring road?" She gave the driver the address in Russian.

"You seen the papers?" asked Charlie.

"Heard it on television, when I was trying to estimate the crowd outside. Your friend Harry's gone ape-shit, along with the entire inquiry team that came in this afternoon. I actually didn't think I was going to be able to get away tonight after all: they've got Sotley in with them now, with Dawkins on standby."

Charlie was intent upon the cab driver's reflection in the rearview mirror, relieved from the disinterest on the man's face that he really didn't understand English. "Who'd you think couldn't keep their mouth shut?"

"If we take you, me, and Halliday out of the frame you've got a fairly short list of suspects. My money's on Reg Stout."

Stout was certainly the most obvious, accepted Charlie. They were on the multilaned freeway now, swept along by the tide of vehicles all around them. Recognizing the landmark of Pushkin's house, Charlie looked to the right where Natalia's apartment was, little more than a hundred yards off the main highway.

"Familiar places from when you were here before?" asked Paula-Jane.

"No," denied Charlie, honestly. The apartment he'd occupied with Natalia and Sasha, an entire floor of a minor, prerevolutionary palace, was on the far side of the city. Wanting to move on from the unwelcomed reminder, he said, "Tell me about the people we're going to be with tonight."

"Tex Probert is from the Company," she said, using spook-speak to identify the CIA. "His wife, Sarah, is over on a visit. Bill

Bundy's his intended replacement, overlapping to settle him-self in. Shirley Jenkins, who's partnering Bundy, is in their legal department. Nice guys, although it takes a lot for Shirley to unbend. . . ." She smiled, the remark prepared. "Although she does quite a lot of unbending in certain circumstances, according to the stories I've heard."

Charlie ignored the innuendo. Instead, he said, "Sarah's over on a visit?"

"From what's officially described as relocation leave," explained Paula-Jane. "Tex is due to go back permanently any time now. He's been assigned a CIA headquarter's posting at Langley so she's house-hunting around Washington and finding colleges for the two kids, who've been at school there. Bill's the eventual re-placement, like I said: third-term assignment, the Company's ac-knowledged Russian guru."

"I know," said Charlie.

"You know?"

"He was on station here the same time as me."

"How about that!" exclaimed Paula-Jane.

How about that indeed? thought Charlie, easing his finger inside his left shoe to massage the discomfort.

Charlie had never understood why nostalgic, back-home theme restaurants and bars in foreign cities never properly replicated back home at all. The American Café, which hadn't existed when he'd lived in Moscow, was designed to represent a 1940s diner that, as far as Charlie was aware, didn't exist anywhere in the United States. This one was complete with blown-up photographs of Lana Turner and Rita Hayworth, and a cigarette advertising poster of a young, Chesterfield-smoking Ronald Reagan. There was even a bulbous, multilighted although silent jukebox. All the tables were covered in red checked cloths, each topped with a to-tem ketchup bottle.

"Cute, eh?" enthused Paula-Jane.

"Fascinating," allowed an unimpressed Charlie.

The American party was already there, around a centrally placed circular table. Charlie instantly recognized Bill Bundy in the middle of the group, guessing from Paula-Jane's rehearsal that the serious faced, dark-haired girl to the man's right to be the lawyer Shirley Jenkins. Which made the man next to her Tex Probert, with blond wife Sarah completing the group. Both men stood to shake hands at their introduction and Bundy said, "Good to see you after all this time, Charlie."

"And you," said Charlie, who couldn't isolate a single apparent difference in the man's appearance from when they'd last met. The preppy, short haircut didn't look out of place on a man who had to be at least fifty. Nor did the regulation Ivy League suit, complete with metal-pin collared shirt clamping the club tie in place.

"You two guys already know each other?" exclaimed the angular-featured Probert, whose accent explained the nickname: the formal introduction had been John.

"From way back," confirmed Bundy. "We two can actually remember what the Cold War was like."

"And dinosaurs," said Charlie, to the laughing appreciation of the three women, giving him the necessary moment to think. Bundy's posting quite clearly had nothing whatsoever to do with what he'd been sent from London to investigate but Charlie had never before heard of a third-time overseas assignment—certainly not one that involved moving such an acknowledged Russophile at a time of impending political change. His professional curiosity was piqued.

The arrival of the waiter stopped the conversation. The women agreed to share a bottle of white wine while they decided the menu. Probert chose beer and Charlie stuck with vodka in preference to doctored scotch, knowing the restaurant definitely wouldn't have a bottle with the correct label, let alone genuine Islay malt, which reminded him to collect his commissary order the following day. Bundy, whom Charlie belatedly remembered never chanced losing control, stayed with mineral water, insisting on breaking the bottle-cap seal himself. The American food order was uniformly T-bone steaks upon Probert's insistence that they were definitely flown in from Texas. Paula-Jane wanted trout, ordering from prior knowledge of the menu without needing to consult it, and when Charlie asked for borscht Bundy said, "Staying native, Charlie?"

"When in Rome," Charlie answered, using the cliché. He started putting people in their pigeonholes. There was very definitely a frisson between Probert and Paula-Jane, which he guessed Probert's wife was as conscious of as he was. Probert also appeared overly deferential to Bundy, even making allowances for the Bundy legend within the CIA. Deciding to use that reputation to goad the man in return, Charlie said, "How about you, Bill? What brings the head of the CIA's Russian desk back to Moscow?"

"Interesting times, politically, don't you think?" said the man.

"I always thought ambassadors and diplomats assessed things politically and that people like you and me were expected to make other sorts of contributions."

"My philosophy has always been that you can't do one without studying the other. You here simply because of your murder?"

"Who said I was here for that?" demanded Charlie, aware of the others shifting uncomfortably at the sudden seriousness between him and the American.

Bundy looked around the table, as if aware of it, too. "Now here's a lesson for all of us, the danger of assuming too much. Charlie's on a mission he obviously can't tell us about."

"Which is another dangerously accepted assumption," said Charlie, raising his delivered vodka in a toast to the group to cover his irritation at losing the exchange.

"Can't say I envy you guys," came in Probert, attempting to lessen the atmosphere. "Must be a hornet's nest down there at Smolenskaya Naberezhnaya?"

"It's kind of busy," agreed Paula-Jane.

"You just won the understatement of the year award, P-J," said Probert, leading the laughter.

"From the outside, looking in, I'd say there's going to be a wholesale massacre," suggested Bundy.

"I'm keeping my office door locked," said Paula-Jane, over-emboldened by her earlier reception, although only Probert laughed again this time.

"From what I've read in the American papers it seems too late for that," said Sarah, adding to her wineglass for the third time. "I thought all this spy nonsense was over: actually I never believed most of it in the first place." She was blue eyed as well as blond, with perfectly sculpted teeth and a milk-and-vitamin-fed complexion. She looked challengingly between her husband and the two other men and said, "Okay, let us in on the secret! How many James Bond coups have any of you had that you know saved the world?"

"Sarah, stop it!" protested Probert.

The arrival of their food contributed to the interruption. Unasked, Charlie took the initiative and ordered his favorite Georgian red wine, intrigued by the total unexpectedness of the dinner party and the vague undertones he was detecting, most surprised—and curious—at facing an adversary he'd never imagined confronting ever again, socially or otherwise. His mind held by Sarah Probert's outburst, Charlie tried to recall a start-to-finish operation of which he was proud, and couldn't. He'd stuck a hell of a lot of wrenches into a hell of a lot of engines, though, and who could calculate their outcome if he hadn't done it? Perversely wanting to keep the uneasy conversation on its present track to see where it might lead, Charlie said, "There's no such thing as a one-man band in our business: it's lots of different people offering lots of different tunes eventually to create a song to hum to. Wouldn't you say that's how it is, Tex?"

Before her husband could reply, Sarah said, "John says very little about anything, to me at least. That's why I'm glad we're moving back to Washington, D.C., where things will be much more normal and I can get my husband back."

"That's enough, Sarah!" said Probert.

"Moscow's not the best foreign posting for a family," offered Paula-Jane.

Sarah looked across the table at the English woman but deferred to her husband's warning, pushing aside her scarcely touched meal and picking up the empty white wine bottle with her other hand to gesture for a replacement.

"Is Ann coming back this time?" Charlie asked Bundy, knowing the man's wife hadn't enjoyed Moscow and spent a lot of time back in America during their contemporary posting.

"Jury's still out on that," said Bundy. "How long are you expecting to be here?"

Charlie shrugged. "Open-ended."

"Why don't we make lunch sometime? Catch up on old times?"

"That would be good," lied Charlie, who'd only ever socialized with the American at mutually attended embassy receptions and even then to the polite minimum.

It was Paula-Jane Venables who recovered the evening, using her enjoyment of Russia in general and Moscow in particular as the springboard—although not in critical comparison with Sarah Probert's obvious disenchantment—to enthuse about the Bolshoi ballet and of a trip she intended repeating to St. Petersburg to again visit the Hermitage and the Tzars' village of Tarskoye Selo and to see more opera at the Mariinsky Theatre, culminating with the announcement that when her tour of duty in Moscow ended she intended going east, not west, to take the trans-Siberian railway all the way to the Chinese border and complete her recall to England via Japan if she was refused a visa into China. She amusingly told stories against herself of misadventures and mistakes during her explorations, to the genuine, Tex Probert–led amusement of everyone with the initial exception of Sarah. Shirley Jenkins took up the travelogue with an account of a college-graduation rail journey the length of Latin America as far as Patagonia, and eventually Sarah—and even Bundy—relaxed sufficiently to keep the conversation away from embassy rumor and gossip, the only real subject all of them had in common.

On the way back to the embassy Paula-Jane said, "That wasn't anything like the fun I'd hoped it would be. Bundy's a stuffy old fart, frightening all of them with a reputation I didn't see or hear much to justify. I think he's stuck in a Cold War time warp, like the way he dresses and how that fucking café is designed."

"He's a very dedicated guy," said Charlie, impressed at her analysis.

"You work a lot with him when you were both here?"

"Not at all. We both preferred to work alone."

"Like you prefer to do now?"

"We've been through that."

"You didn't share anything with Bundy!" persisted the woman, disbelievingly.

"Nothing," said Charlie. "Was it just your idea to invite me along tonight?"

Paula-Jane turned to him in the taxi. "How do you mean?"

"Was my name mentioned, when you were invited?"

Paula-Jane hesitated, thinking. "I don't remember your name coming up. How could it have? No one at the American embassy could have known you were here, could they?"

"Bundy didn't seem surprised to see me. And appeared to know what I was doing here."

"Bundy tries to give the impression of knowing everything before it ever happens," she dismissed. "I thought we came close to an embarrassment with Sarah."

"You did well to save the evening," congratulated Charlie. "You know her well?"

"Hardly at all. This isn't her first extended trip back to the States. From what Tex has told me, she's spent more of his Russian tour back home than here."

As the embassy came into view Charlie leaned toward the windshield and said, "The media siege appears to have been lifted."

"I thought you might have invited me back to the hotel for a nightcap," said the woman.

I'd guessed you would, thought Charlie. "Maybe another time."

"Let's hope there is one."

Charlie eagerly took the offered message slip from the Savoy receptionist, his expectation of it being from Natalia collapsing immediately. The only thing written on the slip was the telephone number of Colonel Sergei Pavel.

★

Charlie's second arrival at Petrovka was very different from his first. On this occasion there was an instant acknowledgement from a different, attentive desk clerk, and at whose bell-pressed demand another escort officer appeared despite Charlie's assurance that he knew how to get to Pavel's office. The bigger surprise, coming close to astonishment, continued when he reached Pavel's top-floor aerie. Already there, waiting with the organized crime colonel, were the weak-stomached Foreign Ministry official of the mortuary visit, together with the suspected FSB's Mikhail Guzov, and two other men whose identities Charlie guessed from their nervous, foot-shuffling deference to be the discovering gardeners, which was a bonus Charlie hadn't expected, but which he decided could more than justify his responding to Pavel's previous night summons. There were thermoses of black tea waiting on a side table that hadn't been in Pavel's office the first time. The voice recorders and film equipment would still be, Charlie knew.

"The situation would appear to have become very complicated," opened the Foreign Ministry's Nikita Kashev.

"In what way?" queried Charlie, intentionally awkward to give himself time to compartment the assembled group in their necessary order of priority. Kashev had to be there, according to the diplomatically agreed protocol, for the questioning of the body-discovering gardening team. And the murder investigation was officially the responsibility of Sergei Pavel. Which left Mikhail Guzov as the only one who didn't have a place. Which put the FSB man in charge. By intruding into the meeting Guzov was positively, although unnecessarily, confirming his own official role and purpose. Why? Could it be a test in reverse, Guzov *wanting* there to be no misunderstanding of who and what he was: confronting, even, any possible accusation of the FSB bugging the embassy? As always, Charlie accepted, he had to dance on ballet points, an agonizing concept with feet like his.

"A lot of media speculation about continuing difficulties at your embassy," offered Kashev.

"I am not concerned or interested in any media speculation, apart from how it could interfere with what I am here to do," Charlie continued with intentional awkwardness. "As I'd hoped to have made clear at our initial meeting, I am here for one specific purpose . . ." He smiled between the gardeners and Pavel. "And I appreciate what I'm anticipating to be our continuing cooperation."

Reluctantly drawn into the discussion, Pavel introduced the two FSB informant gardeners, Boris Nikolaevich Maksimov and Petr Petrovich Denin, formally including their patronymics. Pavel made the identification at the same time as offering Charlie two separate dossiers, concluding, "And here are their sworn statements."

Bulldozing time, Charlie at once recognized, his conviction growing that everything was being orchestrated as well as recorded by Guzov. Disregarding the increasingly impatient fidgeting of his audience, Charlie took his time reading the supposed recollections of each gardener, both of which stopped short of two full pages and roughly—very roughly—accorded with Reg Stout's totally inadequate account of his conversation with Maksimov.

"There are some questions, of course, in light of what was discovered after your crime scene investigation." Charlie briskly set out, docking Guzov two points on the professional score sheet for the man's obvious frown. Talking directly to Maksimov, Charlie said: "How close did you go to the body?"

The thin-faced man hesitated, his look to Guzov for guidance too obvious. Haltingly, weak-voiced, he said: "I'm not sure. Not close enough to touch it."

"You thought at first it might be someone sleeping, didn't you?"

"What!" asked the man, now including Pavel in his anxious look for help.

"You told the head of security at the embassy that at first you thought the man was sleeping. It's not in your statement," said Charlie, waving the folder.

"I don't remember saying that."

"Why should you have thought someone was sleeping in the embassy grounds?"

Maksimov scrubbed his hand across his sweating face. "You see people lying drunk at night."

"What made you changed your mind?"

Maksimov shuddered. "When I got closer . . . saw what had happened to his face . . . that there wasn't a face."

"Were the clothes wet?"

"No . . . I don't know . . ."

"You did touch the body, then?"

"No! I told you I didn't."

"You said the clothes weren't wet. How did you know the clothes weren't wet if you didn't touch the body?"

"He said he didn't know," came in Guzov, speaking for the first time.

"*After* saying the clothes weren't wet," insisted Charlie.

"I meant I didn't know, not that I touched the body. I didn't touch the body."

"How close did you go to it?"

"Not close . . . no closer than a yard."

"Close enough to see that there wasn't a face?"

"That was obvious."

Maksimov was starting to relax, Charlie recognized. "Not at first, when you thought it was someone sleeping."

"I don't remember saying that," repeated the man.

"What about the chip out of the brickwork? You saw that, didn't you?"

"No . . . I don't understand that question."

"You sure you didn't?"

"No . . . I mean I don't know. I can't remember."

"What did you mean by telling the embassy security officer that you didn't do it? Did you mean that you hadn't killed him?"

"I didn't mean to say that. It just came out like that."

"When you got about a yard away you could see the body very clearly?"

The man hesitated, nervously. "Yes."

Time to sow more seeds, Charlie decided. "I know there wasn't a face but on which side was the head laying, to its right or to its left?"

There was another pause. Maksimov looked at his supervisor, who shrugged. Maksimov said, "To its right."

"You're sure it was to its right?"

"Yes," said the Russian, sounding anything but sure.

"That's consistent," said Charlie, as if to himself, looking down again at Maksimov's written statement, to provide the delay.

"Consistent with what?" demanded Pavel.

Looking down as he'd had to, Charlie hadn't been able to see any indication from Guzov for the organized crime detective to ask the question. Charlie said, "The gouge mark in the wall our forensic people believe was caused by the bullet ricochet . . ." He looked from Pavel to the others in the office. "You have passed on what we talked about earlier?"

It was Kashev who answered. "The colonel has, in some detail, which is why we are here and why I think we need to talk very specifically beyond this immediate subject. I want to stress, most forcibly, that my government denies absolutely any knowledge or responsibility for what is being reported in the media as an espionage intrusion into the British embassy. My colleagues also wish—"

"Sir!" Charlie broke in. "And before I continue any further, I apologize for interrupting you. I have no permanent attachment to the British embassy here. I cannot, therefore, discuss anything other than what I have been sent here to investigate. My investigation is, however, overshadowed by the situation to which you refer. And obviously, potentially hampered by it, particularly by the disparities in these"—Charlie fluttered the two inadequate statements—"and what British forensic scientists collected from other parts of the murder scene. And I intentionally use those words, murder scene, because every conclusion British scientists have so far reached is that the crime was very definitely committed on British territory, not somewhere else. I have taken the advice of our embassy lawyer on that . . . the embassy is legally and technically British territory, not Russian."

"None of those conclusions—or the proof that led to their being reached—has been exchanged, according to the cooperation understanding between our two governments," intruded Mikhail Guzov, to Charlie's satisfaction.

It would be wrong to challenge the other man's official reason for being there, too easily dismissed as Guzov being attached to the Foreign Ministry, which technically he probably was. "Another overshadowing but inevitably connected problem."

"So what's the resolve?" demanded Guzov.

"A separation, if it's possible, between the diplomatic and the criminal," suggested Charlie.

"Answer your own question," insisted Guzov. "Is that possible?"

"I, for my part, believe that I can work in total cooperation with Colonel Pavel, quite separately from whatever else is affecting the embassy. I will further undertake to do my utmost to persuade London to make available the results of all scientific tests. And as a gesture of my commitment, I will tell you now that there are definitely images upon the CCTV loops that were intended to be rendered useless by being tampered with. The ricocheting score mark on the wall is still evident and has been extensively photographed, although its immediate brick surface has obvious been scraped away for fragment traces of the bullet that made the mark after exiting the man's head. Also extensively photographed is the second border area from which earth was dug by our forensic experts' team to retrieve blood residue and, hopefully, the bullet."

"I must ask that our forensic officers be allowed back into the embassy for a second examination," said Kashev.

"In the circumstances in which we now find ourselves and which I have made clear to you, that is not my permission to give," sidestepped Charlie. "That has to be an official request from your ministry to the ambassador. The most I can offer is the expectation of sharing with Colonel Pavel the photographs and the forensic results to which I have referred."

He'd been cut off by Guzov before getting all that he'd wanted from the easily manipulated gardeners. But he'd done far better than he could possibly have hoped before entering the room. So why wasn't he feeling far more satisfied?

The doubt vanished an hour later when he entered the Savoy to find waiting for him, on a message slip, another telephone number he recognized at once to be Natalia's.

7

"GOOD TO SPEAK TO YOU AFTER SO LONG."

It had to be close to five months, Charlie reckoned. "And to speak to you. How are you?"

"Fine. You?"

Did her voice sound as distant as it had when they'd last spoken? Too soon to tell. "Fine. How's Sasha?"

"Very well," said Natalia.

Why were important conversations, which he judged this to be, conducted in such mundane, ordinary words? He said: "I'd like to see her while I'm here. You, too, of course. I'm sorry; I didn't put that very well, did I?"

"She's away for a few days on a school trip."

"Isn't she young to be away on a trip by herself?" Alone in his hotel room, Charlie grimaced as he uttered the words, wishing he could have bitten them back. There was a strict rule between them that he never questioned Natalia about the upbringing of their daughter. "Ignore what I just said. I'm sorry." It was the second time he'd apologized in less than five minutes: he was sounding like a stumbling idiot, not someone determined to persuade her against all her previous refusals.

"She's at a regulated camp up in the hills, about ten kilometers outside Moscow. They're in purpose-built barracks, four girls to a hut. There are three permanent staff, as well as security and two teachers. She can telephone me every day, which she's doing *every* day, and she'll be back in two days."

"I said I'm . . ." began Charlie, stopping short to avoid repeating himself again.

"Of course we should meet. Why not?" said Natalia, helpfully.

"My movements are uncertain."

"Of course," Natalia accepted, without needing to ask why. "I'm fairly flexible, although it might be more convenient if we met initially ahead of Sasha getting back."

"Tomorrow," demanded Charlie.

Natalia hesitated. "I'll wait for your call."

Following that afternoon's meeting with Pavel and the others, there was every likelihood that some surveillance would be imposed upon him, acknowledged Charlie, relieved that so far he had not detected any telltale delay in anything Natalia had said to indicate an interception already on his hotel phone. He had to assume, though, that the hotel line was unsafe. And he knew that cell phones could just as easily be scanned. "I'll use public phones to contact you from now on."

"I see."

"And you shouldn't try to call me here again."

"No."

Charlie had forgotten the long-ago subterfuge he and Natalia had needed to stay safe and didn't imagine Natalia would welcome the rigmarole again, certainly not at the risk it created for Sasha. "I hadn't properly thought the nonsense through."

"Neither had I."

"We can make it work, though," urgently insisted Charlie, worried by the difficulty, angry at himself that he hadn't considered it earlier. But then he hadn't expected the reception committee awaiting him in Pavel's Petrovka office, which he'd left less than an hour ago and still had to assess. Not any sort of excuse, he criticized himself.

"We both need to think about that," said Natalia, cautiously. "Particularly where we meet."

She was very sensibly putting her apartment—her and Sasha's

apartment—off limits, Charlie recognized. The hotel would obviously be impossible, too. "We'll talk about it when I phone."

"Definitely before Sasha gets back."

"Definitely," agreed Charlie.

"I'll be waiting."

Charlie remained listening after Natalia replaced her receiver, relieved at not hearing a second intruding disconnection, reminding himself at the same time that Russian technology would have obviously improved since he'd last worked here. Harry Fish, whose knowledge Charlie respected, had described the listening devices at the embassy as state of the art.

★

Which was the expression Fish used again the following day, when Charlie entered the assigned inquiry room at the embassy to find the electronics expert with Paul Robertson, the London director of internal counterintelligence, whose peremptory summons had been awaiting Charlie the moment he'd arrived at the embassy.

Fish had three more pinhead devices laid out, again on a white cloth. Nodding to them, the man said: "One was in the terminal relay to the ambassador's personal phone, the second in that of his personal assistant. The third was on Dawkins's line. All the bafflers on every terminal, put there to defeat just such emplacements, had been removed."

"We've had our differences in the past," Robertson immediately reminded Charlie, clearly expecting to take command and control of everything. "That's where they are, in the past. And where they'll stay. I want this all wrapped up, which also means I want your input. Which further means I want to know everything you've discovered and how it's going to help me. . . ." The sallow-faced man jerked his head sideways, to the electronics expert. "Harry's told me what he helped you do, so I don't want any of that bullshit, which I don't anticipate the Director-General will, either, so we won't involve him in any discussion about it."

Two major differences, Charlie remembered. The first had

arisen when Robertson had suggested the wrong traitor in a long-ago operation which he'd overturned by identifying the correct one. On the second occasion, Robertson had wrongly accused Charlie of security negligence and been officially censured in the subsequent exonerating inquiry. Charlie had suspected then the personal accusation had been in revenge for Robertson's initial mistake and didn't have any doubt about the personal animosity involved this time. How much lower—and heavier—was the sky going to come down on his head? Looking to the other man, Charlie said, "Thanks, Harry, for the discretion."

"Trying to con the Russians as you are doing is a stupid idea that isn't going to work and I'm not going to be pulled down by it. Or by you," returned Fish. "I've got friends now stacking supermarket shelves who got too closely involved with you!"

"Let's not get petulant," warned Robertson. "Tell me what you know!"

Fuck both of you, thought Charlie. "Is this embassy now totally clean?"

"Guaranteed," confirmed Fish.

"Which isn't any reassurance," dismissed Charlie. "They scored ten out of ten, with a gold star. There had to be inside guidance for them to have hit every target like that as well as removing the counterprotection, in the limited times between Stout going back and forth between the control boxes and CCTVs to check they were working properly after they were supposedly fixed."

"Our conclusion, too," said Robertson. "Which gives us a mole hunt and one hell of a problem. The Director-General has told me you're working directly to him, quite independently of what we're trying to do. Which is why it's only you here with Harry and me. And why Harry's shown you what else he's found, to give you some idea of the mess we're in. All I want is your opinion."

Charlie's first thought was that what Robertson had just said was a very bad attempt to give the impression that the Director-General had sanctioned this meeting. Aubrey Smith's edict categorically precluded his cooperation—even his taking part in this conversation—ridiculous though it seemed in the circumstances.

"Do you think the two *are* separate: your murder having no connection whatsoever with the planting of the listening equipment?" demanded Robertson. "Or, from what you've so far discovered, do you think they are linked in some way?"

"You know I'll have to give a full account of this meeting to the Director-General?" said Charlie, determined against a bureaucratic misdemeanor suddenly biting him in the ass.

"I accept that completely," assured Robertson. "I've already told Smith what I'm asking you."

Charlie doubted he had been as specific as that. "Until now, until you showed me those three new bugs and we both reached the same conclusion about the FSB having a source embedded within the embassy, I was working on the assumption—an assumption so far without any positive proof—that the Russian electricians were FSB opportunists, not able to believe their luck at being called in by our idiot head of security with the permission of our equally idiotic diplomats. But I had a problem with that assumption; still do have a problem." Charlie nodded to the miniscule devices on the desk between them. "State of the art, Harry calls them. That's what the FSB electricians who installed them would have been, state-of-the-art experts at their jobs. And having installed them, they wouldn't have left the electrics so fucked up that they continued to malfunction, for the bugs to be found when Harry and his team arrived . . ." Charlie paused, caught by an unprompted thought. "Unless . . . ?"

"Unless what?" demanded Fish.

Charlie waited for the conjecture to get firmer in his mind and when it did, although not completely, he said: "I don't at this moment fully see how this helps any assessment. But how about the FSB technicians not having enough time to do all they wanted at their first opportunity? So they do something to continue the problem, expecting to be called in a second time to get a lot more devices into a lot more sites?"

"But then you arrive to investigate the murder, the security idiots here know they've broken the rules, and they start doing things properly and call in Harry and his team?" anticipated Robertson, smiling.

"No," rejected Charlie, refusing to be tricked into confirming the other man's conclusion. "The way I understand it—and this can be checked—the alert to London that brought Harry here was sounded *before* I arrived . . ." He hesitated again, unsure whether to continue but then asked, "You spoken to David Halliday yet?"

"No," said Robertson.

"He's told me he's been warning London for the past six months that there's virtually no internal security here," said Charlie. "Check his log, to see if he knew locals were being called in *before* they actually arrived to look at the problem. And if it was another message from him, when the CCTV continued to malfunction afterward, that brought Harry here."

"We're throwing up some interesting hypotheses but you haven't yet given me an answer to whether you believe our two investigations are linked or separate," complained Robertson.

Throughout the discussion, Charlie had been sifting what he felt comfortable sharing with the other two men against the risk—heightened now by the suspicion of the FSB having a source inside the embassy—of either Robertson or Fish, or both of them, inadvertently saying something that would ruin his dangerously uncertain bluff. Cautiously Charlie said, "I think there is a link. Whoever killed my man needed to sabotage the CCTV systems to get in and out without being detected. What about there being someone inside the embassy—the mole—who separately carried out the initial entry sabotage?"

"Which doesn't give me any direction in which to work," Robertson continued to complain.

"It does!" contradicted Charlie, at once. "Until now, until Harry found the additional three bugs *where* he found them— and we talked it through—you didn't suspect there was a mole in the embassy. Now you do."

"And wish I didn't," said the counterintelligence director.

★

Charlie didn't immediately access the London messages waiting for him in the communications room, intent upon filing without any interfering distraction his own account to the Director-General of the meeting with Robertson, needing two drafts before being satisfied. The writing and rewriting provided the opportunity for Charlie to assess the impact upon his independent investigation of a potential FSB source within the building, reassured at his eventual conclusion that it affected him very little. He'd neither used any compromised telephone connections nor taken anything out of the secure communications system in which he now sat. Looking up to Ross Perrit, the communications controller, Charlie said, "Who else has access to my Eyes Only password to London?"

"No one *but* you," said Perrit, a vaguely mannered, seemingly distracted man whom Charlie knew to be anything but vague or distracted.

"What about you?"

Perrit sighed, although not offended. "I didn't give it to you, remember? You used your London password when you logged on from here and it was from London that you got your operational code. I don't know what it is."

"So no one here in this embassy, not even you, can read my traffic?"

"You got something specific, something *very* specific, you really want to ask me?" pointedly asked the no longer vague or distracted man, abandoning whatever it was he had been doing at another computer terminal to walk over to Charlie's station.

He had, accepted Charlie, betrayed his knowledge of a so far undisclosed double-agent situation in exactly the same way as he'd feared Harry Fish or Paul Robertson might have let slip anything he told them about the chicanery he was orchestrating. "I was just trying to resolve a question that suddenly came to me."

"And now that you've got my undivided attention, why don't you ask me the question and let me help you answer it?" challenged the man.

"You just have," avoided Charlie.

"I know the meaning of security," belligerently reminded Perrit. "It's what I'm here for."

"My misunderstanding," retreated Charlie. "Let's not let things get out of proportion."

"You're right," said Perrit. "Let's not!"

Charlie was neither intimidated nor embarrassed by the confrontation—rather, he was encouraged at the confirmation of remaining out of danger—and his spirits lifted further when he finally opened his personal, Eyes Only file from the London scientist. All the false enhancement and manipulation he'd asked for, particularly on the CCTV loops, was both technically possible and technically undetectable. It did, though, require the personal authority of the Director-General.

Charlie looked up at the unexpected return of Ross Perrit, who said without any explanation or preamble, apart from indicating the single strut suspended, doubly secure box within the communications room: "You've got Booth Two."

"Who's in Booth One?" asked Charlie, instinctively.

Perrit walked away, pointedly not replying.

★

"I've spoken to Robertson," announced the Director-General, answering Charlie's question that Perrit had just refused. "What the hell's happening over there!"

"Too many things, all of them too quickly one after the other."

"Meaning?" demanded Aubrey Smith. He usually had a soft, never-surprised voice, which Charlie guessed was being stretched to the extreme.

"The embassy's being manipulated, for a reason or reasons I don't at the moment understand," replied Charlie, honestly.

"You in any way compromised or endangered?"

"No," assured Charlie at once, glad of the review time.

"Do you need backup?"

"No," said Charlie again, the refusal more professional than self-protective. "More people would mean more confusion, which might well be one of the several intentions." He hesitated. "On the subject of backup, David Halliday, the MI6 man here, is anxious to get involved. He told me his director was approaching you directly, to talk about it."

"I don't like Gerald Monsford and certainly don't respect his judgement," said Smith. "He did approach me. I told him no."

"Thank you," said Charlie. "I appreciate that."

"But with so much dependent upon your total success, I'm unsure if you can any longer operate alone."

"I can!" insisted Charlie.

"I'm keeping open the option of sending in a team."

"Would I be in charge of it?" asked Charlie, desperately.

"No," refused the other man, without any hesitation. "What's the point of all this you've asked the technical division to create?"

"To avoid being excluded by the Russians claiming it's their investigation in which we have no right of participation."

"No," agreed the soft-voiced man at once. "We most definitely don't want that with everything else that's happening there."

"Technical say it's got to have your personal approval."

"It'll be authorized the moment we conclude this conversation. I don't like so much appearing to happen beyond our control. You any idea, the faintest suspicion, who the traitor might be?"

Charlie was caught by the pedantically correct word. "Finding whoever it is isn't my remit."

"Neither was it the point of my question."

"Not yet," prevaricated Charlie, on this occasion more for self-protection than strict professionalism. "How do I deal with it, if I become suspicious?"

"The way you're being told right now, only and directly through me. I don't want another quiet exchange between you, Fish, and Robertson."

Smith was invoking the most inviolable rule of double-agent penetration, Charlie recognized: slam shut every water-tight door and not answer anyone's knock. "I understand."

"I hope you do. I sent you there to do a job, not to become a puppet."

The self-directed anger at allowing himself to be sidetracked physically burned through Charlie. Robertson had occupied the adjoining compartment ahead of his, Charlie acknowledged, able to get his explanation and story in first. But to whom? Charlie opened his mouth but stopped himself, knowing to attempt a defense would be a further mistake. "I'll call, if there's something positive from what I'm doing."

"I'm expecting you to," said the other man.

★

Charlie had subjugated his irritation at having made the cooperation mistake by the time he reached his rabbit-hutch office, more curious at the first than at the second of the two voice-mail messages awaiting him, although choosing to respond to the second.

"I've pressed the pathologist for more," announced Pavel.

Liar, thought Charlie at once. Pavel was offering everything that had been originally available instead of the scraps the man had imagined he could get away with. But it was looking promising. "And?"

"He's talking about some additional medical findings. And there's a lot more photographs."

"I'll stop by the mortuary first thing tomorrow," tempted Charlie.

"We could go together," said Pavel, as Charlie had expected. "We might as well go through it all together."

Once again bullshit had proved to be the magic fertilizer. "How about my meeting you there at ten?"

"Perfect timing for me," agreed Pavel.

"What about the others who were there the first time?" pressed Charlie, wanting as much forewarning as possible.

"I'll let them all know the arrangement," promised Pavel. "I understand there's been contact between Nikita Kashev and your embassy?"

"I haven't heard," said Charlie, honestly. And wouldn't have confirmed it if I had, he thought. It had been an unthinking question, even from someone as anxious as the organized crime investigator.

"How about your scientific people in London?" Pavel pressed.

"I haven't heard anything from them, either," lied Charlie. Deciding, though, that he should make a gesture, he added, "I'll drop by the embassy before I come to the mortuary to check if anything comes in overnight."

"It would be good to hear something that takes the investigation forward."

It very definitely would, thought Charlie. It would be premature to become overconfident from this very preliminary conversation, but it looked as if he'd kept himself on the inside of the investigation. But in terms of practicality, the inquiry hadn't moved a stumbling step from the finding of the body.

"Surprised to hear from you so soon after our dinner," opened Charlie, finally responding to the other voice mail from Bundy.

"I'd welcome talking to someone whose experience and opinions I respect," said Bundy.

Bollocks, dismissed Charlie. "Been away too long myself to get up to speed yet."

"You certainly hit the ground at a busy time."

"Maybe one that talking about on an open-line telephone isn't such a good idea, unless you're equipped with an intercept white noise cutout at your end."

Bundy laughed. "You're not trying to tell me you're calling on a phone that hasn't been swept clean enough to shine in the dark?"

I'm not but someone else already has, decided Charlie. And it was all too easy to decide who that person was. "I'm still uncomfortable after an episode like this."

"You wouldn't be on top of your job, which you always have been, if you weren't more than uncomfortable," overflattered the American. "We talked the other night about lunch. How about it?"

Charlie's instinctive inclination was to make an excuse, just as quickly discarded. Charlie was as much a learn-everything Russophile as Bill Bundy and wanted very much to discover the reason for Bundy's inexplicable interest in him. He was also anxious to get off the telephone and out of the embassy to make contact with Natalia. "Lunch would be good."

"How about tomorrow? The Pekin on the ring road?"

He now had Bundy's direct line to cancel if the mortuary visit went on longer than he expected. "One o'clock unless I have to cry off."

"I hope you don't cry off," said the American.

To make what he judged the far more important call Charlie used the same telephone kiosk farther along Smolenskaya from which he'd rearranged his dinner date with Paula-Jane, with whom he guessed he was going to have a confrontation the following day.

"How about the Botanical Gardens?" he suggested, when she answered.

He heard—or hoped he heard—her faint laugh at the venue: the gardens, with their huge cultivation greenhouses, had been one of their tryst locations when he'd first maneuverd the posting to Moscow after learning of Sasha's existence. "How long will you need to be sure?"

"Two hours should be more than enough," said Charlie, knowing Natalia wouldn't require the same amount of time to ensure she wasn't under surveillance. He also knew that she would still take every precaution.

"Eight then," accepted Natalia. "The tropical plant greenhouse, as always."

She'd even remembered the specific meeting spot, Charlie recognized, encouraged.

8

NATALIA WAS WAITING ON THE SEAT HE'D EXPECTED, PAR-
tially hidden beneath an overshadowing cedar but with an un-
obstructed view of his approach to establish for herself that he was
not under any surveillance. This was where—and how—she'd
expertly waited in those initial days that now seemed so long ago:
it had been summer then, too, and although it would have been
impossible for it to have been the same one, she was even wearing
a matching light coat that Charlie remembered her wearing then.

She would have seen him enter, of course, but she didn't look
up from her book and Charlie made no acknowledgement as he
continued past to a seat closer to their chosen glassed exhibition
hall where he sat and opened that day's *Pravda*. His position gave
Natalia an even more extensive view from which surveillance
could have been established if any pursuers entered through other
gates; Charlie was sure there was no one after the precautions
he'd taken over the preceding two hours. The Moscow Metro, with
its eight separate but interlinked, people-jammed underground
lines, was an espionage Olympics training ground for trail clearing, and that evening Charlie had used it like the gold medalist
he was.

He'd been alert to everything and everyone around him when
he'd left the embassy, deep within as big a departing group as he
could find among which to hide himself from the remaining

although slightly smaller media melee, knowing there would still be FSB cameramen among the photographers. He kept that danger in mind while making for the already identified telephone kiosk on Smolenskaya. Although not suspicious of any suddenly slowing pedestrian or vehicle during his brief conversation with Natalia, he held back from descending immediately underground at a convenient Smolenskaya Metro station. Forcing himself onto Kievskaya with growing protest from unexpectedly challenged feet, he changed at Barrikadnaya onto the inner-city sixth Tapansko line, disembarking at Tverskaya to change lines again, allowing himself two stops until transferring to the Kaluzsko-Rizskaja route to go north. He became uncomfortable with a bespectacled, mustached man who stayed with him as far as Turgenevskaya, remaining on the train after the man disembarked, and only got off himself at the warning of the doors closing to trap on the departing train anyone who might have worked an obligatory observation switch. Charlie went back and forth between two alternative lines, once coming up to ground level—before going back down again after five lingering minutes—at Poljanka. He'd finally emerged at Botanicheskiy Sad with fifteen minutes to spare before his rendezvous with Natalia, sore-footed but confident he was alone.

It was an additional fifteen minutes before Natalia finally got up from her bench and crossed to where he rose to meet her.

"You're clear," she said.

"I know." She was wearing her hair shorter but otherwise he didn't think she'd changed at all. "You look wonderful."

"You look like you," she said, smiling.

"I'd like to kiss you."

"Do you have to ask?"

"I'm not sure. Do I?"

"I'm not sure, either." She turned her head as he came toward her, offering her cheek.

"We know we're alone but I can't remember anywhere around here where we could move on to," said Charlie. Hurriedly he added, "A restaurant, I mean."

"I know what you mean. There's a place on the next block. I've never been there, so I don't know what it's like."

A discovery she'd made clearing her own trail, Charlie guessed. "Let's look at it."

It specialized in Georgian cuisine, already with enough people inside to recommend it, and able to provide Charlie's choice of wine, which he ordered the moment they secured a secluded table at the rear, against an inner wall. He also ordered chilled vodka with the Beluga, which they both appropriately chose before their fish.

Natalia said: "You ordered caviar for me the first time we ate out."

"I was trying to impress you then, too." It had been Natalia who'd taken the risk then, agreeing to the outing while still officially debriefing him to confirm he was a genuine defector, which he hadn't been, living another professional lie.

"As you are now?"

"Now's a celebration of our being back together."

"In the same city together," she qualified, heavily.

"It's a start."

"You're rushing, Charlie. There's a lot to talk about: maybe too much for one night."

"I've got as many nights as we need."

Natalia made as if to speak but didn't. Then she said, "Do you really know how long you'll be here?"

Now it was Charlie who hesitated. "It'll be some time."

"I didn't enjoy the Botanical Gardens routine," Natalia declared. "I didn't the first time."

"I didn't imagine you would."

"And wouldn't, for all those nights we might need. Nor would Sasha."

They both waited for their main fish courses to be served. Charlie considered a second bottle of wine but decided against it. Natalia had often complained of his drinking too much. When the waiter left, Charlie said: "Of course, Sasha wouldn't be involved in anything like tonight. It just had to be this way, to make contact."

"And?" she asked, laying down her knife and fork unnecessarily to show the importance of her question.

It was a protective demand she was justified in making, not an investigative inquiry into what he was professionally involved. "A possibility at Turgenevskaya. I slipped it, if indeed there was a watcher with me."

"You hope."

"You were the final cutoff check. You know I arrived clean." This wasn't evolving as he'd expected.

Natalia began eating again. "Sasha called, before I left. She's enjoying herself."

The encounter wasn't working out as Natalia had intended, either, Charlie guessed. "What do you tell her, about me? About us?"

"That you're her father but that you have to work away."

"Doesn't she question that?"

"She's starting to. There are other fathers of children in her class who work away but they come home sometimes. She can't understand why you never do."

"Doesn't she remember me at all?"

"Not really. She's got all the toys and dolls you spoiled her with."

"My meeting her now—but then having eventually to go away again—is going to confuse her even more, isn't it?" said Charlie, objectively.

"Yes," agreed Natalia, abandoning her meal altogether.

"Do you want me to meet her now, this time?" asked Charlie, pushing his own plate aside.

"You're her father."

"Who doesn't want to confuse her, upset her, any more than is happening now."

"Any more than I do," echoed Natalia, shaking her head against Charlie's offer of more wine.

"I can't live here again. And it's not primarily a question of my not wanting to—although I don't, as you know—but the practicality of not being *able* to, not anymore," said Charlie, urgently. "The FSB are involved in what I'm doing here. I'm identified to them now. You wouldn't just be dismissed from the service if you and I were found out. You'd probably be arrested. Jailed. I'd be expelled and wouldn't be able to take Sasha with me. She'd end up in a state orphanage. The answer's what it's always been—for you to resign and come to London with me. The question is, who do you love more, Sasha and me? Or Russia?"

"That's a cheap, unfair question!" protested Natalia, only just managing to keep her voice under control.

"It's the practical one," insisted Charlie, unrepentant.

"Do you think your service would let you go on working for them, with me in London?"

"I doubt it. It's not important, not anymore. Terrorism is the new buzzword. With my background—as much of it as I would be able to disclose on a CV—I could get work as an antiterrorist consultant like that"—Charlie snapped his fingers—"at probably three times more money than I'm earning now."

"And hate every minute of it," predicted Natalia.

"I hate every minute of what I'm doing now," said Charlie, having to control the loudness of his own voice. "I want to be with you and Sasha more than I want to be in this fucking job." It wasn't entirely true but it was close enough. Between assignments, his existence was an aching aimlessness of pub closing times and reheated supermarket dinners for one in a Vauxhall flat more resembling a monastic cell than a place in which to live. The apartment would certainly have to go if he could finally convince Natalia. Sasha would need a house with a garden and a good school and . . . and everything that other normal families had, whatever that was.

"It isn't as easy or as simple as that."

"Isn't as easy or as simple as what?" demanded Charlie.

"You think you can appear from nowhere, without any warning after five years, and expect everything to be the same as it was with us?"

Charlie felt physically chilled. "No. I don't think that at all."

Neither looked directly at the other across the table, grateful at the interruption of the waiter clearing their table. Charlie shook his head against their ordering any more, asking for the bill instead.

Natalia said: "I've got to go."

"Can I call you again?"

"I don't know. I'm not sure."

"We haven't decided if I can see Sasha."

"We haven't decided anything."

"I'll call."

"Not tomorrow."

"When?"

"I don't know. A couple of days."

It would be a mistake to ask why, Charlie decided. He wasn't actually sure he wanted to know why. "A couple of days then."

"I'll leave first. Give me fifteen minutes."

"I love you," declared Charlie, a man to whom expressing emotion was always difficult. "I love you and I love Sasha, and I want us to be together."

"Fifteen minutes," Natalia repeated.

"You know you're safe."

"Safe is what I've never been with you, Charlie. And safe with you is all I've ever wanted to be. Safe with you and Sasha."

★

Charlie's very determined effort to separate his personal from his professional confusions wasn't helped by the head-tourniquet hangover from the previous night's consumption of Islay single malt after he'd got back to the hotel from his reunion with Natalia, the ache worsened by the eye-wincing glare of the sun the moment he stepped outside his hotel to hail a taxi.

Charlie, who knew his every natural as well as carefully culti-vated fault, had never included being a fantasizer among them. But that's what he'd been, he acknowledged, accepting Natalia's accusation: a head-in-the-clouds fantasizer in imagining he could pitch up in Moscow as he had and expect everything to be as it once had been between them. So if it wasn't as simple and as easy as he'd fantasized, how—exactly—was it? He didn't know. He was encouraged by her parting remark but unsettled at the thought of some hidden meaning behind her telling him their being together with Sasha in London wasn't easy or simple. Was her remark so hidden, though? Hardly. The impossibility of their being together in Moscow was entirely practicable, for all the reasons he'd spelled out to her. What was not so easy, in Natalia's mind, was surely the mystical obstacle of abandoning Russia, which Charlie had never been able to conceive as an obstacle no matter how many times they'd talked about it from so many different directions. It had to be the suddenness of his being here, Charlie tried to reassure himself. That and the Botanical Gardens reminder of how threatened their existence had once been. Wasn't that what she'd actually said—*safe with you is all I've ever wanted to be.* It would all be different—better—when they met the next time, after she'd had the opportunity to think everything through.

Charlie had intentionally arrived at the mortuary thirty minutes ahead of the time he'd arranged to meet Sergei Pavel, wanting to talk alone with the pathologist, but the organized crime detective was outside, waiting. So was Mikhail Guzov.

"You're early." Guzov's smile combined satisfaction with a rebuke at Charlie imagining he could outsmart him.

"As you are," Charlie pointed out. Give the man all the rope he needs to tie himself up in knots, thought Charlie.

"I think it's impolite to keep people waiting."

"So do I," sparred Charlie. "Thank you for your courtesy."

Guzov's smile faded. "I'm representing the ministry. Secretary Kashev is occupied talking with your embassy."

Why had Guzov volunteered that? Probably to convey the impression of cooperation when he was offering virtually nothing, which made the gesture hardly worth the effort, apart from trying to establish his control of the gathering. "Less likely to upset his stomach as his being here did last time. So it's just the three of us?"

"Let's go in," suggested Pavel, talking to Charlie, not the other Russian.

Vladimir Ivanov was waiting in the postmortem room, the body of the one-armed man already on the examination slab. It had a ghostlike grayness from its refrigeration, a faint mist from the room's warmth wisping from the edges of the cloth in which it had been wrapped. From the disinterested expectancy of the pathologist's greeting, Charlie guessed Guzov and Pavel had already been into the room once that morning, probably to check that he hadn't gotten there ahead of them.

"You've found more to help us?" prompted Charlie.

Following Ivanov's inquiring look to the FSB officer, Charlie caught the nod of permission from Guzov. He was curious at the fixed, almost irritable expression on Pavel's face. The pathologist said, "It's for you to decide how much help it might be." The body had thawed sufficiently for the man to raise slightly the remaining hand. "The fingertips—and therefore any prints—were taken off with sulphuric acid: I lifted traces from the thumb, as well as each finger. And see here . . ." The man isolated the little finger and that next to it, both of which were roughly stitched after incisions. "I originally thought these distortions were contractions caused by exposure to extreme heat but when I found the acid traces I reexamined the hand much more closely. In my opinion, the disfigurement was caused by frostbite a long time ago, possibly even when he was a child. And this . . ." Ivanov turned the back of the hand. "Again, I thought that was a heat burn but it isn't. It's a strawberry birthmark that's been made darker by an acid splash, maybe when he was flailing against the acid being applied to his fingertips—"

"Unquestionably tortured," broke in Charlie, including Guzov in the remark more in challenge to the official casualness of the first dismissive examination than for confirmation of his own early judgment. Remembering his earlier torture oversight, he saw that the fingernails of the right hand were intact but turned brown by the acid.

"Without any doubt," agreed the pathologist. Detecting the possible criticism, he added, "I suggested the possibility when we met before."

Neither Guzov nor Pavel reacted.

"And we have much more now to help with an identification?" persisted Charlie.

"I wouldn't exactly say much more," disputed Pavel.

Briskly, actually turning as he gestured toward the door, Guzov said; "I've had a room made available for us, where we can talk about the London findings."

Far too anxious, decided Charlie, ignoring the invitation. Nodding toward the body and an obvious abdominal incision, Charlie said to the pathologist: "There was nothing in your first report of stomach contents?"

"A partially digested meal, eaten maybe an hour to an hour and a half before he died," replied Ivanov, at once.

"Possible to analyze?"

Ivanov nodded. "I don't think it would have been, normally. There was some in the gullet, as if it was being expelled. I think he died as he was about to vomit from the agony of what was being done to him. I recovered ground beef and some bread residue. I'd say he'd eaten a hamburger. There was also some liquid mixed with the ort, with a high sugar content, which I'd say came from a cola."

"McDonald's is very popular here in Moscow," offered Pavel.

"And our victim wore cheap clothes and shoes, so a man with a limited income would eat in a fast-food outlet, wouldn't he?" said Charlie, familiar with the menu from his own London diet, eaten more for disinterested convenience than economy. Going back to the pathologist, Charlie said: "There is another thing I need to establish. Your first report didn't give a blood grouping?"

"It's in the addendum," said Ivanov, defensively, picking up and letting drop the manila folder at the bottom of the slab. "It's AB."

Charlie nodded, head momentarily forward on his chest. "Of course it is."

"What?" exclaimed Pavel, frowning.

"It's what the British forensic people recovered from the separate soil samples from the area we examined," Charlie lied. Five minutes earlier he hadn't even thought of the need to match the Russian blood findings.

"We really do need to hear what you've got to tell us!" insisted Guzov, the earlier bombast weakening.

"As we really do need to examine one thing at a time," argued Charlie, instantly registering Pavel's apparent smile of approval at the confrontation. "What about toxicology?"

"Also in the report," sighed Ivanov, tapping the folder. "There's evidence of barbitumiv acid in the blood."

"How concentrated?" demanded Charlie, identifying another Russian-convincing bonus.

"Weak."

"Not barbiturates of anaesthetic strength?"

"Definitely not. Is that what your toxicologists found?" asked Ivanov, making it even easier for Charlie's improvisation.

"They wouldn't positively commit themselves," tiptoed Charlie, cautiously. "My impression from the conversation was that it was a little stronger than sedative level?"

"I'd go along with that," agreed the pathologist.

"Are you saying this man was sedated before he was tortured?" demanded Guzov, too eager again.

Charlie was almost too eager himself to put the Russian down but held back for the pathologist. "No, of course not!" rejected the doctor, careless of the obvious exasperation.

"Whoever did what they did to him certainly didn't want to spare him pain," picked up Charlie. "It's an outside guess that his killers used sleeping pills or draughts to sedate him *after* the torture to get him into the embassy grounds without risking an alarm, once the CCTV was out of action."

"It was too faint for that," argued Ivanov. "It's a sleeping preparation."

"I called it an outside guess," reminded Charlie, an escape route prepared. Having established far more than he'd hoped, Charlie turned to Guzov and said, "Why don't we talk things through now?" putting the impending exchange very firmly under his, not Guzov's, control.

★

The room was a marginal improvement upon what Charlie had at the British embassy, but it would have required a micrometer to measure that margin. At least the smell of formaldehyde and disinfectant was less. And his success in reversing how Guzov had clearly intended their meeting to go had done a lot to ease the tightening alcoholic band around Charlie's head: in fact, there was hardly any ache troubling him any longer. Determined to build upon what he had already achieved and using his newly acquired folder as a prompt, Charlie said at once, "This has been an extremely useful, confirming discussion. Our respective scientists have positively but independently matched the blood as well as the barbitumiv content within the victim's body. There has been a very calculated and well-planned attempt to conceal the identity, not just upon the body, but by cutting all the labels from the clothing as well as emptying its pockets. . . ." He looked between the two Russians, refusing to accord seniority to Guzov. "London believes there could be a lot more discovered from the clothes and so far we haven't discussed them. I'm told forensically they could be far more productive, providing dust, fibers, hair other than that of the victim, under detailed analysis. I've been asked formally to request that everything the man was wearing be made available to London when your detailed examination is concluded, so that we can continue the cooperation that we're enjoying now—"

"Let's stop right there!" halted a now very red-faced Guzov, unable any longer to contain the indignation at being so completely steamrollered. "What cooperation? So far everything has come from us, nothing from you. I do not know anything about cooperation being agreed. And—"

"I thought I had explained my operational difficulty very clearly and fully," blocked Charlie, in turn. "And understood from what you told me earlier today that Secretary Kashev was currently involved in trying to resolve that difficulty."

"Until which time and until there is some reciprocity from

your side, I do not consider a case for cooperation has been established or agreed!"

Hardball or softball? Somewhere in between, Charlie decided. "You also told me this morning that you were representing your ministry. Is the view you have expressed that of your ministry? If it is, then it is obviously a matter I shall have to raise with London."

"I am talking of the lack of reciprocity." The man backed off.

Which wasn't an answer to his question but certainly was to Guzov's bombast, thought Charlie. "I find myself at a loss to know how to continue this conversation. I believed I had made very clear the matching medical findings I shall be able to provide from London. As well as the CCTV enhancements that we talked about at the meeting at Petrovka. We're at a stalemate here."

"I am sure it is something that can be resolved, although perhaps not today," came in Pavel, whose irritable looks at the other Russian, as well as annoyed shifting in his seat, Charlie had been aware of during his exchange with Guzov.

"I would certainly hope so, as soon as possible," said Charlie. He'd achieved everything and more than he'd hoped, and there was still time to keep the luncheon appointment with Bill Bundy. He hoped he'd do as well there, too.

9

IT WAS VIRTUALLY INSTINCTIVE FOR CHARLIE TO CHECK FOR unwelcome company, particularly when he was on foreign assignment, and after that morning's confrontation with Mikhail Guzov, Charlie ratcheted up the concentration, not going directly to the Pekin but taking the taxi by a roundabout route to the Arbat shopping area and holding it while he briefly toured the stalls and outlets, ready actually to buy something for Natalia or Sasha if anything caught his eye. Nothing did, but a small BMW he'd isolated close to the mortuary continued three cars behind when the taxi moved off again. The detour and the traffic buildup on the freeway delayed his arrival and Bundy was at their table, mineral water already poured, by the time Charlie got there.

"Bad traffic," apologized Charlie.

"Just got here myself," said the American, which Charlie doubted, guessing someone as old school as Bundy would have given himself at least an hour to clear his trail.

Although not a hair-of-the-dog advocate, Charlie decided the success of his morning—and the gradual settling of his stomach—justified a preprandial vodka. Raising it to the other man in a toast, Charlie said, "To the death of all our enemies."

"Difficult to pick them all out these days, don't you think, Charlie?"

"I guess white hats against black hats or vice versa was easier," encouraged Charlie, relaxing back in his chair like a confident boxer before the first round.

"I think it's more interesting now in many ways."

"How's that?"

"Take your reason for being here. You've got to admit we never had anything like this, right in our own front garden, in the old days."

"You're talking about the murder at the embassy, right?" asked Charlie, unable to find a connection to what Bundy appeared to consider logic.

"What the hell else do you think I'm talking about?"

"I don't recall telling you that's what I'm here for," fenced Charlie.

The American spread his hands in front of him, as if he were pleading. "Charlie! It's me, Bill Bundy, remember? We've been here since the beginning: know all the tricks."

"Difficult to remember them all sometimes," said Charlie, refusing to contribute to whatever the other man was trying to establish.

"It's true," insisted Bundy. "But if you tell me you're here for something else then I'll take it you've got another agenda you can't tell me about."

"Bill!" exclaimed Charlie. "We're not running a joint operation here!"

"Maybe I could provide some input."

"And maybe get burned in the effort."

"I've always thought myself pretty fireproof."

"I'm not," refused Charlie. He found this entire exchange absolutely bewildering except for one thought: Bundy could be a convenient sacrificial escape if the need arose.

"There's a nostalgia about the murder, don't you think?" persisted the American. "Guy gets whacked at the moment of his defection."

"Is that how you think it happened?" queried Charlie, remembering some of the newspaper conjecture.

"I'd give the idea some room to run. How do you see it?"

The waitress's arrival spared Charlie's need for an instant reply, although he didn't need time to consider one. He was enjoying the verbal ping-pong, the vaguest idea of its purpose forming in his mind but in no hurry to confirm it. In deference to the abuse he'd inflicted upon himself the previous night, Charlie restricted himself to pancake-wrapped duck, crispy beef, and spicy noodles, with boiled rice and a bottle of rice wine, despite Bundy's protests that he wouldn't share the alcohol.

"So how do you see it?" repeated Bundy, when the girl left.

"I'm keeping an open mind. Everything's at a very early stage. Still a lot of technical and scientific stuff to be analyzed and assessed."

"So you are here for the murder?" openly demanded the American.

"It's not carved in stone," avoided Charlie. "There seems to be a lot else happening."

"Things good with the local homicide guys?"

"There's some diplomatic protocol to work through; you know what it's like."

"Not helped by your guys finding a big bunch of bugs nesting right there in the ambassador's phone system."

"Not helped one little bit," agreed Charlie, without pausing at the alarm bells that rang in his mind.

"Surprised you don't have help," pressed Bundy. "Something as serious as this, with the bugging on top, strikes me as a heavy workload."

"I'm just about keeping a handle on it," claimed Charlie, hoping his voice conveyed the conviction he didn't feel at that moment.

"I've still got a few open lines here. You wanna bounce anything off me, feel free."

Charlie needed his control to hold back his surprise at that remark. "That's very good of you."

"Maybe it's jealousy at everything happening on your patch and nothing on mine."

Charlie recognized the perfect opening. "I got the impression that you guys were very much caught up with the new presidential elections here?"

"I guess your political section was, too, until last week," said Bundy.

"You keeping out of it?" asked Charlie, risking directness himself.

"Tex has been keeping a tight watching brief."

"You would have been on station here the first time, when Lvov was with the KGB, right?" demanded Charlie, direct again.

"Right, I was here in Moscow," agreed Bundy. "Stepan Grigorevich Lvov was in charge of St. Petersburg. It's a long way away. And I got moved to Cairo after about six months, so I didn't do much but add him to the list of known KGB personnel."

"You run a file on him?"

"We knew who he was, basic biog stuff. Wish we had managed more, now that he's emerged to be the rising star and promised friend of the West." The American shrugged, expansively. "But there it is, all down to the political analysts now!"

Their food arrived. Charlie couldn't remember the last time he'd ever knowingly helped another foreign country intelligence agent he trusted as little as he trusted Bundy. Predictably for someone who never drank anything but mineral water, Bundy had ordered the blandest possible food, steam-cooked vegetables, scallops, and bean curd.

"You want to try anything of mine, go ahead," invited Charlie, wondering why someone who ate like an invalid suggested such a restaurant in the first place.

"I'm okay but thanks," refused the man, measuring out his water.

"You keep in touch like this with Paula-Jane and Halliday?"

"Not on a regular basis. P-J's a cute kid."

"Tex seems to think so," risked Charlie.

"The guy's thought very highly of back at Langley," said Bundy, cleverly choosing an alternative gossip from that offered by Charlie. "I knew P-J's daddy. Davy Venables was a very formidable operator. You ever come across him in London?"

Charlie shook his head, tipping the last of his wine into his glass, eager to get back to the embassy to set up everything he now knew he needed London to arrange. "It's been a good meal. Let's do it again. My treat next time."

"I'll keep you up to that," said Bundy. "It's good to talk to someone who's been around the block a few times."

"I've got your number," said Charlie, enjoying his own double entendre, confident he'd got more from the encounter than the other man.

Charlie didn't detect the already identified BMW until just before his taxi turned onto the embankment. It continued straight on over the Kalininskaya Bridge, sure of his destination. Which wasn't good or proper tradecraft, Charlie recognized, curiously. But there was so much else that had been unexpected during the meeting with the American; so much that it was going to take time to interpret whatever its purpose had been.

★

"It's taken long enough for you to talk to me!" complained Jack Smethwick, the director of the agency's technical and scientific division in London, the moment they were connected.

"Wanted to make sure I had as much as possible before bothering you," said Charlie, soothingly. He'd forgotten the man's almost perpetual irritation.

"I hope you have."

"So do I," said Charlie, from the secure, strut-supported compartment in the communications room. "And I want to get some things clear in my mind."

"That might make a change."

"Let's talk about the loop, which is most important," said Charlie, refusing an argument. "Can't the fact that it's computer-simulated be scientifically detected by the Russians?"

"If it could be, I wouldn't have done it this way," said Smethwick. "The loop will be clearly marked as a copy of the supposed original which we've enhanced here. It's perfect."

So precise was the technical clarity of the line that Charlie could hear the noise of other people working in the MI5 laboratory on the northern outskirts of London: It was another affectation of the scientific director to take phone calls standing up at a laboratory bench rather than in his separate, more confidential office. "Three men looking to be close around a fourth, head bowed as if he's being forced along?"

"That's what you asked for," reminded the scientist, curtly. "We've put a woolen ski cap on the shortest of the three representing the assassins. Another seems to be wearing an anorak, with the hood up. It opens with a lot of broken, zigzagging film, the figures scarcely identifiable through the interrupting tearing. That tearing briefly stops but it's very hazy. And, of course, the light's very bad. It looks as if they were picked up after they've come into the grounds off the embankment. From the photographs of the official opening we've superimposed, with sufficient clarity for it to be positively identified, the ornamental hedge by the exhibition hall. None of the figures is fully framed, leaving the height to be estimated, although the dead man is close to being accurate from the calculations we've been able to make from the Russian mortuary photographs. . . ." The man stopped. "Have you shipped me the new set of photographs you picked up today?"

"In tonight's diplomatic bag, along with the updated medical report," promised Charlie. "The AB blood grouping is listed there, too. And the note about the barbitumiv traces."

"I'm not comfortable about that," complained Smethwick. "Sure we can mix some AB blood with the soil samples you've already sent us from the flower-bed area. But what if they do a DNA typing? It won't match what they've got and your great big scam will be blown sky-high."

Charlie hadn't needed the reminder of the weakest part of what he was trying to set up. "They wouldn't give me the clothes, for me to give you a match. But there's nothing in their medical reports of their having taken DNA."

"Which doesn't mean they haven't typed it," dismissed the scientist. "DNA is the first of any blood tests these days. It would certainly be for me in these particular circumstances."

"It's a gamble I've got to take," admitted Charlie. "You won't forget to mix in some of the soil fertilizer I sent back with the soil?"

Smethwick's pained sigh was audible. "Of course, I won't forget to mix it in: we've already tested some of what you provided and found a previous residue but the fertilizer won't affect DNA."

"I'm taking the gamble," repeated Charlie. "What about the Makarov 9mm shell?"

"It will test to be Russian if Moscow runs a metal comparison," assured the man. "We put a cross in the tip, as they did with the bullet that killed your man, and took most of the slow down wadding out of the butt before backing a steel sheet against which we split it with Kevlar, all traces of which we've taken off the fragment you're going to claim came from your hole in the ground."

"I think we've got enough to convince them," said Charlie, forcing the confidence he didn't fully feel.

"I don't," disputed Smethwick. "I think it'll be exposed for the nonsense it is and actually create what could escalate into an official diplomatic incident in an embassy that has got too many already. And because I think that I'm filing to the Director-General my officially recorded written objection to what he ordered me to do for you."

"Thanks for doing it, despite how you feel."

"Everything you've asked for will be back to you in a couple of days," guaranteed Smethwick. "And comes with the best of luck. You're going to need it."

★

Charlie already knew that, but Smethwick's dismissal deflated Charlie's usual optimism. His hope lay in his belief that he had sufficiently convinced the Russians—Pavel perhaps more than Guzov. But if that hope was misplaced, Smethwick's doomsday prediction could become a reality, and with it his exposure and immediate recall—even expulsion—back to England before any possible conclusion between himself and Natalia.

There were no voice-mail messages on the rabbit hutch

telephone but on the card table there was a two-word note from Paula-Jane: DROP BY.

"I've been censured," she announced at once, not smiling up at his entry. "I'm not sure yet if it's going to become official, from London, or stop here. I was two hours in front of Paul-fucking-Robertson and his inquiry team this afternoon, like a child who'd done something wrong."

A role for which Charlie strongly suspected she might qualify. "Censured for what?"

"Not going over everybody's head here in Moscow to alert London about the security chaos. Appears that Halliday's been doing so for months."

"Why didn't you?"

"I'm just past my first year on my first foreign station. Sotley's fifty-five years old, a senior ambassador. Dawkins served in Rome, Canberra, and Berlin before coming here. Do you think I was going to risk a career that hasn't even started by taking them on, even if I'd recognized how bad things were? Which I didn't, not properly, until all the shit happened at once."

There was a catch in her voice that Charlie feared might be a prelude to tears.

"You heard the other news?"

"What?"

"Sotley and Dawkins have been recalled today, as quietly as possible. The public announcement isn't going to be made from London until tomorrow, by which time they'll be under wraps. Peter Maidment, the *chef du protocole,* is going to stand in until there is a proper replacement."

Was there proof against either man of being the inside source? wondered Charlie. Paula-Jane was very definitely the wrong person to ask. Instead, he said: "What's Maidment like?"

"Bit of a dreamer," assessed the woman. "Passed over too many times for promotion until now and this isn't permanent. I feel sorry for him. He tries but can't sustain the momentum."

"Was he involved with the discovery of the body?" asked Charlie, hopefully.

"Never saw him there," dismissed Paula-Jane.

Timing the announcement, Charlie said: "I had lunch with Bill Bundy today."

"I remember him suggesting it," said Paula-Jane.

"He knew a bug had been found in the ambassador's personal telephone, which hasn't been publicly disclosed."

Paula-Jane remained looking up at Charlie but said nothing.

"And he knew my temporarily assigned direct number, here at the embassy. That's how he got in touch, by leaving a call-back message."

"I told him," she blurted. "He called me the night after we all had dinner together. I didn't think I was doing anything wrong, as you two appeared to go back a long time. But I didn't tell him anything about a bug being in the ambassador's telephone because until you just told me, I didn't know exactly *where* it had been found. You do believe me, don't you?"

"I'm trying very hard," said Charlie.

10

IN ADDITION TO PAUL ROBERTSON AND HARRY FISH, THERE were two other men and a matronly, gray-haired woman—to none of whom there was any formal introduction—when Charlie gained entry into the inquiry room by insisting his need to speak to them was urgent. There were also two technicians to one side of the room, clearly supervising an equipment bank including a polygraph machine and its adjoining, cable-festooned chair.

"This is surprisingly unexpected," greeted Robertson. "Particularly as I personally understood from the Director-General that we were absolutely forbidden any further contact."

From the tone of the other man's voice, Charlie guessed that Robertson had been equally rebuked for their earlier encounter. He looked sideways to the equipment setup and said, "Is this being recorded?"

"Of course, visually as well as audibly," confirmed Robertson. "Has your coming here been authorized by London?"

"No," said Charlie, further reassured by the man's obvious concern.

"Then I don't intend allowing it to continue," refused Robertson.

"And I don't want to be part of it, either," insisted Harry Fish.

"Please leave the room," said Robertson.

Nodding to the recording equipment, Charlie said, "It's my

ass in the air! Everything's being doubly recorded, so none of you are endangered. You're here to expose and arrest an inside source, and I think I know who that source is. You still want me to leave, I will. Your choice, being visually and audibly recorded, as you make it."

The unknown man to Robertson's right came quickly sideways for a whispered exchange, which concluded with a nod of permission for the man to leave the room. Coming back to Charlie, Robertson said, "We'll hear what you have to tell us."

"But not with me participating," refused Fish, rising to follow the other departing man.

The hurriedly leaving investigator was on his way to speak to London, Charlie knew: Fish probably intended to cover his ass, too. Deciding that he needed, belatedly, as much professional protection as possible, Charlie said, "My instructions from London, personally from the Director-General, were not to discuss with you anything concerning the investigation in which I am involved. Nothing I intend to tell you reflects in any way whatsoever upon that. Is that understood and accepted?"

"We're waiting to hear what you have to tell us," said Robertson.

"And I'm waiting to hear the answer to my question," returned Charlie, hoping he wasn't coloring as obviously as the equally furious Robertson. Robertson shifted in his chair but didn't speak and Charlie stood, shrugging.

"Your choice and you blew it. I'll tell the Director-General and he can tell you, and we'll all keep our fingers crossed that nothing else goes wrong while you piss about."

"Wait!" called Robertson, when Charlie was almost at the door. "We understand what you've said, that nothing you're going to tell us will compromise your purpose here."

Charlie took his time walking to the seat and settling himself. Robertson's face remained puce. The anonymous woman had colored, too. Charlie said, "A few nights ago I went out socially with people from the American embassy, accompanying Paula-Jane Venables. One of the Americans was William Bundy, an acknowledged CIA expert on Russian affairs, who has been reassigned here for a third tour of duty, after running the Agency's Russian desk for a number of years. I was on station here during one of his earlier assignments. During that period we knew each other but were never friends. Nor did we liaise, operationally, in any way whatsoever. The most recent evening ended with Bundy suggesting that he and I get together while I was here. No arrangements were made. The following day a voice-mail message from Bundy was left upon the temporary telephone number allocated to me, here at the embassy. I had not given Bundy that number. I responded to Bundy's call. We lunched, yesterday. During that lunch, Bundy made a remark about listening devices having been installed within the telephone systems of the ambassador. To my understanding no mention has been made in the media coverage, either in English, American, or Russian newspapers, of the precise location of any of the devices that were discovered by Harry and his team. . . ."

Charlie paused at the reentry into the room of the man who'd left after his earlier whispered conversation with Robertson, and didn't continue until after another hand-shielded exchange between the two men.

"When I returned from that lunch, I confronted Paula-Jane Venables about the disclosure of my telephone number and of the undisclosed location of the bugs. She admitted providing my number but categorically denied passing on anything about the listening devices, insisting she didn't know where they were placed. I know she has already appeared before you. I consider that from the conversation I have just recounted there is sufficient cause for her recall and reexamination before you."

An echoing silence descended upon the room. It lasted several full minutes before Robertson said; "You believe Paula-Jane Venables to be the traitorous source within this embassy?"

"I believe the indiscretion that I have personally experienced justifies her being questioned further," replied Charlie.

"Apart from Harry and me and a very limited number, you were one of the few to know about the devices," reminded the other man.

The threat churned through Charlie. He said: "Perhaps you should take that remark further."

"We intend to," said the same panel member. "You are to go at once to the communications room to speak personally to the Director-General." The man indicated the recording assembly at the side of the room. "He will instruct you, leaving no doubt of the authority, to return here to undergo a polygraph test to establish the truth of what you have just told this committee and to eliminate you from the investigation in which we are currently engaged—"

"A polygraph test that your colleague, Paula-Jane Venables, underwent yesterday and passed to the complete satisfaction of the technical examiners and the members of this panel," completed Robertson.

"How the hell can I be involved in things that happened before I even arrived here?" demanded Charlie. So angry was he that Charlie failed to detect the approach of the outside office guardian until the man was behind him.

"Shall we go, sir?"

★

Charlie Muffin was the foremost exponent of the credo never to panic but he found rational thinking difficult as he was humiliatingly escorted along linking corridors to the basement descent. He managed it—just—precisely because of his need to keep the secret that no one could learn. Charlie knew all about lie detector tests; he hoped that he could remember how to defeat the supposedly undefeatable machine that distinguishes lie from truth by measuring breathing rate, pulse, and perspiration flow.

Robertson's investigation was restricted solely to uncovering a traitor within the embassy. Which should keep the questioning well away from anything risking Natalia. But would it? Couldn't he, by the strictest interpretation of the word, be regarded a traitor, secretly married as he was to a senior analyst in the Russian Federation's internal counterintelligence organization? Not if he were able to argue semantics. But he wouldn't be, restricted to yes or no. What the fuck were the rules, the protection from being exposed by the machine? Remain calm, allow no anger or agitation, he remembered. Easy enough advice—easily followed advice—in a simulated situation where there was no anger or agitation, the total opposite from how he felt now. Keep what is not to be disclosed firmly out of mind, Charlie further recalled. He'd thought that particular mantra a complete load of bollocks at the long-ago training school and hadn't changed his mind since.

The unsympathetic Ross Perrit was waiting expectantly among all his electronic paraphernalia, the door to the first cubicle in the supported box already open. "The DG's waiting on the line."

"What the hell's going on?" demanded Smith, the moment Charlie identified himself.

"I tried to report things I believed relevant to Robertson's inquiry, things that had no bearing upon what I'm doing here." From the tone of the Director-General's unusually harsh voice, Charlie decided that the prevailing political wind was blowing slap into his face.

"What things?" The man listened without interruption to what Charlie had earlier told the inquiry panel and did not speak for several moments after Charlie finished. Then Smith said: "Venables underwent a polygraph examination. There were no difficulties."

"I know. But at the time the panel was unaware of Bundy's knowledge of where the listening devices were found. The examiner wouldn't have been prompted to ask her."

"She was specifically asked about her associations with the Americans," disclosed Smith. "A liaison was suspected with a married CIA officer, John Probert."

Charlie felt the first stirrings of unease. "And?"

"I told you," said the man, irritably. "She passed the polygraph without any doubts arising."

"Who suspected the liaison with Probert?"

"You've interfered in something from which I categorically barred you," refused Smith. "All I've got so far as the result of your being in Moscow are official complaints from the forensics and technical divisions being asked to manufacture evidence that can be exposed as fake with a schoolboy science kit."

"We've discussed the need for what I want," reminded Charlie.

"You cause any more public embarrassment by what you're doing, this will be your last assignment. You hear what I'm saying?"

"I hear," said Charlie. "I also hear that I have got to undergo a polygraph myself?"

"It's been requested."

"I wasn't even *in* Moscow when the listening devices were installed and the electrical system was sabotaged!"

"Everyone attached to the embassy has to undergo a polygraph test until the apparent inside source is found; even you, pointless though it will be."

Another indication that Smith was accepting defeat in his battle to retain the directorship of MI5 from the internal maneuverings of Jeffrey Smale. "If I don't answer a question honestly— which I might not be able to do if I think it impinges upon my function, which you've ordered me not to discuss with anyone, there will be a reading indicating that I am lying," Charlie resisted, desperately.

"That will be taken into consideration, of course," assured the other man. "And Robertson's people have been told that no questions should be phrased that might lead to that particular conflict of interest."

He had a possible escape, Charlie recognized. But the uncertainties were too many and too great. This was probably going to be the biggest test ever to discover if he were as smart as the smart-ass he'd always prided himself upon being. "I'll get back to you."

"Hopefully with something worthwhile from what you're there to do, for which I seem to be asking every time we talk."

★

"Let me explain the procedure—" managed a polygraph technician before Charlie broke in, "I know the procedure. Arm cuff, chest strap and hand-palm sensors, only yes or no answers and the first question is usually whether I masturbate to which everyone says they don't and gets a lie reading that proves the machine is working properly, so my answer is I did a lot once, when I was younger, but not so much now."

The technician didn't look up from attaching the band around Charlie's chest. "That comfortable?"

"Fine."

"It's better if you relax and don't let yourself get uptight."

"I know." The inquiry panel had all left the room by the time Charlie returned, leaving him alone with the two technicians. The one whom Charlie guessed to be the questioner was sitting facing him, going through a list of questions on a clipboard while his colleague hooked Charlie up to the machine, which was between him and the questioner, positioned so that it would be impossible for Charlie to see any movement or to register from the attached computer-screen tracing its peaks and troughs. Charlie wondered where the film and audio apparatus was, among everything else.

"You ready?" asked the questioner, looking up from his clipboard. He wore a woolen sweater beneath a tightly buttoned jacket and had a spare pen in a special holder on his clipboard.

"When you are." He had to find a way out, an explanation for the inevitable spike that would show up a lie.

"Is your name Charles Edward Muffin?"

"Yes."

"Are you an operative of an organization known as MI5, Britain's internal counterintelligence agency?"

He had reason for the wrong answer, Charlie realized. "No."

There was a pause from the questioner. "Do you tell lies?"

"Yes." How would that be recorded? wondered Charlie, the wisp of an idea threading its way into his mind.

"Was your previous answer a lie?"

"No."

There was another hesitation. "Do you lie to your superiors?"

"Yes." Charlie believed he could see an escape, actually available to him by the one-word answer restrictions.

"Are you an honest man?"

"No." That had to show as a truthful response.

"Are you proud of what you do?"

"Yes." Charlie decided he was confusing the questioner, which was precisely what he wanted to do.

"Have you ever come into contact with or had dealings with members of a foreign intelligence service?"

"Yes." He wasn't endangered by the question that could have encompassed Natalia.

"Have you ever cooperated with a member of a foreign intelligence service?"

"Yes."

The technician shifted awkwardly in his facing chair. "Have you cooperated with a member of a foreign intelligence agency within the last month?"

"Yes." He hoped to Christ it worked.

"Have you ever betrayed your country to a foreign intelligence service or agent?"

"No."

"Have you ever accepted money, financial rewards, or any benefit in kind from a member of a foreign intelligence agency?"

"Yes."

"Are you aware of listening devices, bugs, being installed within this embassy?" There was impatience in the man's voice now.

"Yes."

"Did you have any prior knowledge of those devices being installed in this embassy before they were discovered?"

"No."

"Have you any knowledge of how those devices were installed in this embassy?"

"Yes."

"Have you kept that knowledge from your superiors?"

"No." The questioner was visibly flushed, suspecting he was being mocked: Charlie was surprised it had been so easy.

"Do you believe there to be an informant to a foreign intelligence agency within this embassy?"

"Yes."

"Do you know who that informant is?"

"No."

"Have you ever served a term of imprisonment?"

"Yes."

"Were you guilty of the crime for which you served that term of imprisonment?"

"No."

"Were you subsequently pardoned?"

"No." The other man's exasperation was palpable.

"Do you regard this polygraph examination as a joke?"

"No!" What about remaining relaxed and not getting upright? reflected Charlie, noting the frown toward the questioner from the man who'd attached him to the sensors.

"Has every answer you have given been an honest one?" insisted the questioner, close to a repeat of an earlier demand.

He was rattled to buggery, which would show on the tracing replay of the computer tracing, Charlie knew. "Yes."

"Enough!" decided the questioner, abruptly snapping off the machine, nodding to the other technician to disconnect Charlie from the sensors. "That was ridiculous!"

"What are you talking about?" asked Charlie, in feigned surprise.

"You know damned well what I'm talking about. You were taking the piss, from start to finish."

"I was doing nothing of the sort!" denied Charlie.

"I can't wait to hear the reaction of the panel."

"Neither can I," said Charlie, which was another honest response.

★

He only had to wait thirty minutes for his escorted recall—two men this time, the first indication of what was to come—from his tiny office, knowing the reception to expect the moment he crossed the threshold of the inquiry room. The panel sat with what had to be individual printouts of the polygraph before them.

There were separate sheets of paper with what Charlie hoped to be copies of the questions to which he'd responded. There were matching sets of paper before the questioner and his associate. The escort who had accompanied him to the communications room actually took Charlie by the arm to put him very firmly into the waiting chair. He and his companion stationed themselves directly behind Charlie, one on either side.

Charlie turned to them, smiling, and said, "Don't worry, guys. I can't do a runner, with the flat feet I suffer from." He wasn't suffering any discomfort at that moment, which was a good omen.

"So the cabaret continues!" commented Robertson.

"I'm sorry?" questioned Charlie.

"Have you the slightest idea what you're doing, behaving like this? The slightest idea what's going to happen to you?"

"I'd appreciate your telling me."

"You are being taken, under escort, immediately back to London," announced Robertson. "Disciplinary proceedings are already being formulated, upon the basis of your ridiculous polygraph performance, each and every aspect of which has already been communicated personally to the Director-General, together with my recommendation that it be treated with the utmost severity. Recorded on that recommendation is my personal assessment that you can no longer be considered for any employment within the service, from which you should be dismissed after the most intensive investigation to discover the damage you have caused in the past. You are a disgrace to be treated as such!"

"Gosh!" said Charlie, not believing it possible for the furious man's face to get any redder, which it did.

"That completely absurd, contemptuous remark confirms every assessment this panel and the polygraph team has already arrived at: that you are suffering some mental illness making it necessary for you to be put into protective care," declared Robertson.

"Have you sent that assessment to the Director-General, along with everything else?" asked Charlie, coming forward in his chair, conscious as he did so of the two guards behind him coming restrainingly forward.

"This examination is over," said Robertson. "There is no need or purpose for any further conversation. Someone has already gone to the Savoy Hotel to pay your bill and collect your belongings. You are booked, together with the two escorts who will accompany you, on a plane leaving for London in three hours. We would like you now to leave for the transport that has already been arranged for you."

He was a whisker too close to leaving it too late, Charlie recognized. "Wait—and listen—for a moment longer! If I am taken back to London today, the careers of each and every one of you"—he turned, to include the polygraph duo—"will be over. I am astonished at your collective ineptitude, which might still end your careers, which it should"—he included the polygraph operators again—"the most inept of which has been your analysis of my examination.'

"This is madness!" said Robertson.

"Yours is the madness if you don't hear me out," retorted Charlie, relieved at the shifts and sideways exchanges among some of the panel confronting him, culminating in another whispered conversation between Robertson and the messenger next to him.

Robertson said: "All of this is being recorded."

"Which saves me asking the question to ensure that it is," said Charlie. "And guarantees that I have a complete, untouched copy of every word that has so far been spoken and everything that follows, upon which I am insisting."

"What do you want to say?" demanded Robertson.

"You each have the question-by-question analysis of the polygraph examination together, I hope, with the transcript of the voice recording. I do not, because I don't believe I shall need it but if I omit anything, please question me about it when I finish saying what I have to say, okay?"

Robertson nodded, refusing a spoken acknowledgment.

Charlie inhaled a deep breath, knowing he was going to need it. "I denied being a serving officer in MI5 because denial is the inviolable rule, never to be broken under the severest pressure, even torture. I *do* tell lies. It is an essential necessity in my professional life, as it is now if I am to succeed in remaining part of the investigation with which I am entrusted. And which I did, in answer to the question of whether I lie to my superiors. You, Paul Robertson, are my superior, both by seniority and grade. I am under the strictest orders from our Director-General not to discuss anything involving my separate investigation. If there was not this ridiculous insistence upon yes or no answers, I would not have replied yes to that question. I would have replied that I lie to my superiors when necessary. If I lie I am not, by definition, an honest man. But my answer to that specific question *was* honest if you examine it properly. And yes, I am proud of what I do, lying and deceitful and deceptive though it is and how I have to be, because I believe that ultimately—although perhaps not always—it is for the common good, not bad. . . ."

Charlie had to stop, both breathless and dry mouthed, wishing he'd asked for water before he'd started to talk. There was no offer of any from anyone in the room. "Have I come into contact with foreign intelligence agents? Of course I have. I had dinner with American CIA personnel this week. I believe one of the Russians with whom I am now in contact belongs to the Russian FSB. By a strict definition of a yes or no answer I am cooperating with him and have cooperated with others many times in the past, but always dishonestly on my part, to achieve whatever my objective has been in doing so. Yes, if I have to answer yes or no, I received money and accommodation and rewards from the former KGB. I was a supposed defector who escaped from Wormwood Scrubs with a known and legally convicted British traitor, to discover his secrets. Which I did. But because the sentence that got me into prison was phony, I never got pardoned. I was aware of listening devices being planted in this embassy because you, Mr. Robertson, *told* me when we agreed it indicated an inside source. I do not know who that source is: I thought I did, which was why I appeared before all of you earlier today. But when I spoke to the Director-General, he assured me that Paula-Jane Venables has been exonerated from any culpability. . . ." Drawing to the end of his uninterrupted diatribe, Charlie once again turned to the now tight-faced technicians. "And no, I do not regard a polygraph examination as a joke, although I might wonder about today's particular operation of it and the complete misconception that has been drawn from it. The yes or no restrictions allow grossly misleading readings to be drawn, as they were in this case."

No one spoke when Charlie fell silent but there was a lot of head-turning looks back and forth among the panel as each sought someone who would spare Robertson's very obvious discomfort. When no one else volunteered, Robertson said: "I think we need time to consider our responses so I must ask you to withdraw again."

"Before I do leave the room I need to have my own copy of everything that has been said during this session, to submit in its entirety to the Director-General in London while you reconsider."

"We resent the inference of that demand," said Robertson.

"As I resent, much more deeply, what I have been subjected to," said Charlie. "And while you're discussing things, it might be an idea to have my things returned to the hotel and for another room to be reserved for me." *That* had been too smart-ass, acknowledged Charlie, in immediate regret.

11

WHILE CHARLIE DIDN'T GO AS FAR AS CONCEDING IT TO BE A
Pyrrhic victory, he didn't expect a Christmas card from anyone
on Paul Robertson's investigation team. And even less from the
Director-General. Aubrey Smith's acceptance of Charlie's defense
had been begrudging in the extreme, tempered with accusations
of arrogance, insubordination, and camera posturing, with a repeated warning that Charlie's future employment depended on
results that had been too long in coming. Apart from all of which,
Charlie consoled himself, he'd survived.

Charlie encountered David Halliday on his way from Smith's
tirade to check his voice mail, his mind equally split between doing something as quickly as possible to impress the distinctly
unimpressed Director-General and making the promised contact
with Natalia.

"You looked outside?" greeted the MI6 officer.

"I've been so long underground I'm not sure if it's day or
night," said Charlie.

"Then you're in need of a reviver, even though it's not yet midday," said the man, jerking his head back toward his own quarters.
"I duplicated your Islay single malt order and I'm glad I did."

Charlie gratefully followed, welcoming the drink and the familiar "death to our enemies" toast.

Halliday said, "We're virtually under siege since the London announcement of Sotley and Dawkins's recall. Reg Stout says his outside guards estimate the media mob at more than fifty."

"Stout's still on duty?" queried Charlie, surprised.

"Apparently he took the Nazi defense of strictly obeying orders."

"That's neither a defense nor an excuse."

"Which I've been telling London for months."

"Was it you that finally got things moving?" asked Charlie, openly.

"I'd like to think so but for anyone in London finally to admit it would be to concede that they'd been hibernating, wouldn't it?"

"You going to argue against Stout remaining on station?" pressed Charlie, accepting a top up from the offered bottle.

"Specifying names could risk a libel or slander accusation," said Halliday.

Charlie didn't believe it could but he was more interested in pursuing the conversation than in challenging it. "You been before Robertson's inquisition?"

"P-J got a mauling, apparently. Seems to be pissed off with me for not telling her I was ringing alarm bells."

"You didn't answer my question."

Halliday smiled at Charlie's persistence. "Underwent the whole yes or no shebang, survived without losing a single fingernail or crushed testicle."

"So who's whispering all the secrets?"

Halliday shrugged. "How do I know? All I do know is that this embassy has been wide open to any sort of infiltration for months. Against which, how about the finding of the listening devices where they were being a complete coincidence? The FSB gets a chance they can't believe and are doubly lucky when their guys hit all the right places entirely by accident?"

"You believe in that sort of coincidence?"

"No," admitted Halliday. "I'm just pointing out that lucky coincidences sometimes happen, like miracles."

"What about Paula-Jane?" said Charlie, consciously ignoring every London edict.

"What about her?"

"She have any bother?"

Halliday smiled, knowingly. "What have you heard?"

"I haven't heard anything," denied Charlie. "You told me you came out smelling of roses but she was pissed off. Just wondered if things went badly for her. This is her first posting, after all."

Halliday shrugged again. "She didn't go back on the same plane as Sotley and Dawkins, so I guess she's okay. She didn't tell me anything specific apart from getting a bollocking about lack of earlier warning but let's face it, that's not her function here." The man offered the bottle again.

Charlie, who disagreed with that assessment, shook his head in refusal. "Still got things to do."

"How's it going?"

"Slowly."

"My offer still stands. I'm not exactly overstretched and you know my director is more than willing to get me involved."

Which was what Bundy had said, remembered Charlie: he could set up a sideline business selling tickets. "London's orders are to keep everything strictly compartmented, certainly until Robertson's inquiry is resolved."

"The bastards in London expect too much from ground soldiers like you and me," sympathized Halliday, the slightest of slurs to his words. "Things go right, they get the glory; things go wrong, we get the shit."

Why was it, Charlie asked himself as he made his way along the corridor, that he still didn't like Halliday, even though he was now serving Islay single malt?

★

Charlie wasn't surprised to find his roughly packed suitcases tossed carelessly into his office, nor to be told when he called the Savoy Hotel that no new reservation had been made for him. Charlie took the offered suite, all that was available, when he was told his original room was no longer vacant. His initial amusement at wondering what innocent conversations the FSB was going to hear from its new occupant became serious at the realization that until Guzov learned of the change he'd probably have an untapped telephone line. There was one call on his voice-mail register but when he accessed it there was no message, just the click of a telephone being replaced. It wouldn't, he knew, be Natalia. He called Sergei Pavel's personal number at Petrovka but got no reply and matched his unknown caller by deciding not to leave a message.

Knowing that no local taxis were permitted within the embassy grounds and with no intention of making himself the focus of the waiting photographers by leaving the embassy like a refugee carrying his possessions on his back, Charlie called the transport office for an embassy car and wasted an additional twenty minutes arguing with Harold Barrett to get one.

Charlie's telephone rang the moment he replaced it after the transport dispute. Sergei Pavel said, "What's going on? The hotel told me you'd checked out."

"It's a misunderstanding," said Charlie.

"I want to stop another one from happening," said the Russian.

Charlie became aware of traffic noise in the background of Pavel's call and realized the man was telephoning from the street.

★

Charlie was confident he could juggle the newly added ball without dropping any of those he was so far managing to keep in the air. There was still an explosion of camera lights when the car left the embassy, but Charlie was sure that while not making the evasion suspiciously obvious, he'd sufficiently obscured his face to avoid any identification on the FSB cameras. The media horde actually helped in that, overflowing on to the embankment road to slow the traffic and give Charlie more than sufficient time to check for pursuit. Nothing was obvious so Charlie ordered the English driver off the river road as quickly as it was possible, using his knowledge of the city to twist and double back until he was sure they weren't being followed.

Charlie hurried his reregistration at the hotel although taking his usual care reestablishing his room traps, and was back on the hopefully watcher-free street within half an hour. He kept to the outskirts of Red Square, using the tourist groups for cover but holding back from getting too immersed, not wanting too many faces from which to pick out the one more interested in him than in St. Basil's cathedral, the Kremlin, or Lenin's tomb. Satisfied after half an hour that he was not under surveillance, Charlie moved in the direction of Ulitsa Varvarka and the side-alley rendezvous chosen by Pavel, although not immediately searching for either. He found the street telephone just off the main Varvarka highway, ideally wedged into a corner formed by two side roads that gave him a vantage point from which to continue searching all around him after dialing Natalia's number.

"I thought you'd call before now?" she challenged, at once.

"We agreed two days. Is there a problem?"

"No."

"Is Sasha back?"

"Yes."

"Have you told her I'm here?"

"Not yet. I wanted us to talk some more, before I did."

"Talk about what?"

"I'm not sure I can do it. Leave everything. Not sure I *want* to do it."

Charlie wished there wasn't so much traffic noise. "It's the only way it can work for us."

"Sasha's happy at her school. I'm frightened it would be too much of an upheaval for her."

"Children are resilient, adjustable, aren't they?"

"Not like this. This would be like taking her to the moon."

"We can't make decisions like this, on the telephone. We need to meet again." Charlie waited and when she didn't respond, said, "Natalia?"

"We have a routine," said Natalia. "If she's done well, which she did with the summer school project, I take Sasha to the central park of culture to let her enjoy herself on the rides and amusements. We're going there tomorrow afternoon."

Everything was arriving from London tomorrow, Charlie

remembered. And he still didn't know why Pavel had approached him as he had, insisting upon the Varvarka rendezvous. "You want us to meet there?"

"No," said Natalia, sharply. "I thought you wanted to see her. I don't want you suddenly to appear, like a ghost. I want to prepare her, before any meeting."

"There might be a problem with tomorrow. Some things might be happening."

"It won't matter if you can't make it," said Natalia, realistically. "We're going anyway, around three o'clock. Be by the Ferris wheel if you can: Sasha always likes to ride it. If I don't see you, I'll know you're held up and I'll wait for another call, like this."

"I'll be there," promised Charlie, unsettled by the arm's length dismissal.

"If you're not, call."

It hadn't been the sort of conversation he'd expected or wanted, Charlie thought, as he continued on toward Varvarka, sure from watching everything around him that he remained quite alone. Natalia had obviously acknowledged their only chance of being together permanently was for her and Sasha to resettle in England. So why wasn't he feeling encouraged? Because, he supposed, of the reservations in almost everything she'd said, capped by her idea of his seeing Sasha from afar but not meeting her. But Natalia was right about preparing the child. Perhaps, even, it was a good idea that he be prepared, too. He hadn't done anything about a present, for either of them. Plenty of opportunity for that. Better, probably, not to go bearing gifts the first time they got together as a family.

Charlie had no difficulty locating the workers' café in the side street off the main road. In these casual, inexpensive bar/cafés, there was normally a scattering of places to sit but the preferred way of eating and drinking appeared to be standing up at small, mushroom-style tables. Pavel was already at one, a salami sandwich before him. There was no recognition. Charlie bought himself a coffee at the counter, intent upon any warning gesture of refusal from the waiting detective as he went toward the rear of the smoke-fogged café, finally going to Pavel's stand.

"This might have all been overdramatic," apologized Pavel, at once.

"What, exactly, are we doing?" opened Charlie, cautiously.

"Meeting properly by ourselves, as we should be doing, not having everything monitored and orchestrated by Mikhail Aleksandrovivh Guzov."

Pissed-off policeman or poorly prepared provocateur? wondered Charlie. Whatever, he had to go along to see where it led but watch his back even more closely and carefully than he was already doing, if that were possible. "You got a professional problem?"

"You know he's FSB, don't you?"

"It wasn't too difficult to guess," tiptoed Charlie, waiting for the question about his own genuine profession. Which, surprisingly, didn't come.

Instead Pavel said, "The way things are going—or rather *not* going—this will end with me being the take-all-blame victim of a failed investigation Guzov is doing his best to sabotage, with whatever shit that doesn't get dumped on me poured all over you."

Which in general terms was what he'd already worked out for himself, decided Charlie, becoming increasingly bewildered by the conversation. "Why does he want to sabotage everything?"

"I don't know, not completely," admitted Pavel. "But there's one thing that I think might be an indicator. Guzov is absolutely insistent that the listening devices weren't planted by the FSB. Or by the *Sluzhba Vneshney Razvedki,* because the foreign service doesn't have internal authority or remit."

"How else could listening devices get into the embassy unless FSB officers put them there!"

Pavel shrugged. "I don't have an explanation for that, either, but if the murder investigation ends in a mess then so, too, do allegations of planting bugs and spying. Leaving you and me, the two failed investigators, taking the blame for each and every failure. I don't want that—couldn't professionally survive that—and I don't imagine you want to fail, either."

Certainly not after the litany of complaints and criticisms

he'd endured from London over the last few days, acknowledged Charlie, that thought colliding with another, that no provocateur could be as inept as Pavel was showing himself to be. "What do you want me to do?"

"Start making things happen, the way they should be happening. Despite Guzov's interference and obstruction, I've done all the routine stuff: missing persons, gang feud rumors, informer whispers. I've gone through forensics until I can recite every finding practically from memory. And got nowhere: we're looking at the perfect murder. There's got to be something innovative to break it open and I don't know what it is. Or could be. And even if I did, Guzov would overrule whatever I suggested. . . ." The Russian paused, smiling tentatively. "But he couldn't do anything to stop you, which is why he wants to be at your shoulder every time we meet."

Charlie found a lot—most—of Pavel's reasoning convoluted and obviously unsubstantiated, leaving him with only one point of total clarity: he couldn't for a moment professionally risk everything collapsing as the Russian was predicting. But could he remotely consider exposing himself in the way Pavel was suggesting? There was a way, he supposed, although it would expose him to public recognition, which he'd never done before and had argued against so very recently. But did that matter if he were going to resign the service to make possible what he wanted with Natalia and Sasha?

"If I do something to exclude Guzov, he'll exclude me from anything you're going to do."

"He's doing that anyway. But I wouldn't exclude you: we could go on like this."

"Why are you taking such risks?"

"I stand to lose either way," Pavel pointed out.

"I need to think things through," said Charlie, consciously avoiding the commitment.

"If Guzov knows we've met like this he'll get me off the case, which he's already tried to do," disclosed Pavel. "He wants to replace me with his own tame militia man."

"How can we stop him from doing that?"

Pavel shrugged. "Lose me and you lose any possible cooperation."

In how many different ways could he lose? Charlie asked
himself. And didn't bother to start counting.

12

FOR SOMETHING UPON WHICH CHARLIE'S FUTURE, IF NOT HIS actual existence, still depended, the supposed forensic evidence of assassination appeared remarkably inconsequential, apart from the totally manufactured CCTV record and its freeze frames showing the entry into the embassy grounds of the victim and his killers. The only other tangible evidence was a comparatively small vial of provable embassy soil, into which AB blood had been introduced and a sliver of provable Russian metal from a provable 9mm Makarov bullet. There were also photographs of the supposed score mark caused by that ricocheting exiting bullet. There were also duplicated stacks of technically phrased forensic tests and findings, in Russian, to accompany and support every exhibit.

Charlie ran the loop through the replay machine several times before going just as exhaustively and individually through every exhibit and report, finally convinced, despite the reservations of technical director Jack Smethwick, that with the exception of DNA testing it was all unchallengeable.

Positively separating the professional and personal dilemmas with which he was confronted, Charlie concentrated first upon the bizarre café confrontation with Sergei Pavel. And always arrived back at the conclusion he'd reached walking with aching feet back along Varvarka the previous evening: that Pavel's approach and reasoning was so open to question and doubt that it had to be genuine, not a layered deception devised to eliminate him from an investigation the Russians were determined to keep to themselves.

Which was how he put it to the Director-General from the familiar communications room, reluctantly making the approach not so much from the need for a general sounding board but very specifically to relay Guzov's disclosure to a fellow Russian that the FSB was not responsible for bugging the embassy.

"The devices are provably Russian!" exclaimed Aubrey Smith, impatiently. "Who else but the FSB put them there?"

"I'm not inviting a debate because I think the denial is as absurd as you do," said Charlie, matching the impatience. "You've ordered me not to talk to Robertson so I'm passing it on for you to tell him. Guzov is technically Pavel's superior. He's got no reason to try to persuade Pavel."

"It's part of the same patchwork," dismissed Smith. "Nikita Kashev has summoned the acting ambassador twice to the Foreign Ministry to make the same denial. The Russian ambassador here has sought two meetings at our Foreign Office, with the same message. Now Guzov joins the chorus, for Pavel to tell you, hoping that you'll tell me—London at least, because I hope there's no way they know you and I are liaising directly—for it to be spread as fully and as thickly as possible."

"Isn't that unusual?" asked Charlie.

"I don't understand the question."

"Every Western embassy has had listening devices installed by the Russians. And we've done our fair share in return," Charlie pointed out. "The embassy protests, Moscow denies it—as we do when we're caught—and in a few months it's all forgotten until the next time. Why the continued, persistent denials this time?"

"Because everything is supposed to have changed since the demise of communism, which we all know it hasn't," said Smith, still dismissive.

"I felt I should pass it on," said Charlie, reminding himself it was not his investigation and that his day had to run on a strict timetable.

"You've got all you wanted," said Smith. "Now I want results—some significant developments—pretty damned quick."

"I've got some things in mind," said Charlie, disliking the vagueness but not wanting to risk the Director-General counter-manding what he was considering.

★

Charlie phoned ahead and by the time he arrived at Petrovka, a replay machine was already set up in Pavel's office, cramped by the two rows of chairs arranged in a viewing semicircle. Charlie accepted without protest his relegation to the second row, leaving those closest to the screen to Mikhail Guzov and the assembled but unidentified forensic specialists and technicians. Pavel positioned himself behind them, alongside Charlie but gave no indication of any prior contact. They all watched the two-and-a-half minute tape without comment but immediately after it faded a heavily bearded forensic officer demanded a replay, coming intently forward to watch it for the second time: once he leaned sideways to mutter to the man next to him something that Charlie strained to hear but missed. He didn't hear the conversation between the man and Guzov when the second viewing ended, either.

Turning to Charlie, Guzov said, "The CCTV copy isn't of much practical use."

Charlie had spent both replays intently studying the FSB officer for the slightest facial indication that the café encounter had been a setup and detected nothing. Charlie said, "Together with what London identified as part of a Makarov bullet, it proves the victim was alive when he was brought into the embassy grounds by at least three men and that the murder was committed there, positively establishing that the crime was committed on British territory, which further establishes that it is primarily a British investigation."

"I meant, of practical use in identifying the victim or the men who killed him," corrected Guzov.

They'd accepted the phony CCTV film as genuine! realized Charlie. "They won't know that, though, will they?"

"What? Who?" Guzov frowned.

"I intend to hold a press conference at the embassy," announced Charlie. "I consider the CCTV to be a breakthrough in the investigation, showing the murder in the process of it being committed."

"You'll be asked if you can identify the victim and his killers," said Pavel, nodding to the freeze frames stacked on a side table, together with all the other London material. "There will also be demands for those photographs to be released."

"Of course I'm going to be asked," agreed Charlie. "And I am going to describe what we've got as vital evidence that cannot be released for fear of affecting the outcome of any trial."

"In the vain hope that the killers, frightened of being identified, will make the mistake that'll do just that?" queried Guzov, the sneer very obvious.

"That would be a little too much to expect, but not totally beyond the realms of possibility," said Charlie. "What we do have is a reasonably good physical description of the dead man, and what's definitely not beyond the realms of possibility is that it will be recognized by someone who will come forward to identify who he is. And that would very definitely be a breakthrough, wouldn't it?"

Guzov's face hardened at the awareness of how easily he was being outmaneuvered. Trying to make it sound more like an already agreed decision rather then the question it really was, the Russian said, "The press conference panel will need particular and careful planning."

"Very particular indeed," picked up Charlie. "The film very positively establishes the United Kingdom's primary legal jurisdiction, which requires that any public discussion has to be conducted on British territory . . ." He hesitated, the affect timed to the ticking second. "Which presents a difficulty of your participating in view of the current diplomatic problem between our two governments."

"Are you trying to tell me that no Russian participation will be allowed?"

"I'm just pointing out that the degree of participation has to be diplomatically agreed."

"I shall need to discuss the legality of the situation with lawyers at our own ministry," said Guzov, trying to make it sound like a challenge.

"Of course you must," agreed Charlie. "As I will with my embassy." How much of an obstacle were temporary ambassador Peter Maidment and his own Foreign Office going to be to the media proposal, wondered Charlie.

Guzov swept his arm to encompass the CCTV tape and everything else that Charlie had brought to Petrovka. "And there may be further need to discuss everything you have provided, after closer study by our scientists."

Shit, thought Charlie.

★

Charlie accepted he could not have expected it to have gone better—although being a pushy, foot-in-the-door optimist he'd hoped that it would—but Mikhail Guzov's implied threat nagged at him, despite Charlie's balancing belief that Pavel's café approach had been professionally genuine.

And he was thirty minutes behind schedule getting back to the embassy, with only time to check his telephone messages before his courtesy appointment with the acting ambassador. Again, the one call routed to his voice mail disconnected without identification.

When Charlie was ushered into the ambassador's suite, Peter Maidment was at the window overlooking the river and didn't immediately turn. There was a weariness about the man when he finally did so, waving Charlie to the waiting chair. "Your Director-General sent me a message that you wanted to see me?"

And he was taking his biggest risk yet, not clearing his intention first with Aubrey Smith, conceded Charlie. "I want to conduct a press conference for the media camped outside the gates."

There was no outrage or theatricality at the idea from the lank-haired man. "To tell them what?"

"I need to identify the victim," said Charlie, encouraged. "There are some physical characteristics I hope might be recognized by a wife or a girlfriend or a work colleague."

"There'll be Russians among the media? Journalism is a very common front for the sort of people who installed the most recent listening devices."

"The conference could be very strictly controlled," pressed Charlie. "They could be escorted to the conference hall quite separate from the embassy building itself. And escorted directly out again at the end. All the accreditation could be thoroughly vetted. And the local Russian staff is still being allowed in and out."

"What's wrong with simply issuing a statement, listing what you want someone to recognize?"

"I'm looking for the maximum response from the maximum publicity," said Charlie. "Bringing them in—holding the conference in a building close to which the body was found—will be far more effective than a printed statement."

"Under the circumstances, this isn't a decision I can make alone. It'll have to be approved from London."

Everyone ducking responsibility, as usual, Charlie realized, except himself, who couldn't. "But you won't oppose it?"

"Not upon your assurance that it will clear up at least one of the problems we're facing here."

"It could," qualified Charlie. Now to the more difficult part, he thought. "There's something more you—and London—needs to know. I believe the Russian coordinating their side of the murder investigation is, in fact, an officer of their counterintelligence service. And that the Russian intention is not to solve the crime but make the failure a British responsibility. If the conference is approved, I intend that man be excluded."

Maidment remained silent for several moments. "I will not be drawn—I will not allow this already embarrassed embassy to be drawn—into any further difficulties."

"It won't be," insisted Charlie. "It's to avoid any further difficulties that we're having this conversation."

There was another pause. "Are you convinced this whole thing is necessary?"

"Beyond any doubt. I don't believe the Russians have made any progress whatsoever, despite a genuine effort from the militia officer involved."

"Have you got any evidence to substantiate that belief?"

"None."

"This isn't going to be an easy discussion with London."

"I wish there were more I could offer," said Charlie, sincerely. "I expect there to be a lot of pressure for it to be a joint British-Russian affair."

"What will you do if you're refused permission?"

It would be the easiest—and safest—course for the man to take, accepted Charlie. "If I am refused, I will lose the control I want—I *need*—over the investigation. Which means we go on being manipulated by the Russians, to whatever end or purpose they intend."

"And you've no idea what that is?"

"Absolutely none."

"We might even return to London together, both empty-handed," reflected the man.

"Quite possibly," accepted Charlie, fatalistically.

★

Charlie was in Gorky Park's cultural center with time to spare, despite the necessary Metro-dodging trail clearing, on a bench that gave him a view of every path approach to the Ferris wheel over a concealing copy of that day's *Pravda*. Charlie was cautiously encouraged by Peter Maidment, although objectively accepting that if he were in the diplomat's position, he'd probably play it safe, reject the suggestion, and blame it all on London. Which he'd tried to anticipate by sending as cogent a written argument as he could asking Aubrey Smith to support the whole fragile proposal.

Charlie told himself he'd done everything and more to push-start his role in the investigation. The rest of the day was person-ally his. He was going to see for the first time in five years the daughter he adored. And the woman with whom he was determined to spend the rest of his life, wherever and whatever that life might be.

There was a physical stomach jump when he saw them. Natalia was wearing a cream skirt and a deeply colored shirt, dark blue or maybe even black, Sasha's hand in hers. Sasha was taller than he'd expected from the photographs, up to her mother's waist. She was wearing light-colored trousers, faded jeans perhaps, and a roll-necked sweater as dark as her mother's. Her blond hair was long, practically to her shoulders, in a ponytail that jumped and tossed in time as she skipped at Natalia's side, gesturing excitedly toward the slowly revolving Ferris wheel.

There was not the slightest recognition, but Charlie was sure Natalia had isolated where he sat, watching. He kept to their arrangement, remaining where he was as they joined the short queue, not getting up to move closer until they were next in line to get into their gondola, moving close enough to the ride, the better to see Sasha before it rose above him. Natalia looked very directly at him then but still showed no recognition; Sasha was looking up, to see how high they were going, still gesturing for Natalia to look, too.

Charlie backed off, although not as far as his original bench, stopping about five yards away. That was close enough to see them both when they got off, see them practically near enough to touch and imagine what it was going to be like when they were all together in England—or wherever Natalia wanted them to live. Charlie followed their ascent until his neck ached from how far back he had to strain and picked them up again on their descent, seeing Natalia pick him out as the gondola got closer to the ground. At first, she remained as impassive as she had been when they lifted off but when they were at the point of getting off, Natalia's face broke into a frown and Charlie hurriedly, although as unobtrusively as possible, shook his head in reassurance that he wasn't going to attempt any encounter, physically pulling back farther.

It was Sasha who got off the ride first, obviously saying something to her mother as she did so, and not stopping on the raised platform but running down the steps with her arms outstretched toward a fair-haired, Slavic-featured man in jeans who held his arms out toward her, lifting her, laughing, high in the air and twirling her around and around.

13

CHARLIE MUFFIN DRANK FOR ENJOYMENT, NOT OBLIVION, which kept the bottle of Islay single malt untouched upon the bureau of the Savoy suite in which he slumped, the conflicting half thoughts jostling in his uncertain mind.

This wasn't Natalia; couldn't be Natalia. Or could it? She was a KGB-schooled debriefer, trained to suspend all personal operational feelings: that was how they'd met when she'd been his relentless interrogator determined to discover if his British jailbreak and supposed defection was genuine or phony. He'd professionally cheated her then, not just by convincing her he was an authentic defector but by persuading her and her superiors that the real defector with whom he'd fled England was the fake. He'd cheated her again, on that occasion personally as well as professionally, when—not knowing she was pregnant with their child from their Moscow affair before he escaped back to England—he hadn't trusted her sufficiently to keep their London rendezvous from which, just once, she *had* decided to defect from a KGB escort assignment, which had her monitoring visiting Russian politicians.

He'd atoned, Charlie mentally insisted, seeking a balance to his own deceits and failings. When he'd learned about Sasha—no, he stopped himself, refusing the self-serving excuse: when, belatedly accepting his being in love *and* learning about Sasha—he'd connived the Moscow embassy posting and married her under

Russian law in the Hall of Weddings and set up home to create an ultimately unlivable, knife-edged existence that neither could possibly have sustained. And so, again, he'd left to go back to London, swapping one unsustainable existence for another.

Could—should—he really be so surprised that after suffering all those abandonments Natalia had chosen the revenge she had orchestrated those few hours ago in the park? Yes, he answered himself. Despite what had happened he could never—would never—conceive Natalia to be a vengeful person.

So what had it been? Why had she set up the opportunity for him to see their daughter—virtually choreographing the situation—to include a man whom Sasha very clearly knew and trusted and into whose arms she'd so unhesitatingly ran?

Charlie didn't know, no matter how many different conflicting, contradictory arguments he advanced to himself. And so he couldn't conclude it to be anything other than understandable and ultimate revenge for all the hurts and fears and uncertainties he'd inflicted upon her. Which inevitably brought more conclusions, the most numbing of which was that she'd forced herself to make the nostalgic Botanical Gardens reunion—nostalgic for him, if not for her—to set up the scourging Gorky Park proof that everything was over between them: that she'd found another man—a younger, even more presentable Russian man—whom she loved and whom Sasha very obviously loved.

Which he could do nothing but accept. Charlie acknowledged that it was finally time for long overdue reality. He'd have to convince her it wouldn't be difficult for him to make everything as easy as possible for her and Sasha, although in reality, it would be impossibly, achingly difficult. He didn't know anything about Russian civil law but they'd been apart for five years, without any cohabitation, which should make grounds for a divorce straightforward enough for her. Desertion was the most obvious, he supposed, if it existed on the Russian statute books. If it didn't there was sure to be something similar that would fit. Would he surrender Sasha for adoption, if Natalia wanted to remarry? That wasn't even a question. Of course he would. He'd have to, to make everything complete for them. That's what he had to do, make everything complete for both of them, as easily and as smoothly as possible.

Which required, of course, his making contact with Natalia: talking to her, discussing it all with her. Being adult. But not yet. Certainly not tonight—that was unthinkable—and probably not tomorrow, either. Or the day after that. He had other things to do, not more important things but necessary arrangements to take the assignment forward.

He didn't any longer have the option—the reason—to quit the job he'd been prepared to abandon. So he needed at least to get the assignment right to avoid losing his job as well.

★

The two-word command—CALL NOW—awaiting him the following morning scarcely needed the your Eyes Only security designation. Before obeying the instruction Charlie logged his request for a meeting with the temporary ambassador and when he did call London, Aubrey Smith, without any greeting, declared: "I don't like the idea. Neither does the Foreign Office. Why didn't you discuss it with me first?"

"I need room to work. And room, a lot of room, from Mikhail Guzov," Charlie said, fighting back, realizing the other man had already made up his mind. "You've read my reasoning?"

"Of course I've read your reasoning. It'll cut you off from any future Russian cooperation."

"There isn't any Russian cooperation, not now or in the future. I'm risking nothing." Charlie hadn't included anything about the café encounter with Sergei Pavel in his overnight argument and didn't intend mentioning it now, not wanting to give the Director-General any further opposing reason.

"What about obviously revealing your personal identification, which seemed to worry you a lot about a week ago?"

"The concern then wasn't personal identification: the FSB will have already run their checks. The concern was that I didn't have a clue what the hell was going on. I still don't but I've got enough for a description of the dead man for somebody to recognize. It's his identification I want and can't make any progress without getting it."

"You'll be inundated by cranks," predicted the man.

"Of course there will be cranks. I'm not suggesting it's going to be easy." What could he do—what was there—to reverse Smith's opposition?

"What happens if cranks are all you get?"

"I'll be answering all the questions," reminded Charlie, heavily. "So I'll get at least some direction toward the answers I need."

There was a momentary silence from the London end at the obvious inference. Smith said: "If Guzov and the FSB are determined somehow to obfuscate the bugging with your failure to solve the murder—and I still can't understand how they're going to use one to achieve the other—they're going to go through everything you've had fabricated here with damned more than a toothcomb."

"That's clearly what you are more worried about than what I want to get from a press conference!" openly accused Charlie, his instant regret at the outburst worsened by Smith's totally controlled reaction.

"Not more worried," corrected the Director-General. "Equally worried at the fallout from your being publicly exposed as a liar and a cheat in a situation from which it would be impossible for you to recover. That would sweep away any chance of our resolving either the killing or the bugging."

Your being exposed...impossible for you to recover isolated Charlie, accustomed to the abandonment rules in his particular workplace: not *our* being exposed or impossible for *us* to recover. Then, with abrupt awareness, he thought, you've shot yourself in the foot. "Then *I've* got very little personally to lose by publicly identifying *myself* in front of a group of inquiring journalists, have I?"

"*You* haven't," matched the other man, careless of the threat being made obvious.

"Which virtually brings it down to being my decision, reached after the required consultation," seized Charlie: got you, provably recorded on the statutorily insisted upon, inquiry-producible re-cording.

The further pause was the only indication of Aubrey Smith's realization of Charlie's verbal entrapment. "Is what you propose essential to continue this investigation?"

"Absolutely," said Charlie.

"Then you must go ahead."

You again, not *we*, noted Charlie. But then Smith had made it glaringly clear that was how it was going to be: how, realistically, it was always going to be if Smith's personal survival required his sacrifice. "Maidment wants the Foreign Office's approval, which I doubt they'll give without knowing the decision *you've* just reached." Charlie's stress on the identifying word was intentional.

"I see," said Smith, after yet another pause of awareness.

As I'll see whether you've passed it on if I get a rejection from the acting ambassador, thought Charlie. "I want to get every-thing underway as soon as possible."

"I understand."

"It's good that we both understand each other. And thank you, for your support." That final remark hadn't been necessary—too smart-ass again—Charlie accepted. But it sure as hell made him feel better.

★

There were two calls on Charlie's voice-mail register but no mes-sage on either when he accessed them. It reminded him, though, that if approval came from the Foreign Office, which he still wasn't totally confident it would even if Aubrey Smith did offi-cially endorse the idea, he was going to need a separate dedicated line and a message service—possibly even two—to accommodate the hoped-for responses.

Could Guzov and the FSB get around their intended exclusion by somehow tapping into the numbers that would have to be made publicly available for him to receive incoming calls? Harry Fish would know, and have the expertise to prevent further bugging or cell-phone interception from scanners. Charlie hoped he wouldn't have to go through any more get-permission-from-the-head-teacher nonsense when he asked Fish but thought it probable that he would. As well as having to ask Harold Barrett for the apartment he had earlier refused and for special telephone facilities. Pain in the ass, compounding pain in the ass. And he still had warning discomfort in his awkward feet.

It was another hour before the summons came from Peter Maidment and as soon as he entered the ambassadorial suite, the man indicated a gray-haired, fixed-face note taker and announced: "A written account of everything that's said *will* be kept."

Which had to auger in his favor, Charlie thought, at the same time disappointed that the man needed the visible threat, like a stage prop, in a room which all of them knew to be fitted with automatic recording apparatus. "If that is your wish," Charlie flattered.

"It is," claimed the man. "It has not been an easy permission to obtain: there was opposition."

Let Maidment have his brief moment, Charlie decided, recalling the diplomat's passed-over disappointment. "Thank you for the effort you've made on my behalf."

"There are essential strictures."

"I expected there to be."

"There will be separate film and audio records of the entire event."

Which would disclose all his intended manipulations, accepted Charlie. "Essential."

"Everything will be confined to the conference hall and every accreditation of every person attending has to be submitted, listed, and approved before monitored admission into the embassy precincts."

Which would ensure the required publicity buildup, although create a delay he hadn't wanted, recognized Charlie. "A worthwhile restriction."

"Those checks will be carried out by Robertson and his team."

What about the separation of investigations? Charlie wondered, surprised for the first time. "Is that a London decision?"

"Yes," confirmed Maidment, after a pause.

Another change of direction in the prevailing wind, accepted Charlie, recognizing it amounted to his being monitored, too. But there could be advantages. "Has Robertson been told?"

"His meeting follows this."

"Is he to participate in the conference?"

From the man's hesitation, Charlie knew it was a question that hadn't been considered. "That is something that needs to be discussed with him. Would you have any objection?"

"None whatsoever," responded Charlie, seeing the first possible benefits.

"But no one diplomatically accredited to the embassy will participate."

"Of course not."

"Questions must be restricted to the murder investigation. There must be no discussion whatsoever about listening devices or withdrawal of embassy personnel."

"Questions will inevitably be asked."

"And must be refused."

"An outright refusal could result in a misleading misunderstanding," risked Charlie, nervous of erecting any barrier but wanting to log a minimal warning.

"That's the ruling," insisted the ambassador.

"Which of course I will observe," emptily promised Charlie.

"There have also been further representations both to me here at the embassy and in London, through the Russian ambassador, denying any Russian knowledge or responsibility for the listening devices," said Maidment. "In each approach there was a demand for participation in the press conference."

"I advised you to expect that," reminded Charlie.

"And I warned London," said Maidment, looking more toward the note taker than Charlie. "No one suspected of any involvement with any Russian security service will be allowed within the embassy precincts. Which is the purpose of the accreditation confirmation."

Charlie decided against bothering to remind the other man

that it was he who had talked earlier of excluding Guzov. "What's the official response going to be to Moscow's representation?"

"An acknowledgement of their Note."

Which was fence sitting, not a response, Charlie recognized. Could he risk including Sergei Pavel, without actually mentioning it? He could by the strictest interpretation of Maidment's caveats. "I'll announce the conference for Wednesday."

"It's important that you understand that everything about this is your responsibility," insisted Maidment.

What, wondered Charlie, was the collective noun for a group of shit-scared diplomats: a cower of diplomats was all that came to mind. "I totally accept that."

"And I am declining any further involvement," added the frightened man. "From now on everything goes direct to your Director-General, who in turn will deal with the Foreign Office."

"Of course," said Charlie, snatching a benefit he hadn't imagined possible.

★

Unsure from which direction the next problem might come—simply resigned to the inevitability that one would—Charlie did his best to cover his back with his own account to London of the encounter with Maidment before moving on to his dedicated apartment and telephone requirements, sparing himself the playground petulance by e-mailing his demands to Harold Barrett. He posed his telephone interception queries to Harry Fish the same way as well, copying London's authorizing approval to both men. Charlie completed his computer correspondence by announcing the press conference on the TASS, RIA Novosti, and Izvestia online news agencies and duplicated the information to the Associated Press wires for the Western media, although knowing that they would pick up the constantly read Russian news services. In every e-mail, he identified Paul Robertson as the man to whom all necessary accreditation information should be addressed. He also set out the admission and exit restrictions and stipulated that the conference would be strictly limited to the murder investigation. Finally, he duplicated everything to London. And then he sat back to wait, wondering who would be the first through his door.

It was Paula-Jane Venables. She burst into the room, without knocking, the slip from the TASS service still in her hand and said: "Hey! We got a breakthrough here?"

"We've got enough hopefully to unlock some doors."

"Like what?"

"I want to keep that until Wednesday."

"For Christ's sake, Charlie!" she protested.

"No one officially accredited to the embassy can be involved, for obvious reasons."

"What's official got to do with it!"

"How it's got to be."

Her face hardened. "And I was prepared to forgive and forget!"

"Forgive and forget?"

"I know."

"Know what?" Charlie frowned, genuinely confused.

"How you tried to stitch me up a second time, with Robertson."

"I didn't try to stitch you up," denied Charlie. "You did wrong and in these very particular circumstances, it was right to do what I did."

"Which was to prove you're a bastard."

"Which was to behave professionally, which you hadn't been doing. And we're not achieving anything debating it."

"Fuck you!" She was red faced now, her hands trembling as if with the effort of holding back from hitting him.

"Quite a few people seem to be trying to do that, one way and another," remarked Charlie, mildly.

Paula-Jane remained where she was, shaking and with no words left but reluctant to retreat the loser. The impasse was broken by Robertson's entry, again unannounced. The man looked between Paula-Jane and Charlie before saying: "I'm sorry. Am I interrupting something important?"

"Not at all," said Charlie. "Paula-Jane's just leaving, aren't you?"

She took the offered escape but paused at the door and said, "Bastard! Sneaking fucking bastard!" before slamming it closed behind her.

Charlie said, "Did you tell her I'd suggested she be recalled?"

Robertson's face opened, in understanding. "Not personally. I did recall her, though. It came out during her reexamination. Which she passed the second time, to everyone's satisfaction. She's not our inside source."

"You found out who is?"

Robertson shook his head. "The concentration's now on Dawkins, back in London. I hope there aren't any bad feelings about that polygraph business."

"I hope there aren't at the way it ended," responded Charlie, who didn't care a wet fart about Robertson's feelings but was intrigued at the man's surprisingly changed attitude.

"This conference is going to be very much your show," said Robertson. "You'd better tell me what you want me and my guys to do."

His performance wasn't just going to be monitored by film and audio recordings, Charlie decided. Like Sinbad the Sailor, he was going to have Robertson on his back just as Sinbad had the clinging old man of the sea.

★

Harry Fish was added to the mix within fifteen minutes to answer Charlie's queries in person. It took another ten to go through the no-hard-feelings bullshit before Fish insisted that he could defeat any Russian scanner interception with white noise equipment, which would at the same time detect Russian eavesdropping attempts. Additionally, he could attach to Charlie's phones recording apparatus sensitive enough to pick up extraneous and, hopefully, identifying background sounds—to establish whether the incoming calls were from a pay phone from a street kiosk, a cell phone, or a landline—that would normally be inaudible to the human ear. In certain circumstances, landline calls would be traceable.

The e-mail from the facilities and housing officer allocating Charlie his two requested telephone lines and numbers, both within the available compound apartment, arrived in the middle of the discussion with Fish.

"My people will install both connections and everything else you'll need to block any intrusion," guaranteed the electronics sweeper.

And install his own duplicate eavesdropping equipment, Charlie accepted, unconcerned. "It's good to be part of a team: none of this will work without your help," lied Charlie, to make them believe he didn't suspect the bullshit they were shoveling.

"It's still got to work," cautioned Robertson.

"It will," insisted Charlie, feeling as claustrophobically enclosed as he had in the communications compartment in the embassy basement. But not, Charlie was determined, in the way that these two men planned for him to be.

14

CHARLIE GOT HIS PREFERRED CORNER STOOL IN THE HOTEL bar, with its fuller view of anyone who might approach from behind reflected in the glass-fronted bar mirror. He was as expectant of an approach as he had earlier been for the first entry into his office, although as equally unsure now as he had been then as to who might come. He knew only that it most certainly wouldn't be Paula-Jane Venables. Which was a comfort.

Charlie still wished he'd known about her second clearance, not from any mistaken interference on his part but rather for its reassurance. What he didn't find reassuring—or even believable—was that Jeremy Dawkins could possibly be the spider in the middle of any embassy web.

He was more than content for Robertson and Fish to be co-opted although, unsuspected by them, on his terms, not theirs. He needed people to sift the hoped-for kernels from the chaff, for which Robertson's investigators were preeminently suited. Charlie was reasonably confident he could manage the essential secondary sieving to separate those leads he intended personally to pursue from the cranks he'd leave to Robertson's team. The further, even surprising, benefits from their embassy planning session had been Robertson's apparent expectation, before it being suggested, that he should appear on the conference podium and Fish's insistence that he could generate during the conference sufficient white noise to defeat any mobile or landline spying interception of all communication.

Charlie nodded his acceptance of another vodka from the attentive bartender, finally confronting the reflection he'd consciously refused to consider all day, trying to convince himself that he hadn't expected contact from Natalia. For him to have done so would have been like budgeting to win a lottery. The approach had to come from him and with the press conference not scheduled until Wednesday, there was no reason why he shouldn't initiate it, apart from fear of rejection.

Drink in hand, on the point of finishing it before making the call, Charlie turned more fully into the gradually filling bar, curious about which of the supposed relaxing drinkers was the watcher assigned to him, professionally sure that there would be one: possibly even one of the assembling working girls, grouped conveniently for an easy exit close to the door in the hope of early evening trade. Charlie raised his glass to drain it but abruptly stopped, halted by the most unexpected approach of all.

"I'm glad I found you," said Mikhail Guzov.

From their obvious reaction to Guzov's appearance, Charlie decided his surveillance was a dual operation between a bearded man and a full-breasted blond girl who'd ruined the charade by snatching her hand from her pretend lover, as if embarrassed at being caught out by her FSB superior.

★

Charlie began to doubt his expectations when, instead of choosing mineral water at his drink invitation, Guzov asked for vodka, suggested a toast—to friendship—and settled comfortably on the adjoining stool without following up on his opening remark.

To fill the gap, Charlie said: "You've got all my numbers."

Without looking away from his drink, Guzov said: "And you've got all mine. And didn't call any of them about the press conference."

"You knew I was organizing it."

"And you knew we wanted participation."

"I also told you of the problem with that. Which I can't do anything to reverse."

"You know none of our intelligence agencies had anything to do with planting those devices."

"I know you continue to tell me that: to tell the same to the embassy here and the Foreign Office in London." This was going beyond—far beyond—the normal diplomatic denials, almost into the realms of farce, thought Charlie.

"It's true."

Charlie spread his hands, palms upward, in a gesture of helplessness. "It's an impossible situation. And one I can't do anything about."

"You could authorize our attendance."

"Our?" queried Charlie, pedantically.

"Myself and Sergei Romanovich. This is supposed to be a joint investigation. If we are not publicly there, it amounts to a positive accusation and will be interpreted as such."

The man was genuinely concerned at the personal, professional damage of his being excluded, Charlie suddenly decided, warmed by the further, unnecessary recognition that everyone at their level lived at the receiving end of the shit sluice. With that reflection came another, far more important awareness. This encounter wouldn't be taking place if the Russians had subjected his phony forensic material to DNA testing. Charlie said, "Surely it won't be a personal accusation against you and Sergei Romanovich?"

"There needs to be a Russian presence," insisted Guzov, giving Charlie the cosmetically salvaging cooperation opening he'd never anticipated getting.

"I'm not handling the attendance applications," said Charlie. "But the conference is sure to be covered in its entirety by Russian television. A full tape—not an edited transmission version—will provide you with every question and every answer. I also undertake to make available the embassy film and audio recordings."

It was Guzov who gestured for more drinks before sourly looking sideways. "The purpose of press conferences is to generate public response. What's your undertaking about that?"

"Responses will be made available, along with everything else," replied Charlie, expecting the demand. For you to chase the chaff behind Robertson's crew, Charlie thought.

Guzov looked back into his drink. "I was forbidden from making this sort of approach."

"Why did you?" asked Charlie, astonished that Guzov was shoveling the special relationship, professional-to-professional crap.

"It was a mistake to try," admitted the Russian.

"I've given you every possible undertaking that I can. There isn't any more." Charlie had turned more fully into the bar for the conversation with the Russian and got an impression—which was all it was, the barest flicker of a face, of a person—at the entrance to the bar, which he imagined to be Natalia.

"Things aren't as they seem," declared the Russian.

"I don't understand," said Charlie, dismissing the distraction.

"And I can't explain."

"That's even more difficult to understand."

"I know."

Charlie gestured for more drinks but Guzov covered his glass with his hand. "Can we meet, officially, tomorrow?"

"Of course," agreed Charlie.

"Petrovka, at noon?"

"I'll be there." For what? wondered Charlie, deciding not to ask, his mind still held by the split-second image of Natalia, knowing that was all—the only thing—it could have been, a mental trick.

It was an additional ten minutes, the time it took him to finish his drink and get to his suite floor, before Charlie learned, after the briefest of alarms, that it was nothing of the sort.

★

It was not a shifting sound or the faintest breathing but instinct alone and Charlie stopped his hand short of the light switch, knowing at once there was someone already in the room. And when the single sidelight clicked on it was not he who caused it but the momentarily still unseen intruder who said, "Close the door," and Charlie finally knew who it was.

"You frightened me," he said.

"Guzov frightened me." Natalia moved from the shadows, for Charlie to see her at last. She was wearing a hat that hid her hair and a dark, tightly belted raincoat.

"You know him?"

"He was once my section leader."

"I only just saw you; convinced myself it was a mirage. Guzov didn't see you. But there were others in the bar who must have alerted him I was there. And who might have seen you."

"There was no one else who could have recognized me."

There was no guarantee of that, Charlie knew. "You shouldn't have taken this risk."

"I wasn't getting any reply at your embassy number and couldn't leave a message someone else might have accessed. I didn't want to leave things as they are."

"Do you want more lights?" asked Charlie, giving himself time to analyze what she'd said.

"No," Natalia refused, shortly. "It shouldn't have happened, in the park. I didn't know . . . didn't mean . . ."

Charlie at last moved farther into the room, standing directly opposite Natalia. "Who is he?"

"His name is Karakov. Igor Anatolivich Karakov."

"How long?"

Natalia shrugged. "Six months, maybe seven."

"Are you together?"

Natalia frowned. "Not living together, no. It would confuse Sasha."

"What have you told him about her?"

"He knows I am married but separated. But nothing about you, obviously."

"It is serious?"

"I think so."

"What do you want me to do?" The usual ordinary, inadequate words.

"I don't know. I never thought you'd come back; didn't expect ever to see you again. I was going to write, try to explain. I actually tried to write but nothing sounded as I wanted it to."

"I'll do whatever you want . . . I mean—"

"I told you I don't know what I want," she stopped him.

"It's important that you know . . . for me to tell you."

"What were you going to do . . . about the park, I mean?"

"Call you. Ask to meet, to talk like this. I was going to do it tonight but Guzov arrived."

"I'm sorry . . . very sorry . . . that it happened as it did," she said.

"You explained."

"He's a teacher, at Sasha's school. That's how we met. He was one of the escorts on her trip."

"She seemed fond of him. Comfortable."

"He's very kind."

"Is he married?"

"No."

Why should he simply give up? Charlie abruptly asked himself. "Do you love him?"

"I don't . . ." started Natalia, but she stopped, appearing to change her mind. "It would be easy to."

He'd lost her, Charlie decided, but then he'd already come to that conclusion. "It seems to make everything pretty clear."

"I'm not sure that it does," said Natalia. "You haven't told me how you feel."

Charlie curbed the instant reply, not wanting it to degenerate into an argument. "I thought I had. I understand what has happened: it was almost inevitable that it *would* happen, because of how we are . . . how we've been . . . but—"

"What about you?" Natalia broke in. "Have you got anyone?"

"No. But I don't think that comes into it . . . not into what you've got to decide. Which I guess you've already decided."

"I haven't decided anything yet!" said Natalia, her voice angry for the first time. "I'm going around in circles, which I have been ever since you came back."

"I don't see . . . can't think . . . that there's anything else I can do to help . . . to say . . ."

"Don't call . . . not for a few days . . ."

"I'm worried you might have been recognized."

"Guzov was the only danger."

"Be very careful."

"I have worked in the field, don't forget. How do you think I got in here, to be waiting for you?"

And I outmaneuvered you twice, thought Charlie. "Let the move come from me. Don't come anywhere near here again. Guzov is going to pack this hotel with eyes and ears: probably already has." It was conceivable the man would even have live microphones in the suite, if he'd discovered the room transfer. He'd have to check his intruder traps when she'd gone.

"Not for a few days," Natalia repeated.

"I'll run hare," Charlie announced. "Don't leave here for thirty minutes after me. I'll have one more drink in the bar, for them to get organized and in position. I'll leave by the main exit, going right toward Sverdlova Square and the Bolshoi. You go through Red Square, in the opposite direction."

"You really sure all this is necessary?"

"I wouldn't be suggesting it if I weren't."

Charlie isolated the bored-looking man in a lobby armchair, directly facing the elevator that he left and knew he was right when the same man, no longer bored, came into the bar behind him within minutes, now with a dark-haired woman whom he'd earlier decided to be one of the working girls and who took the most obvious table closest to the door. Charlie chose Armenian brandy and talked about a nightcap as he ordered it, using the bar clock to count off the time schedule he'd given Natalia. The initial team remained at their table when Charlie left but there were three replacements, a couple and a woman by herself, close behind when he went out through the main entrance. Sidelights immediately went on a parked car outside. Charlie paused, as if undecided in which direction to walk. He identified the solitary woman and the slowly cruising car as he entered the square, unhurriedly strolling passed the Metropol Hotel, pausing again as if undecided to enter before continuing on to study the program offerings outside the brightly illuminated theater. He used every pause and halt to monitor the time, not turning back toward the Savoy until a full twenty minutes had elapsed beyond the time he'd given Natalia to leave. All his intruder traps were in place and undisturbed when he checked them but Charlie wasn't reassured that the rooms remained untouched.

But then, he reminded himself, he had nothing whatsoever about the evening to be reassured about.

15

BY THE TIME CHARLIE REACHED THE EMBASSY THE FOLLOW-
ing morning, just after nine, there had been 138 press conference
applications, 26 of them from television companies, which included every Russian channel, all American, British, and satellite
majors, and every leading European national and commercial outlet. There were three television requests among the nine Japanese
submissions. A minor conference room within the main embassy
building had to be made available for Robertson and his team, two
of whom were additionally assigned permanently to the basement
communications room transmitting accreditation photographs,
names, and identification documentation of every Russian journalist, photographer, cameraman, and technician to London for
vetting by MI6, which called in exchange cooperation from CIA
record duplication. That second check duplication, under similar
cooperation agreements, was extended to the external intelligence
agencies of Germany, France, Italy, Spain, and Japan.

So widespread was the attempted trawl that media leaks were
inevitable. The first came from Paris, quickly followed by a longer and more detailed account in *The New York Times* and *Washington Post. Liberation,* in Paris, wrongly reported that two agents
from the external KGB successor, the *Sluzhba Vneshney Razvedki,*
had been discovered among the applications, which London refused to confirm or deny. Because of the varying time differences

throughout the world, Moscow's positive denial was the initial lead item in more than fifty European, American, and Asian day-time radio and television news bulletins.

Associated Press was the first international news agency to create a composite file of the global reaction, which Halliday brought into the embassy hall in which Charlie stood with Robertson, watching the applications in the process of being sorted into their security level checks.

Robertson said, "I wasn't told London was going to go into this degree of duplication, and I don't believe anyone anticipated this sort of result. This could turn the conference itself into an anticlimax if you don't have enough to say."

Charlie's concern had already gone way beyond that awareness, to the fear that it might diminish the all important public response. "It wasn't properly thought through."

"How many times have I heard those precise words at the beginning of a disaster assessment?" said Halliday, whose in-house MI6 embassy records were the first to be consulted for application comparison, before their onward submission to London.

"It's a fuck-up before it even gets started," judged Robertson.

"Only if I allow it to be," said Charlie.

"There are two logical interpretations from all this," speculated Robertson. "One is that the Russians gained something of enormous importance from the embassy bugging. The other is that it's the dead man who's important. You going to be able to answer either of those questions?"

Those weren't the priorities in Charlie's mind at that moment. In little more than an hour, he had to confront Guzov and God knew who else and whatever demands they might make. One uncertainty prompted another. Surely he wasn't being set up in some way! He couldn't see how but then he wouldn't—shouldn't— be able to. It was on London's orders that everything had been so abruptly turned on its head with the involvement of Robertson and Fish, and he hadn't expected that, either. Where was Fish? came another question. "I think I can do enough to ensure it won't turn into a disaster assessment."

"Which I'm glad I'm not going to be part of if you're wrong," said the MI6 *rezident*.

"I won't be," insisted Charlie, thinking that Halliday was the sort of man he'd always want to have in front rather than behind him.

"At least it'll ensure you come out on top of the local viewing figures, which I never imagined you would," said Halliday.

"What's that mean?" demanded Robertson, his voice indicating the annoyance at the man.

"Your timing's head to head against Stepan Lvov's major—live—election address to his party conference," said Halliday. "Didn't you realize that?"

"No," admitted Charlie.

"Who the hell's Stepan Lvov?" asked Robertson.

"The guaranteed new Russian president, who's going to turn the world into a better place," identified Halliday.

"Does that include not having his people bug our embassy?" asked Robertson.

"Top of his list, along with a cure for cancer and the common cold," persisted Halliday.

Reminded by Robertson's remark of the initial reason for the man and his team being there, Charlie said, "Where's Harry Fish?"

"Isolating the embassy's conference hall from any electronic intrusion into the main building," said Robertson. "He's apparently got some gizmos that'll shatter the eardrums of anyone trying to tap into any embassy system."

And others that detect a lot more electronic intrusion, suddenly thought Charlie, reminded of his bugging concern when Natalia had been in his suite the previous evening. "You think all the accreditation checks will be completed by Wednesday?" he asked the man.

"We'll probably manage the clearances, providing we don't get more than another fifty to sixty applications," undertook Robertson. "The problem already looks like equipment accommodation. Even with handheld cameras and minimal sound booms, it's going to be a crush getting all the television crews in. And then there's the radio station gear."

"There'll have to be pool agreements, two or three stations using one group of technicians and equipment," decided Charlie.

"They don't like doing that," Robertson pointed out.

"And if you impose that restriction on any Russian station, there'll be the automatic assumption—and accusation—that the excluded technicians are suspected of being intelligence agents," added Halliday.

"Let there be," dismissed Charlie, most of his concentration still upon Harry Fish. "This isn't a friend-winning exercise."

"I'm still not sure what sort of exercise it is," complained Robertson.

"Winning precisely the right sort of friend," provided Charlie.

★

Which he wasn't going to do at Petrovka, Charlie guessed, hunched in the back of the now readily available embassy car, which was blocked for more than ten minutes getting through the media siege directly outside the embassy gates that spilled over onto the gridlocked embankment road. That delay, compounded by the time-consuming detour to locate Harry Fish, meant he was going to be late getting to the headquarters of the organized crime bureau, but Charlie was encouraged by the necessary conversation with the electronics expert.

An impatiently waiting Sergei Pavel was actually at the point of going back inside the police building when Charlie arrived, only just managing to bring Pavel back by shouting as he got out of the car, which on impulse Charlie asked to wait.

Pavel said at once, "What in the name of God is happening?"

"London miscalculated."

"They're planning something inside. I don't know what but a colonel from the *Sluzhba Vneshney Razvedki* arrived with Guzov, so you're facing both intelligence agencies. And someone from the Kremlin itself."

"What about forensics?" risked Charlie, a DNA challenge at that moment his main concern.

Pavel frowned. "None. Why?"

"It's not important," hurried on a relieved Charlie. "Whatever happens inside now I will personally get you into the conference, freeing you from Guzov's control and satisfying a Russian presence, which is his argument. But I don't want to announce it to him or anyone else today. How would it affect you, personally and professionally? Would it be a problem, at either level?"

"From what's already happened today I don't know—can't know—until we meet the others. I'll call, afterward. It's chaos up there."

The group gathering in Pavel's office numbered the same as those of Charlie's original confrontation there, but the three he didn't recognize replaced the earlier forensic scientist. Charlie said, "I apologize for my lateness." It was a full fifty minutes, he calculated.

To Charlie's surprise, it was not the baleful Guzov who opened the expected attack but the Foreign Ministry's Nikita Kashev. "Everything's been escalated, beyond any common sense," complained the man, at once. "We have done everything possible to maintain an amicable working relationship. The United Kingdom has done everything to sabotage it with false and unfounded accusations."

"And I for my part have done everything to make clear to you, to everyone, that I am in no way responsible, nor can I in any way influence or change London's response to what the British embassy here in Moscow has been subjected to," argued Charlie.

"I am attached to the legal department of the president's secretariat," identified the youngest of the three strangers. "My name is Semon Ivanovich Yudkin. I am authorized to ask you to communicate both to your acting ambassador and to your Foreign Office in London the opinion of our president and our government that the current difficulties are being intentionally exacerbated and manipulated to influence the forthcoming elections in this country. That opinion—and protest—was officially communicated an hour ago to your ambassador here and to your Foreign Office to London."

"This . . . what you have said . . . is nothing I can . . . to do." Charlie stopped, forcing some cohesive control. "This is nothing, nothing whatsoever, to do with me; nothing, as I have tried to make clear, that I can control or influence. I am here to investigate a crime, nothing else."

"We know your accredited function," dismissed Kashev. "You are the only person who has been made vocally available: communication to the ambassador and your Foreign Office has degenerated to the point of formally exchanging unanswered Notes. You plead that you are little more than a messenger boy, which is what we consider you to be. In addition to what we've already told London, there will be no further cooperation or communication whatsoever in the murder investigation in which you are supposedly involved. And further, that every detail of British obstruction and inconsistency will be made publicly available to counter whatever diplomatic difficulty is currently being cultivated by London."

It would be his name publicly attached to the Russian complaints, Charlie immediately realized. "I have made it abundantly clear to your representatives attached to the murder investigation that I will make available each and every response the embassy conference generates. It is an undertaking I repeat now."

"This meeting is over," declared Kashev. "And you," completed the man contemptuously, "can leave now to deliver your messages!"

★

With the fortunately retained embassy car waiting outside Petrovka, Charlie was back at Smolenskaya long before Harry Fish left for their earlier arranged sweep of his hotel suite.

"We got another problem?" asked Fish.

"I don't know what the hell we have," admitted Charlie, continuing on to the basement. Unsure what the Russians intended to announce, Charlie included in his warning to London every accusation, threat and challenge he'd faced at the Petrovka confrontation, as much as possible—which was a lot—verbatim. He was near the end of his second revision when the hammered summons came at his cubicle door and when he opened it Ross Perritt said: "Get up to your *rezidentura, now*!"

Paula-Jane, Halliday, Robertson, and Fish were already there when Charlie arrived, grouped unspeaking around the widescreen television. P-J needed both hands to gesture him in at the same time as warning against his saying anything to overlay the program-interrupting news announcement. Charlie at once recognized the bespectacled, solemn-faced anchor of the main Rossia news channel.

". . . can only be interpreted as an intentional and provocative determination to interfere in the internal democratic activities of the Russian Federation," Charlie picked up. "Concerted and genuine attempts by members of the Russian Federation to understand the escalation of the intrusion by the United Kingdom have either been rebuffed or ignored, imposing upon the two countries the severest strain over recent years. That strain culminated earlier today in a recorded confrontation between a representative of the British government and officials of the Russian Federation, up to and including the president's office, in a final attempt to rectify a deteriorating situation . . ."

The picture switch to Pavel's Petrovka office of four hours earlier, dominated by Charlie isolated against the Russian phalanx he'd faced, was so abrupt that both Paula-Jane and Halliday audibly gasped.

Harry Fish exclaimed: "Jesus!"

Charlie said: "Fuck!"

It was a montage but Charlie at once acknowledged that the editing was so brilliant—photographically as well as verbally—that only he and the Russians who'd been there would have recognized it as such. Apart from an opening shot of the assembled Russians, the camera concentration was entirely upon Charlie and he cringed inwardly at the variety of facial expressions he had been totally unaware of making. There was the wide-eyed surprise of his entry into the room, despite Pavel's warning, but by far the worst was his brief, blank-minded reaction to the statement from presidential lawyer Semon Yudkin, which had been retained in full. Charlie judged to be the most devastating of all the editing of his initial response to Nikita Kashev's opening attack, which had been cut to just *I am in no way responsible, nor can I in any way influence or change London's response.*

When the transmission reverted to the studio commentator, Charlie was identified by name and portrayed as an ineffectual dupe who could be recognized as such by his contribution to what was referred to as a high-level government meeting. The segment ended with a separately recorded statement by Yudkin declaring that the strongest possible protest Note had been delivered by the London ambassador to the British Foreign Office and repeating the suspension of all cooperation between the two countries until a full explanation, accompanied by an apology, was made.

An aching, embarrassed silence, disturbed only by more embarrassed foot shuffling, descended on the room the moment the news break faded. Charlie broke it. He said: "I have just been sucked up and blown out in bubbles."

"That doesn't even come close to describing it," said the resentful Paula-Jane. "That's going to become an idiot's guide training film for every intelligence agency for at least the next hundred years."

"Didn't you guess you'd be filmed and recorded?" asked Harry Fish, more professionally.

"I didn't need to guess: I *knew*," Charlie flagellated himself. "I fucked up, big-time." Except for transmitting his account of the meeting before responding to the summons here, he thought hopefully.

"We're on the third floor," persisted the woman. "With luck you'd probably kill yourself outright if you jumped. We won't stand in your way."

"They've been incredibly clever, generalizing every accusation and even making it sound as if the presidential elections were in some way involved!" assessed Halliday, reflectively. "*Years,* the commentator claimed. That covers them for whatever they want—the murder and the bugging and any other embarrassment since the end of communism—and a London denial will simply be laughed at, just as you're being personally laughed at right now."

The MI6 officer was right, conceded Charlie, running the realities through his mind until he came to one that stopped him. Would Natalia have seen him wriggling like a worm on a hook? It was too forlorn to hope that she wouldn't.

"You'll obviously have to cancel your precious conference," insisted Paula-Jane. "What the Russian have just done turns it into a farce."

"Does it?" challenged Charlie, back in control. "Or is that *precisely* what they expect to happen: why they staged what they just did, because they weren't going to be part of it and wanted to stop whatever I might have said, in answer to something I was asked?"

"You surely don't expect London will allow it to happen now!" demanded the woman. "You'll be eaten alive."

"I just have been," admitted Charlie, again. "If the conference is canceled, they win. And I might as well jump, as you suggest."

"I think she's right," came in Robertson, speaking for the first time. "London's only thought now will be containment."

"Containment of what!" refused Charlie. "That's the Russians' strategy."

"I think you should talk to London," suggested Robertson.

"So do I," agreed Charlie, fervently wishing that he could have avoided doing so.

★

But yet again he was surprised, to the point of bewilderment, when he did. Having by now come to know the Director-General's emotional-controlling demeanor, Charlie didn't expect a shouted tirade but he hadn't anticipated Aubrey Smith hearing him out as patiently as the man did, thinking again as he anxiously explained his side of the debacle how lucky it had been to send his recollected account of Petrovka ahead of his televised humiliation.

When Charlie finally finished the other man said, "You've still been made to look absolutely stupid: a naïve, stumbling idiot."

"I know," accepted Charlie. "But I won't continue to appear that way if you let me go ahead."

"I know the basis upon which you've planned everything. You can't possibly guarantee any sort of exoneration!"

"They're gambling that we'll cancel," insisted Charlie. "If we do they will have won; beaten us." Not beaten us, beaten *me*, he thought.

"By elevating everything as they have, talking about affecting Russia's supposed internal democracy, they've taken any decision totally away from me, personally: it's government to government now."

"You could argue the point. And the impression that will be created if we back off," risked Charlie.

"And I will argue it," promised the man. "But that argument, logical and realistic though it is, won't necessarily prevail with politicians who think and act in sound bites."

"Then what the hell can I do?" asked Charlie, hating the sound of his own inadequacy.

"Pray," replied Smith, unhelpfully.

"To whose God?"

"The One who's best at miracles," said Smith, which helped even less.

★

Bill Bundy was the only one of his three listed callers to have identified himself with a message, and the American answered his phone the moment Charlie returned it.

"You managing to stay sane?" greeted the American.

"I'm not sure."

"You going to go ahead with the press conference?"

"It's not been decided yet." Why was Bundy interested, wondered Charlie.

"I'd like to be there if you do."

He had to ruffle his feathers, start acting professionally, Charlie decided. "I'll let you know if it's decided we go ahead."

"So you might not?" persisted Bundy.

"I said it hasn't been decided."

"You'll fix my admission, if it does?"

"Yes," promised Charlie. To try to work out your reason for being so anxious to be there, he thought.

"I can't imagine how it might help, but my offer to pitch in still stands."

"I appreciate it," said Charlie, emptily. He really could have sold tickets, he thought.

"What are you going to do—is London going to do—if you don't go ahead?"

"We haven't decided about whether or not to go ahead," wearily reminded Charlie.

"You want a break, someone to relax with, you've got my number, okay?"

"I appreciate that, too," Charlie lied again.

"Look forward to your call, whatever's decided."

Charlie pressed back in his inadequate chair in his inadequate office, deciding the dedicated number and its answering facility should be transferred to the comfort of the compound flat in which the hopeful response lines were being installed. He was about to concentrate upon the American's approach when the telephone rang once more, the traffic noise obvious the moment Charlie lifted the receiver.

"I didn't know what they were going to do," apologized Sergei Pavel at once, from his untapped phone from the street kiosk. "I realize now that telling me to wait outside for you was to get me out of the way while they set everything up—in my own fucking office!"

"You did warn me they were planning something," said Charlie, as confused at the Russian's approach as he had been by that of Bundy's, just minutes earlier. "There's nothing you could have done if you had known."

"Except given you a better warning," said Pavel. "I didn't want you to think I was part of it: tricking you like that."

"I wasn't thinking that," replied Charlie, honestly.

"You said I could get into the conference with you?"

It took Charlie several moments to reply. He'd believed the man up to now but couldn't any longer. Pavel had to be a plant, to discover what the British response to the television broadcast was going to be. Which meant, Charlie realized at once, that he couldn't indicate any uncertainty about the conference. "How can you hope to be there, beside me, after what Kashev and Yudkin said?"

"I'm not part of anything they said or did, or the trap they set. I told you before, none of them wants the investigation to continue. And if it doesn't, I'll be held ultimately responsible for its failure."

"You can't confront *both* intelligence agencies *and* the office of the president itself!"

"Things aren't that bad, not like they were in the old days."

"They're not that much better, either!" argued Charlie.

"I want to be there!"

"Then you shall be," decided Charlie. Having Pavel publicly at his side would make the Russian televised denunciation of non-cooperation almost as ridiculous as its portrayal of his stumbling inadequacy: almost, he qualified, but not quite.

"How?"

"Call on this number, this way." Unless a London-ordered cancellation were announced in advance there would not be enough time for any further sabotage to be mounted, even if Pavel were a provocateur.

"Thank you," said Pavel.

"Let's wait to see if you've got anything to thank me for."

★

The car had the now familiar difficulty getting through the thronged embassy gates and it hadn't gone more than 100 yards along the embankment road when Charlie's now regular driver said, "It could be two cars following us: one certainly, a BMW again."

Harry Fish swiveled to stare out of the rear window. Charlie didn't bother. The electronics expert said, "You actually think the FSB are tailing you!"

"It would be pretty standard practice, after everything that's happened: we'd do it if it were London."

"I most certainly wouldn't . . ."

". . . like to do my job," Charlie finished for the other man. "At the moment I don't like doing it, either." He hoped the intended hotel-room sweep wouldn't take too long. He had a lot to think about and work out. And the urge to call Natalia was becoming stronger, despite his undertaking not to attempt contact so soon.

"It's definitely two," reported the driver. "The BMW and what looks like an old Skoda."

"What do you want to do, if I do find something?" asked Fish.

"Nothing," said Charlie, frowning toward the man to indicate his discomfort at the driver being able to hear the conversation, even though he probably wouldn't understand it. "Just show me where." If the suite were bugged, he'd have a genuine and essential reason to speak to Natalia.

Fish nodded in understanding, and said nothing more until they were crossing the hotel foyer. "Sorry about that. Stupid of me."

"No harm done," said Charlie, standing back for Fish to enter the elevator ahead of him, glad they were alone. "If you find anything I want to use it to my advantage, which is why I want it left. Is there any way they can detect your searching for it?"

"Only if we speak, if and when I do find something. I'll indicate it and mark it. We can talk later, out of the room."

The briefcase-sized bag that Fish opened was sectioned to hold and clamp various instruments—including a doctorlike stethoscope—and yards. It was a yard with an elongated attachment, like an elephant's trunk, that Fish extracted and looped around his neck by a thin strap. There was a regimentation in the way the man operated, with virtually immediate results when he put the nose of the attachment to the telephone, turning to Charlie and nodding. In thirty minutes, he detected six emplacements, three in the living room and three in the bedroom. Having sticker-marked the location of each, Fish unscrewed the first detected telephone handset, pointed into the diaphragm to the sort of pinhead device Charlie recognized from the embassy search, and examined it, in situ and from several angles through an intensity-enhanced magnifying glass before looking up, both frowning and shaking his head. After a further, even more concentrated examination, Fish handed the glass for Charlie to look in detail for himself. Charlie was able under the enlargement to see that the device was not completely cylindrical, which he'd imagined it to be, but had an extension, like a finger, from its left side. Several times, unnecessarily gesturing Charlie against any utterance, Fish painstakingly opened every identified location and subjected each bug to the same intensive scrutiny, finishing every one with the same frowned head shaking.

There were people in the outside corridor and again in the descending elevator so it wasn't until they were in the familiar bar, Charlie in his back-protective corner seat and the drinks ordered, that Charlie was able to say, "What's all the head shaking about?"

"They're not the same," declared Fish, with another appropriate head movement.

"What's not the same?"

"The listening devices," said Fish, patiently. "Remember I told you those in the embassy were state of the art, which I thought they were because I'd never seen anything like them before? These are even better! They're fantastic and I'd sell my soul as well as my body to get hold of one to dismantle and reverse engineer."

"What are you telling me?" persisted Charlie, feeling another sink of unwanted bewilderment.

"*These* are state of the art: I've never seen anything so sophisticated, even without taking them apart. Why weren't those the same in the embassy, potentially a far bigger and more important target?"

"You tell me," invited Charlie.

"I can't," admitted Fish. "But I'd like to be able to."

So would he, Charlie decided, adding it to his list.

16

CHARLIE WAS GLAD HE'D PROTECTIVELY WARNED THE TELE-
vision media of the likelihood of pooled arrangements because
overnight, effectively with just six hours before the start of what
he realistically accepted to be one of the greatest gambles he'd
ever taken, forty-three more attendance applications, ten of them
from additional stations, were logged at Robertson's embassy vetting room. By that time, Charlie's painstakingly created priority
list was mentally shredded by Harry Fish's discovery in the Savoy
Hotel suite, and Charlie personally and arbitrarily decreed the
share between Russian, American, and British TV stations, rejecting any decision-reversing arguments against his edicts with
the warning that any station refusing to accept his ruling would
be refused attendance altogether. Anxious not to miss Sergei
Pavel's expected approach, Charlie accepted Fish's offer of a pager
attachment to his dedicated apartment telephones, as well as his
previously allocated line, his suspicion of the man's overall monitoring confirmed by Fish not asking for an explanation for the
request. Charlie was surprised to the point of astonishment—
although in turn not seeking an explanation—that Reg Stout was
included by Robertson for their final tour of the specially assigned conference facility and the route to it from the gatehouse,
accepting Fish's assurances without fully understanding the detailed explanations that the embassy and its ancillary buildings

were totally secured against electronic intrusion. Charlie did understand how completely those attending the conference would be recorded from the three television cameras presenting a 360-degree surveillance within the hall, in addition to those temporarily added to the now fully operational outside cover. There still hadn't been any contact from Pavel when they ended the tour back in the conference chamber, with a complete rehearsal of the embassy secretaries who were to be stationed throughout the room with handheld microphones for individual questioners and a final check of the translator's booth.

Charlie waited until Stout left for his self-appointed supervision of the gatehouse arrivals before saying, "Why's Reg to be included?"

"He's officially responsible for embassy security," said Robertson.

Charlie's intended protest at not being consulted was stopped by his pager's vibration, its source registering on its screen. Charlie at once recognized the street phone number.

"It's your now transferred original line: it's not secure if it's transferred a second time through the switchboard," hurriedly intruded Fish.

"You've just told me everything electrical is totally secure behind a white noise barrier," said Charlie, as the pager continued to reverberate.

"There's a risk with a double transfer," insisted the other man.

Mumbo-jumbo bullshit, decided Charlie, picking up the conference-hall extension and telling an immediately responding operator to put the call through.

The voice Charlie instantly recognized to be Pavel's said: "Fifteen minutes."

"Yes," acknowledged Charlie, though unsure if the Russian heard him so quickly was the outside street telephone replaced. Turning back to the other two men, Charlie said, "Your secondary monitor, the one I'm not supposed to know you've attached to the apartment lines, wouldn't have got that, would it, Harry?"

"A backup is an obvious precaution," tried Robertson.

"Why play silly buggers and not tell me there was one?" demanded Charlie.

"We're not spying on you," insisted Fish.

"I would, if I were in your position," said Charlie, sardonically. "I just wouldn't be so bad at it."

"Who was it?" demanded a tight-lipped Robertson.

Charlie's hesitation was more to continue the other man's annoyance than to avoid the answer. "Sergei Pavel."

Initially, there was blank-faced silence from the two men, until Robertson said, "It was my understanding that no one officially involved in your murder investigation was to attend."

Your isolated Charlie yet again. "Pavel's militia, not FSB."

"Working entirely independently from the FSB?" questioned Robertson.

"It's my decision and my responsibility," stated Charlie. He was unsure approaching the thronged entrance if the already assembled media were early arrivals or a separate assembly of FSB agents and informers to record and identify those arrivals. Within the gatehouse, in addition to its now totally functioning CCTV system, Reg Stout was virtually at attention behind Russian-speaking embassy staff there to confirm that every attending journalist and technician was listed against their official accreditation documentation. The setup reminded Charlie of the passport controlled and suspect-indexed checks at the long ago Checkpoint Charlie crossing between East and West Berlin during the numbing days of the Cold War. He'd once had to let a man be killed there to prevent being shot himself, he further recalled. It was wrong to remember; to invite ghosts.

It was difficult through the gate office window to isolate the face for which Charlie was looking, but from the main, better windowed exit and entry section he at last saw Pavel, trying to keep himself apart from the ebbing and flowing melee while at the same time hopefully using its protective concealment from the sweeping camera lenses. The Russian detective located Charlie at the same time, hurrying through the door Charlie opened to an instant explosion of camera lights.

"I didn't expect this," greeted Pavel. The man's excitement was obvious.

"Who is this? I need an identity!" officiously demanded Stout.

It was Charlie, caught by a sudden idea, who answered, although in the Russian Stout was supposed not to understand. "Colonel Pavel is attending upon my authority," Charlie told the registration clerks.

"I need to see some provable ID," insisted the clerk, also in Russian.

"You're looking at it. It's me," said Charlie, impatiently.

Stout shifted, as if to intrude further, but didn't.

Pavel nodded back toward the gatehouse as they emerged into the crash-barrier controlled walkway. "Was that a problem?"

"We'll see," said Charlie. He was conscious of one of the temporary camera installations keeping them constantly under observation as they approached the hall. Neither Robertson nor Fish were there. Charlie led the way past Fish's monitoring technicians making their last-minute equipment adjustments into a rear anteroom in which three closed circuit screens were already operating, although without sound. One showed the approach from the gatehouse along which they had just walked. The other two were focused on the inside of the hall from two different angles, totally covering the area. At that moment on both were pictures of sound technicians moving along the already set-out chairs, depositing on each ear pieces for simultaneous translation.

Pavel looked briefly at the screens. "It all looks very impressive."

"It's got to be impressive," said Charlie. "If something doesn't come out of this, I don't see a way forward. I've lost any contact, certainly any cooperation, with Guzov: with everyone, except you. And what *about* you? What's your position going to be, after today?"

"It's a gamble I had to take. If they believe I'm the only conduit, being here today is my best guarantee to be kept in the investigation. I'm betting on their not being able to risk pushing me aside anymore."

"Here they come!" said Charlie, attracted by the sudden in-flux through the gatehouse, led by the first group of equipment-burdened television and radio engineers. There was a bottleneck at the very entrance to the hall and almost immediate shoving.

Charlie looked away at Robertson's entry, unexpectedly fol-lowed by Stout. Robertson said, "I want Reg on the platform with us."

This wasn't a last-minute move, Charlie knew. Any more than Stout's earlier inclusion hadn't belatedly occurred to the spy hunter. "I'm not allowing any questions about the bugging. It's strictly limited to the murder," he told the security chief.

"I've already made that clear," intruded Robertson.

"I'm making everything even clearer," said Charlie, still talk-ing to the ex-army major. "Don't get in the way by trying to in-volve yourself in any English exchanges."

"What if there's something I need to make clear?" asked Stout.

"Pass me a note," ruled Charlie. "Unless I have your absolute guarantee that you'll say nothing—just sit there—you're not coming on to the platform."

"Reg has got every official—" started Robertson.

"I'm setting the rules and this is what they are," halted Char-lie. "You don't like it, you're not coming on the platform, either."

"I won't try to contribute," promised Stout.

Charlie remained staring at the man for several moments. "That's a positive order! One word that fucks up what I'm trying to achieve, you're on tonight's plane back to London."

"I don't think . . ." began the ex-soldier but abruptly stopped. Then he said, "I understand. I won't say anything. Just be there."

The confrontation was broken by the arrival of Harry Fish. The man said at once, "We didn't build in enough time for all the gatehouse checks. There's got to be at least fifty still waiting to be processed. And God knows how many more not yet in the hall . . ." He waved his hand toward the television screens. "Look at it!"

The jostling line outside stretched unbroken the complete length of the forecourt from the gatehouse to the hall, the inside of which was shown by the internal cameras still to be only half full. Despite Charlie's insistence upon pooling same-country television and radio technicians, the area directly in front of the raised stage was already a thicket of trailing television cables and there was a hedge of station-identifying microphones running the entire length of the official table. From the number of chairs at the table Charlie realized a space had been set for Stout before their argument.

From beside him Pavel offered Charlie a slip of paper and said: "These are the two headquarter lines dedicated exclusively for any response we might get from today."

"I'll have them included on the list to be distributed," said Charlie. "I'll leave it to you to announce it, from the platform."

Robertson turned from the television sets. "We need to announce a delay."

"We'll make it together," insisted Charlie, telling Pavel what he was going to do as he moved toward the door, gesturing Robertson ahead of him. Directly outside, in the linking corridor, Charlie said, "What the fuck game are you playing?"

"It's necessary," said Robertson, awkwardly.

"What is? Why wasn't I told?"

"It came up. There wasn't time."

"Bollocks! What is it?"

"I need to keep Stout on a leash. Harry thinks one of his tracking devices has picked up something. He and his guys want time."

"I should still have been told," repeated Charlie, sure Robertson had manipulated the episode to establish his seniority.

"You just have been told. Let's get on with it, shall we?"

Charlie accepted, leading the way out into the hall. Charlie had expected the immediate eruption of noise but not the sunburst of blinding lights that almost made him stumble into the waiting, empty chairs. He gestured Robertson down beside him and said, "My senior colleague and I, on behalf of whom I speak, are delaying the start until everyone gets into the hall. We don't expect that delay to be more than half an hour. We're not imposing a time. Everyone will get their opportunity to ask their questions."

There was an immediate protesting cacophony and Charlie rose, hearing words like "deadline," and "murderer," and "mafia," and "spy," and "Cold War," and a lot more in several other languages. Robertson momentarily remained where he was, only rising at Charlie's encouraging nudge and even then slowly, turning to put both of them facially beyond any camera focus. Few but someone of Charlie Muffin's experience would have recognized Robertson's look to be one close to hatred.

Back in the linking corridor Robertson said, "You just made me a bigger target than yourself, identifying me as your superior. I'm going to bring you down for that; do everything I can to destroy you."

"You know the problem with bad gangster movies, Paul? They all have that sort of crap dialogue: turns them into comedies instead of being frightening."

★

The noise at their reentry was an unintelligible roar, which visibly startled Stout and Pavel. Charlie managed to avoid the blinding brightness of the strobe lights. The three looked to Charlie for seating directions. Charlie put Robertson beside him, at the center of the table, with Pavel flanking him on his left and Stout on the other side of Robertson. It took several minutes for the uproar to subside and when it did, he still had to shout into his microphone, flapping waving-down motions with both hands. Charlie identified the three other men and insisted the conference was restricted solely to the murder of the one-armed man; any other questions on anything else would be refused. There would be simultaneous translation through the available earpieces into Russian, English, French, German, and Italian and within the hall were six embassy officials with handheld microphones for individual questioners: those questions would be amplified for the benefit of everyone. There would be no individual, one-to-one television interviews after the main conference. Nor would any photographs be released of the murder scene or of the body. Deferring to Pavel as he spoke, Charlie said the joint British and Russian investigation had so far been extremely productive, which would become obvious during the conference but that they were still seeking help from the public. To receive that help three dedicated telephone lines had been established at the embassy and two at the Petrovka headquarters of the Organized Crime Bureau: after slowly reciting each—and repeating each—Charlie said information sheets listing them would be available to everyone upon departure and he was asking that the phone numbers be printed in all newspapers, their Web sites, and repeated on television and radio broadcasts as well as being published on their Web sites, too. No identification of any caller would be publicly disclosed; anonymous calls could be made. There would be recording apparatus on every listed line.

Along with the telephone list would be separately printed information, which the joint investigation hoped would lead to the identification of the victim. Another sheet would illustrate the precise spot where the body had been found, showing its proximity to the hall in which they were assembled and its relationship to the main embassy building and the entry gate into the forecourt.

The victim was male, five feet eight inches tall, weighing 164 pounds, and was aged between forty-five and fifty. The left arm had been surgically amputated between ten and fifteen years earlier. He had been killed by a shot in the back of the head from a Makarov pistol, its bullet made to flatten on impact, to destroy all facial and dental features. He had also been tortured, and the fingers of his surviving right hand had been burned by acid to remove all fingerprints. All makers' names had been removed from his Russian-manufactured clothing: a brown, polyester mass-produced suit, a blue shirt, and a red-and-black-striped tie. The lace-up shoes, which were well worn and also of Russian manufacture, were brown. All the suit pockets had been emptied. There was a red birthmark, affected by the acid burning, on the right hand, and the little finger of that hand had been distorted, possibly since childhood, by what forensic pathologists believed to be frostbite. In the past, again possibly in his childhood, the man has undergone an appendix operation. There had been traces of a barbiturate in the man's blood.

"Let's start the questioning," invited Charlie.

There was an immediate burst of inaudible shouted questions, which Charlie had to again subdue by shouting louder and standing to gesture the noise down. Shielding his own microphone, Robertson said, "This is a farce, a waste of time."

Needing his amplification, Charlie still had to yell. "This is going to be canceled right now if everyone doesn't start behaving sensibly!"

A woman in the third row gestured for a handheld microphone, identified herself from *The New York Times,* and said, "Are you treating this as an assassination?"

Charlie deferred to Robertson, who appeared startled. Leaning hesitantly forward he said, "It is certainly one avenue of inquiry."

"So the man could have been an informer—a Russian spy—pursued into the embassy by Russian security officers?" seized the woman, refusing to surrender the microphone.

To Charlie's gesture, Pavel said, "We have been officially assured there is absolutely no involvement of any State security organization, so that is untrue."

"You would be, wouldn't you?" said the persistent woman, to isolated sniggers at the mockery.

"There is also no involvement of any British intelligence organization," came in Charlie, to help Pavel.

"We'd be told that, too, wouldn't we; *have* been told that already," said a man in heavily accented English—an Italian, Charlie guessed—who reached across from his seat directly behind the woman to take the microphone.

"Nothing can be ruled in or out of the investigation until we get the victim's identity," said Charlie.

"So it is a possibility—a strong possibility—that it is an intelligence assassination?" persisted an NBC reporter from the middle of the hall.

"Nothing has been ruled in or out," repeated Charlie, identifying Bundy next to the questioner, relieved at the comparative order that had finally settled. There'd be a publicity benefit from the inevitable concentration upon an intelligence-organized assassination.

As the thought came to Charlie another woman, this time from the *London Times,* demanded, "Which British intelligence organization do you, Mr. Robertson, and Mr. Stout represent?"

"That is not a question that will be addressed," refused Robertson, without any prompting from Charlie.

"Why not?" pressed the woman.

"Next question," insisted Robertson.

"MI6 or MI5?" came a shouted question, not needing amplification.

"Next question," repeated Robertson.

Charlie had to listen intently to his own earpiece for the translation from German of the question. "What other lines of inquiry are you pursuing, apart from it being a State-approved killing of which, comparatively recently, there is evidence of the Russian authorities being prepared to sanction?"

After a momentary hiatus, Pavel said, "Regrettably, there is a great deal of organized crime in Russia, particularly in Moscow. Assassination of this sort is a very common method of settling gangland feud and disputes."

"How many others have there been in the grounds of the British embassy?" immediately demanded the German, to more mocking laughter.

"None," quieted Charlie. "But it would be a very effective way of misdirecting an investigation along the espionage lines that appears to be the media preference."

"What's your preference?" asked the determined German.

"I have none," responded Charlie. "With my colleagues I am conducting this investigation with an open mind, with no preconceived impressions or theories."

There was more disbelieving laughter, which brought a heavy sigh and a pointed sideways look from Robertson. Charlie was happy for the next question to move away from the espionage fixation, a demand for more evidence of the murder having been committed within the embassy grounds, which enabled him to expand upon the supposed discovery of part of a 9mm Makarov bullet and the score mark on the outside wall of the hall in which they now sat, which inevitably brought the question of how the killers and their victim got into the embassy grounds unseen.

"The killers weren't unseen," snatched Charlie, seeing the first opportunity to stage manage the event as he wanted. "Despite a partial malfunction of the entrance security cameras, the actual moment of the murder, by a number of men, was indistinctly recorded. The images are being scientifically enhanced and the hope is that such enhancement will be sufficient to identify the killers, although from the position in which the victim is shown, on his knees, no recovery of his features will be possible."

The hall erupted into a far noisier outburst than any previously and it took Charlie a full five minutes to once more subdue the babble sufficiently to continue. The most obvious and frequent demand was for the CCTV and stills from it to be released for publication, which Charlie refused with the easy escape that as the film was in the process of being sharpened, hopefully to form the core evidence in a prosecution, any release was legally impossible. He refused, too, any verbal description of those featured on the loop, apart from saying that all appeared to be male. He—as well as Robertson and Pavel—were able to avoid any demands that didn't serve their purpose by refusing to let the questioning go beyond the actual murder, despite determined and repeated attempts to get a response to the bugging. Charlie was, however, selective in his refusals, alert to whatever maximized his chances of getting that one essential, victim-identifying response.

When no opportunity presented itself after almost another hour, during which the predictable insistences expanded into the recurring possibility of the victim being a Russian intelligence officer killed at the point of an intended defection, Charlie decided to bait his own manufactured hook.

To a question that had been phrased in varying forms at least three times before—how endangered were relations between the

United Kingdom and the Russian Federation—Charlie replied, "The successful conclusion of this investigation, toward which we are moving, ensures there is no risk whatsoever to that relationship."

"What successful conclusion?" insisted the original questioner from *The New York Times*. "You're asking for help: that doesn't convince me you're anywhere close to solving this!"

"I have already told you why we cannot release the surviving images on the CCTV film," said Charlie. "You will surely understand and accept that there is other evidence we cannot make publicly available. We might be able to come some way towards providing more—making arrests even—once we have named the victim."

The fresh outburst was less strident than those that preceded it. "You've already got enough for an arrest!" demanded the woman.

"The answer to that will have to wait for the next conference," evaded Charlie, rising to bring the other three men up with him, to yet another protesting uproar.

★

"That was a disaster!" insisted Robertson, back in the anteroom.

"It did everything and more to achieve what I wanted," rejected Charlie.

"What if you don't get a name from it?" persisted Robertson.

"Today will bring something out of the woodwork."

Robertson appeared, oddly, to become aware of Stout listening to the exchange. "Let's hope so."

"I'll walk you to the gate," Charlie told Pavel. As they went across the forecourt, Charlie spoke to the other man of his rejection of Robertson's assessment, which he translated.

Pavel said: "He's got every reason to be doubtful. To be honest, so am I."

"We laid out enough bait," insisted Charlie, wishing he sounded more confident.

"We need to establish undetected personal communication," said Pavel. "What about individual cell phones?"

"We might as well stick tracking devices up our asses," dismissed Charlie. "In England, we foiled dozens of Islamic terrorist plots before they had been mounted and captured the perpetrators of a lot more that we missed the first time through mobile phones. Once detected by scanners, they can be listened to and the users traced to within fifty yards by the electronic signals they emit. We'd be more discreet standing on street-corner boxes, with megaphones."

Pavel lifted his shoulders in an awkward shrug. "Stay with phones at street kiosks then?"

"By far the safest."

When they stopped, just before the gatehouse, the Russian suggested the already used café as another unmonitored meeting place, allowing an intervening gap of two days for incoming calls to begin on the publicly announced numbers. "During that time we can make our choice of telephone kiosks; get some numbers to exchange. From now on, Guzov's people are going to permanently be just one step behind both of us, probably literally."

"Which will make the Varvarka café an important test," acknowledged Charlie, confident of his own trail-clearing ability but wondering about Pavel's.

One of the designated telephones was ringing when Charlie entered his assigned embassy apartment and, for the briefest moment, he hesitated before snatching it up.

From the unexpected internal line Robertson said, "Something's come out of the woodwork."

17

CHARLIE MUFFIN WAS ENGULFED BY A FEELING OF DÉJÀ VU on the threshold of the spy-catchers' inquiry room. Paul Robertson occupied the chief inquisitor's position from which he'd conducted Charlie's interrogation, flanked by the same male and female team. The two polygraph technicians were at their momentarily quiet equipment, but looking far happier than during Charlie's session and Charlie recognized on either side of the door the two heavy-handed guards who'd stood threateningly over him before he'd ridiculed his polygraph examination. Harry Fish was to the left of the judgemental bench; in front of him, the familiar white handkerchief upon which lay three pinhead bugs. As Charlie came fully into the room, Reg Stout, in the same chair upon which Charlie had sat, was saying vehemently, "I have only ever seen devices like these once before in my life, when the original six were discovered in the telephone relay box."

"And I've already told this inquiry I found them in your compound flat, taped to the underside of a chest drawer," insisted Fish. "And shown you the Polaroid photographs, prior to those we also digitally took later as part of official evidence."

"What's your explanation for the bugs being where they were?" demanded the unnamed man who had orchestrated Charlie's confrontation.

"I'm being set up!" protested Stout, his voice rising. "You won't find my fingerprints on any of it."

"The surface of the devices is too small to register fingerprints: they have to be handled with tweezers," dismissed Fish. "There's enough surface, though, on tweezers we did find in your apartment. There's only one set of prints—yours."

"What about the logs?" demanded Stout, desperately.

"Your fingerprints are on the spirals and the log cover," said Fish.

"I want a lawyer," demanded Stout, his voice wavering almost beyond control. "You're framing me, with an illegal search. Planted stuff. You need a warrant."

"You will be appointed a lawyer when you arrive back to London, under arrest," came in Robertson. "And to help you when you meet with your lawyer, it was not an illegal search. We have a warrant to search wherever and however we want in this embassy, including all staff accommodation."

Abruptly, in Russian, Charlie said, "It'll go easier for you, Reg, if you make a full confession."

Attracted by Charlie's voice, Stout turned to the side of the room where Charlie stood and said: "I should have guessed you'd be part of it, too."

"What did you say?" Robertson asked Charlie.

"You tell them what I said, Reg," hopefully suggested Charlie, in English.

"How the hell can I?" protested the man. "You know I don't speak the fucking language!"

"I know you've told me you don't."

"And I don't! I'll go to the papers about this—expose you all."

"You're a signatory to the Official Secrets Act, which precludes you or your representatives speaking about anything official to any media outlet or organization," said the woman panelist, whom Charlie presumed to be a government lawyer.

"You will remain overnight, under guard, in your apartment, from which the telephone will be disconnected preventing your contacting anyone outside this embassy," officially recited

Robertson. "You'll be repatriated, still under guard, on the first direct London flight tomorrow. In London, you will be formally arrested and will appear, in camera, before a magistrate. A lawyer will be present to represent you at this and any subsequent hearings."

"I'm being set up," repeated the ex-army major, in a near hysterical babble. "I've served my country, loyally, all my life . . . got medals . . . decorations . . . this isn't right."

"Take him back to his quarters," ordered Robertson, gesturing to the two waiting guards.

Stout twisted, his face contorted, to the advancing men. He stood, obediently, at the gesture from the larger of his two custodians and was led, unprotesting, from the room.

"What did you say to him in Russian?" Robertson again demanded of Charlie.

"I told him it would be better for him if he made a full confession."

"Why did you tell him that?" asked the woman.

"He's always insisted he can't speak Russian," reminded Charlie. "He was distressed . . . disorientated. I thought there was a chance he might have slipped up and answered me in Russian. It would have undermined his denials, don't you think?"

The three at the table frowned between themselves. Dismissively Robertson said, "Not particularly. But thanks for your effort."

"Why'd you go back to Stout after clearing him the first time?" asked Charlie.

Robertson hesitated. "We didn't clear him absolutely: his original polygraph was better than Dawkins's or Sotley's and that's all we had, contradictions and inconsistencies in their separate statements. No supporting evidence. London's decided that was because of their arrogance: that they were affronted having to undergo the polygraph at all. They performed much better under more formal investigation in England. They're both being prematurely retired, of course, because of their obvious incompetence but there were some inconsistencies between what Stout told us the first time and what Dawkins said, under reexamination . . ."

". . . so we decided to go back to Stout," picked up Fish. "As small as they are, these bugs have miniscule transformers, to connect with their outside receivers. And they generate a pulse, which we picked up when we swept Stout's apartment. We found them within an hour of your press conference getting underway."

"Confronted with the positive evidence, Stout came close to collapsing, although he recovered by the time you came in," resumed Robertson. "He was all over the place on his second polygraph."

"He certainly wasn't admitting anything from what I heard," challenged Charlie.

"He doesn't have to," insisted Fish. "We've got the evidence."

"Which isn't enough, by itself, is it?" challenged Charlie, again. "You've got to sweep the entire embassy all over again, to ensure Stout hasn't replaced the first lot of bugs you found."

Robertson gave Charlie a condescending look. "What, exactly, do you imagine Harry's people are doing right now?"

"It's good to know everyone's staying on top of their job," said Charlie, unabashed. "And when that's done, I guess you're all looking forward to going home?"

Robertson slowly shook his head. "You think that all by yourself you can monitor three contact appeal phones and what might come in on them—sift the cranks from what could be your breakthrough call—as well as liaise with whatever your Russian militia friend might get from his end? The Director-General himself thinks you need help."

"He hasn't told me that," said Charlie. Was this another act of desperation by the losing Aubrey Smith?

"He will when you speak to him; he's expecting your call. I've arranged five o'clock, his time."

Looking toward the electronics expert, Charlie said: "You staying on to hold my hand, too, Harry?"

"Obeying orders, as we all have to do," replied the man.

Ignoring the inquiry panel, Charlie walked the length of their table to look down at the still displayed listening devices. To Fish, he said: "You got a glass?"

Fish paused, frowning, before handing Charlie the magnifying glass. Squinting down through it, Charlie said, "They're not the same as those you found in my hotel, with the spur to their left. These are the same as the others that were found here the first time."

"Of course they're the same," echoed Robertson, impatiently. "What else did you expect?"

"You're right, of course," agreed Charlie. "What else could I have expected?" More professionalism, he thought, answering his own question.

★

"I'm relieved that Robertson and Fish have solved their problem," announced the Director-General.

"Have they?" questioned Charlie, from his suspended telephone booth.

Aubrey Smith hesitated. "They will have when the new sweep is completed and if we locate some fresh bugs that will give us even more evidence."

"I would have appreciated being told directly that they'd been seconded to my investigation."

There was another pause from the London end. "Let's not get petulant. Robertson called to tell me what had been found in Stout's rooms and how Stout being kept at the press conference helped. There was a natural progression to the conversation that followed. You can't be expected to handle everything by yourself. I thought Paula-Jane could be brought in, too. Her speaking Russian would help, wouldn't it? Maybe Halliday, too. MI6 have offered their help."

"I don't want any permanent embassy staff included," argued Charlie.

"Why not?"

"There's been very little so far to give me any confidence or faith in existing staff here. I want to maintain the separation."

"Robertson and Fish are sure Stout's their spy."

"I'm not," disputed Charlie.

"Is there something you're not telling me?"

"This was—and still is—an appallingly mismanaged embassy," reminded Charlie. "My investigation should remain entirely independent from anyone here. Unquestionably the people with Robertson and Fish are sufficiently security cleared, but I need a system under which I personally examine and assess all recorded messages without my authority being questioned, apart from by you." Charlie's irritation was growing. "I know a secondary recording system has been installed ensuring calls will be taped to provide you with immediate access to every contact. I would like your guarantee that you will not instigate any action whatsover, as a result of what I have begun today, without prior discussion with me—"

"That is impudent insubordination!" interrupted the Director-General.

"That is a very necessary operational request, expressed as directly as it was to prevent the slightest misunderstanding between us," persisted Charlie, glad that as always the exchange was being automatically recorded in London. "You have gone with me—trusted me—so far in risks that I have accepted to be entirely my responsibility. If I fail, I want that failure to be of my own mistakes and making, not through the interference of others following their insufficiently prepared initiatives or an agenda of which neither you nor I have prior knowledge."

"I've read your file, know your history: Charlie Muffin, the maverick loner bucking all authority and opinions other than his own," warned Smith. "And I've backed you all the way. Sometimes I've got to defer to collegiate pressure here."

The internal counterintelligence department in which Robertson and Fish operated was under Jeffrey Smale's direct control, Charlie remembered, many unexplained irritations abruptly becoming clearer.

The Director-General continued, "I think, upon reflection, that misunderstandings have occurred. Robertson can come back with his other two adjudicators, leaving his support staff with Fish and his people to provide your backup."

Was Smith according him the battle honors? Or allowing Paul Robsertson a tactical retreat? "I'll let Robertson know you want to talk to him again." If he hadn't won the battle he'd at least come out best in the skirmishes, Charlie decided.

"Don't, for a single moment, forget anything I've told you," pressed the man.

"Not for a single moment."

★

Hunched on his bar corner stool at the Savoy Hotel, Charlie resisted the sink into self-pity, surprised at the feeling: self-pity wasn't an emotion he very often, if ever, allowed himself. Of all his feelings after such an overfilled day—Natalia still firmly compartmented—the hovering depression was the easiest to identify. When he'd finally left the embassy, less than an hour ago, there had only been six calls to his dedicated telephone numbers: four of them, predictably, had been from journalists, seeking the earlier-refused personal interviews or follow-up information. The other two, predictable again, had been from cranks, a woman complaining that she was being sexually motivated by the FSB with a mind-controlling laser beam, and a man who interspersed his insistence upon a return to communist rule with a slurred rendition of one of the former Soviet Union's marching anthems. Charlie had tried Pavel's personal line as well as the two publicly supplied Petrovka numbers and got the answering service on all of them.

Working to retain his momentarily lost objectivity, Charlie acknowledged that it had been ridiculous to expect a worthwhile response so soon after the press conference. As yet, the appeal with its all-important contact numbers was virtually confined to television coverage and the late editions of two evening newspapers, and so far the TV coverage would not have been seen by anyone working normal office or factory hours. Charlie was encouraged by the one early evening TV repeat he had already seen in his suite by the station's assurances of two additional and longer segments later that night, and the promise of an extended, although edited, version being carried the following day. He wasn't, though, encouraged by his own hesitant stumbling and very visible perspiration during the press conference questioning. By his own judgement he'd appeared amateurish, suspiciously ill at ease, and haphazardly disheveled alongside the other three men. Briefly allowing a thought of Natalia to emerge from the locked part of his mind, Charlie hoped she would not have watched the full live coverage.

"The victor, savoring his triumph," said the easily recognizable voice, behind him.

"You staying with fake scotch?" Charlie asked Halliday, not needing to turn to identify the man.

"It's an acquired taste," accepted the MI6 man, settling on the adjoining stool.

"What's the triumph?" asked Charlie, ordering from the attentive bartender.

"Been watching satellite TV," said Halliday. "CNN got hold of the viewing figures for your event to compare with those of Stepan Lvov's keynote speech to his party's annual assembly. You got 76 percent against Lvov's 24. His people are going to be pissed off with that."

"The success or otherwise of Stepan Lvov's election isn't in the forefront of my mind," dismissed Charlie.

"It's picking up elsewhere," remarked Halliday. "*Time* magazine made him and that gorgeous Marina their cover story this week—THE MAN TO REVOLUTIONIZE RUSSIA FOR THE SECOND TIME. Thought you would have seen it."

"I've had a few others things on my mind," said Charlie, sourly.

"And now you're going to get a hell of a lot more," predicted Halliday. "Really thought Paula-Jane and I would be seconded to help with the workload."

There was a throb in Charlie's left instep, along with the thought that he'd be running out of come-join-me tickets if he'd turned it all into a commercial venture. "You know the problem involving embassy personnel in high-profile situations like this."

"Paula-Jane's really upset; thinks it's personal."

"Do you and Paula-Jane get included in everything that London decides here?"

"I'm sure I do: it's a question of courtesy."

"What about Paula-Jane?" questioned Charlie.

"I get the impression she does, too," said Halliday. "What do you think about Reg Stout?"

"What about Reg Stout?"

Halliday actually turned for a more direct confrontation, glass suspended before him. "Charlie! I'll give you the benefit of the doubt—*just*—for keeping Paula-Jane out. But *I* know that *you* know about Reg: it's the only thing anyone's talking about at the embassy! You ask me, Robertson and his band of merry men were pretty fucking inefficient, taking so long to expose the obvious. At least now the embassy is finally secure."

"Is it?" asked Charlie, doubtfully.

He had his question answered when, back in his suite, he tuned into the late evening ORT station's news which, quoting "informed sources," led with the disclosure of Reg Stout's arrest and the suggestion that the embassy security man was involved in the murder investigation as well as the spy hunt.

18

BY THE TIME CHARLIE REACHED THE EMBASSY THE FOLLOW-
ing morning, just after seven, the message capacity on one of his
dedicated telephones was blocked by the overflow of incoming
calls, and the register on the second showed there was less than
two minutes recording space left. There were just three minutes
remaining on his personally assigned line. It only took seconds for
two of Fish's technicians to download the messages from all three
instruments, each of which was switched to speaker reception.
Practically every call they reviewed was a media demand—
worldwide approaches almost equaling those from within Russia—
for comment or more information on the previous night's ORT
disclosure. So were all but seven on the overnight tapes. Three of
the outstanding seven were cranks, one again from the singing
communist zealot. Charlie ordered all but four of these calls—
each duplicates from ORT—to be wiped, with no intention of responding. Of the four that remained, three were from men, the
other from a woman. Two of the men insisted the murder of the
one-armed man to be a gang killing, offering an identity for
money—one for £5,000, the other for £1,000—which had to be
left in advance at designated places before they'd call back with
the name. The third man, who didn't leave a return number,
said he personally knew the victim and would make contact
again. The woman, who sounded old, thought the one-armed

man was her husband who hadn't returned from the siege of Leningrad during the Great Patriotic War.

One exception, on Charlie's personally allocated line, was from Bill Bundy. The CIA man said: "You feel in need of a sympathetic ear, you've got my number, Charlie."

"Robertson was as pissed off as hell at being called back to London," said Fish, who'd remained in the room with his technicians listening to every playback. "He'll be even more upset about the TV disclosure."

"I'm sure he will be," agreed Charlie, philosophically.

Fish indicated the tape still containing the television station approaches. "You going to return those?"

"I need to know who's still leaking from inside this embassy."

"You think the station's going to tell you!"

"I won't know unless I ask, will I?" said Charlie.

A woman answered the ORT number, her voice lifting the moment Charlie identified himself. "We very much appreciate your calling back, Mr. Muffin."

"You are?"

Harry Fish turned from the apparatus he was now operating alone, nodding confirmation that the sound levels were providing a perfect recording.

"I am Svetlana Modin, ORT's main news anchor. Your information at yesterday's conference was extremely useful."

Fish gave a thumbs-up, nodding approvingly at the identification and mouthing that they had her image on film.

"You called me?" invited Charlie, his feet beginning to throb in warning.

There was just the slightest uncertainty in the laugh. "We certainly have a lot to discuss."

"About what?"

The laugh was stronger this time. "About your security chief, Reginald Stout, the man close to you on the platform yesterday."

"Are you recording this conversation?" demanded Charlie.

"I can assure you that we at ORT are jealous of our integrity and consider accuracy the cornerstone of our journalism."

"That's not an answer to my question."

"Do you want me to stop the recording?"

"Your integrity didn't extend sufficiently to your telling me what you were doing."

"I've stopped doing it now."

"Why don't you come to speak to me here, at the embassy?"

"With a film crew?" the woman asked, urgently.

"No, definitely not with a film crew," refused Charlie. "I will see you here in one hour. I have also recorded this conversation. You will not be allowed to bring any recording equipment into the embassy. Don't attempt any hidden devices, after openly surrendering an obvious machine at the gatehouse: the room in which we meet will be electronically protected against any attempted recording."

"I can't accept those restrictions," the woman tried to argue, hurriedly.

"Then there is no purpose in continuing this conversation or in your coming here. Good-bye—"

"No!" blurted Svetlana, anxiously. "Okay! I accept the conditions."

"That sounded pretty good to me," suggested Fish, as Charlie replaced the telephone. "But I still don't imagine she'll give you her source."

Reflectively Charlie said, "I think Svetlana Modin's a very, very clever lady. And that she thinks I am a very, very stupid man, which is hardly surprising after my performance. Can you get me a written transcript of that conversation?"

"Did I miss something?" Fish frowned.

"I think the definite intention was that I should," judged Charlie. "We still got yesterday's cameras on the gatehouse."

"Yes."

"And they're still operational in Robertson's inquiry room, with all the recording gear there?"

"Yes," said Fish.

"Can you record whatever conversation I have with her there while at the same time preventing her using a concealed device?"

"It won't be perfect," said the electronics expert, cautiously.

"But still audible?"

"I can enhance it, later. Why don't you tell me what's going on, Charlie?"

"I will when I'm sure myself."

Charlie watched Fish hurry from the room, adding another uncertainty to all his others: Why hadn't Pavel made contact by now? It was irrefutable logic that the Russian would—should—have done so, after the television revelation, quite irrespective of all the Petrovka lines being tapped by Guzov's FSB.

When Charlie got the answering machines on two of Pavel's numbers and an unavailable signal from the third—which Charlie assumed to be jammed to overflowing—he rang the main Petrovka switchboard. The operator insisted that no one in the headquarters building knew the militia colonel's whereabouts. There was no reply from the personal line Charlie had for Mikhail Guzov and although there was a listed number for the *Federal'naya Sluzhba Bezopasnosti*, Charlie held back from ringing it, reminding himself that he was not officially supposed to know that the man was a serving officer.

Charlie's frustration was broken by Harry Fish's return, two closely typed foolscap pages in his hand. "Now I've read what she said as well as hearing it. I'd say Svetlana Modin is one hard-assed bitch."

Charlie didn't speak until he'd read the transcript through himself, twice. On his third reading he worked on the typed pages, deleting and rearranging the context. Finally looking up at the other man, Charlie said, "I'd say she's a hard-assed *professional* and that she's going to think she's got me by the balls even before she gets here." He handed the marked pages back to Fish and said, "You think you can keep our master copy but make another record, still in our respective voices, what I've written there?"

Fish looked quizzically up from what Charlie had created. "They surely wouldn't do this! You told her yourself that we were making our own copy: We could refute it."

"Remember the golden rule of propaganda," urged Charlie.

"Tell a lie enough times to a big enough audience and it'll become the truth."

Both men looked toward the suddenly ringing telephone, at once recognizing Halliday's voice on the speaker phone. "For Christ's sake, turn on your television!"

The picture that flickered on to the screen was a virtual replay of the media scrum outside the embassy gates the previous day, the frenzy greater now because of Reg Stout and his two escorts being the focus in its very center. Robertson and his two panelists were separately surrounded by more jostling, yelling journalists and cameramen. There were two uniformed British Airways stewards attempting as ineffectually as three uniformed Russian militia officers, to force a path along the airport concourse to the waiting London flight. As Charlie and Fish watched, the TV camera abruptly zoomed in upon the embassy security officer tight enough to show his escorts were gripping Stout by either arm to force him on and that the man was struggling against them, his head thrown back as he shouted inaudibly. The Russian voice-over commentary was of Stout demanding protection by the Russian authorities and for the militia officers to intercede to prevent his kidnap, back to England. "He is saying," reported the commentator, "that in London he will be put on trial for his life. The charge will be treason, the maximum penalty for which is the death sentence, despite the United Kingdom supposedly no longer having capital punishment on its statute books. . . ."

"Jesus Christ!" exclaimed Fish.

"I'd like what I wrote back on the recording and ready for replay before Svetlana Modin gets here," said Charlie. "She's due in fifteen minutes and I don't expect her to be late."

★

She wasn't.

From the concealment of the gatehouse Charlie decided that if Svetlana Modin was indeed as hard-assed a professional as she was attractive, he was confronting a formidable adversary. The jacket of her full-skirted, dark brown business suit was cut wide to make the brown-trimmed yellow shirt a part of the ensemble, one too many buttons unfastened to hint at the deep cleavage beneath. The blond hair, meticulously fashioned by an attendant hairdresser, brushed her shoulders, and on the second by second countdown to a live transmission a makeup girl applied last-minute touches to an eyebrow that arched questioningly on cue as the woman began her piece to camera. Enclosed as he was, Charlie was unable to hear what she was saying but saw almost overexpansive gestures toward the embassy and from the reaction of other journalists and cameramen closest to her guessed the woman was announcing her impending, exclusive entry into the embassy. He was proved right when, with her camera still running, Svetlana Modin handed her microphone to an expectant sound recordist before walking to the gatehouse door where she stopped and posed before pushing into the entry control area. Once over the threshold, she relaxed the tightly fixed presentation smile, twitching the cramp from her face, and began, "I have an appointment . . ." before she saw Charlie at the far side of the shadowed cubicle.

She said: "Thank you, Mr. Muffin, for inviting me here to talk at length about the murder and everything else that has happened in and around the embassy."

"There was an agreement about recording," reminded Charlie.

"Because of which I have not brought a machine with me."

"You have no recording equipment whatsoever?"

Smiling, Svetlana held her arms away from her body, stretching the shirt further over the impressive breasts and said, "Search me, if you wish."

"Let's go into the complex," invited Charlie. He remained silent as they crossed the forecourt. At the main building he said, "No unauthorized electronic equipment works now."

"I told you I don't have any electronic equipment."

"I heard what you told me," assured Charlie, ushering her into Robertson's interrogation room.

Svetlana said at once, "This looks like a torture chamber."

"Nothing electronic works in here, either."

"You really don't believe I'm clean, do you?"

"Did you really expect me to?"

"Not if you're the intelligence agent I believe you to be. That's what you are, aren't you? An agent?"

To Svetlana's obvious bewilderment, Charlie said, "We're ready."

Her frown cleared at the entry of Harry Fish, a flashlightlike device in his hand. "A club to beat me with?"

"Are you still willing to be searched?"

Now her face hardened. "Why shouldn't I be?"

"Are you still willing to be searched for electronic recording equipment?" repeated Charlie, formally.

Svetlana smiled, once more extending her arms in an expansive invitation. "Enjoy."

Harry Fish was professionally, painstakingly thorough, standing behind her to sweep every inch of Svetlana's back and sides, even going over the curtain of hair beneath which something might have been concealed, reversing from the heels of her shoes to their toes to start ascending from her front. A bleep accompanied the sharp flash on Fish's sensor when he got to the top of the woman's thighs. "There it is," said the man, unnecessarily.

"You'll be escorted to a cloakroom to take off whatever recording apparatus you've got under your clothes," announced Charlie.

Slowly, provocatively, Svetlana lifted her skirt above her waist. She wasn't wearing any underwear. The brown stockings were supported by a black lace suspender belt, framing her natural blondness. The device was strapped around her right thigh, tight against her crotch.

Not looking at the woman exposing herself, Harry Fish said, "It's a microphone."

Ignoring her, too, Charlie said, "Would it have transmitted from the gatehouse and coming across the courtyard?"

"Yes," confirmed Fish, at once.

Eventually looking back to Svetlana, who was letting her skirt gradually drop, Charlie recited, "*Thank you, Mr. Muffin, for inviting me here to talk at length about the murder and everything else that's happened in and around the embassy.* That really was too scripted, although I didn't expect the pubic demonstration as well. Take the microphone off."

The skirt rose again. "Why don't you help me?"

"Both of us or do you have a preference?" asked Charlie.

She shrugged. "I'm a fun person."

Charlie jerked his head backward. "Your vagina's been on camera now for close to five full minutes, maybe longer. You look closely you can see the fish-eye lens just above the light switch on the wall opposite you. And my sound system isn't affected by what will have destroyed yours, once you got inside the embassy. I can't imagine that you thought you'd get away with it. I even warned you!"

The microphone came away from her groin with a crackle of torn-apart Velcro with the second descent of the skirt. "Motherfucker!"

"Listen," said Charlie, smiling, and nodding to Harry Fish. At Fish's press of the replay button the room was filled with the sound of Charlie's edited version of his earlier telephone conversation with Svetlana Modin, dominated by her voice.

Svetlana Modin: *We very much appreciate your calling, Mr. Muffin. I am Svetlana Modin, ORT's news anchor. We certainly have a lot to discuss about your security chief, Reginald Stout. I can assure you that we at ORT are jealous of our integrity and consider it the cornerstone of our journalism.*

Charlie: *Why don't you come to speak to me here, at the embassy? I will see you here in one hour.*

Svetlana: *Okay! I agree and accept the conditions you set out earlier.*

"I'm not suggesting that is precisely how you planned the edit, but it's pretty close, isn't it? Screened with the scenes at Sheremyetevo Airport this morning you'd have had another world exclusive, wouldn't you?"

"You really are a motherfucker, aren't you?"

"We'll complete the check, shall we, Harry?"

The second microphone was between the fulsome cups of her bra, black lace to match the suspender belt. Charlie said, "Let's not fuck about with helping you disconnect it. Just take it off."

As she did so, quickly buttoning her blouse afterward, Svetlana Modin slumped into the interrogation chair, legs splayed but covered. "What do you want?"

"The name of your informant."

"You know I won't do that. I've got a much better idea. You give me something, I'll give you something. If you're as clever as you're making yourself out to be, you'll have the name and I'll have the exclusive I hope to get. How's that sound?"

"You were too obvious with the way your framed your questions, from the word go, on the telephone. But I never expected the pussy-peek."

"You'd be surprised how often it's worked before."

Charlie turned to Harry Fish. "You think you could run that part of the film on which Svetlana's proving herself to be naturally blond?"

Fish made the connection within minutes, beckoning the Russian to the small viewing screen, from which she very quickly looked up. "Very enticing, even if I say so myself. What's your point?"

"Your international as well as national fame. If I released that footage to all your rival Moscow TV stations, as well as those throughout Europe, America, and Asia, your vagina—even with the necessarily discreet editing—would have phenomenal viewing figures, alongside the edited and unedited tape of our telephone conversation. We'd describe it as evidence of how far—up to and including blackmail and sex, with your invitation to Harry and me to take the first microphone off—you're prepared to go to get what you want."

"I've got enough to face you down, you bastard!"

"And I've got film of your openly offered and freely displayed crotch. Whose face is going to be redder, yours or mine?"

★

"It was an anonymous caller," said the woman, tightly.

"Male or female?"

"It sounded male but it was difficult to be sure."

"Why?"

"It was distorted through a synthesizer."

"In Russian or in English?"

"Russian."

"A genuine Russian speaker or with an accent?"

"There was an accent."

"What sort of accent?"

"The synthesizer made it impossible to guess."

"Try."

"I can't."

"How soon after the press conference here?"

"An hour; maybe an hour and a half. I'd just gotten back to the studio. I'd told the switchboard to put any calls that referred to the press conference directly through to me. We'd made an appeal for callers, throughout the morning."

"Tell me—the actual words the caller used."

Svetlana gave another of her familiar, open-armed gestures. "I can't remember the exact words!"

"Try," Charlie said.

"It was something like, 'I have information about the conference at the British embassy. The man on the far right of the platform, the one who didn't say anything. He's been arrested for spying. It's to do with the listening devices that were found earlier.' That's as much as I can remember."

"You're lying," accused Charlie. "That sort of conversation couldn't have been within a ninety-minute time frame. Stout was still being questioned an hour and a half after the end of the conference."

"Maybe it was longer than an hour and a half."

"Doesn't your recorder have a time counter?"

Svetlana's face twitched. "I don't remember the precise timing! There was sufficient time for me to catch the main news bulletin."

"You went to a lot of trouble when I first called you today, telling me how important integrity and accuracy is to your station. So, set out the sequence in more detail for me. You get an anonymous call from someone whose gender you can't even identify, because they're using a synthesizer?"

"I asked him questions."

"So tell me the *first* thing he said."

"It was something like 'I have information about the murder at the embassy.'"

Charlie made as if to speak but didn't, not immediately. Then he said, "Let's go back to integrity and accuracy. What did you do to substantiate the information you got from your anonymous caller, before going on air?"

Svetlana looked steadily across the space separating them, her mouth a tight line only broken when she said, "I'm getting very pissed off with this."

"Don't, for a single mistaken moment, imagine that I won't do what I warned you I would if you tried to fuck me about . . . as I think you've tried to fuck me about ever since we began talking. So you know what we're going to do, to achieve a lot more a lot quicker. We're going to stop now. You're going to go back to the station and you are going to get me the tape you recorded—the original, not a copy . . ."—Charlie gestured to the silent Harry Fish—"I know you'll take a copy, but he'll know if you've doctored it in any way and if you do, I'll expose you more effectively than you've ever exposed yourself before. And you're going to tell me who you called here at the embassy to confirm Reginald Stout's detention. Is there anything I've said that you don't understand or need me to explain in more detail?"

Svetlana's face had been reddening as Charlie talked and now it was blazing. "You shouldn't talk to me like this . . . *imagine* you can talk to me like this!'

"Noon!" stipulated Charlie. "I'll be waiting."

★

Charlie was halfway back across the courtyard after escorting Svetlana Modin to the gatehouse, having enjoyed her furious gestures to her crew to stop filming her emergence outside, when Harry Fish came hurriedly out of the embassy, waving him back into the building.

"What is it?" demanded Charlie.

"Hear for yourself," said the electronics expert, bustling

Charlie into the elevator to the apartment where the dedicated telephones were recording incoming calls. One of Fish's technicians was by Charlie's personal line, and as they entered the room the man depressed the replay button.

The voice, in Russian began: "Charlie! I've got . . ." before the room reverberated with a deafening roar.

Charlie said: "That was Pavel's voice."

Fish said: "And that was a gunshot."

19

CHARLIE MUFFIN WAS AGAIN SWEPT BY A FEELING OF DÉJÀ
vu, the comparisons everywhere: the same mortuary in which
he'd first seen the body of the one-armed man, facing across his
dissecting table the same pathologist, with Mikhail Guzov hovering at the man's shoulder, as he'd hovered then.

And Sergei Romanovich Pavel had been killed the same way
as the first victim, by a single shot to the back of the head, although this time the bullet had not been hollow-nosed or had
dum-dum crosses carved into its tip, so the face, apart from the
absurdly neat exit wound to the forehead, remained comparatively
intact, although the man's nose was broken and his left cheek lac-
erated from the force with which the impact had smashed him
into the wall of the telephone kiosk. Charlie wasn't sure if the
death-mask grimace had also been caused by that impact or if
Pavel had felt a brief second of agony.

Mikhail Guzov said, "He'd been searched, pockets pulled inside out but he wasn't robbed. Some coin was lying around the
body, as well as his wallet with some rubles still in it. Twenty dollars in American money, too."

"What about his militia identification?"

"Still in his jacket pocket. And his gun was in its holster."

"He was most likely killed by a Makarov, too," offered Vladimir
Ivanov. "I'll confirm that when I complete the autopsy: forensic

will positively identify the compressed remains of the bullet they dug out of the kiosk frame."

"Where was it, the kiosk?" asked Charlie, the questions more instinctive than formulated to a pattern, the greater part of his concentration on why Guzov had so quickly included him, particularly after the previous TV entrapment at Petrovka. By the time Guzov arrived personally at the embassy, an hour earlier, Charlie had already been alerted to Pavel's murder by the obediently returning Svetlana Modin, with the tape of the anonymous tip of Stout's detention. She'd still been there when Guzov arrived at the embassy, recognized the man at once, and just as quickly addressed him familiarly by his patronymic, which was another memorized-for-later curiosity. As was Guzov's apparent willingness to confirm to the woman that Pavel's murder was unquestionably linked to that of the one-armed man, which had provided her with another exclusive to mitigate Charlie's earlier outmaneuvering.

"At the junction of Bogoslovskij and Palashevsky," identified the Russian intelligence agent, without hesitation.

"Two busy, inner-city roads in broad daylight!" exclaimed Charlie, knowing the location.

Guzov shook his head. "Bogoslovskij is closed off, for roadwork. There's a lot of drilling, which would have covered the sound of a shot. We haven't been able to find any witnesses: no one who heard anything."

"Wouldn't the roadwork and the drilling have still made it a bad choice?" persisted Charlie, hoping to encourage the Russian further. Was it a good idea to have brought Pavel's murder tape with him?

"There's no indication that he had made a call. The telephone was still on its rest when his body was found by one of the workmen farther along the street: if it hadn't been it might have given us a lead. It's possible he was lured there."

Charlie briefly hesitated before taking from his pocket the CD Harry Fish had copied from the master tape of Pavel's call. Offering it to the Russian, Charlie said, "He did make a call, to me.

He manages three words—*Charlie. I've got*—before the sound of the shot. There's no disconnection sound but there's noise in the background, which I now guess was the roadwork."

"'Charlie, I've got . . .'" echoed Guzov. "What the hell had Sergei Romanovich got?"

"I doubt we'll ever know," accepted Charlie. "If he'd written it down it would have been found by whoever went through his pockets: maybe *why* he was searched."

"Why replace the telephone?" persisted Guzov.

"To prevent the call being traced," said Charlie. "I didn't get the impression of anyone listening, trying to discover if he'd made a connection. There was a noise, which until now I couldn't identify. Then silence."

"I've been put in charge of the investigation into Pavel's murder," disclosed Guzov, straightening at his side of the dissection slab as if expecting a confrontation.

"Which you told Svetlana Modin was connected to the first murder. Why'd you do that?"

"Hopefully it'll make the killers think we know more than we do: that Pavel told others what he was doing."

Charlie didn't completely follow the other man's reasoning but decided against questioning it. "Let's hope you're right and they make a mistake we can follow."

"My being put in charge of the Russian side of the investigation means we'll be working together, sharing everything," said the Russian, staring very directly at Charlie across the corpse.

Which the FSB had been determined to achieve from the outset, recalled Charlie. And which probably explained Guzov's quick arrival at the embassy, the obvious preparedness to include him in the most preliminary of medical examinations. Surely not! Charlie thought, as his reflection lengthened into a possible conclusion: surely the FSB wouldn't have taken their determination to the extreme of sacrificing a militia colonel who'd openly opposed them, as Sergei Romanovich Pavel had done! Why wouldn't they? Charlie at once asked himself. Pavel had even suspected he was being set up as a sacrifice, although not literally.

There was an unarguable logic in Guzov taking over Pavel's role, the switch from militia to FSB cosmetically easy to adjust by stressing Guzov's prior participation.

"I look forward to that."

"If the head of your embassy security is responsible for planting the listening devices he'll break under interrogation?" suggested the other man.

"I would expect him eventually to make a *confession*," mildly qualified Charlie.

"When he does you'll have to finally concede that no agency of the Russian Federation is in any way involved in a security breach within your embassy, nor in the death of the still unidentified man," said Guzov. "When that is accepted we'll be able to make progress in solving both crimes instead of constantly wasting time."

★

Charlie Muffin knew all his faults and failings, but hypocrisy was not on his self-criticizing list. Neither was it a factor in the unsettling uncertainty that he began to feel as the day progressed.

Which was, inconceivably, that Russian intelligence might not be implicated in the bugging of the British embassy and genuinely sought not just to resolve the murder of the one-armed man but now that of militia colonel Sergei Romanovich Pavel.

From the mortuary he drove with the Russian directly to Petrovka where he was presented with sheaf after sheaf of transcripts of telephone responses to the press conference and with a minimal selection of actual tape recordings. The overwhelming majority of the printed log contained exactly the same—déjà vu again—press approaches with a similar sprinkling of crank and confidence trickster demands for money in advance of information. There were six separate sheets, each with its relevant tape segment, that were selected as possibly informative, although none was sufficiently complete to be acted upon. Three had been traced to public telephones and Guzov anticipated Charlie by saying that none was that of the kiosk in which Pavel had been shot.

Charlie was impressed by the infrastructure assembled to monitor the inflow, the assigned telephones all in a large room Charlie guessed normally to be a conference facility but manned now by a staff of predominantly male operators on one side, divided from its other by a pool of mostly female typists maintaining a simultaneously transcribed record of the tapes' contents. Six people—three men and three women—were in the center of the room, pointed out by Guzov as trained interrogators ready instantly to take a call from the initially alerted telephone operator who judged it sufficiently important to intercept and hopefully extend before any nervous disconnection. None was summoned during the time Charlie was in the room: all were in civilian clothes, as further confirmation that all were FSB.

After the practical demonstration, Guzov led the way back to Pavel's office, which he'd clearly commandeered. It appeared much tidier than when Pavel occupied it, even during the ministerial-attended conferences. On the desk was a wooden frame, its back to Charlie. Intercepting Charlie's look, Guzov turned it to show Pavel in the center of a family group and said, "He had three daughters. The youngest will be six next month."

The month of Sasha's birthday, too, Charlie recognized. He was a day late with his promised call to Natalia. He said, "That looks an impressive setup," speaking of the telephone room.

Which Charlie didn't imagine Pavel having either the resources or the authority to have established. Nor did he believe that Guzov and the FSB would have been able to create it in the short time—a matter of hours—since Pavel's murder. Was that what Pavel had been so anxious to tell him—warn him—that the FSB were, quite literally, in total control of the Russian investigation, irrespective of Pavel's attempted independence: reducing that effort to irrelevance, in fact? It was an unavoidable speculation that at the same time did nothing to undermine Charlie's nagging thought that Guzov's denials might be genuine.

Guzov said, "Does what you saw help to convince you?"

"Of what?" stalled Charlie.

"That we are as anxious as you are—as your country is—to

bring this investigation to its proper and hopefully quick conclusion," said Guzov. "As I believe is the case in your country, there is always a greater, more personal commitment to solve a murder in which a law officer is the victim. Shouldn't we stop dancing around a situation and stop distrusting each other until there is a real and positive reason for that distrust . . . ?" The Russian smiled. "Which we both know and expect to happen before it's all over."

"I think perhaps we should," allowed Charlie.

★

"The tip about Stout was definitely made through a synthesizer," confirmed Harry Fish. "I've already had it transcribed in full. It's pretty much as Svetlana Modin paraphrased."

"What about the sex of the caller?" asked Charlie, accepting the transcript.

The electronic expert shook his head. "It's not the usual sort of synthesizer: there seems to be an additional distorting device that jumbles the tonal range."

"You telling me you can't decide whether the voice is male or female!"

"It renders what's recorded to be virtually androgynous."

"And you're also going to tell me you've never confronted anything like it before," said Charlie, sighing.

"Right," confirmed Fish, hefting in his hand the Russian recordings. "What do you want me to do with these?"

In an uninterrupted rush of impatience, Charlie said, "Run every check to establish if they've been tampered with, whether they're genuine—particularly if the callers were indigenous Russian or from any of the other republics or outside foreigners—whether the calls were from public telephones or private lines, anything identifiable in the background that can't ordinarily be heard without enhancement to suggest a location, and whatever else you think might help."

"You going to work with Guzov?" demanded Fish.

Charlie was surprised there hadn't been any response by now from the Director-General to everything he'd filed to London after his return from Petrovka: surprised, too, that it had taken Fish so long to start asking the recorded question to be relayed back to Thames House on channels to which he had no access. "With Pavel lying dead in the mortuary, Guzov is now my only link to the Russian investigation."

"Don't you find it curious that Pavel had U.S. dollars in his wallet?"

"What's your point?"

"Just that."

"There's nothing whatsoever to be curious about," insisted Charlie. "U.S. dollars are the currency of Russia, Moscow particularly. It has been since 1991: before that, even." He pulled out a bundle of mixed notes from his own pocket. "I've probably got fifty dollars or so myself." It was the currency he provided Natalia, in cash and by post, and at irregular dates and amounts to avoid creating a pattern, judging a regular electronic transfer from an English to Moscow bank too liable to arouse suspicion over time. So far, surprisingly, nothing had been lost.

Fish shrugged, no longer interested. "Surely you don't think Guzov's given you these to prove the Russians are genuinely going to work with you?"

"It would be stupid to turn my back on anything without seeing what's in it for me." Which was, Charlie accepted, the central core of his rigidly followed survival credo.

"I really wouldn't . . ."

". . . like to do my job," Charlie wearily finished for the other man. "You told me. Now tell me something else. The leak of Stout's arrest came from inside the embassy. So who, in this embassy, has the need for or access to a voice-distorting synthesizer?"

Fish considered the question. "Paula-Jane Venables and David Halliday. But as far as I know—and it's my job to know—the synthesizers that we and MI6 supply to its officers do not include the gender distortion facility."

"We both also know Reg Stout couldn't have been ORT's source: he was already incommunicado, with Robertson's heavies at either elbow. There's another source within this fucking embassy!"

"I'm going around in so many tight circles I'm expecting to disappear up my own ass!" protested Fish, just as exasperated. "You survive this—and I don't think you've got a chance in hell of surviving—and I'm told I've got to work with you on something else, I'll do whatever I can, up to and including killing myself, to avoid it! You contaminate and bring down everyone and everything with whom you come into contact!"

Charlie let some silence into the cavernous room, intrigued at the unexpected outburst. "You got something more you want to tell me, Harry?"

"Point *out* to you," qualified the other man, quiet-voice now, seemingly embarrassed. "Don't you think you might be next on the murder list after Sergei Pavel?"

"I certainly believe it's a possibility I might be *expected* to think."

"Let's hope some poor innocents don't get caught up in the crossfire."

Some poor innocents like Natalia and Sasha, thought Charlie. And wished he hadn't.

20

NO LONGER OPPOSED—NOT EVEN QUESTIONED—BY TRANS-
port officer Howard Barrett, Charlie improvised on basic tradecraft, dispatching three unoccupied embassy pool cars in three
different directions before uncomfortably hiding himself in the
rear of the fourth to run the embassy gauntlet, redirecting his first
time driver after awkwardly hauling himself up from the concealing foot well. He halted the car in less than a mile, descending to
the Metro on the Sokolniceskaja line at Park Kultury, and carriage
jumping between stations and three interconnecting lines for an
additional thirty minutes before finally, with aching feet, regain-
ing ground level at Kitay-Gorod, satisfied that he was alone. He
was lucky with the guess initially to go along Novaka, almost at
once locating a telephone kiosk at its Staraja intersection.

"It's me!" proudly announced a child's voice, on the second ring.

Charlie swallowed against the unexpected difficulty in his
throat. "Is your mother there?" He consciously turned, protectively to put his back toward the wall against which the kiosk was
built. There was a swirl of traffic but few people, none showing
any interest in him.

"Yes."

Charlie could hear Sasha breathing, not calling for Natalia.
"Can I speak to her?"

"She's in the kitchen."

"Will you ask her to come to the phone?"

"What's your name?"

Charlie had to swallow again. "Please call your mother to the telephone."

Charlie heard the sound of Natalia's approach and of Sasha's voice, away from the mouthpiece, say: "It's a man."

"Who is this?" demanded Natalia.

"Me," said Charlie, unthinkingly repeating Sasha's identification.

"Oh."

"Sasha's very good on the telephone."

"She likes answering it." Natalia's voice was neutral, neither welcoming nor rejecting.

"I'm sorry I didn't call when I said I would."

"I didn't expect you to."

"I guessed you'd understand."

"I feel . . . it doesn't matter."

"It matters a lot," said Charlie.

"What's happened hasn't made things any easier."

"I told you I'd get out of the business." Had he? Charlie asked himself: he couldn't remember. When she didn't respond he said, "Natalia?"

"I'm in a mess . . . don't know what to say . . ." she suddenly blurted.

Charlie was surprised, not able to recall Natalia ever sounding so uncertain: lost even. Another impression, a hope, began to form. "We were going to talk about meeting."

"You sure you can safely do that now?"

He'd never been safe in his life, reflected Charlie. "You know I'll never put you or Sasha at any risk; wouldn't ever endanger either of you."

"I'm not sure."

He couldn't let her uncertainty grow, give her any reason to refuse: "I won't allow any risk!"

"I've promised to take Sasha to McDonald's on Saturday."

Charlie was jolted by the recollection that McDonald's was

where the one-armed man had most likely eaten his last meal. Bulldozing her, not allowing her any escape, he said, "How do you want me to do it? Be there and approach you?"

Natalia hesitated. "Just come in. I want time to be sure: you take time ordering. Look about for a seat when you get your meal. If I look directly at you, it'll be okay. If I ignore you, it's not. Or at least I don't think it's okay." There was a muffled sound of someone calling, which Charlie didn't hear, not sufficiently even to decide if it was Sasha. Clearly turning away from the telephone, Natalia said, "In a minute."

Charlie began: "Who was . . . ?" but abruptly stopped.

There was another pause before Natalia said, "No one's here with me, apart from Sasha."

"I'm sorry."

"So am I."

"How will you explain to Sasha what I'm doing at McDonald's?"

"That you're someone I know. It will be all right. But you must be sure you're clean."

There was nothing to be gained from trying further reassurance. "How long does it take you to get there?"

"Half an hour."

"What time will you arrive?"

"Lunchtime . . . say twelve."

"Don't leave the apartment until I call, to tell you it's okay . . . that I can make it."

"I'll still take her, of course. Even if you say you can't make it. That's why it's important."

"You don't have to tell me the importance of anything."

"Maybe I just need to keep telling myself," said Natalia.

Better—far better—than he'd hoped, assessed Charlie, as the conversation ended. This, right now, would have been her moment: her arm's length opportunity to tell him everything was over between them. But she hadn't! More than that, even; very much more. She'd agreed to meet him with Sasha. She wouldn't do that—even contemplate that—if she'd already made her final, irrevocable decision. But enough, for the moment. Until Saturday.

Charlie got back to the Savoy in time for the main evening news, which as he expected was led by anchorperson Svetlana Modin's overexaggerated claim to have another world exclusive based on her fortunately coincidental encounter with two of the senior investigators into both murders. There were photographs of Pavel but neither Charlie nor Guzov were initially named, although there was footage of the press conference and of the kiosk in which Pavel had been shot. There was also, predictably, a lot of location-establishing footage of Svetlana going in and out of the embassy: she relied heavily upon impressive-sounding although empty clichés like "major international exchanges" between Moscow and London being considered at "the highest levels," and used the word "major" again—as well as sensational—when she hinted at impending developments. Just as Charlie believed he'd escaped identification there was more footage showing him dismissing a question about "a highly trained, international and professional Murder Incorporated assassination squad"—which at the time he'd refused even to speculate upon—edited to appear instead as if he'd suggested such a ridiculous possibility and that there was indeed an international search for such a group with airline checks and requests to worldwide intelligence agencies.

Charlie was conscious of several looks of recognition as he went through the lobby on his way to his nightly bar-stool ritual, sure that in turn he recognized the girl—although tonight with a different surveillance partner—who'd played the role of a hand-holding lover the night of Guzov's unexpected visit. Sure of Guzov's professionalism, Charlie knew her repeated presence was not an oversight but something he was intended to recognize. Maybe even a warning against established routine. They'd briefly discussed such precautions during the drive between the mortuary and Petrovka. It was perhaps something to which he needed to pay more and closer attention, although not so much for his own safety—which he never endangered—but for the now absolutely essential security for his Saturday rendezvous.

The bartender and the already poured vodka were waiting when Charlie got to his wall-protective stool. As Charlie settled himself the man said, "I reserved it for you. I'll do that from now on, shall I?"

"I'd appreciate it," accepted Charlie. The program being shown mute on the bar television was that which followed the evening news, so the man would have seen the transmission. Charlie guessed at an approach from the way the bartender's attention switched beyond him and turned from his corner before Bill Bundy reached him. Charlie said, "I think I need to employ an appointments secretary."

"What?" the American frowned.

"I seem to get a lot of visitors here."

"I'm not surprised. You're getting enough publicity to stand against Stepan Lvov," smiled Bundy.

The predicted new Russian president and reason for Bundy's return to Moscow, Charlie remembered, after a momentary blankness. "It'll be mineral water, right?"

"I'll break the seal," reminded Bundy, in Russian and loud enough for the bartender to hear. More quietly the American said, "Tried you earlier at the embassy to make sure you were all right . . . not involved, I mean."

"What do you mean?" queried Charlie.

"The accident. Haven't you heard?"

"What accident?"

"One of your embassy cars got driven off the embankment road. There was a piece on the TASS wire. When I couldn't get you I spoke to Paula-Jane. She told me the driver was pretty smashed up—might have broken his back even. She said she hadn't heard from you all day."

Charlie swallowed against the sudden nausea. "What about the other car involved?"

"Didn't stop," said Bundy. "The militia are looking for it. You catch tonight's television news?"

"There wasn't anything about it on the channel I saw."

"I wasn't talking about the accident. I meant Svetlana Modin's."

"I knew it was going to be screened," said Charlie, forcing the calm. Why hadn't Paula-Jane or Halliday—anyone—made contact to tell him about the accident, which hadn't been an accident at all. Because he hadn't told anyone about the exit subterfuge and no one had made the connection yet.

"Why are you feeding her exclusives?"

"I'm not. It's a confused story."

"Which you're not going to tell me," anticipated Bundy.

Charlie didn't bother to reply, gesturing instead for another drink.

Bundy said, "You know Guzov, your new partner, is big time FSB?"

"Of course I do."

"He tell you himself?"

"He didn't have to. Pavel did." And could have been killed for doing so, Charlie thought.

"Did he tell you Guzov's a general? Sits on the top floor?"

"No, he didn't," admitted Charlie. There'd only be the night-duty officer at the embassy this late, Charlie calculated. He'd have to wait until tomorrow to find out anything more.

"Guzov will use you, in each and every which way he can," warned the American.

"As I'll use him," said Charlie. "We all know the rules, Bill!"

"You're here all by yourself. You really think you can compete with the resources he's got?"

"I'll do my best."

"You know why Pavel got whacked?"

"You got any theories?"

Bundy shook his head. "The most obvious is that he had something. And from your hugger mugger press conference performance and how Svetlana spun her piece tonight, the even more obvious inference is that if he did have something, you've got it, too. Which I'd say makes you target numero uno, wouldn't you?"

"It's crossed my mind." And was now very firmly fixed in the forefront of it, threatening the determination not to panic.

"You're not impressing me with all this flip talk, Charlie. You're in the crosshairs and you know it."

So did Natalia, Charlie knew. And would think so even more if the accident was reported in any media. "Like I said, we all know the rules."

"I also know we didn't hit it off in the past to become friends. But I'm talking to you now at least as a colleague in the same business . . . a concerned colleague."

"I appreciate that," said Charlie, keeping the disbelief from his voice.

"But I didn't come here tonight to tell you that. Or about the accident."

It had taken the American long enough, thought Charlie. "What then?"

"You didn't call me back."

"I was getting round to it."

"You heard from London today?"

"No," said Charlie. Which he'd expected to, after Pavel's killing.

"My people at Langley have officially approached yours—MI6, too—with an offer to help in any way we can. Let's face it, Charlie, you need all the help you can get."

And probably a lot of protection, Charlie thought. "I don't like armies. People get in other people's way and mistakes happen. I've never liked the phrase 'friendly fire.'"

"It was Langley's idea. I just thought you should know before being told officially."

Charlie was disappointed Bundy didn't lie more convincingly. "You going to show Guzov the same consideration?"

"You know as well as I do how well—and how much—we've worked with the Russians in the past. As you have. But that's not the game plan this time."

"What is the game plan this time?" Charlie echoed.

"We work through you."

"Without telling Guzov?"

"This investigation has become too public. The FSB couldn't

risk the embarrassment of it becoming known that we're on board too. Let's face it: this thing is leaking faster than the *Titanic*."

"Much faster," accepted Charlie, at least recognizing his way out of an American involvement, even if there were an official edict from Aubrey Smith.

"That's another good reason for the linkup. You could transfer everything to the leak-free security of our embassy here: cut that problem out of the loop."

For linkup read takeover, thought Charlie, astonished at the unashamed hubris. "You seem to have thought it through to the end."

"We're offering help, Charlie."

"I'm sure London will appreciate that as much as I've already told you I do."

"I look forward to talking more tomorrow."

"I guess we will."

Bundy, who hadn't bought a drink, fingered the till receipts of those that Charlie had purchased. "You need these for your expenses?"

"Be my guest," invited Charlie.

"Remember what I said about taking care . . . physical care, I mean," said Bundy, pocketing the slips.

"I will," promised Charlie.

★

It was very easy after an almost sleepless night for Charlie again to be at the embassy by seven the following morning, sitting low but alert in the back of a taxi he'd insisted draw right up to the Savoy steps. The overnight duty officer didn't know anything more than Bundy, the previous night, nor was there any further information on the Tass slip, which Halliday had left in his original office, inscribed with his name and a lot of question marks.

To fill in the time, Charlie coordinated the advantage of his early arrival with the time difference between London and Moscow to reach the Director-General the moment the man arrived at Thames House, and sat unspeaking for thirty minutes listening to Aubrey Smith's account of Whitehall and American embassy meetings the previous day. When Smith finished, Charlie bluntly declared: "No!"

After a moment's surprised silence, Smith said, "Bringing in MI6—despite my personal dislike and suspicion of MI6's Director Gerald Monsford—and the CIA are convincing arguments. We get a lot of extra manpower without risking any more from our own department. We get out of a leaking embassy, to which I'm sending Robertson back to finish the job he clearly hasn't. And if it ends up in a disaster, which there's every indication it will, we offload a hell of a lot of responsibility on to the Americans and our doubtful MI6 friends across the river at Vauxhall Cross."

"It's a bullshit argument that scarcely stands examination," rejected Charlie. "It's an attempted takeover of an investigation that has to remain under our control. Were you told at the American embassy that Langley wants to work unofficially, without telling the FSB?"

From the silence Charlie knew the Director-General hadn't been. "Not in as many words."

"Let me spell it out without any inference," demanded Charlie. "Okay, I know Guzov will cheat on me just as I'll cheat on him if it's necessary or advantageous for either of us. But at the moment we are talking as fully and properly as we can expect: Harry Fish tells me the material Guzov made available hadn't been tampered with or doctored in any way. If the Russians learn we're letting Washington in by the back door, the slamming of the front, right in our faces, will make a noise you'll hear all the way over there. There's a 101 percent chance I'd be expelled, along with a diplomatic Ice Age that will take years to thaw. And Moscow will be in the position they've wanted to be from the beginning of this, in charge of everything, able to fudge everything and anything they want, particularly the bugging of the embassy in which there's still an undetected informer. And Washington will lie, insist we'd asked for unofficial help on the side, and come out squeaky clean. Which is probably their intention from the beginning: my guess is that the Russians would learn about it *from* Washington. And from, what you've inferred about Monsford, Christ knows what MI6's contribution would be!"

"You lost me about three turns back," complained Aubrey Smith, although without any irritation.

"What reason is there for America getting involved in something that has nothing to do with them? The CIA and the American administration aren't charities, for Christ's sake! Try this scenario. We accept the American offer, they leak it to Moscow claiming we sought their help, which they refused. Russia gets full control, we get frozen in the new and personal Cold War, and in a matter of months a new Russian president—a new Russian president who seems to be the only item on the agenda of the American embassy here—gets sworn into office. Who do you think's going to be invited to form a new special relationship, London or Washington?"

Almost reflectively, Smith said. "This all began with the shooting of a one-armed man in a £20 suit and cardboard shoes."

"The First World War began with the shooting of an Austrian Archduke by a student in a £5 suit and cardboard shoes," reminded Charlie. "It's not the perfect analogy but it's the closest I can think of, so it will have to do."

"We've got more meetings scheduled today," disclosed the Director-General. "I'll raise your points."

"I'd like to be told at once of the final decision."

"*If* any final decision is reached," heavily qualified Aubrey Smith.

It was still only 8:45 when Charlie reached his compound apartment but Harry Fish was already there with his two monitoring technicians. The man said at once, "I'm glad you're early. Knowing about the bugs in your hotel suite I held back from ringing you there."

"Is it the accident?" anticipated Charlie, who'd put the reason for his being so early out of his mind during the confrontation with the Director-General.

"No," said Fish, frowning.

"What?" Keep everything separately compartmented, Charlie told himself: he had to stay on top of whatever confronted him.

"Something I think could be important," said the electronics expert, pressing the replay button on a recording machine. "This is before enhancement but with the volume at its highest. . . ."

There was intermittent sound but Charlie couldn't decided what it was or represented, although twice he thought he heard what could have been a human voice. He looked between the three other men, shaking his head.

"Now the enhancement," announced Fish, in his conjuror's voice.

There was still a lot of indistinguishable sound but the human voice was identifiable now. So were two outbursts of crying. Charlie positively translated from Russian "please, oh please," followed by weeping, then "do it." There was a burst of recognizable words—"please . . . have to . . . make . . ."—more sobbing, noise that meant nothing, and finally the repeated click of a lost connection.

Charlie again looked questioningly to Fish. "So what is it?"

"A compilation of three calls, the first within two hours of the press conference and initially dismissed as a crank approach, someone ringing the number for no reason: there've been at least twelve and I've had every one reexamined. Which is how we picked up the other two, over following days. The noise is traffic sound, so it's a public street telephone, always put down before we can get number traces. The timing is always the same, though: precisely ten minutes past noon and always on the first of our listed numbers. It's a woman's voice: I haven't had it voice-printed, not yet, but I'm going out on a limb to say it's the same voice. I'm also suggesting it's a Russian woman brought to tears trying to force herself to make the call but not being strong enough when the connection is made . . ." He paused. "I'm suggesting a pattern."

Charlie considered what the other man had said. "The last call on the compilation? That was yesterday, right?"

Fish nodded. "Her lunch hour, I'd say. I thought it might be an

idea to have a human voice—your voice—answer the first number on our list at precisely ten minutes past noon today."

"So do I," agreed Charlie, looking at his watch. There was just
over three hours to fill, before the possibility of her calling again.
Coming back up to Fish, he said, "Now tell me about the accident."

★

Fish had just begun when Halliday came into the apartment, instantly picking up the conversation and nodding for the electronics sweeper to continue. It only took minutes. It had been the
second of the decoy cars Charlie had dispatched ahead of his own
hidden departure. The vehicle had got less than two hundred
yards in the direction opposite from that in which Charlie was
traveling when an overtaking car cut in too sharply. At that point
the camber of the embankment road dipped toward the Moskva,
close to where the argument had been staged to distract the gate
guards the night the body of the one-armed man had been
dumped at the embassy. It had been instinctive for the driver to
swerve in the direction of the river. He'd clipped the low embankment rail but the force of the collision had tipped the embassy car
over. It had rolled four times before coming to a halt, at the water's barrier.

"What about the other car?" demanded Charlie.

"Hit and run," said Halliday.

"Traced yet?"

Halliday shook his head. "The only description was that it was
big, something like a four-by-four."

"Registration?" persisted Charlie.

"Too dirty to be read," said Halliday.

"What about the driver of the embassy car?"

"He's got a fractured spine. Already on his way back to London
in a hospital plane that came in overnight," said Halliday. "The
prognosis is that he'll certainly be paraplegic . . . possibly quadri-
plegic."

"Who is he?" asked Charlie, expectantly.

Halliday hesitated. "Jack Hopkins. That's why I came up here when I heard you were in the embassy. He was . . ."

". . . my regular driver," finished Charlie. "It had to be, didn't it?" The man had only talked of just failing to qualify for the Tottenham Hotspur junior soccer squad, Charlie remembered, but of being determined to coach his son to succeed where he hadn't when his Moscow tour ended.

21

"I'M HERE, TO TALK TO YOU: THE ENGLISHMAN YOU SAW ON television. Read about in newspapers. You can talk to me. Just to me." Charlie spoke in Russian, very consciously keeping any urgency from his voice, anxious that she didn't detect the other emotion surging through him, even after the hour there'd been for him to rationalize the only possible interpretation from the car ramming. The reception volume was tuned to its highest without risking an ear-splitting playback and Charlie could clearly hear heavy breathing: quick, jerky, gulping snatches. Magnified as the receiver was he could very definitely detect traffic noise, the sticky tire sound against the street, an occasional impatient horn burst. "Don't be frightened. You mustn't be frightened. I promise nothing bad will happen. I'll look after you." Better that time: proper, comprehensible sentences. Her breathing sounded heavier, positively panting. "Talk to me. Tell me you understand what I'm telling you."

From his equipment bank, Harry Fish hand signaled that the connection had been kept for two minutes.

"Not safe . . ." The words hissed out, scarcely above a whisper. It was a hoarse voice, a smoker's voice.

"I'll make it safe. Keep you safe."

"Can't."

"I can. And I will."

"Ivan said . . ." she began, before stumbling into a coughing fit. It was definitely a smoker's cough, a discernible wheezing.

"What did Ivan say . . . ? Tell me what Ivan said." He'd spoken too loudly, too demanding, Stop thinking about the car crash!

". . . safe . . ."

"That he'd be safe?" groped Charlie, hopefully. Concentrate on one thing; only one thing, he told himself.

". . . killed him . . ."

"Help me catch who killed him . . ."

"Can't."

"I can!" insisted Charlie, wanting the forcefulness in his voice now. "If you help me I can catch them."

"No!" refused the voice just as forcefully, and the line went dead.

"Hello? Hello?" repeated Charlie.

"She's gone," announced Fish, unnecessarily. "You did well, holding her as long as you did."

"Did you get a number?" demanded Charlie. "We know the time she's going to phone, if she phones again. If we could find the kiosk we could stake it out; identify her!"

"I told you that was what I was going to try to do!"

"Did you *do* it?"

Fish shook his head. "I think the Russians are trying to monitor the line."

"Can they?" asked Charlie, even more demanding.

There was another head shake. "I've 'washed' all the lines, to stop them being able to do that. But their device blocks me in return. Electronically it's a standoff."

After a pause, Charlie said: "I think she was genuine . . . not a crank."

"I'll need a translation of the actual words," said Fish, guardedly. "The tone—the fear—certainly sounded genuine. Unless . . ."

"Unless what?"

"While you were talking, it suddenly occurred to me that it could be an FSB trick, testing you out."

"You just told me they can't monitor the line, hear what's said."

It was a reasonable suggestion from the other man. From the accident report on Hopkins they'd know they'd failed. If it was a ploy, they could plan it better the next time.

"They'd know the call was made," Fish pointed out. "They can count them, quite easily, now that the calls are trailing off. And just as easily know how long they last." So far that day there'd only been eight incoming contacts—four from journalists, two cranks, and two seeking money in advance of imparting promised information—in addition to that which Charlie had just finished.

Now Charlie shook his head. "If Guzov challenges me I'll dismiss it as a crank: a hysterical woman I didn't believe. But I think she's our most likely . . ." He hesitated. "Our *only* possibility, in fact, apart from the silent ones who didn't call back."

"Twenty-eight who didn't call back," itemized Fish, pedantically.

"Will this one?" asked Charlie, in self-reflection.

"I think so. You kept her on far longer than I expected: that's what made me wonder if she might be a plant. If she isn't, she's someone who wants to talk but is too frightened."

"And our one-armed man was named Ivan," Charlie remembered. Would he ever know the name of his attempted murderer? At once, irritation overwhelmed the thought. He wouldn't be able to protect himself—survive even—if he allowed himself to think nonsense like that.

"What about her voice? You've got the language, I haven't. Well educated, high born, low born, what?"

"Difficult, from what little she actually said, the hoarseness with which she said it. My impression is well educated."

"You intend telling anyone?"

"There's nothing *to* tell." Which wouldn't stop Harry Fish navigating his back channels to London, Charlie accepted. And probably Halliday, who'd fortunately left the apartment before the call, would have already told his MI6 case officer in London of the car crash, just as Charlie was sure that Fish would already have done.

"All we can do now is sit and wait, hopefully no longer than just after noon tomorrow."

Maybe all *you've* got to do, thought Charlie. He had a hell of a lot more than that to do and at that moment wasn't at all sure where to start.

★

Paul Robertson's returning inquiry team arrived during the course of the afternoon, each traveling separately, routing themselves through Paris, Amsterdam, and Frankfurt. Only Robertson came direct from London, getting to the embassy ahead of the rest.

"It was the Director-General's idea, hoping to avoid the sort of identification debacle we had going out," explained Robertson. "That was an absolute bloody nightmare."

"I'm surprised he didn't send a different team," said Charlie. Harry Fish had already been with the other man when Charlie arrived in the retained inquiry room and he was curious if the man had already told Robertson of that morning's telephone call. Or of the embankment crash.

"You all right?" Robertson asked Charlie, answering Charlie's uncertainty.

"They failed," said Charlie.

"This time," said Robertson. "What's the Director-General say?"

"We haven't talked about it yet."

"You'll be going back to London, of course."

"No," said Charlie.

"Don't be ridiculous," said the man.

"What's ridiculous?" demanded Charlie. "I'm reading it that I am close to something or someone: they're frightened that I'm too close. This isn't the time to run: that's what they'll be hoping, having missed with the crash."

"You think the Director-General will risk another killing?"

"We'll see," said Charlie.

"He's under a lot of pressure in London," said Robertson. "He considered sending in an entirely new inquiry team to find this inside leak. I argued against risking different people. My group and I are already blown."

Robertson was desperate to recover from his mistake, recognized Charlie. "And you've limited the number of people who've been told in advance, so if the rest of your people get in unspotted and your return leaks, you've got your list of suspects?"

Robertson smiled, humorlessly. "And I know he only told you he was *thinking* of sending us back."

"Where's this new indication of an inside whistleblower leave Reg Stout? And all the others, for that matter?" asked Fish, entering the conversation.

"They're all bound by the Official Secrets Act, under which we use different rules before we actually get into court; until then, they're all guilty until proven innocent."

"But Stout can't be your man, even though I found those bugs," Fish pointed out. "He was incommunicado, from that moment on."

"That's the defense he's trying, ahead of even seeing a lawyer," offered Robertson.

" 'I'm safe' calls," dismissed Charlie.

"Exactly," agreed Robertson.

"What?" questioned Fish.

"The embassy was known to be under investigation," reminded Robertson. "If Stout didn't make a call, any sort of contact, at or on a rigidly fixed time schedule—miss one, it could be circumstance, miss two, it's alarm bells, miss three, he's in the bag—his Control knows he's lost him. He didn't make his 'I'm safe' call."

"It's a basic tradecraft routine," added Charlie. "You've never heard of it before?"

"I'm not operational," indignantly protested Fish, flushed at the reaction from the other two men. "This is the closest I've ever got. Or ever want to be again."

"I wish we were closer," picked up Robertson. "None of us is winning accolades at the moment back at Thames House."

"It's a common concern," said Charlie. There'd be a concerted effort to get him withdrawn, he accepted. Which, perhaps absurdly, strengthened his determination to stay. To rebase would obviously be the safest thing to do but despite his apprehension he didn't want to run, which was probably pride and common sense gone mad. And, came the ever-looming awareness, selfishly unfair on Natalia and Sasha. Fish, who was nearer, answered the telephone but handed it immediately to the spy-catcher. Robertson smiled, said "good," and smiled more broadly as he replaced the receiver. "All in, undetected, including the guards and the polygraph technicians."

"Let's hope our luck holds," said Harry Fish.

It didn't.

That night Svetlana Modin once more led the ORT main evening news bulletin with the disclosure of London's rejection of CIA assistance, predicting that it would result in a deterioration now of relationships with Washington, because of the refusal, and with Moscow, who had been unaware of any possible collusion between the two Western governments. Her report concluded with the announcement of the inquiry team's return to Moscow, which included footage of Robertson's earlier airport departure melee.

"Fuck!" said Charlie, aloud, in the solitude of his hotel suite. And hesitated, undecided, when the telephone rang five minutes later, finally snatching for it.

22

AND WAS GLAD HE DID.

"Son of a bitch!"

"Bill Bundy?" loudly questioned Charlie, audibly to establish the caller's identity. Was the American going to join the long line of commentators on the embankment crash?

"You know damned well it is! Just as you damned well know how much shit you've dropped me in!"

"Actually, Bill, I don't know that at all."

"I told you in advance what Washington was doing—the offer we were making—as a friend. Your intervention to London has totally screwed me!"

Not the crash at all, acknowledged Charlie. And there was no way the American could know of his conversation that morning with the Director-General. "I did nothing of the sort, Bill. I said it would be London's decision, remember?"

"All the vibes were good and then suddenly, bang, the door gets slammed in our faces. You telling me you didn't have anything to do with that?"

"That's exactly what I'm telling you," lied Charlie. He'd never imagined there was going to be this amount of benefit from having Harry Fish leave the FSB listening devices in place. Recalling his doubts about the man, Charlie wondered if Fish had installed his own bugs to record incoming conversations to the Savoy suite.

"Trying to run everything as a one-man band, as you're trying to do, is going to fuck up big-time. I think this is something that's actually going to kill you!"

So did a lot of others, some actually trying very hard to make it happen. "I'm not trying to conduct a one-man band. It's a joint operation with the Russians; you know that."

"Mikhail Guzov wouldn't give you a head cold, unless it was guaranteed to turn into a fatal pneumonia."

"I thought a pretty good relationship was developing."

"Okay, so you tell me one, just one, useful scrap of information you've got from him."

"We're talking; liaising."

"I've heard you called many things over the years, Charlie. Until now naïve wasn't one of them."

"Don't you think it was naïve of you to expect that you could have worked unofficially with me without Guzov discovering what was going on?"

"It stood a better chance of producing something than what you're left with now."

"What I'm left with now is what I've got to live and work with, I guess."

"You're not going to live with it: you're going to die *because* of it."

"Don't you think you're getting a little overdramatic here, Bill?"

"You suffering amnesia or Alzheimer's, forgetting what happened to Sergei Romanovich Pavel?"

"You got a theory about that?"

Bundy snorted a jeering laugh. "Jesus H Christ, I don't think you're suffering amnesia! I think it's Alzheimer's! You sucker me like you've just done and then expect me to offer you murder theories!"

"Had London accepted your approach I would have expected you to bring something to the table."

"Now you're never going to know what help I could have provided, are you, buddy!"

The American's vernacular, like his dress sense, really was in a time warp, thought Charlie. "It's unfortunate you brought a decision between our two governments down to a personal level."

"Your loss, Charlie. We could have walked away covered in glory!"

Now who was sounding naïve? thought Charlie.

★

Whatever he might minimally have gained from managing to extend his stumbling conversation with the terrified woman, he could far too easily have lost by that evening's television disclosure, which would have already been picked up for repetition in every newspaper the following morning, when it would doubtless be repeated yet again, not only by ORT but by every other TV and radio station in Moscow. It was impossible for the caller to remain unaware of the latest twist in the already overtangled killing of the one-armed man. Would it frighten her away; destroy any fragile confidence he might have instilled? It was the most obvious possibility. But then again, there was an alternative. The television presentation could work to his advantage rather than disadvantage if the unknown caller had seen it. Its thrust had been entirely upon the collapse of cooperation not just with America but with Russia. Would she be able to rationalize through her fear that she'd be safer—more protected even—by his being ostracized by the Russians?

Charlie's hesitation was longer when the telephone rang for the second time, reluctant to talk on a line open to the FSB but conscious of the benefits if it were something he could use, as he'd just used Bundy's diatribe.

Curiosity won over caution and the concern ebbed away at the voice of Harry Fish, who knew of the Russian bugging.

"Did you see ORT?"

"Yes," said Charlie.

"All our dedicated lines are in meltdown: everyone's asking for you. I'm referring them all to London."

Surely the man hadn't forgotten what he'd personally located here! "That's what I want, all press calls referred to London."

"Four have been from your favorite TV anchorwoman, who says she's going to go on calling every fifteen minutes until she gets to you personally. I thought you'd like to know."

"What else did she say?" Could he use her, as he'd used Bundy?

"Just that, apart from leaving a number."

"Why don't you let me have it?"

"You going to talk to her?"

"Maybe."

"Shouldn't you get clearance from London? She's . . ." Fish paused. "Her story's attracting a lot of attention. Maybe you should come back here."

Now the man was trying to warn him about the listening devices, Charlie realized. "I might, if I decide to call back. Give me the number anyway."

Charlie dialed from the public telephone kiosk closest to the hotel, the one near Red Square, glad it was enclosed, again with a protective wall to his back, and with a view of about twenty-five yards over which to see any suspicious approach. Svetlana answered personally. Charlie said, "I don't want my phones blocked every fifteen minutes. It might be someone important."

She laughed, unoffended. "I really didn't expect you to come back to me."

"What do you want?" Despite the video recording he held as insurance, he still had to very carefully weigh every word he uttered.

"I'd say the points were about equal in the teaching-each-other-lessons league, wouldn't you?"

From the background sounds Charlie guessed she was talking from an open newsroom phone. "I didn't know it was a competition."

"You're making it one. I really don't want to screw up your investigation: you know the arrangement I'm offering."

Based upon her success over the past few days, she had every cause for arrogance. "Which is?"

"Why don't we meet to talk about it?"

Charlie thought there was an eerie familiarity about the conversation. "You won't forget that I know where you keep your microphones hidden, will you?"

"Are you ever going to let me?"

"The bar, at the Metropol, in an hour," suggested Charlie.

"Why not your room?"

"The bar."

"I'll be there."

★

She was ahead of him, although Charlie got there early. She wore the clinging black dress in which she'd appeared on the screen earlier but now high on her left shoulder there was a jeweled clip of what Charlie was sure were genuine diamonds. She sat majestically in the very center of a banquette, champagne already poured from a bottle—French, not Georgian—resting in its cooler. His concentration, as he made his obvious way toward Svetlana, was as much upon identifying potential danger around her as it was upon the woman herself.

"I tried to call your room but the desk told me that you weren't staying here."

"Neutral territory," said Charlie. Which she'd taken over by being first. There was a second glass already waiting but Charlie shook his head against champagne, ordering vodka. "Mikhail Guzov's taken to dropping in, unannounced. I thought it would be better not to be interrupted, although I got the impression at the embassy that you knew him quite well?"

"Quite well," she agreed, cautiously.

"If you've got with him the same sort of deal you're going to put to me, he might have thought you were playing one of us off against the other."

"Did it occur to you he also might have thought you were my source?"

"No," lied Charlie.

Svetlana touched her glass against Charlie's when his vodka was served and said, "You stay pretty concentrated upon the job, don't you?"

"I got the same impression about you."

"Which makes us well matched."

"What's your suggested deal?"

Svetlana waited for their attentive waiter to top up her glass. "How about you and I speaking before every evening transmission. I tell you what I'm going to say. You tell me anything that might seriously impede or endanger anything you're doing. I cut it out."

Surely she couldn't be serious! If he accepted her offer it would give her a spread-open map along which to track, from what he asked her to omit, every twist and turn of the investigation. But by the same token she was offering him a map of her own, which could lead him directly to the embassy informant. Which wasn't his investigation. But also something he wasn't going to ignore. "Give me an example."

"How about the killers of your first victim, and Sergei Pavel being so worried how close you are to them that they tried to kill you on the embankment?"

He'd got it right by agreeing to meet her, Charlie decided. "I don't want that broadcast."

"It's a good story that no one else has picked up on."

"I thought the idea was not to screw my investigation?"

"As well as for me to get exclusives."

He had to be careful not to show his desperation. "You broadcast it, I lose the lead I've got," exaggerated Charlie.

"Are you threatening me with the video recording?"

"Are you going to make me?"

Svetlana regarded him expressionlessly for what seemed a long time. "If I hold off, we agree to my deal?"

From scouring the Russian papers as intently as he had, Charlie knew she was right about no one else picking up on the connection, and his concern was as much to avoid Natalia learning about the attempt as the hoarse-voiced woman. And if Svetlana kept her promise, there could be the other opportunities to manipulate things to his benefit. "I agree to the deal."

Svetlana smiled, gesturing the waiter to replenish their drinks. "And I get my exclusives."

He couldn't risk her having a change of heart, Charlie decided. "Since Putin got to power a lot of the freedoms achieved by

Gorbachev and Yeltsin have been taken back or eroded, particularly press freedom. How long do you think you can go on like this?"

She laughed, genuinely amused. "Think back *before* Gorbachev and Yeltsin, to the bad old days. How did the famous dissidents and nonconformists stay out of the gulags? By becoming—and staying—famous in the West, too well known to be moved against."

"That's my point!" risked Charlie. "If you keep cutting things when I ask you, you could end up nights in a row with nothing to say."

"Okay, so I've made the first concession," accepted Svetlana. "But I want the big ones, those that'll make me untouchable forever! I help you, as I've just agreed to do, and you give me your solemn undertaking that you'll repay me at the end. I get something that's going to keep me on TV screens around the world. When you learn whatever the hell's going on, you tell me. You also tell me how you finally got all the answers. I get my global exclusive, with enough to produce the supporting documentary. You get your man and I give you all the credit. How's that sound?"

Better than he could have hoped, conceded Charlie. Could there be some physical protection in it for him, as well? He couldn't at that moment imagine what but it was something to keep in mind. The only obvious drawback was the one he'd already identified, that she had the same sort of arrangement with Mikhail Guzov. Not a problem, Charlie decided. He was feeding the source, not drinking from it. "It sounds like something to explore, to our mutual benefit. Let's see how it works."

"I'll make it work."

So would he, determined Charlie.

★

Since the relocation of the monitored telephones to the compound apartment, Charlie had virtually abandoned his original assigned rabbit hutch, but on his way to the embassy the following morning he decided to check for any misdirected written messages—or anything else—that might have been misdelivered. Nothing appeared to have been disturbed but on the card table, to its left, were neatly stacked by date Halliday's English-language publications. To its right, set out on a white sheet of A4 paper upon which was drawn a large question mark, was a polished brass bell.

Charlie was reaching hesitantly for it when through the left-open door behind him Paula-Jane said, "If it weren't for those raftlike shoes, which I'd recognize anywhere, I'd believe I'd caught the embassy spy himself, breaking into offices."

Charlie turned, leaving the bell. "How are you?"

"Me? I couldn't be better. Which I guess you'd very, very much prefer to be." She was designer-dressed as always, the interlocking C of the Chanel logo on the jacket buttons matching those on her suede loafer. For the first time Charlie acknowledged the coquettish similarity between Paula-Jane Venables and Svetlana Modin, who'd predictably ended their previous night's encounter with the clear invitation, which he'd just as clearly declined, to share either her bed or his. He wondered where P-J hid her recording equipment, sure there wouldn't be too much objection to his making his own discovery.

"I assume you're talking of the car business?" invited Charlie, wanting to get it out of the way as soon as possible.

"Among other things," said the woman. "You trying to convince me it really was an accident!"

"You wanted to see me?"

"I was sneaking in to get it back."

"What?" frowned Charlie.

"The bell. I put it there as a joke when I got back last night, the lepers' bell or for whom the bell tolls: whatever. I'd been to that American Café with Tex: his final farewell and I'd drunk too much. This morning I decided there was nothing funny about anything that's happened to you and wanted to get it back; stop the whole stupid thing. I'm sorry."

She appeared contrite, which was something else he didn't expect. "It's not the best joke that's ever been tried on me, but thanks for trying to lighten the burden."

"It should be me, thanking you, for not involving me. You're probably well enough established to survive this other business with America, as Bill Bundy is. Or would have been if you'd let him in. I'm sure as hell not."

Charlie was immediately attentive. "Was Bill with you last night?"

Paula-Jane shook her head. "There was a big crisis meeting at the embassy, apparently, after the television broadcast. Tex was only able to make it because he wasn't any longer officially attached to the embassy; he's flying back to the States today."

There'd been an inference of an affair between P-J and the American, Charlie remembered. "I'm not sure I can survive if I don't wrap it up soon."

The woman looked very directly at him. "I've heard things about you."

This wasn't P-J the coquette. "Things like what?"

"That you don't like to lose. Which is why you so rarely do, irrespective of the shortcuts you take."

"What do you want me to tell you?" demanded Charlie, trying to jar the innuendo into something more recognizable.

"If you're not going to trust me—which I know you don't from what you did during Robertson's first investigation—I can't expect you to tell me anything, can I?"

"I thought you were grateful not to be involved?"

The woman smiled wanly. "Grateful doesn't begin to describe it. I'm sad we got off to such a bad beginning and lost the colleague-to-colleague relationship, though. I could have learned a lot."

"Or lost a lot, if you believe the car accident wasn't an accident."

The smile broadened. "How long's it going to be, Charlie?"

"How long's what going to be?"

Paula-Jane shrugged. "I suppose I should have known better. But I thought I'd worked it out; thought I'd run it by you, see what you'd say."

"Run what by me?" Charlie continued to question, refusing to volunteer anything.

"London wouldn't have knocked Washington's offer back and you wouldn't have been isolated for so long by yourself—my even being excluded, despite all the diplomatic bullshit—if you weren't on the very edge of the big denouement that's going to knock everything, and everyone, on its ass! What do you say to that?"

Charlie's first reaction was to say that the vocabulary of people to whom he'd spoken over the preceding twenty-four hours appeared to be remarkably similar. Instead he said, "I say that it's very fanciful and I wish it were more realistic."

The woman remained silent and solemn faced for what seemed a long time. "So much for my trying to make things a little more pleasant between us! I suppose I should have expected it." She made another vague gesture behind him. "Time to get back to the office work."

Charlie glanced behind him. "What office work?"

"If you bother to look through what Dave's left, you'll see that the Western media have well and truly adopted Stepan Lvov as their own, even before he's elected. The buzz phrase is 'Russia's New Camelot.' Inevitably London is asking for a full profile."

"Halliday told me he's already provided one."

"For his people. Apparently we need our own. Dave's given me all his stuff and Tex passed on a lot more . . ." The smile was a frigid one. "Some people work quite harmoniously with others."

As she turned to leave Charlie said, "Don't you want your bell?"

She paused at the door. "You keep it, Charlie. You might want to ring for help. Let's hope someone hears."

★

Charlie made his way slowly from the main embassy building into the residential compound, trying to decide if the previous thirty minutes really had been a genuine olive branch offer from an inexperienced operative on her initial overseas assignment. First-time appointees—certainly to a high-profile embassy like Moscow, which was rarely if ever a beginner's posting—were rigidly vetted for any personal weaknesses and there certainly hadn't been any weak frailty during their initial encounter. Why then the near embarrassingly inept act? Not something to be mulled over at any length but perhaps mentally filed for later reference.

Both duty operators—one male, one female—were lounged in easy chairs, disinterestedly flicking through out-of-date newspapers, their boredom shown in the log listing only four incoming calls after the tidal wave of the previous night's TV broadcast. One of the four was from the familiarly ranting communist zealot, two were new Japanese press calls, and the fourth was a heavy-breathing blank.

The man said, "Harry told me to tell you he'd be along later, around eleven. He's with Robertson, in the inquiry room, if you want him."

Mikhail Guzov wasn't at his Petrovka telephone when Charlie called. He told the woman who answered that he'd courier transcripts of the overnight contacts, although there was nothing of significance, and asked that Guzov return his call, slumping into another easy chair. He managed to go through Halliday's newspapers, relieved there was still no reference to the embankment crash, before Fish's arrival.

"What's Robertson doing?" asked Charlie, expecting the mole-hunter to be in tow.

"His job, starting the reinterviews," retorted Fish, more belligerent than unhelpful.

"You tell him about the hopeful call?"

"You didn't ask me not to."

"Or that you should."

"You're surely not expecting her to call again, after last night? And today's newspaper follow-ups!"

"That's not really the point, is it?"

"I don't think there's any longer much point in anything we're doing here," dismissed the electronics specialist. "Did you call that anchorwoman back?"

"That's not a point of discussion, either," refused Charlie, raising a three-day-old copy of the *Daily Telegraph* to create a physical barrier between himself and the other man. An odd, uncertain silence settled beyond Charlie's screen. The operators found unexplained reasons to check and recheck their equipment, and Fish very obviously, close to mockery, constantly checked the time as it approached noon, once loudly calling for the two operators to synchronize their watches with his. Charlie kept checking, too, at the same time as forcing himself to read the newspaper comments and poll predictions of the landslide victory in the forthcoming presidential elections of Stepan Lvov.

"A minute to go, if she's going to call," announced Fish, unnecessarily.

Charlie finally lowered his newspaper and said "thanks," disappointed he didn't convey the intended sarcasm.

All four watched 12:10 register on their individual watches. A full minute later, Fish said: "You've lost her, as it was obvious you would."

The woman monitor coughed and began rummaging in her handbag.

Fish said, "A good job you didn't tell London."

"I'm pretty sure they know, aren't you?" said Charlie.

"How could . . . ?" started Fish, but was stopped by the telephone.

★

"I couldn't decide."

"I'm glad you did," said Charlie.

"I'm frightened." It was more a wheeze than hoarseness.

"I know. Don't be. We have to meet."

"I need to be sure."

"Whatever you want. Tell me and I'll do it . . . whatever you want."

"Need to be safe."

"I'll make sure you're safe. Kept safe." It wasn't so difficult for him to say today.

Charlie could hear the growl of her breathing, which sounded as if it was quickening, as if the fear was building, but he held back from speaking, waiting for her, tensed against the line suddenly going dead. The other three in the room were tensed forward, too, the female operator with her cupped hands to her mouth. Charlie didn't understand the single word the hoarse-voiced caller said, despite the magnification. Forcing the calmness, he said, "What was that?"

"Arbat," she repeated. "You know the Arbat?"

"Yes, I know the Arbat." Moscow's tourist flea market, jammed with people, the best place for a jostled, easily escapable assassination, he thought.

"Saturday. Go there on Saturday."

Natalia's day! was Charlie's immediate thought: the day he had to meet Natalia and Sasha—after now trebly ensuring he was free of any unwanted company—to make all the promises he intended to keep, make any concessions she demanded to persuade her to come with him to London. "What time on Saturday?"

"Be there at ten."

"Where? What part? It's a long street."

"Just walk. Look at the shops and the stalls."

"How do we meet?"

"I'll decide. Don't be surprised."

"I need—" started Charlie but the line went dead.

"It's a hoax," declared Harry Fish. "You're going to be made to look a fool again. Or be killed."

The bastard was probably right, conceded Charlie, before the other thought registered. "I didn't think you could speak Russian?" he said to the man.

23

DURING THE INITIAL SECONDS THAT FOLLOWED CHARLIE RE-
gretted his challenge. His intuition was that the hoarse-voiced
woman had something to offer. But objectively he had to recognize that Harry Fish could be right and that it could all be an
elaborate hoax or, he had to accept, another attempt on his life.

Charlie contemptuously refused Fish's near incoherent insistence that what he had intended to convey was not so much a denial of the language but a qualification that his superficial
restaurant-Russian was insufficient for him properly to discuss
and assess the shaded nuances of any exchange. In an insistence
of his own, Charlie demanded the names of both monitoring operators to be witnesses at any future inquiry that might be con-
vened by London after the documented protest he intended to
make to the Director-General.

Which he did.

Consciously invoking more clichés, Charlie wrote of climates
of suspicion, vindictiveness, unjustified internal spying and distrust, exacerbated by a still undetected internal informant, positively obstructing every investigatory move he attempted and
further endangering any continuing, already fragile cooperation
with the Russian authorities. It was not until his second complaining page that Charlie mentioned the contact from the hoarse-
voiced woman, inferring London's awareness of everything he did

having been under constant observation by warning that if the woman suspected for a moment that he was not entirely alone for their arranged encounter, as he'd promised, any chance of maintaining that contact would be lost. For that reason, he intended employing even more evasion to keep the hoped-for appointment than he would normally have done to defeat any Russian surveillance, which he had to anticipate, the more so since the most recent publicity about the American approach. Since that publicity, he had not been able personally to reach his replaced Russian liaison, indicating further exclusion as the result of the debacle.

Charlie concluded the unaccustomed officialese by formally requesting that his protest—to which he added the addendum that it was being copied as a matter of courtesy to both Harry Fish and Paul Robertson—be attached to his personnel file, for production at any future inquiry into the manner and outcome of the investigation.

So protectively cocooned was the communications room against any outside electronic intrusion that it was not until Charlie got into the corridor outside that his pager showed two calls from Mikhail Guzov, the second within fifteen minutes of the first. Harry Fish was no longer in the set-aside apartment when Charlie reached it. The earlier operatives had been replaced by two men, both of whom regarded him sullenly. Without speaking, one offered a log of eight new incoming calls, all from journalists, in addition to the two from Guzov.

The FSB general personally answered the Petrovka phone, immediately breaking into Charlie's greeting. "We know who your dead man is. Everything's wrapped up."

★

The man was in the former office of Sergei Romanovich Pavel when Charlie arrived at the headquarters of the Organized Crime Bureau. There was another plainclothes man introduced as Leonid Toplov, from the Interior Ministry, and two in militia uniform. Nikolai Yaskov wore the epaulets of a colonel, Viktor Malin those of a major. Slightly behind the four stood the pathologist, Vladimir Ivanov, whom Charlie at first failed to recognize out of his stained autopsy scrubs. An extremely attractive blond stenographer was at a side table Charlie could not remember being there before, notebook open in readiness, which Charlie thought an unnecessary prop. On Guzov's commandeered desk was an already diminishing bottle of vodka, its cap discarded Russian-fashion: once opened, a bottle's contents had always to be drunk. All five men held glasses and as soon as he saw Charlie, Guzov filled a waiting glass and said, "Join the celebration!"

Charlie accepted the drink, touched invitingly offered glasses from the other men and cautiously said, "Everything seems to have happened very quickly?"

"And proven us right from the beginning," insisted Guzov.

"Who was he?"

"Maxim Semenovich Poliakov," announced the uniformed colonel. "Professional criminal, major activities include pimping prostitutes and trafficking heroin from Afghanistan. Ran with a Chechen gang that we finally broke up entirely three days ago. We wouldn't have been able to do so, without Poliakov. We got him a month ago coming into Moscow with two kilos of heroin and did a deal, information in return for no prosecution."

"But missed out protection?" observed Charlie.

"He thought he could look after himself," said Guzov.

"You got an admission of the murder from other members of the gang?" asked Charlie, intentionally ingenuous.

Guzov gave a derisory laugh. "These guys are too professional to confess to anything. They're actually claiming not to know anyone named Maxim Poliakov. But they've given away enough for us to realize they'd discovered Poliakov was our original source. We're sure three of them were involved in planning the Beslan school massacre, too."

"It all seems to have been resolved remarkably quickly. And completely," encouraged Charlie. He was reminded of a theatrical production in which everyone knew their scripts but recited rather than performed them.

"It almost seems"—Guzov searched for the expression—"an anticlimax, after all that's happened over the last few weeks."

"Any theories why they killed him in the British embassy? Have they said?"

"Something we'll probably never know," dismissed the colonel, Nikolai Yaskov, shaking his head.

"Maybe to cause all the distractions by making it an international incident, bringing your country into the investigation," suggested Guzov. "They certainly succeeded in doing that, didn't they?"

The absurd suggestion was undisguised mockery, Charlie accepted. They were baiting him.

"These people believe they're above any law," offered the colonel. "They like making grandiose gestures, aping the gangster movies they try so hard to model themselves on."

"Isn't murdering senior militia detectives more than grandiose?" asked Charlie. "I'm assuming, of course, that you believe they also killed Sergei Pavel?"

Guzov nodded. "Sergei Romanovich was the investigator who personally arrested Poliakov: persuaded him to turn informant. Killing Sergei, as well as Poliakov, was their settling every score. And of showing their derision of us."

"That's how we got them," came in the colonel. "Going back through all Pavel's cases. There it was, someone who perfectly matched the description of your dead man. Everything fell into place."

It was a lie, a setup, from start to whatever finish they intended, Charlie realized. Pavel would have at once remembered personally arresting a one-armed man; he would have recognized the body even without a face that very first day in the mortuary. And then Charlie remembered Pavel's assurance that he'd found no similarities in the complete archival search he had personally carried out. But why? Why the hell were Guzov and his team of amateur actors putting on this performance? Playing the part in which they'd clearly cast him, Charlie said, "What proof is there that the gang killed Sergei Romanovich Pavel?"

Guzov, who was going around the group adding to their glasses, snorted another laugh. "We're hardly likely to get a confession, are we? Even without charges, no one in the court is going to be left in any doubt who killed both men. But we're going to get the proper, fitting punishment even if we can't proffer the actual charges of murder: heroin trafficking on this scale carries the death penalty. And we've got enough proof of that against every single one we've arrested. It's going to be a show trial!"

Stalin was good at show trials, reflected Charlie, on even less manufactured evidence than this. He still couldn't understand why they were doing it! "I should congratulate you on such a successful investigation. I'm sorry—embarrassed perhaps—not to have been able to contribute." He hoped the attractive note-taker behind him hadn't missed the denial of any part in the farce.

"You've had a lot of side issues to distract you," emptily sympathized Guzov.

Was that a reference to the embankment incident? Hardly, decided Charlie. In fact, the belief that it had been a Russian initiative didn't square with the bullshit they were shoveling now. If they were setting out to smother the two murders this way, there would have been no point or purpose in mounting the embankment crash. From the almost imperceptible lisp, Charlie guessed the Russian was getting slightly drunk. "I'd appreciate a complete dossier. I'll obviously have to submit a full report, despite being able to contribute so very little."

"We anticipated that you would," said Yaskov. "Everything's being duplicated."

"I'd also like a full copy of Poliakov's criminal record."

There was a hesitation from the uniformed colonel. "I'm not sure . . ."

"Of course you can have it," came in Guzov. "And we can also provide you with a more complete medical report—more complete, even, than that which your medical examiners in London gave us—can't we, Dr. Ivanov?"

The chill began to envelop Charlie.

"Yes, we can," said the rehearsed pathologist, the nervousness making his voice almost as hoarse as the unknown woman on the phone.

"Dr. Ivanov realized there was no DNA recorded, on either his initial report or that from your people," expanded Guzov. "He and other specialists carried out tests on hair follicles and skin tissue, as well as the blood, which in your case was heavily contaminated. Now you'll have everything to take back to London."

They knew what he'd done! How he'd faked everything to stay involved in the case, Charlie accepted. And they'd neutered him against any possible challenge because by making one, arguing against anything they intended to say or do, he would expose himself and his own attempted deceit! And not just himself: London and the department, as well. Forcing himself to go on, Charlie said, "You're making an official announcement, I suppose?"

Guzov looked theatrically at his watch. "In an hour's time." He came back to Charlie. "And tomorrow we're holding a full press conference, although I don't imagine it will be as extensive as yours at the embassy. I'm presuming you'll want to attend with me?"

They weren't just boxing him in, Charlie acknowledged: by appearing on the same platform, he'd be confirming that every claim the Russians were making to be the truth and that the investigation was over. "That's very generous of you, considering it's come down to a successful Russian investigation with virtually no input from me."

"Our agreement was full cooperation," mocked Guzov. "And there's something else. The conference is at eleven. Sergei Romanovich's funeral is in the afternoon."

Not just boxed in, thought Charlie: the lid was being firmly hammered down as Pavel's coffin would be! "I would, of course, like to attend that, as well."

"I expected that you would," said Guzov. "You have already been included on the list of those officially attending."

"Has London been informed of these developments?"

"They will be, before the formal announcement," said the Interior Ministry official, Leonid Toplov. He smiled as he added, "As a matter of courtesy."

"Continuing that courtesy," picked up Guzov, "I'll ensure you receive all the official reports at the embassy before the end of the day. We wouldn't expect you to appear before the world media without being fully briefed."

"Thank you," said Charlie, with little else left to say. "Publicly, at least, it will appear to have been a very successful and well coordinated joint operation between our two countries."

"I presume you'll be returning to yours very shortly?"

The first possible crack in Guzov's confidence, picked out Charlie. Why did the man need to know how quickly he would be leaving Moscow? "There's no hurry, now that the murder investigation has been resolved, is there? There might be a few things I still need to tidy up."

As he spoke, Charlie recognized it to be a pitiful attempt to have the last word and wished he hadn't bothered.

★

"They've beaten you," judged Aubrey Smith. "Wiped you off the board. And me and the department with you!"

"It looks like it, at this moment." The admission came out of his mouth like a bad taste.

"This and every moment that's going to follow," insisted the Director-General. "You can't recover from this!"

"I haven't received all their promised documentation yet."

"You think they're likely to have left you an opening there? They've done it all perfectly. What if there is something that doesn't make sense or add up? You can't challenge them without destroying yourself and all the rest of us. They've been brilliantly clever!"

"Which a lot of other people here seem to have been trying to be."

There was a silence from London. Then Smith said, "There have been some contrary instructions to Moscow of which I have been unaware, until now. The situation, as far as you are concerned, has been corrected. Or had been. It hardly matters anymore."

"I'd like you to explain that," said Charlie, who believed he understood completely but wanted confirmation.

"You've been caught up more than I suspected in internecine maneuverings here in London. I regret that."

The first open reference to the power struggle between Aubrey Smith and the disgruntled Jeffrey Smale, Charlie recognized. It would account for his being the choice for the Moscow assignment in the first place.

"Has whatever's been happening in London been blocked?"

"I'd hoped it had been, until this conversation," said the other man. "Now it's academic."

"I'm still going to keep the appointment with the woman."

"Do you genuinely imagine that she's going to keep any appointment after the publicity there's going to be over the next few days?" demanded Smith. "She could even be part of all the Russians have done to trap you."

"I need a way out," said Charlie.

"Maybe your return is that way out."

"I don't follow."

"Hopkins has been interviewed as far as the doctors had judged it safe to do so," said the other man. "He's adamant that the other car drove into him intentionally to force him over the edge: that they, whoever they are, believed you were in the car, too. It was a deliberate assassination attempt."

"How is he?"

"He'll live but he'll never walk again."

"Is he going to be looked after?" demanded Charlie, refusing the dismissal. "Medically and financially, I mean?"

"I know what you mean, and of course he is," said the other man, impatiently. "And now I want you out."

"Let me see this through," pleaded Charlie.

"I'll not be responsible."

"I'm not asking you to be. This is being recorded: there's no responsibility on the department."

"No!"

"We both need my resolving this. And I can do it."

There was a pause. "Day to day. I'll judge it day by day."

★

"No one could have anticipated this!" opened Svetlana Modin.

"No one did," agreed Charlie, accepting the desperation of his making the contact they'd agreed. Could he use the broadcaster: find an escape or at least a stay of execution through her? He had been quite prepared to resign if that was what it would have taken to get Natalia and Sasha with him in London, but he'd wanted the decision to be his, at his timing and on his terms, not ignominiously thrust upon him with accusations of gullible incompetence and failed professionalism. And unfair to Natalia and their daughter though it was, it was still what he wanted.

"How much were you involved?"

Charlie shifted in the telephone box, alert to everything outside. "There has to be no indication that we've spoken."

"I want to go with what I've got tonight, which you're not going to like. It is that you've been intentionally humiliated, because of what happened—or rather didn't happen—with America."

The wrong reasoning but she was certainly right about humiliation, conceded Charlie. But she had kept her part of the deal making no mention of the embankment collision. And there could conceivably be some physical safety in that being promoted. "I certainly had no input in whatever the official communiqué says: my first and only awareness of the murders being solved was when I was summoned to Petrovka today to be told, an hour before the official announcement. But I haven't yet seen any evidence to support the claims."

"Are you suggesting the investigation *isn't* over?"

He hadn't been but an idea began to wisp in his mind. "I'll answer that after I've seen the evidence."

"Do you believe you were excluded because of the proposed inclusion of America's CIA?"

Could he maneuver her in the direction he wanted, his idea settling. It was important to put the CIA more firmly in her mind. "If that were the reason, it was misguided or perhaps misunderstood. The approach came *from* Washington, as far as I am aware: it wasn't considered in any depth by London."

"You're going to be at tomorrow's press conference. And also be at Sergei Romanovich's funeral. Why exclude you one moment and include you the next?"

Neither of which had been mentioned in the official communiqué, Charlie at once isolated, his disappointment that she hadn't picked up the lead-in as he'd intended, tempered by the suspicion that she'd come close to confirming an arrangement with Mikhail Guzov.

"That's a question for Moscow to answer, not me."

"I don't think they believe London has genuinely rejected the American approach: that London still hoped to work with Washington in the background. But that they've beaten you—not you personally, your people—by solving everything first."

That had to come directly from Guzov! seized Charlie. And fitted perfectly with what he was trying to implant in the woman's mind. "If they are, then I know nothing about it. But then perhaps I wouldn't."

"I don't understand?"

You're going to right now, determined Charlie. "Perhaps I was never intended to be the proper investigator, just the person everyone, including the Russians, were supposed to believe had been assigned to the case."

"Are you suggesting there was—still is—an entirely separate investigation that no one knows is going on?"

"It would explain a lot of strange things that have happened in the investigation up until now."

The word "humiliation" did not feature in that evening's ORT broadcast, and Charlie was only mentioned once by name and without a photograph being shown. It was the lead item, fronted by Svetlana Modin, and once more claimed to be a world exclusive. A combined and absolutely covert investigation between British and American intelligence had been defeated by the brilliance of Russian detectives who had solved both the murder of the mystery man at the British embassy and that of the originally appointed Russian investigator. The revelation, insisted the woman, would further worsen diplomatic relations between Moscow and the two

Western capitals, both of which had issued statements strenuously denying any such joint operation when it had been put to them. A Russian presidential spokesman was quoted that, despite the already issued denials, formal explanations were being demanded from Washington and London.

Had he manipulated the program sufficiently to deflect any further physical attacks? wondered Charlie, hunched over a tumbler of Islay single malt in his firmly secured hotel suite. Still too unsure to relax, he decided, turning to the promised and combined Russian dossiers that had arrived an hour before he quit the embassy and carried back with him to the Savoy. It took Charlie three hours fully to read the dossiers the first time and an additional two to reread everything for a second before finally pouring himself his second Islay single malt of the evening, his minimal satisfaction at manipulating the television broadcast muted by the Russian material.

Charlie had seen weaker evidence, some of it more obviously fabricated, overwhelm barristers in English courts. In what passed for justice in Russia, total victory was a forgone conclusion. The Russians hadn't missed a single trick.

It was to take another twelve hours for Charlie to change his mind. There was one trick, which even Charlie couldn't at that moment have imagined. Or hoped for.

24

CHARLIE CHANGED DIRECTION, REACHING FOR THE RINGING telephone instead of the television remote control for the first broadcast of the day. David Halliday said, "Have you seen the news?" and Charlie pressed the power button in time to see a photograph of Svetlana Modin fading from the screen and to catch "strongest protest" as the commentator's voice-over finished, too.

"What's happened?" demanded Charlie.

"According to the broadcast, she was arrested at four o'clock this morning," relayed Halliday. "The station says they've no idea where she's been taken or what charge is being made against her, if any. One suggestion was that she is being accused of acting for a hostile foreign power in the dissemination of false information."

"Is there such a charge?" So much, thought Charlie, for fame keeping her safe.

"Probably. I haven't checked."

The TV picture now was of ORT's senior newsreader, Svetlana's photograph in the background. The man expanded the protest statement beyond that from the station itself to include the Moscow journalists' union. There was a reference to that morning's scheduled murder press conference, which the anchorwoman had intended covering, with the speculations that Russian journalists might boycott it in protest at her arrest. That was followed by stock footage of Svetlana's most recent appearances, accompanied by a commentary describing them as a series of unrivaled world exclusives.

"They're going to sweat her, for her sources," predicted Halliday. "You think they'll disclose them, when she tells all?"

He had to be wary of the recording equipment in the suite Charlie reminded himself. "They might, if it serves their purpose." And totally destroy him in the process if they chose to do so, he accepted, if his belief of Guzov initiating Svetlana's approach to him the previous day was right.

"You think it could cause us more problems here at the embassy?" asked Halliday, with unknowing prescience.

"It could, I suppose. I'll just go to the conference, see what I can pick up there," said Charlie. And lay himself out for sacrifice if Guzov were listening, which Charlie was sure the FSB general was. It didn't really matter whether the Russian press boycotted the event. The rest of the world media most definitely wouldn't and there he would be, displayed for all to see, if Guzov chose that moment to denounce his contact with the woman.

"You spoken to London since last night's broadcast?"

"No," said Charlie.

"Don't you think you should, particularly now that she's been arrested?"

"I intend to."

"Harry Fish has been withdrawn, incidentally. Did you know that?"

The planted bugs! Charlie thought, deciding the conversation had to end. "No, I hadn't heard. I need to get going. I'll see you at the embassy." Could he infer Fish's removal to be a victory for Aubrey Smith? At that moment, Charlie didn't think it was safe for him to assume anything. And even if he did—and was right—he couldn't imagine that it would indicate anything to save or protect him.

It was a last-minute thought to order an embassy car to collect him, and Charlie was glad he had as he approached the legation. It was once more under media siege, the embankment road close to being impassable. He was recognized during the vehicle's slow progress through the crush and it took several moments for Charlie to recover from the flash and strobe-light blindness when they finally reached the sanctuary of the inner courtyard. Charlie asked his driver to wait to take him to Petrovka, unsure what to expect within the building.

The answer to which appeared to be very little. Neither P-J nor Halliday—despite his earlier conversation with the man— were in their offices, although in Halliday's there was a pile of that day's newspapers, all headlining the TV program. There was already waiting for him in the communications room a message from the Director-General that the claim of a covert American/ British operation was being officially denied and an instruction that he should not become embroiled in any public or private discussion whatsoever about it. The message concluded that the man would be unavailable the entire day which, without conceding paranoia, Charlie took to be abandonment, compounded by his being told when he called the ambassador's suite that Peter Maidment was at the Russian Interior Ministry and not expected to be available until late in the afternoon. Neither in the rabbit-hutch office nor in the set-aside apartment was there any message or notification of Harry Fish's withdrawal. The same two sullen operatives of the previous day were on duty again. The overnight log, again offered by the elder of the two, listed seventy-eight press calls in the two hours following Svetlana Modin's program.

An obviously alerted Paul Robertson arrived at the apartment five minutes after Charlie, just as Charlie was replacing the phone from being told that Mikhail Guzov was also unavailable.

"Has there been a nuclear explosion I didn't hear? Everyone appears to have been vaporized," Charlie greeted.

Robertson ignored the remark, going instead to the other two men. "Why don't you two take a break? We'll handle anything for the next fifteen minutes." The man waited until the door closed behind them before coming back to Charlie. "Maybe people don't want to become contaminated by the fallout you've caused. And on a very personal note."—the man nodded generally around the room "—which you know is going on record as we speak, I resent and refute all the inferences in your note to the Director-General. I'm not part of any cabal or conspiracy, and I'm demanding a formal personnel inquiry when I get back to London into any suggestion or claim that I am. I don't know—and don't want to know—what games are going on back there. Or here, apart from what it's my function to uncover and expose. That clear?"

"Good for you," mocked Charlie, refusing the rehearsed attack. "Harry Fish isn't here any longer though, is he? And how are your own inquiries going?"

Robertson swept his hand toward the recorder-linked telephones. "I'm now responsible for the duties of Fish's technicians here. That's where any contact between you and me begins and ends."

"Comforting for me to know I've got your help and support," said Charlie.

"You've got—and will get—absolutely fuck all from me."

"You got all your explanations and excuses ready for that inquiry panel you're demanding when they ask why it's taken you so long and why you've fucked up so many times trying to find the inside source here, Paul?"

"Most of it could be in the material in which you feature in the diplomatic bag going back to London with Harry Fish."

"No they can't and you know it: the sequences don't fit in times or dates or events or leaks. . . ." Charlie made his own movement around the wired-for-sound room. "And don't forget that all that's being recorded now will be available as a reminder for that inquiry panel of yours."

There was a sound at the door, directly followed by it being opened by the elder of the two sound technicians. Hesitantly the man smiled, "You said fifteen minutes?"

"Perfect timing," said Charlie, before Robertson could speak. "Best of luck, succeeding eventually in your function of getting your still-free-to-operate informer."

For the first time Charlie welcomed the camera flash gauntlet getting out of the embassy and into the similarly media-cordoned Petrovka, confident of its physical protection although finding it difficult to focus in the sudden darkness of the building. He did not immediately recognize Mikhail Guzov waiting for him just inside the entrance. Guzov said: "All this is ridiculous! Absolutely and completely ridiculous!"

Believing as he did that the FSB officer had been involved if not totally in control of Svetlana Modin's approach and of the ORT broadcast, Charlie had anticipated a tirade of supposed outrage for the man to distance himself from it but not by this degree of vehemence.

"I tried to reach you," embarked Charlie, cautiously.

"Everything and everyone's gone mad! I haven't been able to talk to anyone, reach anyone!"

The outrage definitely wasn't faked! Charlie wouldn't have risked his lunch money on the bet, wanting more time to be sure, but his initial impression was that the red-faced Russian was genuinely furious. "I haven't seen or heard a full newscast. I don't know everything that's happened."

"You know at least that the militia arrested Svetlana Modin in the middle of the night!"

"I didn't know who initiated it," encouraged Charlie.

"The interfering militia commandant, that's who! Acting without reference to anyone. The Russian media are threatening to boycott the conference, which we decided to cancel until we sorted out the mistake. But now Lvov's involved himself!"

"Lvov! How can he involve himself!"

"Easily. And brilliantly. He's declared it an attack, an infringement, on the supposed freedom of the press. It's a platform he's made all his own, chasing publicity like a dog after a bitch in heat."

"Are you still going to cancel?"

"How can we now?" demanded Guzov, exasperated. "If we cancel, Lvov can—and will—claim the currently elected government can no longer properly run the country and that canceling everything is a panicked reaction to a mistake they shouldn't have made"—he hesitated—"which the militia certainly shouldn't have made."

Guzov was echoing a politician's—maybe even a ministerial—judgement, Charlie guessed. Where was his benefit apart from the most obvious that an assassination attempt was unlikely here? It was an additionally hopeful thought that his personal humiliation was being overshadowed, at least for the moment. Unless, perhaps, Svetlana was coerced into naming him. Unlikely, came the reassurance. From his experience, Svetlana Modin wasn't easily coerced. Rather than being frightened by her detention, the self-promoting woman would be reveling in it, already having calculated how it would increase her fame and notoriety. "So what are you going to do?"

"Wait. It's being discussed elsewhere," disclosed Guzov, leading the way farther and down into the building into what, from its lingering smell, Charlie assumed normally to be a staff canteen, although any trace of its use had been removed. Charlie thought there was something almost pitiful about the very obvious anything-you-can-do-we-can-do-better determination to improve upon the facilities of the British press conference. The improvised Petrovka facility was actually bigger, with far more attendance-recording cameras and the addition of four huge instant-replay screens at the front, sides, and even rear of the room. Each back-padded chair had its individual translation earpiece and microphone in its holster, with a separate already assembled but uncertain-looking group of backup microphone runners to be ready if the main questioning system broke down. There was another group of men and women moving along the lines of set-out chairs, distributing press packs in manila folders. It was impossible to see into the temporary, smoke-windowed translators' booth, but Charlie guessed it could accommodate at least a dozen linguists. Charlie wondered if the Russians had also copied the internal video and audio recording equipment that Harry Fish had assembled at the embassy. The elevated dais was a goldfish bowl of even more lights and cameras.

Charlie turned to the FSB general but at that moment Leonid

Toplov hurried into the room and without any explanation Guzov moved toward the man. The discussion between the two Russians began quite calmly but within minutes degenerated, Guzov making expansively sweeping movements about the room before trying—and very clearly failing—to reach someone on his cell phone. With a very visible shrug of despair Guzov bustled out through the door, followed by the hapless ministry official. They did so with difficulty, struggling against the flow of early arrivals who at once began to spread out throughout the hall, quickly overwhelming the place-allocating greeting officials. At the initial influx Charlie very quickly attached himself, although not closely enough for conversation, to the momentarily unoccupied backup group of additional microphone distributors. Charlie's impression from the incoming flow of journalists was that the threatened Russian boycott hadn't materialized, although from the muted outside broadcast being relayed upon the wide screen on the far wall of the hall the now banner-carrying crowd outside appeared greater than when he'd arrived. On the perimeter of the demonstration there was a disjointed line of confronting, uniformed militia officers as well as plainclothes officials but Charlie could not locate either Guzov or Toplov among them.

As Charlie watched, more confronting uniformed officers began to move in from either side of the headquarters building which, oddly, appeared to be matched by the growth in the number of protesters, creating surge and countersurge to a silent-movie background of arm-waving, fist-shaking, banner-fluttering jostling. Charlie had intentionally positioned himself to keep the entrance partially in his eye line, so he saw Guzov the moment the man reentered the hall, like a piece of flotsam on an incoming tide. For the briefest moment inside the hall, the FSB general appeared disorientated, gazing around until establishing the raised stage area and, as he moved toward it, where Charlie stood. The Russian, sweat-streaked as well as visibly flushed, escaped from the flow and said, short breathed, "A fiasco! We couldn't stop it . . . nothing we could do."

"What?" demanded Charlie.

"Lvov," managed the Russian. "Heading a demonstration here ..." The rest of what Guzov said was drowned by the increasing outside noise and there was briefly the surreal combination of silent television footage on the inside screen accompanied by the permeating uproar. Stepan Lvov, his surprisingly still immaculately designer-dressed and coiffuer-intact wife by his side, was clearly visible on the screen now, the surrealism heightened by their being in the middle of a marching, chanting crowd but separated and untouched by it, protected as they were by an inner cordon of bodyguards. The militia barrier melted in the face of the oncoming tidal wave of people, which was on the screen one moment and the next, sweeping into the hall. Charlie later reasoned that the politician must have had advance scouts already inside because without pause Lvov and his inner caucus turned as if choreographed by unseen directions, toward the raised area where a man already stood, handheld microphone ready for Lvov to reach out and take as he mounted the small stage, which immediately became an oasis of calm just slightly ahead of the room quietening.

"Svetlana Modin is a brave and courageous woman, a symbol, a visible and recognizable face, of the oppressive, brutish, and even murderous attacks of the government I am going to sweep from office," declared Lvov, illuminated by a thousand cameras flashes as he turned to suddenly raised photographs of Svetlana. "Her fight for the freedom of the press is my fight for the freedom of this country and when I am elected we will work together to achieve and enjoy both."

There had, Charlie supposed, been time enough for Lvov to formulate at least a framework, but the speech itself had to be virtually impromptu and verged on oratorical brilliance. Each attempted and successful act of censorship after the early perestroika spring of press freedom was recited by Lvov in perfectly dated sequence and outcome, each arrest, suspicious death and unquestionable murder of investigative journalists dated and itemized. The "rasping keys to journalistic shackles" was a familiar sound in every newspaper office in the land, a chorus to the cracked songs of a communism desperately trying to regain its former tyranny and to enslave its people as it had once done, but must never be allowed to do again. There should not just be a media strike until Svetlana Modin was freed. Every industry and shop and workplace should stop, immediately, until she was released from illegal arrest and detention. And all those who had tasted the brief democratic freedom piece by piece, inch by inch, being daily taken away from them should show their determination that it stop, never to be imposed again, by registering their vote for him.

Lvov's exit was as triumphal and swift as his entry, trailed by the majority of people in the hall, all attempts at a formal press conference abandoned. Charlie allowed himself to be carried along, unresisting, in the exodus. He did not detach himself until he was well outside, isolating David Halliday on the periphery of the watching crowd and then, nearby, saw first Paula-Jane Venables and just beyond her, Bill Bundy: none gave any sign of recognition but Halliday said, "You know what the stupid bastards of a government did! They were taken so completely by surprise they didn't jam the already set-up television satellite feeds, worldwide. The next, absolutely guaranteed leader of the Russian Federation has just delivered his winning presidential address to a global audience of five billion people." The man smiled directly at Charlie. "And at the same time, you, Charlie, got let completely off the hook."

★

Charlie thought a further comment of Halliday's—that Lvov's protest matched that of Boris Yeltsin in 1991 being carried to presidential victory after boarding a government tank threatening the Russian White House—to be an exaggeration until he learned that the seat of the elected Russian parliament was the destination of the continuing peoples-power protest. And it didn't stop there but meshed together with the stage managed continuity of a Hollywood blockbuster. From the White House, order-imposing stewards now quite clearly in evidence, the march proceeded in perfect coordination to Vagankov Cemetery at which Pavel's wife, three daughters, and a small group of officers—not one in militia uniform—were gathered for the funeral of Sergei Romanovich Pavel. The crowd control was absolute, Lvov and his wife and just four others—with Charlie tagging himself on until he separated to join a suddenly emerged Mikhail Guzov. None of the huge, no longer banner-waving crowd attempted to enter the cemetery, instead completely encircling it in silent, respectful solemnity, creating for the banked cameras a burial tableau at the center of which stood Lvov, now as silent as his followers, his wife with one supporting arm around the sobbing widow, the other stretched out in comfort to the children.

The politician's total hijack of the day—and the government's equally total ineptitude—was completed with the release of Svetlana Modin just two hours before ORT's main evening broadcast. Stepan Lvov and the attentive wife, not a hair misplaced or an ugly crease marking the virginal white suit, were waiting with their inevitable crowd outside the finally identified militia detention center to receive her. Svetlana, carefully crumpled, disheveled, and dirt-smeared as befitted someone presumed to have been incarcerated in a dank and filthy cell, disdainfully and on camera waved away an approaching makeup girl to remain as she was for a live broadcast, which completely filled the transmission slot. She used an impromptu interview with Lvov to hint heavily—but not positively to claim—interrogation under physical and sexually threatened torture and picked up like the accomplished performer she was on Lvov's repeated diatribe against official media censorship, intimidation, violence, and murder.

To approving roars and applause from the crowd threatening to drown out her words, Svetlana concluded, "I resisted it all, refused it all, and did not break. They learned nothing from me, nor will they, apart from the truth."

There were matching shouts and applause in the packed Savoy bar, in which Charlie and Halliday watched her release. Halliday said, "You ain't seen nuthin' like that before in your entire life and you never will again."

"You're probably very right," accepted Charlie.

"It certainly took the focus—and any threat—off you," remarked Halliday.

For how long? wondered Charlie.

25

CHARLIE BEGAN HIS DAY TENSED AGAINST THE IMMEDIATE setback of Mikhail Guzov personally responding to his Petrovka phone when he called from the bug-monitored Savoy suite, relieved there was no reply. He told the duty officer who answered that Guzov could reach him at the embassy about the rearranged conference, and quit the suite at once. He used the stairs instead of the elevator and took the side corridor to the baroque dining room and its conveniently separate entrance and exit without needing to go through the central lobby and its main door. As he knew from his previous three days' reconnaissance, there were no cars in the outside slip road and only a few disinterested people. He got a taxi at the corner and gave the driver a destination that took them through side streets until the Precistenka turn to go south in the opposite direction from the Arbat, to follow the gradual loop north again. Charlie divided his attention between his deadline and the following vehicles: upon such a crowded, multilaned highway it was impossible ever to be absolutely certain but Charlie remained reasonably confident there was no pursuit. He waited until they climbed as far as the Kurskaya Okalovskaja Metro sign. At the last moment, double fare ready and the door ajar, he ordered the stop for his hurried dash to the Metro escalator. He was fortunate with an Arbat-bound train coming into the platform as he reached it, but traveled only one stop on the fifth line to switch south as far as Kitay-Gorod, where he disembarked to return northwest on the sixth line as far as Tverskaya Puskinskaya for the final line change and the Arbat. It was exactly five minutes to ten.

Charlie had preferred the Arbat as the flea market it had been when he'd first known it, not the hybrid now of doubtful antique galleries, Western designer shops, Russian bric-a-brac and icon stalls, artist-attended—and eagerly selling—exhibitions and tourist-trap outlets. And most definitely not the soccer-crowd volume of people from which to stage the perfect assassination. As he stepped out into the throng his apprehension began to tighten like a spring, his skin reacting into something like an itch at the jostling, inevitable physical contact, the irritation so immediate and intense he had to feel out, to scratch his arms and shoulders.

He moved as instructed, the wandering pick-up-and-put-down loiterer, unsure after so much and so many public interferences—and not one single confirming telephone approach since the rendezvous was arranged—if his was not an entirely pointless performance to a nonexistent audience. He guessed the crowd at this particular midpoint was as dense as that at Lvov's demonstration and even more difficult to be part of: the previous day, those demonstrators had all moved in one direction but now there was a constant ebb and flow of people struggling every which way. To get himself out of the crush Charlie frequently detached himself from the main, outside stream and went off the stall-cluttered road into some of the more established and permanent shops and boutiques, constantly checking the time either from his own watch or available clocks.

At 10:35, he finally allowed himself the thought of his other rendezvous. Natalia had said it would take her an hour to get from her flat to McDonald's. Which only gave him thirty-five minutes to be at one of the two public telephones he'd already isolated to warn her of his inability to keep their meeting if there hadn't been a personal approach from the hoarse-voiced woman. But Natalia had told him she'd be going to the fast-food restaurant anyway. And it would only take him thirty minutes, less even, to get there from the Arbat.

He was being stupid, unprofessional, Charlie accused himself. What if the woman in whom he'd put every hope of survival *did* make contact? He had no way of judging what she had to say or would want to do: whether she'd be a crank. Or a would-be killer. If she were neither and he for a moment believed she were genuine it could—inevitably *would*—take hours, days, to gain her confidence and trust.

Natalia and Sasha had to be a secondary consideration. No! Charlie refused at once. Not relegated to second place: put in their *rightful* place, that of being of absolute personal importance to him but separate from what was professionally essential. Separate, too, from the potential danger at that moment burning through him.

Their meeting had to be postponed. Maybe only put off for a day: freed from the noon deadline he could remain in the Arbat for the rest of the day and if there was no approach he'd know the episode had been a hoax or a crank or that the woman had been frightened away.

He reached the closer of his two chosen telephone phone booths at 10:45, to find it occupied by a woman with a notepad and a heap of replenishing coin on the ledge in front of her and an increasingly fidgeting man waiting ahead of him. The milling crowd in which he'd so recently immersed himself for its concealing protection now became an obstructive, delaying interference.

When it came it wasn't the tight-together pressure of people jamming him between them for a quick, agonizing knife thrust or the hard jab of a silenced pistol. It was a tug, a dip into his jacket pocket. He started to snatch toward whatever had been planted and he only just managed to turn it into the jerk of someone colliding into him, the hoarse-voiced telephone warning— *don't look or act surprised*—echoing in his head as if he were hearing it at that moment. He didn't stare about him, either, but forced himself on, leaking perspiration but not touching his pocket until just before he reached the intended telephone. The interior of Charlie's pockets invariably resembled a schoolboy's treasure pouch, which like so much else about the man was intentionally misleading. He was aware of everything in every space and immediately detected the folded piece of paper, taking it out as if it were a reminder, which it could easily have been, a telephone number which Charlie instantly recognized to be another street kiosk, that day's date and a time: 1700. The numerals were written in a Russian hand.

It was five minutes before eleven, Charlie saw. He could get with time to spare to where he knew Natalia and Sasha would be. He needed time to calm himself, as well as a drink, to help. Probably two, to help even more.

★

And because he had that much time, Charlie chose again to fill it line-hopping across the Metro's central-city spider's web, the tradecraft dance subconsciously prompted by what he'd recognized during the preceding hour and now wanted more reassurance, fully confronting what he was contemplating. He'd lied to Natalia—again—and was about to lie further after promising he never would again: that, instead, he would always put her safety and Sasha's safety before anything or anyone else. It was ridiculous for him never to accept the possibility of failure or to delude himself into thinking the car crash might have been a coincidence. Ridiculous, too, to believe he'd always be able to lose a surveillance tail and the possibility of another assassination attempt, an assassination attempt in which Natalia and Sasha might all too easily be caught up, and even die, with him. So why was he going on as he was, thinking more of himself—*only* of himself—and what he wanted instead of how he should be thinking, of what he should do if he loved them both as much as he insisted that he did? He didn't have an answer. Not one that came even half close to justifying anything.

There was one thing he did know, from the Arbat experience. The hoarse-voiced woman's apparent nervousness during the arranging telephone conversation might have been genuine but her claim not to be sure of a rendezvous definitely hadn't been. She'd planned the Arbat as she'd planned everything else—the concealing crowd on the busiest day of the week, the protective watch for which she would have been in place long before ten to ensure she wasn't risking a snatch squad, and the brush contact drop within a yard or two of the escaping Arbat Metro.

She was, Charlie recognized, a professional intelligence operative with the knowledge and ability of operational field-level tradecraft. And could so easily have been a killer, he reminded himself, refusing to push aside the self-accusation of cheating Natalia and their child. Everything was planned, he further reminded himself. He knew he was clean, that he wouldn't be endangering them today. Just this one more time then, maybe the last—his only chance—to be with Sasha. He'd see them today, judge how the encounter went and then find the answer eluding him.

He scuffed on aching feet up the slightly inclined Kreschatik Square upon which he saw the line stretched at least twenty-five yards from the entrance of the McDonald's, out into the square, and which didn't appear to be moving. And then he saw Natalia close to its front, Sasha's hand obediently in hers. He knew Natalia'd seen him virtually at the same moment, although she gave no indication of doing so. Neither did he, happy that the delay would give her all the time she needed to satisfy herself he had not been followed. If he had been, he would have been hit by now.

★

Natalia had secured a corner table, her large briefcase-sized valise securing a third seat, which would put Sasha between them. She'd already finished whatever she'd eaten and had her coffee cup before her. Sasha was still eating a hamburger, but her attention was upon one of the restaurant-supplied coloring books. Natalia gave him the briefest welcoming smile, moving her valise from the third chair, and said something to Sasha. At the counter he ordered the obvious. His McMuffin was soggy and the coffee was a gray color.

When Charlie reached the table Natalia said, "I told Sasha we might be meeting a friend."

"Hello," said the child. "I'm Sasha. What's your name?"

Charlie looked inquiringly at Natalia, who shook her head. Charlie couldn't think of an appropriate Russian transliteration and said, "Ivan," sure it wasn't a pseudonym he'd forget after the morning's still hopeful expedition.

Natalia's forehead creased as she raised her eyebrows at the name, smiling down at his choice of meal. "I guessed that's what you'd order."

"What else could it have been?" Charlie smiled back.

Sasha made an attention-gaining slurp, sucking at the straw in her cherry milkshake, and said, "Would you like me to color you a picture?"

"I'd like that very much," said Charlie. How could it be like this? Small talk, easy words that ordinary people said in ordinary situations: he didn't have to sift and scrape every word for a second or third or fourth meaning.

"You choose," Sasha insisted. "An elephant or a giraffe or a lion? It will have to be one of those because they're all I've got."

"A giraffe, please," said Charlie.

"You wouldn't like a lion, instead?"

"All right, a lion."

Sasha smiled. "The giraffe is for Mama and the elephant is for Igor. He's my teacher at school and our friend."

"I . . ." started Charlie, stopping himself from saying he knew. ". . . He'll like that," he finished. He'd seen Natalia's wincing frown.

"How are things?" she asked, as Sasha began scribbling with her crayons.

"Confused."

"You look terrible. Drained. Are you all right?"

"There's a lot happening." He was glad there was a wall behind him.

Natalia frowned again. "From what I've read and seen on television I believed it to be all over: I thought you'd be going back very soon?"

"Not yet." Innocuous though the words sounded, they marked a change from neither ever discussing work with the other.

"It seems bad, for you?"

"It could be. I could be recalled." Not instantly forgotten small talk after all. But she would have surely mentioned the embankment ambush if she'd known about it: rejected his even approaching them. Now he was lying by omission, he recognized.

"How would you feel about that?"

Natalia didn't want small talk, either, Charlie accepted. "It could make a lot of things easier."

"Could it? Really, I mean?"

"I think so. And I have thought about it, very seriously thought about it." He'd done the right thing by keeping the meeting, despite all the deceit and soul-searching.

"So have I. Although not to the extent of your quitting."

"It might not even be an option of my choosing."

"You wouldn't like that."

"Perhaps I wouldn't," Charlie agreed. "The circumstances, I mean. Not the result."

"What are you talking about?" unexpectedly demanded the child.

"Something a long way away," said Natalia.

"Not here, you mean? Not in Moscow?"

"No, not in Moscow," said Charlie.

"Don't you live here?"

"No," said Charlie. "I live somewhere else."

"My papa lives somewhere else, a long way away. I don't see him but Mama says she might take me there one day."

Charlie was conscious of Natalia flushing, very slightly. To his daughter Charlie said, "Would you like that?"

"I'm not sure," said Sasha, with the serious-faced sagacity of a child, returning to her coloring.

"I wish that hadn't been said."

"I don't have a problem with it," said Charlie. "The opposite, in fact."

"It doesn't mean anything . . . that I've decided anything. Now I'm even more unsure."

"Don't be," urged Charlie. "It really could be so much easier now."

"You couldn't live without the job. You know you couldn't and I know you couldn't."

"I could," insisted Charlie. "And will. By choice or otherwise."

"Finished!" announced Sasha, triumphantly, offering Charlie the crayoned image. The lion's mane and feet were colored green, its body yellow. She'd strayed over most of the guiding outlines in her eagerness to complete it.

"It's the best picture of a lion I've ever seen," enthused Charlie. "May I keep it?"

"I want you to," insisted the child. "Are we going to see you again?"

"I hope so," said Charlie.

"So do I. Next time you can have the giraffe and Igor can have the lion."

"We have to go," abruptly declared Natalia, the flush returning as she collected up her valise.

"We haven't properly talked," protested Charlie. This could be the last opportunity it would be safe for them to meet, for him to persuade her!

"You knew we couldn't, not today. That wasn't what today was about."

"I'll call again, when things get clearer. But don't forget what I said. And that I meant all of it."

"You've told me you meant what you said a lot of times before, Charlie. And haven't meant them."

"This time I do. I really do."

"I've got a call to make" insisted Natalia, ushering Sasha before her.

So had he, thought Charlie. And a hell of a lot depended on it.

26

"HELLO!" A MAN'S VOICE, SLIGHTLY SLURRED.

Charlie said, "I have this number to call?"

"This is a public phone."

"Who are you?" Surely not a hoax! It couldn't be!

"Get off the line. I want to use the phone." The voice *was* slurred, the belligerence rising.

"Did you answer because it was ringing?"

"Get off the fucking line!"

"I will when you answer the question. Otherwise I'll keep it open: blocked."

"It was ringing as I got into the kiosk. Now get off the fucking line!"

Charlie did, stepping away from the telephone for a woman who was waiting with a tugging child on reins but stayed close enough to hear her voice when she spoke in case the contact was planned differently from how he expected. It was high pitched, a complaint about a gas installation, not at all the tone he wanted to hear. There could be a simple, easy explanation. The belligerent man could have got to the telephone seconds before the woman, no thought of politely deferring to her using it first. Probably wouldn't have wanted him to, hanging around to hear everything she said. Made every sense for her to be the one to hold back. She would have heard the ringing: know he'd understood and was trying to reach her. All he had to do was wait. But not too long. The woman for whom he'd stepped aside appeared to be having an argument with whomever she was talking; the tugging child was pulling away, distracting her. Charlie walked to and fro in her eye line, to remind her he was waiting. Pointedly she turned her back on him. It was six minutes past five. His feet throbbed. The child became entangled in its reins and fell, pulling the woman off balance. He began screaming and she finally slammed the phone down, dragging him away.

Charlie wedged himself into the kiosk, determined against abandoning it again, and dialed out the number from the paper slipped into his pocket. The line was engaged. He had to redial continuously four times before he got a ringing tone, counting each separate sound. He got to six before the receiver at the other end was lifted. No one spoke.

Charlie said: "Hello?"

There was no response.

"I have this number to call."

"You're late."

The relief surged through Charlie at the recognizable hoarseness. "A man answered when I called before, right on time."

"I saw him."

"Then you know I kept my word."

"Yes," she agreed.

"Do you now trust me?"

"I don't know."

"It's a decision you've got to make."

"Yes."

"I promised to be alone at the Arbat. And I was. And I'm alone now: no one with me."

"I know."

"How can you know?" demanded Charlie.

"I can see you."

Again Charlie avoided any startled reaction. Confident that he'd lost any pursuit, he hadn't bothered to check out the streets directly around Hlebnyj pereulok, the street from which he was speaking. "Then you must know you're safe."

"It's not true what they're saying: about gangs and drug running and whores. They haven't even got the name right!"

He had to put pressure on her, Charlie decided: imperceptibly, to prevent her panicking but sufficient to get out of this conversational cul-de-sac. "We have to meet; start talking differently from this. You know you're not in any danger."

"I don't know that at all!"

At last Charlie looked around him, casually. There was what could be another public facility in the shadow of a building about thirty meters to his right. It was too dark for him to be sure, certainly to distinguish anyone inside. Good tradecraft again. "What do you want? If you want the proper retribution against the people who killed Ivan, I'm the man who can get it for you: the *only* one."

"I don't know that at all," the woman repeated.

"You're running away!" Charlie openly accused, conscious of the risk he was taking. "You keep running away from me you're going to let those who killed Ivan escape. Is that what you want, for them to get away, never be punished?"

"No!"

"Then you've got to meet me. Talk to me. Tell me as much as you *do* know and let me take it on from there."

"They're too powerful; too influential." She broke into a coughing fit.

"You don't have anyone else. Can't trust anyone else." There was loud knocking from outside the telephone kiosk that made Charlie jump. He ignored it.

There was silence from the other end but another rap against the glass.

"Tell me how to meet you. *Where* to meet you."

There was a sound that didn't form into a word, something like a sigh that grew into a groan.

"What was that? What did you say?"

"Where the road joins Rizskij pereulok, on the left. The café there. Tonight. Seven. Wait for me to come up to you."

"I need . . ." started Charlie, but the line went dead. His clandestine meeting with Sergei Pavel had been in a workers café, arranged over public telephone lines. And now Pavel was dead, Charlie thought.

★

The café was not quite a step but at least a ledge above that in which he'd met Pavel, but thicker with cigarette smoke. The concentration of virtually everyone was on an ice hockey match showing on the screen behind the counter, one group of men enthusiastic enough to shout at goal attempts and the more violent clashes. There were three women already there when Charlie arrived, two gossiping at one table and immediately behind at another, a babushka heavily muffled in a coat and scarf and woolen hat, despite the warmth. All three ignored him. As he had for his meeting with Pavel, Charlie chose a pole-supported stand-up table closest to the wall farthest from the door, where he was able to see everything and everyone inside. He decided the coffee was better than in McDonald's but the baklava was stale. He still nibbled at it, hungry after ignoring his McMuffin. He wasn't convinced she would come. He'd decided the unintelligible sound at the end of their conversation had been a sob of fear at edging closer to a decision she was terrified of making, cutting off the words she couldn't at first utter, a refusal maybe. Charlie didn't know what to do if she didn't come now. She'd cut him off before he'd been able to suggest a fail-safe, which he'd anyway been reluctant to do because it would have given her an escape. Now he wished she'd given him the chance. He supposed he could again try the public telephone kiosk for which he had a number, promptly at five: she seemed to need the regularity of time. Or hope she would call the embassy again.

Would Mikhail Guzov have tried to reply to his early morning call? They'd surely make some attempt to restage the press conference; not to do so would give Stepan Lvov another victory. Charlie reasoned there was the danger of a further hijack by the world media ignoring the declared purpose of the conference and instead demanding from Guzov and Interior Ministry officials answers about the arrest and detention of Svetlana Modin. Would she have expected calls from him, even though it was a Saturday? Charlie thought she probably would. Automatically he looked at his watch, realizing the ORT main news was in thirty minutes, and just as automatically glanced toward the television, guessing it unlikely the channel would be changed from the ice hockey coverage.

So engrossed in the match was virtually everyone in the café—and so unobtrusive her entry—that Charlie thought he was probably the only person there to register the arrival of the woman he instantly and intuitively was sure to be his caller: it took several moments for the man behind the counter to become aware of her standing, waiting, and Charlie thought there was a professionalism about her nonentity cultivation. She was slight and very thin, anonymously dressed in a buttoned-to-the-neck gray linen coat and gray woolen hat pulled too low to give any indication of her hair shade. Her only distinctive feature when she turned away from the counter was her facial coloring. Charlie didn't think there was any makeup and was surprised, if anonymity were what she wanted, because it could have reduced the strange mottled brownness to the left of her face. If she were who he believed her to be, he accepted that some of the coloring could have been apprehension but her appearance was that of someone who had spent the majority of her life in perpetual sunshine from which she'd made little effort to protect or shield herself.

She hadn't appeared to look for him as she'd entered and continued to concentrate, head bent forward, over her cup as she came farther into the café, not bringing her head up until she sat at the table directly beside him, nodding then as if in permission for him to join her. As close as she now was, Charlie could see nervousness was trembling through her, the cup she'd carried from the counter puddled in a moat of spilled coffee.

Charlie said: "Relax. Nothing can happen to you."

"I'll be all right in a minute." It didn't seem possible for her to look directly at him. She coughed, clearing her throat.

"You know who I am. Can I know your name?" It was going to take a long time, Charlie guessed. He would have to be very gentle, not rush anything.

The woman hesitated. "Irena."

"Irena . . . ?" encouraged Charlie.

There was another hesitation. "Irena Yakulova Novikov."

"And Ivan . . . ?"

Her hands were clenched, to control the shaking. "Ivan Niko-laevich Oskin."

She wasn't wearing a wedding band, Charlie saw. "Tell me about Ivan Nikolaevich."

She jumped at the sudden roar from people watching televi-sion. A man's voice from the crowd said, "Giving the fucking game away!"

Irena coughed again and said, "We were together. Had been, for a long time. Before Afghanistan even."

"He fought in the Afghanistan war?" The missing arm, Charlie thought at once.

"He was there." She fumbled for cigarettes from her bag, the cheapest that minimized the tobacco with a hollow tube half its length, and had to steady the match with both hands.

"Is that where he was hurt?"

She nodded, not speaking. There was another roar from the ice hockey watchers. This time she didn't jump.

"What was he doing there?" asked Charlie, registering her qualified reply.

The hesitation was the longest yet. "KGB."

"He was a KGB field officer?"

"He was Georgian, as I am. He had the complexion . . ." Her hand came up to her own face as she spoke, quicker now, her con-fidence growing. "He was very good at language. He had Pamini as well as Pashto; a lot of Middle East languages. He was highly regarded, because of his ability."

"He had to infiltrate the mujahideen?" guessed Charlie. The most difficult and dangerous of all field assignments was trying to adopt the disguise and culture of an enemy in a war or hostile situation.

She nodded again, looking directly at him at last. "He was at-tached to the military headquarters in Kabul, even though he was

KGB, not the military *Glavnoye Razvedyvatelnoye Upravlenie*. He wasn't popular, because he wasn't one of them, either: considered an outsider. And he was too honest, insisting that Russia couldn't win the war. Something happened. He never knew how. He was betrayed. There was an ambush, near the compound in Kabul. Three generals, air force as well as army, were killed. Ivan lost his arm."

"Were you in Afghanistan with him?" asked Charlie, aware now that the skin on the left side of her face was puckered, as well as mottled brown.

"Does my face distress you?" she asked abruptly, her hand up to her cheek again.

"Not at all," insisted Charlie, unhappy at the sideways drift of the conversation. Her pace, he reminded himself.

"It does some people," she said, accepting his denial. "Ivan and I met on station in Cairo. That was where this happened . . ." She laughed, without humor. "The lobster was being flambéed, at the table. The chef poured on too much brandy and somehow the flame blew into my face . . ." There was another humorless laugh as she gazed around. "It's safer here. They don't go for flambé cooking."

They were straying even further sideways. He had to get things back on track without appearing impatient. Groping, he said, "Did Ivan go to Afghanistan direct from Cairo?"

"He'd fixed it—Ivan was a good fixer—that we'd get married in Cairo and go to Kabul together: the KGB liked husband-and-wife teams. But I got medevaced back here to Moscow: the concern was not my face but that I'd lose the sight of my eye. They managed to prevent that and did the best they could for the burn scars but it took a long time. The marriage was rearranged here, during Ivan's leave from Afghanistan, once I got better. Then Ivan was caught in the ambush and he was brought back and was in the hospital for even longer. . . ." Irena came to a gulping halt, her throat working, and Charlie realized she was close to breaking down. He held back from filling in the silence between them. She fumbled another cigarette alight, wincing at the sound of a goal being scored on television.

"I'm sorry. It's just that . . ." She had to stop again. "Sorry. The wedding was finally planned for the Saturday after he was found dead, in the embassy. . . ." Irena began to shake again.

"Can I get you something?" offered Charlie, not knowing what.

"Sometimes they have brandy here."

They did and Charlie bought two glasses. It was gritty and probably home distilled and caught Charlie's throat, almost making him cough. It didn't seem to cause the hoarse-voiced woman any difficulty.

"Things haven't been good for you," Charlie sympathized.

"No," she agreed. The shaking was subsiding.

Everything still had to be at her pace, Charlie warned himself again, nervous of another near collapse. "What about the KGB? Were you and Ivan kept on after the change to FSB?"

Irena shook her head. "I wasn't, because of the circumstances in which I was hurt. It was bourgeois; criminal, even—enjoying myself at KGB expense. I was dismissed, on reduced pension."

"What about Ivan Nikolaevich?"

"He was kept on, of course. He'd been injured on assignment: he was even awarded a distinguished service medal."

He was getting closer, thought Charlie, more apprehensive than encouraged but deciding to take the risk. "When he was fully recovered, was Ivan Nikolaevich kept in the First Chief Directorate?"

Irena looked at him wide-eyed, open-mouthed. "You know . . . the structure . . . Directorates and Departments!"

Shit! thought Charlie. "It's all right! You're not betraying anything . . . anyone. All I want to know, to find out, is who killed Ivan Nikolaevich . . ."

"No!" she refused. "If they find out—"

"They won't find out," insisted Charlie, desperately. "No one will find out."

She'd had both hands cupped around her brandy tumbler, but the renewed shaking made it rattle against the tabletop, so she released it. "Ivan Nikolaevich wouldn't want me to talk to someone like you . . . he was loyal . . ."

"He was killed, murdered," argued Charlie, his desperation growing. "And nothing's being done to find out who did it. Why they did it. Officially they're lying: you know they're lying, with stories of Ivan belonging to a gang. Pimping whores. And you know Mikhail Alexandrovivh Guzov is FSB."

"I know why they did it," declared the woman, suddenly calm and under control.

"Why, Irena?" pressed Charlie, quietly and controlled. "Why was he murdered?"

"He found out something that he shouldn't have; shouldn't have known about. Tried to do a deal."

"What was it he found out?"

Irena remained silent for a long time, both hands back around her glass, sipping from it once, seemingly unaware of the continued noise from the ice hockey fans. She straightened, suddenly and said, "I'm tired. I don't want to talk anymore."

"You've got this far. Been this brave," pleaded Charlie. "I won't betray you, like Ivan was betrayed." He reached across the table, taking one of her hands away from the glass to hold it to reinforce what he was saying. "I will find out who killed Ivan. And make sure they're punished. But I can't do it without your help. Things went bad for you, both of you, all the time. Don't let this go bad like all the rest, now that you don't have Ivan anymore."

"I need to think. Will think," she said, defiantly.

If he pressed her any harder he'd lose her, Charlie knew. "Promise me we'll talk again." When she didn't reply he repeated, "Promise me!"

"I promise. I'll call the embassy."

"No," refused Charlie. "No more telephoning. Give me a place: somewhere we can meet like this."

There was another long pause. "Here."

"Tomorrow," insisted Charlie. "Give me a time to be here tomorrow."

"I have to work on Sundays."

From the coarseness of the hand he'd briefly held, it could

even be close to manual labor, a machinist in a factory perhaps. "You have a lunch break: you always telephoned at ten past twelve. Let's meet here during your lunch break."

"Twenty past. But maybe not tomorrow. Monday."

"Tomorrow, Irena," insisted Charlie. "Don't run away. If you run away you'll be betraying Ivan Nikolaevich."

"Tomorrow," she finally capitulated.

★

Charlie acknowledged the difference—only four or five first-to-arrive-last-to-leave journalists and one television cameraman—the moment he approached the embassy. There were fifteen press approaches logged in the set-aside apartment, none of them from Svetlana Modin. And Mikhail Guzov had not returned his early-morning call, although waiting for him was a torn-off TASS news agency release, topped by Halliday's name and six exclamation marks, of an official Interior Ministry statement expanding its earlier claim that the British embassy murder had been solved with the arrest of a Chechen drug-smuggling gang. It concluded with the further announcement that the planned press conference had been postponed to a date yet to be decided. There were no messages awaiting him from London when he reached the communications room.

He hadn't been forgotten, Charlie reluctantly accepted: just momentarily ignored, put aside because of other more important pressures. He should, he supposed, be grateful for the respite, which to a degree he was, very grateful indeed. The reservation was prompted by his uncertainty about how successful his over-crowded day had been, by comparison.

Charlie objectively scored himself 60 percent out of a hundred from the meeting with Natalia, largely based—despite Natalia's warning not to overinterpret it—upon Sasha's childishly inno-cent remark about being taken somewhere far away from Mos-cow. The 40 percent reduction came from Natalia's continued reluctance to step out into the unknown and Sasha's apparent closeness—or accustomed acceptance—to Igor Karakov. There was nothing he could do, no tweak he could attempt, to improve his self-assessed ratings, until their next contact. But it *had* been right to keep the personal meeting. Sasha had been wonderful and despite her warning, he'd been encouraged at how concerned Natalia had been about him.

Charlie forced his mind back to Irena Yakulova Novikov. Charlie acknowledged that he still had little more than instinct to trust her disjointed story. But instinct had rarely—and never completely—failed him in the past. And the very disjointedness of their conversation rang truer in his mind than a coherently timed and dated account could or would have done. Apart from his own physical safety the most pressing professional problem was finding the slightest corroboration of anything she'd told him. Neither the name Irena Yakulova Novikov nor Ivan Niko-laevich Oskin came up on Charlie's KGB or FSB search of MI5 records, which didn't surprise him because he knew intelligence officers in both organizations always operated under pseudonyms, as did every other espionage and counterespionage body through-out the world: despite publicly identifiable headquarter buildings and publicly named and identified Directors and Directors-General and Chairmen, intelligence organizations did not officially exist to spy and murder and suborn and infiltrate and manipulate. So how could nonexistent entities be staffed by real, flesh and blood people?

Russia's war in Afghanistan! The possibility burst upon him, not the possibility of obtaining a name—Ivan would have oper-ated in Kabul under an identity different even from his pseud-onym at Lubyanka headquarters—but the disastrous Russian incursion gave Charlie one dated marker, and Irena's account of the ambush in which Ivan lost his arm further refined it. Charlie concentrated his Internet search among publicly available and openly provided strategic study groups in America—knowing no such facility existed in the Russian Federation nor the Soviet Union that preceded it—and located the incident in two hours. It was in a newspaper cutting from *The New York Times,* dated March 15, 1989. It was a very short, two-paragraph report, still with no names, but with the identifying fact that three generals—one air force, two army—had been killed at the same time, the only occasion of such a simultaneous loss of three senior officers. A Russian driver also died in the ambush. Ivan was described as a Pashto-speaking Russian interpreter. In a much longer op-ed commentary feature, again in *The New York Times,* the incident was referred to as a turning point in the Russian disillusionment with the war and Ivan more positively identified by his injury being described as the loss of an arm.

Charlie was warmed by the feeling of satisfaction at his instinct proving right, although realistically acknowledging that it barely took him half a step forward. He needed Irena to keep their meeting the following day—and be prepared to talk far more fully—to do better than this. And he wasn't at all sure that she would. He did, though, know that she worked—and possibly lived—within an area very close to the café, with which she was obviously familiar, by getting her to agree to meet him there during a lunch hour. Charlie hoped that she didn't realize how he'd tricked her into disclosing it and giving him the minimal advantage.

27

CHARLIE ALLOWED HIMSELF A DISCOMFORTING HOUR BE-
fore finally approaching the café in which he'd arranged to meet
Irena Novikov. It was less crowded than before, the permanent
sports channel showing a soccer match featuring Moscow Dynamo.
The clothes-cocooned babushka was at the same table and Charlie
wondered if she'd even left the previous night.

Charlie risked the brandy and chose the same table as before,
able from where he sat to watch the café clock as well as the door.
There had only been six press calls and two rambling cranks
when he'd checked the embassy earlier. But nothing from Mikhail
Guzov, Svetlana Modin, or London, which gave a chance for him
to consider how to utilize each, when they came. And how to
prompt them, if they didn't. It was 12:15 according to the café
clock. The place was filling, for the midday break. The majority
of customers wore workmen's overalls and heavy boots, and by
Charlie's estimate more vodka than beer was ordered. The vodka
was in unmarked, unlabeled bottles and very visibly the yellow of
alcohol-concentrated home distillation. Charlie decided he'd been
wise to stay with the brandy.

By 12:35 Irena still hadn't arrived. He'd give her an allowance, Charlie decided: there could be reasons, even for someone
as time-conscious as she appeared to be. How much allowance? A
lot. She'd had to force herself yesterday, constantly wavering;

would have run—avoided things—if he hadn't gently pushed. The noise in the café was irritatingly rising in proportion to the vodka intake. His own brandy glass was virtually empty. He didn't want to lose the symbolic table by going to the counter for another but was tempted. It was now 12:45 and the place was becoming crowded, three people needed behind the counter now, the noise—spiked by shouted outbursts—growing at the soccer action on TV. It wouldn't be easy to maintain unnoticed surveillance outside the café if Irena reneged. After his earlier location reconnaissance Charlie had naturally continued to check the surroundings of the café as he'd approached. It was situated slightly to the right of a far too expansive square directly overlooked by too many Brezhnev-era apartment blocks and house conversions and, illogically, far too few shops or other bars: there were side alleys and streets but insufficient concealing activity among which he could stay unnoticed.

At 12:50, Charlie tilted his chair against the table, to mark his occupancy, and eased his way through the noisy, tight-packed counter crush. That tightness—and the noise—eased during the time he stood waiting to be served and he realized why when he looked again at the café clock registering 1:10 P.M., marking the end of the break.

She'd run, Charlie accepted, as his brandy was finally poured. He'd give Irena the time it took him to finish this drink, maybe even another, but then have to accept what he'd been refusing to contemplate. He'd lost Irena. But only temporarily, he determined, with customary obstinacy. Whatever—however—it took he'd find Irena Yakulova Novikov again and try to convince her again.

And then he saw her.

He was at the edge of the thinning counter group, his first impression only of a figure at his table. Then his vision cleared sufficiently for him to realize who it was. Charlie didn't hesitate, though, but continued on and by the time he reached her the doubts and the reflections had gone.

"Now you're late," he said, relieved that there was no vibrating nervousness today. She was wearing the same coat as the previous night, over what appeared blue canvas work trousers. The auburn hair, no longer covered by the woolen hat, was flecked with gray and in better light, Charlie guessed she was in her early fifties.

"I'm glad you waited." There was even a wisp of a smile but no immediate explanation.

"What would you like?"

"That looks good," she said, nodding to the brandy glass he was still holding.

"Would you like any food?"

She shook her head. With even fewer people at the counter now, it didn't take him as long the second time to get another brandy. There was another soccer match showing on the television screen.

Irena said, "I worked an extra hour, and started two hours earlier this morning, so we'd have the afternoon." She was already smoking her first cigarette.

"I wish you'd warned me last night."

"Last night I didn't intend coming back today."

"What changed your mind?"

"I decided you'd try to find me. And probably succeed, eventually. So it would only be delaying things. I changed my mind about a lot of other things, too."

"Like what?"

"That I don't really care if they do find out and kill me."

It wasn't the answer Charlie expected. Or wanted. "That's depressingly fatalistic."

"No, it's not," she denied. "It's decisive: my deciding what I want to do and will do, get the people who murdered Ivan brought to justice. That's what you've been trying to persuade me to do, isn't it?"

"I'm surprised by the change," Charlie admitted, honestly.

"Let's both hope I don't change my mind again."

"Let's," agreed Charlie, wondering if this were Irena's first brandy of the day. Not trusting the covering sound of the television Charlie came closer over the separating table and said, "You were telling me last night that Ivan had found something?"

"I don't know it all," qualified the woman at once.

"Tell me as much as you do know," encouraged Charlie, gently, unsure which of Irena Novikov's shifting attitudes he preferred.

"It was to do with his job," she began. "It took a very long time for Ivan to get properly well . . ." She stopped, reflectively. "I don't think he ever got properly well. The field hospital operation was botched and there had to be more surgery when he got back to Russia: he spent months in hospitals and after that in KGB recovery and rehabilitation centers and as I'd been dismissed because of how I'd been injured in Cairo—and that they *were* KGB places—I couldn't visit him, even after the KGB became the FSB. He told me later he became convinced that I'd left him because of how he'd look after losing his arm. . . ."

She was straying off on a tangent again, Charlie realized: too soon yet to bring her back on course.

"He was worried, too, that there wouldn't be a job for him when he finally got better, because of the arm," Irena was saying. "But there was a job, although obviously no longer in the field. Everything had become FSB by then, of course. But a lot of the changes were cosmetic, for outside—mostly western—consumption. One of the divisions that didn't change, has never changed since the first name switch from the Cheka, was the Registry and Archives Department . . ."

Charlie felt a lurch of grateful satisfaction at holding back earlier from any interruption but risked it now. "Ivan was assigned to archives?"

Irena shook her head. "Not current, ongoing records, although the division to which he was assigned is always ongoing. Ivan was put in charge of the bureau keeping up to date the official history of the Russian intelligence service, from its foundation under Feliks Dzerzhinsky by Lenin. Ivan was an ideal and very obvious choice, of course, with all the languages he could read and so easily translate."

"What period was Ivan responsible for?" interrupted Charlie again, conscious of his voice sounding almost as hoarse as Irena's in his excitement.

"I'm not sure of the actual dates," said Irena, lighting another cigarette. "I guessed from what Ivan used to say from time to time that it spanned the last ten to fifteen years: it could have been longer. It certainly overlapped the KGB becoming the FSB."

Charlie coughed, to clear his throat, almost frightened to ask the question to which he might not get the answer he wanted. "Did Ivan tell you how he worked?"

"Yes," replied Irena, seeming to know the importance of the demand. "He had to go through all the old, raw case files and distill everything into a comprehensive, consecutive account for entry into the official history of the Soviet and now Russian Federation intelligence organizations." She smiled. "He used to laugh that the remit was always to make it appear that we were the best and always won."

Irena *had* given him the answer he'd wanted! It wasn't actually the key, but it could be a window into the biggest and richest intelligence gold mine in the world!

★

In her seesawing mood swings, one moment appearing confidently determined, the next relapsing into twitching uncertainty, it was as if Irena had geared herself to go as far as disclosing Ivan's job reassignment but then no further, similarly to her abrupt cutoff the previous night. He worked hard at soothing her suddenly returned fears, reluctantly letting the conversation stray from what he was anxious to concentrate entirely upon by letting her ask questions. He explained away his involvement in a murder investigation initially with no apparent intelligence connections as part of the British service's hugely expanded role countering Islamic and other potential political fanaticism, repeatedly insisting there had been no prior identification of Ivan Nikolaevich Oskin—and most definitely not of Irena—before she'd responded to his television appeal.

"You weren't linked to Ivan Nikolaevich by the KGB after your Cairo accident, or by them or the FSB after he was wounded in Afghanistan and spent all the time he did convalescing," reminded

Charlie, in support of his argument. "And not an hour ago, you told me you didn't care if they discovered your involvement anyway. Which I promise you again, they won't!"

"It was easier for me to *think* brave than it is to *be* brave, when I confronted the reality of what it could mean as I talked to you," said Irena, the slur easy to detect in her hoarse voice.

"You can't stop now."

"I want to." She was smoking what had to be her fourth cigarette.

Her conviction wasn't absolute, judged Charlie. "No, you don't. You want Ivan's killers punished."

"I want another drink."

"Let me get you some food, instead."

"The food here's shit."

"We'll go somewhere else."

"You want to be seen with someone with a face like this!"

"You've probably got more reason for self-pity than most, Irena. Don't use it to hide behind. Your face isn't disfigured, just marked."

"Bastard."

"Not as much of a bastard as those who murdered Ivan."

Her throat began to work as she swallowed against an outburst, which Charlie was frightened would be yet another breakdown. Instead, seesawing again, Irena said: "Okay."

Charlie was unsure what she meant. Guessing, he said: "So let's go on. Ivan discovered something he shouldn't have seen in the raw case files he was going through to prepare the official intelligence history?"

"Yes."

"What?" demanded Charlie, tensed forward.

"That's what I don't know! *What* it was, specifically."

"What did Ivan tell you?"

Irena hesitated. "You've unsettled me, from what you've just told me."

Charlie smothered the frustration. "What unsettles you from what I've just told you?"

"About political fanaticism."

"Go on," urged Charlie.

"It was political, whatever Ivan discovered. He called it sensational: that was the actual word, sensational."

"But he didn't tell you what it was?"

"No."

"He didn't even give you the slightest indication?"

Irena shook her head. "What he did say was that it was payback time. That what he could get for what he knew would set us up in luxury for the rest of our lives. You know what his words were? That we could get married and live happily ever after."

Charlie remained briefly silent, unsure how to phrase his next question, not wanting to drive her backwards. "You told me yesterday that Ivan was a fixer. How was he going to fix it that you lived happily and in luxury for the rest of your lives?"

Now it was Irena who paused, arranging her words. "He told me he was going to do a deal. That he held all the cards and that they didn't have any alternative but to agree to whatever he asked." The woman gave another humorless laugh. "But they did have an alternative, didn't they?"

Avoid the word blackmail, Charlie warned himself. "Ivan was going to deal, bargain, to keep you both comfortable, for the rest of your lives after you got married?"

"Yes,"

"Because he'd learned something politically sensational?"

"Yes."

"But he didn't tell you what?"

"No."

Charlie was unsure which or what to offer next from his mental selection. "Neither the KGB nor the FSB ever discovered you and Ivan were together, for all these years?"

Irena shifted, uncomfortably. "No, they never did."

"You never lived together? Had the same address?"

Irena stared into her empty brandy glass. "We were going to, of course, after we got married. Ivan said that to do so before wouldn't be safe: that we'd compromise ourselves if we set up home together."

She was lying—lying badly—and Charlie was sure he knew why. "Ivan was already married, wasn't he, Irena?"

"Only on paper. There were no children. It was over years ago, before Cairo even."

"His wife wasn't in Cairo with him, was she? She was kept back here, in Moscow. And again when he was in Afghanistan." Unless husband and wife were both KGB, it had been standard KGB operational procedure to hold spouses hostage in Russia against overseas defection. In the case of husband and wife, their children were detained under the guise of receiving a better education than would have normally been available.

"No. She was always here."

"Which was why you couldn't visit him, when he was repatriated from Afghanistan, wasn't it? It was his wife who was able to visit and his wife to whom he went home when he was finally and fully recovered?"

"Yes."

"Do you know if she's been hurt, killed even, after Ivan was murdered?" Whoever killed him would have torn apart the house or apartment in which they'd lived.

The hoarse-voiced woman sniggered. "The first mistake in your grand deduction! She died, two months ago. She'd had cancer for years. That's why Ivan wouldn't divorce her . . . abandon her, even though we'd been together in every other way for so long. He was a good man: intended to make sure she was comfortable from the money he was going to get."

Could a potential blackmailer be a good man? If Ivan had stayed with a terminally ill wife and undergone all the misfortune than he and his mistress had suffered? "But officially, on all the records and registers, Ivan's address is where his wife lived?"

Irena nodded, not speaking.

"So you must have it, Irena! Whatever it was that Ivan found among the raw files and smuggled out of the Lubyanka, knowing its significance. Yours was the obvious—the *only*—place where it could be hidden."

Irena began to cry at last but soundlessly, without any sobs, tears just coursing down her face, oddly spreading out to wash completely over her scarred left cheek.

"You know more, Irena," directly challenged Charlie. "And I need more, properly to understand. If I don't, everything else you've told me is meaningless."

28

CHARLIE BELIEVED HE NOW UNDERSTOOD A LOT OF IRENA'S topsy-turvy behavior but just as quickly—and positively—decided it would be a bad mistake openly to challenge her further. If he was right—as he was sure he was—the prize, incomplete though it might be, was very close now.

"I think we are beginning to understand each other?" he started out, cautiously.

Irena shrugged, not replying.

Not a good start. "You do trust me, don't you?"

With another shrug she said: "Having got this far I don't think I've got any other option."

Minimally encouraging, but only just, Charlie thought: but he hoped she realized how accurate she was. "Certainly there's no one else who guarantees your safety as I do. But is that all you set out to achieve, Irena, apart from getting those who killed Ivan? Or is there something more?"

She had finally begun looking fully at him but now she turned away. It was difficult to tell, because of her skin discoloration, but Charlie thought she was blushing. "I don't know what you mean."

"It's not a criticism," Charlie said, taking a chance.

"I still don't know what you mean."

The advantage was slipping away from him. "Ivan was good,

wasn't he? Apart from his expertise in languages he was a very good, very competent, intelligence officer?"

"Everything would have been different, better, if he hadn't been hurt as he was in Afghanistan: losing his arm and having to undergo so many operations."

"I know that," sympathized Charlie. "You—and Ivan—had more bad luck than most people suffer. But as good as he was, Ivan misjudged things at the end, didn't he?"

"Do you think I don't realize that now!" she flared.

It wasn't the best opening but he had to take it. "Of course I understand that you recognize it now. And I'm glad you have. Ivan couldn't by himself do what he thought he could, no matter how good he was. You most certainly couldn't, not all alone as you are. You've done the right thing—the safest thing—coming to me. And I really do understand."

"I'm embarrassed," she said, suddenly. "Embarrassed and ashamed."

"Why should you feel either?" said Charlie, soothingly. She was definitely flushed. It wouldn't—or needn't—be long now.

"It was the people who killed Ivan who should have to pay, no one else."

He had to steer everything the way he wanted: in her reluctance, Irena was making things more awkward than they needed to be. "How much was Ivan going to ask for?"

"I don't know," admitted Irena. "A lot, I think, because of how sensational he thought it was. He had the key: knew the full story."

"How much were you going to ask, if you'd got to them instead of coming to me?"

She looked away again. "Do you despise me—think I'm a fool—for imagining I could take over: get the money that Ivan believed he could to set us up, as he thought he could?"

"I'm not going to risk the trust I hope I've now got with you by lying," said Charlie. "I don't despise you, for imagining you could still do a deal for enough money to get you out of where and how you are here, now. Particularly having lost Ivan. But I do think you were foolish, believing that you could succeed where

Ivan failed. And you don't have to feel embarrassed or ashamed in hoping that I'll pay for whatever information it is that you're hiding. There! You didn't even have to ask me."

"Could you . . . can you . . . I mean—"

"I know what you mean," cut off Charlie. "And I won't lie to you about that, either. I don't know if—or how much—money I might be able to arrange for you because I don't know what you've got to sell. But I will make you a promise—and you know I keep my promises—that if it is as sensational as Ivan insisted it to be, I will do my best to get you as much as I can."

"Thank you," she said, clearly uncomfortable despite Charlie's insistence that she had no reasons to be. "Thank you very much."

So far so good, thought Charlie: correct analysis all the way. He had to ensure it went on. "Now I've got to see what it was Ivan found and hid with you, haven't I?"

★

It was yet another of the Brezhnev-era apartments that still disfigure Moscow like the last decaying teeth in an old man's mouth, yellowed and black-stained by neglect. The vestibule stank of piss and shit and the graffiti-daubed elevator was out of order, doubtless rusted and clogged by more of both. The graffiti, and lavatory use continued up the stairs and apart from the normal protest from his feet Charlie was glad he only had to climb three flights. The inside of Irena's apartment was in total contrast to its exterior. The entrance hall gleamed from its obvious constant polishing, as did the living room table and chairs and glass cabinet that displayed its prized foreign travel collection of wine and cocktail glasses.

The shrine to the man Irena had loved was directly alongside, a table festooned by photographs and memorabilia of Ivan Nikolaevich Oskin. He had been an extremely handsome man, blond and blue eyed in the color prints, with high Slavic cheekbones and very even, almost cosmetically sculpted teeth. Irena, who was featured with the man in all the photographs, had also been attractive to the point of being beautiful before the Cairo accident, her hair very dark before the now fading grayness, slim but heavy breasted. There were pictures of them both in swimming costumes on unidentifiable beaches and others, obviously dating from their Egyptian assignments, beside pyramids and of Ivan on a camel. At the very front of the exhibition were three medals, their citations set out before each. The presentation was completed by three obviously recent photographs in which it was virtually impossible to see Irena's burned face or Ivan's missing arm from the way each had posed, the dark, nighttime backgrounds showing white-clothed tables with wine bottles and glasses.

"That was our hobby," said Irena beside him, pointing to the formal pictures. "We loved dancing. Ivan was good at it, even after he lost his arm: it's difficult to balance without an arm but he learned how it was possible. We could dance so well, my holding him, not he holding me, that people never realised his deformity. In the darkness, people often didn't see that I'd been burned, either."

Irena gestured him towards the couch that ran the length of the main window and Charlie hesitated before it, able easily to see the telephone box he'd used for their contact, understanding how she'd been able so safely to see him and know he was alone.

"Would you like a drink?" she asked, indicating the decanter on the open-fronted cabinet.

The vodka was the yellow of home distillation, as it had been in the café. "I'd prefer to see what you were keeping for Ivan."

She was back very quickly from what Charlie assumed to be the only bedroom, carrying a large manila envelope, inside of which were four separate, smaller envelopes in which Charlie guessed Oskin had divided what he'd discovered in the archives more easily to smuggled from the Lubyanka headquarters of the FSB. Each was marked by a symbol Charlie didn't understand until he'd taken out the A4-sized contents and realized the markings indicated a sequence, glad he'd kept the packages separate and was able at once to restore each batch to its original envelope.

The material was photocopies of raw but code-deciphered

traffic, the majority cable transmissions interspersed by hand-written telephone or radio communication. The cabled messages were both timed and dated, enabling continuity, but some of the handwritten notes on them were not and Charlie was even more relieved that he had not mixed up the order. If he had compiled it all together, with no way of knowing how Oskin had established his sequence, it might have actually been impossible ever to work out what the Russian believed to be his sensational discovery.

Every printed cable and every handwritten note or memoran-dum was stamped with the highest security restriction, with its access and readership strictly limited to specifically code-named individuals, both inside the Lubyanka and the sending and re-ceiving field stations. Each code-hidden individual had personally signed their code designation for receipt and dispatch and each inscription had additionally been time stamped. Every document was heavily annotated, and every annotation and comment again personally marked.

There were, in total, thirty-two A4-sized sheets but Oskin had sometimes arranged as many as six original cable slips or handwritten notes on one sheet, both to create some further chronological continuity and to minimize the bulk of what he took from the headquarters building at the end of each smug-gling day.

It took Charlie only minutes to locate from the cable dates the first envelope in the series and put the following three into se-quential order and from those dates to realize that the material was not confined to a strict period of time but covered, in total, a possible range of eighteen years, beginning with a cable sent on December 15, 1991. The date of the final cable was July 24, 2006. At once Charlie was swamped by several realizations, the excite-ment moving through him. Although at that moment he hadn't the slightest idea of its importance, he was physically holding material, albeit once removed from its finger-touched original, not just of a well established and entrenched Russian intelligence operation of the highest, your Eyes Only secrecy, but one that could conceivably be currently ongoing: two entire pages in the last batch were crowded with a total of fourteen undated and momentarily incomprehensible telephone and internal memorandum slips.

Throughout Charlie's initial examination, Irena sat motionless and unspeaking on the nearest chair, her entire concentration upon him. As he looked up, she said: "Well?"

"I've got a lot of copied documents the significance of which mean absolutely nothing to me," began Charlie. So secret were the transmissions that every dispatching *rezidentura* was encoded, in addition to everyone mentioned in every exchange.

"No higher security designation has ever been used before, not by the KGB or any of its predecessors," declared Irena. "That's what Ivan told me."

"I haven't properly read—and even less understood—a single thing I've looked at yet. But if I had the slightest idea even after a dozen readings—no matter how many dozens of times and how many readings—it would still and will always remain meaningless without the identifying code key to those involved and of the various overseas stations, over what seems to be a period of more than fifteen years."

"You telling me it's useless?" demanded Irena, anguished.

"I'm telling you nothing of the sort," denied Charlie. "I'm not telling you anything, in fact, that you haven't already told me—without the code key it's useless: impossible to understand. And probably always will be. At this level of security, it'll be a code known to half a dozen people, probably electronically changed during transmission from the code grid in which it was sent to that by which it was received."

"Your people have got computer as well as human code breakers."

"I'll need to take it all, even for them to try."

"I know."

"I'll keep my promises. All of them."

"You talked earlier about our understanding each other?"

"Yes?" agreed Charlie.

"I want you to understand totally everything I want."

"Yes?" repeated Charlie, the curiosity deepening at another topsy-turvy change.

"What is going to happen to Ivan's body?"

Charlie, who was rarely rendered speechless, was stunned by the question. "I've no idea," he finally groped.

"The Russians—the FSB—have it? Along with their bullshit story of drug smuggling gangs?"

"Yes," stumbled Charlie, for the third time.

"They'll toss Ivan's body into an unmarked grave. Or maybe not even bother, just incinerate it without even a proper crematorium. I want Ivan properly laid to rest."

"What are you asking me to do, Irena?" demanded Charlie, striving for control. "You can't take custody of the body, even though Ivan's wife is dead. You're not legally next of kin. And by trying, you'd identify yourself."

"His body was found in the British embassy," set out Irena, her argument clearly prepared. "At your press conference you twice, maybe even more than twice, explained British participation resulted from the embassy technically being British not Russian territory. I've done research. A body found on British territory is, again technically, the responsibility of Britain, whatever its nationality. I want Ivan's body given back to the embassy and repatriated to England, for a proper, civilized burial. In return for what I am letting you have I want enough money to live well, if not in luxury, which Ivan promised. I want to live in London or wherever Ivan is buried, so that I can mourn at his grave every day for the rest of my life."

"That is . . ." started Charlie.

". . . what I want," finished Irena. "Make it happen for me."

★

Charlie ignored the waiting messages and contact-insistences waiting for him, descending at once to his communications cell in which he remained for more than three hours recounting the approach and final encounter with Irena Novikov, up to and including her concluding asylum demands. He also attached scanned

copies of the thirty-two pages of the stolen KGB and FSB material, designating Director-General Aubrey Smith the sole your
Eyes Only recipient. He did so with increasing reluctance, pride-
fully, even conceitedly, wishing he could have kept everything to
himself until he was able to deliver a complete and comprehending
solution to the murder investigation and the eighteen-year-plus
Russian intelligence operation. But with professional objectivity, he
accepted that he couldn't without the essential code key.

It was not until the end of those three exhaustively concentrated hours that Charlie allowed himself to think beyond the topmost secret Russian intelligence material and its potential
significance, to his physical possession and the overwhelming need
for it to be totally safeguarded. In normal circumstances that would
not have been a consideration, let alone a problem, but with an
apparent spy still deeply embedded within the embassy, circumstances were far from normal. There was no one that he could trust.
Except, as always, himself. But that would require his permanently
carrying everything with him at all times, as he'd briefly carried
it from Irena's apartment, by taxi to avoid the constant danger of
Metro pickpockets if not physical attack and robbery as the assassinated Sergei Pavel had been searched, if not actually robbed.

To pad himself like that again would not only attract the attention of Mikhail Guzov and his watchers outside the embassy
but the quizzical curiosity of everyone, including the undetected
mole, inside it. To carry constantly the thirty-two sheets in a never-
surrendered briefcase, an encumbrance with which he rarely
bothered anyway, would create the same Russian interest and
conceivably FSB robbery, either in a street or far more likely from
his Savoy suite.

Could he chance the complete opposite from permanently
keeping the material with him by creating his own dead letter
drop, an unguarded, insecure hiding place known only to himself? Dead letter boxes, contact caches between spy and controller,
were tried and trusted tradecraft facilities which Charlie had uti-
lized but never trusted, but from which, in objective honesty, he
had never once lost an exchange.

Not a decision he had immediately to make, Charlie reminded himself. Tonight and tomorrow, every available minute of which was going to be devoted to Ivan Oskin's hoard, a briefcase would go unnoticed. As anxious as he was to start his examination, Charlie hoped that any waiting calls wouldn't take much time or throw any surprises.

It didn't take long to be disappointed.

★

"It will probably go beyond postponement," announced Mikhail Guzov when Charlie asked the obvious question. "Everything's resolved, after all. The thought now is to let the court hearing provide all the answers."

Charlie's instant thought was of the disposal of Ivan Oskin's body and Irena's determination that the murdered man should be buried in England. His next and almost as quick awareness was that it would spare him the Russian's intended humiliation. "There are still a lot of questions to which I don't have answers."

Guzov didn't reply at once. "A complete case file is being prepared for you."

The cancellation had to be connected with the Lvov demonstration hijack, Charlie guessed. But how? "I—and through me, London—don't have any evidence that everything has been resolved. Until we do—and there is complete and mutual agreement that it *is* resolved—I am going to work on the understanding that it remains an ongoing, combined criminal investigation. . . ." Now it was Charlie who paused, thinking again of Ivan Oskin's remains. "Which means I expect every item of evidence, including the body to support whatever medical evidence is produced at the trial, to remain intact and available."

"That's ridiculous!" protested Guzov, the condescension finally going. "I've told you how it's all been sorted out. It's over!"

"A lot of accusations were made by Stepan Lvov when he took over your press conference," reminded Charlie. "Won't abandoning it altogether be a virtual confirmation of those accusations?"

"That's a political consideration," dismissed Guzov, badly.

"Canceling altogether an international press gathering intended to illustrate the professional ability of Moscow police isn't a political consideration," easily contradicted Charlie. "That's a militia and special investigatory consideration and decision, surely?"

"I have not been included in the discussions."

"Perhaps you should have been, as much to protect your personal reputation as that of the organization you represent."

"If I'm consulted I will make your opinion known: certainly your belief that the investigation has not been concluded," said Guzov, with forced formality.

Guzov was ducking everything! "This number you left for me to call? It's not what I had before for your Petrovka office?"

There was a further hesitation from the other end. "We've closed down the incident room at Petrovka."

Which effectively ended any further contact, acknowledged Charlie. "I'm keeping everything running here. There could be some reaction to your drug gang announcement. Where shall I courier it to you, if it does?"

"Perhaps you'd call me on this number," said Guzov, after another long pause.

"And perhaps you'd call me when a definite decision's reached about the press conference?" pressed Charlie.

Charlie was glad he'd spoken to Guzov ahead of returning Svetlana Modin's call, sure as he was of a link between the two. The broadcaster instantly answered her direct line, the impatience in her voice going the moment she recognized his. "I'm just about to make the pre-recordings, before going on air."

"Do you want me to call back?" asked Charlie, sure of her reaction.

"No!" Svetlana snatched, anxiously. "We haven't spoken for a couple of days."

"No," agreed Charlie, waiting for her lead.

"Did you see and hear all about my arrest?"

"It would have been difficult not to."

"What about Lvov's move today?"

At last! thought Charlie, hopefully. "I haven't heard about any Lvov move."

"He's demanded more about the covert investigation between Britain and America, pointing out that what London and Washington have so far said isn't a positive denial."

"He won't get a response," predicted Charlie. And wouldn't expect one, he guessed. It was a political stunt, to continue embarrassing the existing government and keep his name and face on international television screens. But it explained the possible press conference cancellation, to prevent it being hijacked a second time by the presidential contender.

"Why not?" questioned Svetlana.

"He's not the Russian president yet," argued Charlie "So why should they respond? Lvov hasn't got authority officially to demand any sort of explanation, nor the right to expect one. He's just keeping up the pressure on the government here because of the election."

"Or perhaps Britain and America don't want to make an outright denial, only later to be publicly caught lying," she suggested. "That's the angle of my exclusive interview with Lvov tonight."

She was trying to authenticate the story he'd implanted in the first place, Charlie realized, smiling at the irony. "Another exclusive! Congratulations."

"You think Britain and America are frightened of being caught lying."

He wouldn't be lying giving her the inference she so desperately wanted, Charlie decided. Why not go on stirring the pot? "No one, certainly not governments, like being caught avoiding the truth, do they?"

She laughed. "Should I draw a conclusion from that remark?"

"I can't see what conclusion you could possibly make from what I've said."

"*Thank* you!" said Svetlana, stressing the sincerity.

"Thank *you*," said Charlie, just as sincerely.

He got safely back to the Savoy in time to see Svetlana's broadcast and to hear her quote his reply verbatim to continue her fact-by-innuendo reportage. But then he remained staring, frowning, at the screen for the unexpected live interview from Washington with an American State Department official who actually identified Stepan Lvov by name insisting that there was no truth whatsoever in any suggestion that the American government or its CIA were conducting a clandestine operation in Russia.

29

CHARLIE WAS MILDLY DISCONCERTED AT GETTING WRONG what he considered an obvious prediction but his success at keeping Svetlana Modin's disinformation pot bubbling outweighed his one miscalculation, and at that moment, there was another uncertainty occupying his concentration above all others. Why hadn't there been another attempt to kill him? He'd certainly taken every precaution. Charlie recognized that despite all the dodging and weaving, a professional assassin would have by now tried again. And possibly succeeded. Had it really been a proper, determined attempt? Or had it instead been intended as nothing more than a warning, a back-off threat?

Still not relaxing, he not only locked the door of his suite but further secured it with the triangular door wedges he always carried to prevent its innocent but unwanted opening by room servicing staff. He cleared the sitting-room coffee table to set out the four separated and sequentially ordered envelopes, working through one at a time. He did not, on first reading, attempt to analyze any one item or message but tried to get a general overview of the entire haul, hoping for a clue to a common direction to their contents, his initial bewilderment growing until he isolated what he believed to be an incongruity. Encouraged by it—and other dissimilarities specifically in an increasing number of other sometimes single-line slips—Charlie made his first but absolutely essential discovery.

He'd begun by assuming that each communication in all four packages was exchanges between KGB—and latterly FSB—Lubyanka headquarters, recognizable from its obvious and unvarying CENTER code identification, and at least five if not more code-obscured foreign field stations or *rezidentura.*

It was only when he separated the slips from the fuller messages that Charlie was guided to the all-important different language terminologies. Every code-deciphered word in every communication was an absolutely literal translation into Russian. But from the awkwardness of that translation, or at least thirty of the smaller slips, they had to have originated from radio intercept of a foreign language. But that's exactly what at least thirty of the smaller slips were, not deciphered from their first-time transmission codes but initially translations from foreign language radio intercepts.

That very first item of December 15, 1991, was not technically a message, which Charlie first construed it to be. The literal translation into Russian appeared clumsily stilted because some of the words didn't have a precise trans-literal match. The first impossible match that Charlie stumbled upon was the phrase *walk-in,* which no Russian would have written. It was tradecraft terminology of American CIA origin that Charlie immediately and easily understood from its adoption by at least four European intelligence organisations, including both Britain's MI5 and MI6. It was a term describing a foreign national approaching an American source to offer him or herself—or information he or she possessed—either for money or ideology. *Asset* was another Americanism, which Charlie picked out from another radio intercept dated February 1992, and knew also to have been adopted by other Western intelligence agencies to mean a foreign national suborned or willing to inform or spy upon his country. Both were sourced from the same KGB field station concealed behind the numeric code 68. The next communication was a reaction from CENTER to the alerting field station allocating the word AMBER as a case code. It included the word "struggle," which at first confused Charlie until he remembered being told by Natalia when they were together in Moscow and he was learning the Russian language to be occasionally used colloquially to mean "search," which appeared as search several more times in messages not only to and from Moscow but to and from a wider spread of field stations, some numerically coded—72, 48, 10, and 58—and others under a variety of worded identifications: AJAX, TROJAN, OMEGA, and MARS. In several, another recognizable tradecraft term, *sleeper,* appeared apparently as a supposition or a suggestion. A sleeper was a committed spy not actively engaged in day-to-day espionage but left buried—sleeping—until the reason or decision arose to wake him to begin work.

Increasingly Charlie came to believe he was looking at a surprisingly simple—although still totally incomprehensible—pattern: rapidly escalating, frustrated KGB alarm confirmed by an equally sharp rise in the secrecy and readership restrictions throughout the KGB and FSB hierarchy. Over the last eighteen months available to him, the access limitation appeared to have been confined to six recipients, with the topmost authorizing and questioning participant identified by the code word ONE, written in words, not numerals, on every your Eyes Only exchange. Throughout the exchanges there were six code series included, which, from experience, Charlie knew to refer not to people but to actual espionage operations.

It was just past three in the morning when Charlie finally straightened, cramped and gritty eyed, from the thirty-two pages finally restored to their specific envelopes, minimally satisfied with what he hoped to have established. By listening in to American intelligence radio traffic, most likely between CIA field stations and their headquarters in Langley, Virginia, the KGB had discovered a Russian mole to whom they'd allocated the code name AMBER, but which possibly had been changed to ICON. That American asset appeared to be operating from within KGB ranks itself and, judging from the rising priority—toward the end verging on panic—of those involved in the hunt for him had as recently as 2006, a period of roughly eighteen years since his first location, had still not been found. And who, over those eighteen years, had disclosed or participated or had information about at least six, maybe more, Russian intelligence operations.

And everything contributed absolutely nothing to any under-standing without his knowing or being able to break the conceal-ing codes. Worse, even. If he were even half right in his interpretation, it raised a dozen more questions instead of providing one single answer.

With whom had Ivan Nikolaevich Oskin tried to trade the gold lode he believed he had found? The most obvious answer was the CIA, to keep their asset protected. But according to Irena, her lover would not have betrayed his country. Could one of the wilder speculations about the embassy murder be true after all, that Ivan had been trying to sell the information to the British but had been stopped and killed by pursuing FSB at his moment of contact? No, rejected Charlie at once. He knew, as an indisputable fact, that Ivan had *not* been killed in the embassy grounds but elsewhere before being dumped where he had been found. And he surely wouldn't have been sent from London—unless, of course, as an intended sacrifice—as totally blind as he had been, if Os-kin's approach had been to the sister service MI6? Not such an easy assurance here because MI6 only cooperated with MI5 if there was some beneficial advantage and MI5 operated on the same imbalanced principle: and if MI6 had had an asset like Ivan Oskin they certainly wouldn't have shared him. But they would have definitely tried to discover his killer, which would have in-volved David Halliday, even if the rest of their investigatory team had been covert. And despite—or perhaps *because of*—the chaos within the embassy Charlie was convinced he would have detected some sort of awareness from the contact he'd had with Halliday. Why were the FSB so anxious to close the murder investigation down with a bullshit story of Oskin being a member of a drug-smuggling gang and Sergei Pavel being assassinated in gangland retribution? It might just be conceivable that the FSB had linked the disappearance over the past near fortnight of one of its own Lubyanka operatives with the embassy murder and wanted to resolve an awkward international problem. Still they, or the uni-formed militia, would surely have wanted to find Pavel's killer? Was he right in believing the material lying on the table before him was about a Russian or KGB defector to the CIA? From what he knew at that moment, there couldn't be any other conclusion. The CIA would unquestionably have killed Oskin instead of paying him off if they believed he knew the identity of their deeply embedded ICON. But they wouldn't have killed him *before* getting what Oskin had taken from KGB and FSB records. And that still left Pavel's murder unexplained. What connection with anything was there in the CIA's attempt to get involved but cut the Russians out of the link-up? If the Agency had killed Oskin, they'd surely want to distance themselves from everything about it.

Their own spy in the embassy! Charlie felt a jump of irritation that the possibility of a connection hadn't occurred to him before now. There most definitely was a hostile source whose activities had reduced the British legation to a laughingstock by remaining undiscovered despite every single person within it being interrogated by the best and most experienced mole hunters in the British service. And Oskin's information was of another undetected spy. Could that be beyond a coincidence—the phenomena he distrusted—and be in some way part of the same enigma? But how? And why? The spy within the KGB had remained undiscovered for eighteen years. The hunt for the British embassy mole hadn't yet been running for eighteen weeks. The connection could only be coincidence, nothing else. Or could it?

Circles within circles, blocking his mind until he was incapable of thinking or rationalizing anything, Charlie decided. As an incalculable number of KGB and FSB minds had seemingly been blocked for eighteen years and the minds of Paul Robertson and his mole-hunters remained blocked.

Which could be an answer to so much! One, Charlie remembered, that he'd actually suspected days ago! Creating for himself yet another circle, Charlie confronted his earlier speculation that while not knowing what it was an answer *to*, the constantly unremitting avalanche of apparently unrelated facts and events was creating an impenetrable mental fog through which it was impossible for him and a lot of other people to focus upon what they were trying so desperately to see! And then he remembered the cliché that had escaped him when the idea had first come to him. No one was being able—or allowed—to see the wood from the trees because of the ever and constantly growing forest in front of them.

★

"The code-breakers and analysts have managed to get some way further than you, while at the same time completely agreeing and confirming every one of your interpretations. But by any assessment not far enough," declared Aubrey Smith, when Charlie finished enumerating his overnight impressions from the Russian intelligence archives.

"How much further *have* they got?" asked Charlie.

"Station code names, which we had on record in our own archives," enlarged the Director-General. "The first mentioned, 68, is—or rather was—Beirut. It was changed to MARS, during the civil war there, so we've got a double confirmation. The KGB field station in Cairo is 72, Teheran is 58. Athens is TROJAN."

"All Middle East, where Oskin worked," identified Charlie.

"The connection's been made here, too. And the fact that Oskin was fluent in the languages in the region."

"Could it have any connection with the Islamic terrorism we're facing?" questioned Charlie. "A sleeper operation conceived a very long time ago, coming to fruition now."

"Not from non-Islamists," rejected Smith.

"He and Irena were actually based in Cairo," Charlie pointed out.

"Also flagged up here," assured Smith. "We've managed, as well, to identify three of the six operations itemized in Oskin's stuff. OPERATION MIDAS was a KGB effort to penetrate the banking links between America and Saudi Arabia. OPERATION OSCAR was to get, through KGB nominees, control of two Greek tanker companies which would have given Moscow a limited window into world oil movements. They tried to extend that oil monitor with OPERATION BORE, which was targeted from Beirut after its code change to MARS, by infiltrating tanker companies worldwide."

"You're talking past tense?" questioned Charlie.

"That's how they got into our archives, the tanker operations particularly: Lloyds of London was an obvious priority infiltrating objective because of its insurance records. All three operations were discovered and blown once we got involved."

"Discovered?" queried Charlie.

"The lead, against all three, came from the CIA."

"Who got it from their KGB asset," completed Charlie.

"Where else?" agreed the Director-General. "By giving it to us they protected him. Incidentally, we also agree with you here that AMBER is the Russian code name for the mole they cannot catch but that they changed it to ICON. And we know that ONE, as the secrecy determination ratcheted up, is the chairman of the KGB himself and continued on into the FSB."

"Making ICON—and the need to uncover him—also number one of the Russian's Most Wanted list."

"Which it would be, wouldn't it, for someone they've known about for eighteen years, done incalculable damage and who they still haven't managed to catch?" suggested Smith. "ICON is up there with the all-time greats in the spy ratings. My guess is they'll have a full-time section permanently hunting him."

"*If* they still haven't caught him?" qualified Charlie.

"The analysts here don't think they have," said Smith. "You didn't mention the gaps in the intercepted CIA radio traffic?"

"Because I didn't isolate them," admitted Charlie.

"I didn't, either," said Smith, equally honest. "Because the gaps were filled with KGB and FSB traffic, giving an impression of unbroken continuity. You did isolate *sleeper*, though. And that's what our provisional assessment is. That the CIA has put ICON to sleep, until they choose to activate him. And while the Russians go on looking for him."

"They—or he—are expecting something big: maybe a transfer back here to Moscow headquarters?"

"It could be," agreed Smith. "The FSB will be going even more frantic at the possibility. Anyone being brought in from outside will be put through more loyalty tests than you can imagine."

"None—or any—of which gets us any closer to understanding why Ivan Nikolaevich Oskin came to be found dead in our embassy grounds," reminded Charlie. "Do the analysts think they've got it all? Or could there be more?"

"No one is going to admit we've got it all in less than twenty-four hours: what I've told you is basic, surface stuff. Of course they're going to go on."

"Any thought of a link up with MI6: maybe Oskin was negotiating with them, even though we know he wasn't actually killed in the embassy grounds. His being dumped there could have been a message to them, although I don't believe the resident MI6 officer here knows anything about it. But it would explain MI6's efforts to get involved, wouldn't it?"

"You've asked the station officer directly?"

"Not since getting this material," said Charlie, sensing the concern in the man's voice. "We obviously discussed it before that. I'm sure he doesn't know anything."

"If MI6 already had Oskin they wouldn't admit it or share anything in a million years. And I don't want to share anything with them or anyone else yet, as I've already made clear. Things are still far too uncertain, both here and where you are."

Aubrey Smith saw this as his way to win the power struggle in London, Charlie recognized at once. "What about Irena Novikov's demands?"

"I'll pay her, of course. How much depends upon the ultimate value of what she's given you. And I could also arrange her asylum."

Smith was ducking the most important part of his question, Charlie acknowledged. "What about the body? She wants the whole package, not part of it."

"It's a technical situation that's never arisen, as far as I am aware. And I certainly haven't had time to discuss it with anyone yet. In fact, I can't think of anyone with whom I *could* discuss it."

"I promised I'd give her a reaction as soon as I could." He'd also promised to make contact with Natalia, Charlie remembered.

"She can't expect a decision this soon on something as complicated as she's asked," complained the Director-General. "Neither can you. What's the situation with this damned Russian press conference that could make us all look absurd?"

"As confused as everything else."

"I'm not sure of the benefit of keeping this joint American-British covert business running. Or using this Svetlana woman," said Smith. "It could be exacerbating a situation that doesn't need to get any worse."

Was that a genuine remark or a way of letting him know that all the recorded conversations were still being forwarded to London? "It generates a little confusion."

"Don't we have enough confusion already?" asked Smith.

"Hasn't it occurred to you that there's almost too much of that coming from somewhere?"

For the first time there was a reflective silence from the London end. "Are you suggesting there's a positive disinformation operation going on?"

"I don't know what I'm suggesting, if anything," avoided Charlie. "It could be a possibility."

"By whom? To achieve what?"

Charlie started to regret beginning the exchange. "I can't answer that, either. Maybe I'm imagining there's some kind of orchestration in a lot of things that have happened."

"Maybe you have," said Smith, his tone indicating the exchange was coming to an end. "I'll get back to you if anything comes up from this end that would take us forward in a more positive way."

"I'd like something positive to move things forward." It *had* been a mistake to offer an amorphous idea without anything to substantiate it, Charlie acknowledged.

★

The embassy was still only waking up when Charlie ascended to its more regular working area, skeleton night staff handing over to the day workers and diplomats, although neither Paula-Jane nor

Halliday were in their offices. That day's unread newspapers—including those brought in on the early-morning flight from London—were still in their undisturbed stack in Halliday's outer, unrestricted access room, the English ones uppermost. Only the *Times* and the *Telegraph* maintained their Moscow coverage and both their single-column stories were on the inside foreign pages, but datelined from Washington, pointing up the unusual diplomatic response from the State Department to Stepan Lvov's demand.

Charlie hadn't expected to find Robertson waiting there when he got to the compound apartment.

"We're well met," announced Robertson. "I was looking for you; the hotel said you'd left at dawn."

"Not quite dawn," said Charlie. "Early, though. You're looking for me?"

"I've slotted you in for this morning."

"What?"

"To come before the inquiry panel. We're getting toward the end: you're among the last."

"After the previous charade? Don't be ridiculous!"

"You can't refuse," insisted the man.

"I can and I do," said Charlie. "And don't fuck about like you did last time, threatening arrest and my being taken back to London under escort."

"I will and I can," Robertson mocked back.

"Go outside for a moment, will you?" Charlie said to the four awkwardly, foot-shuffling telephone monitors witnessing the confrontation.

"You don't have the authority to get them to do that," said Robertson.

"Their security classification isn't high enough for what I am going to tell you."

"Don't be . . ." started Robertson but the bravado faltered. To the other four men he said, "Give us a moment, will you?"

"Something has started that's far more important than my fulfilling some piss-willie regulation that can't apply to me because as you already know I don't come into your time frame. I'm not trying to undermine your authority or what you're trying to achieve here. If you're determined to persist with this nonsense I want the personal order from the Director-General—and I mean Aubrey Smith himself, no one else—to appear again before your panel."

"I insist upon knowing what it is you're involved in."

"You know I am not going to tell you."

"Are you sure you've got the backing in London to behave like this?"

"No, I'm not at all sure," admitted Charlie, honestly. "But it's the stand I'm going to maintain until, again, I'm personally authorized by Smith to tell you any more."

30

IT HAD BEEN A RIDICULOUS DISPUTE, ACHIEVING NOTHING except his being backed by the Director-General, but Charlie didn't believe Paul Robertson would have invited the humiliation of being overruled for a second time. Robertson hadn't made any secret of his resentment at his ridicule of the first examination, or of his uncovering Harry Fish's duplicity. Could it be as simple as the man trying to even a score? Robertson and Fish were, after all, part of the same internal counterintelligence division. Of which, taking the possibility further, Robertson was the director and by association shared some of Fish's caught-out opprobrium. Possible but still infantile, which Charlie found difficult to imagine Robertson would risk appearing.

Unless, of course, the man had been forced into the confrontation. If Harry Fish had been part of the Jeffrey Smale faction in London, it wasn't a leap to think that Robertson was a fellow traveler and part of the same headquarters conspiracy. If Robertson were, he could have been obeying the instructions of the protection-promising deputy director in staging today's debacle. But to gain what? Although he'd guaranteed by his sole your Eyes Only designation that the Director-General would be the only recipient of Irena Novikov's story, the fact that there had been an exchange between them extending over almost three hours would have been visibly evident upon the London transmission log. There was every understandable reason for Smith's enemies to want to discover as quickly as possible as much as they could about such a long conversation. But could Robertson or anyone else have conceivably imagined they'd learn anything from yes or no polygraph answers no matter how cleverly they'd phrased and posed their questions? Perhaps not under the polygraph routine. But they might have believed they'd learn something in a more open, free-ranging session, just as strongly as Charlie believed he would have instantly recognized what they were trying to achieve and amused himself by misleading them. Whatever, Charlie positively decided he wouldn't allow it to grow into another distraction.

Charlie's determination to avoid attracting attention to the contents of the briefcase overwhelmed his preference for comfort and directly after hearing Aubrey Smith's decision—a telephone message from Robertson's inquiry clerk, not personally from the man himself—Charlie quit the compound apartment and its too attentive telephone supervisors, and descended to his original rabbit hutch, employing the door wedges to ensure there was no unexpected intrusion. There was less room here than he'd had the previous night in his hotel suite and it was particularly difficult setting out the stolen KGB material, forcing him to spill over onto the floor.

During his first rereading, Charlie factored in every addition he'd learned that morning from London, more fully realizing the importance the Russians were attaching to the hunt for their traitor by its stalled progress being personally controlled by the chairman, first of the KGB and now the FSB, an echelon he'd never before encountered, not even in anecdotal reference in training or instructional lectures. An asset remaining undetected for so long—even one put into inactive hibernation—was unquestionably of major importance but Charlie found it difficult to accept that the chairman himself would participate. His own Director-General was participating in this operation, Charlie reminded himself. But Aubrey Smith had a personal survival interest as well as the initial circumstances of Ivan Oskin's murder having potential political ramifications, heightened by the bugging of the embassy, and maintained by the huge international media spotlight. Having a CIA informant within the Russian intelligence apparatus, although serious, was far more straightforward and capable, Charlie would have thought, of being handled at a lower operational level. The most obvious and logical conclusion had to be that there were additional reasons— further electronic interceptions not being included in the material he had topping the list—to add to all the other competing unknowns.

Charlie read and reread for another two hours without adding anything more to his list of unanswerable questions and had just, fortunately, packed the envelopes away in his briefcase when there was a knock as well as an unsuccessful attempt to open his blocked door. He pocketed the wedges before he noisily unlocked it for Paula-Jane Venables.

"You make a hermit look like a party animal!" she said, smirking, with her usual coquettishness. Today's designer creation was beige, the top button of the cream shirt beneath the pipe-edged jacket predictably unfastened.

"Needed a quiet time and place to think," dismissed Charlie.

"I tried the compound apartment first."

"I checked your office earlier, too."

"I know. You're on my CCTV. That's why I came looking for you, to see what you wanted."

Charlie hadn't known there was an internal television security system: it certainly wasn't openly visible. "I was just passing."

"Why don't you buy me lunch? Or I'll buy you lunch. We could even arm wrestle for the bill."

He had more than enough time before speaking again to London and possibly Irena if Smith offered anything further to justify talking to the Russian woman. What about endangering her by association? Wasn't it the association with him that had crippled Jack Hopkins? "I don't want to appear ungallant—and I will stand treat—but why should I pay?"

"Because I've got something to tell you that I think you should know. And maybe you'll have something to tell me."

"Your choice of restaurant, as long as it's not the American Café," said Charlie, his curiosity piqued.

"The Pekin, off the ring road: it's a favorite of yours, isn't it?"

The embankment episode still in mind, Charlie insisted they travel separately, checking his own journey for pursuit—which he didn't detect—and glad that if there were a reason to talk to Irena about anything from London, he could do it by telephone and not dance around the Moscow Metro system. Charlie intentionally arrived first at the Chinese restaurant and limited himself to one vodka—clear, not home-brewed yellow—from the aperitif carafe, intrigued by the woman's surprising approach but determinedly refusing any preconceptions. She arrived earlier than they'd arranged, too, at once locating their table and as she crossed toward it, aware of the sexual fantasy of at least five separate male diners, Charlie thought again how similar he found her to Svetlana Modin. Who, he supposed, would expect contact sometime that day.

Paula-Jane accepted vodka, touched glasses, and said, "I'll let you order for me."

Charlie did, and chose Georgian white instead of its heavier red or rice wine. "What makes you think this is one of my favorite Moscow restaurants?"

"You introduced Bill Bundy to it, didn't you?"

Charlie's recollection was that it had been the American's choice. "I don't think he liked it very much."

"He's an all-American steak-and-salad guy, light on the mayo, and I'll open my own mineral water, thank you," she mocked. "He does remind me of you in some ways, though."

"Which ways?"

"Certainly not the mineral water! But you're both always looking to see who's behind you."

"Perhaps I've got more reason for caution than he has."

"You changed your mind about it being a coincidence?"

"Not really."

"I'd still like to think it was."

"You seem to know Bundy quite well?" probed Charlie, wanting to move her on.

"Shouldn't a girl know her own godfather well?"

"Bill Bundy's your godfather?" exclaimed Charlie, in genuine surprise.

"He and my dad went way back, as far as Vietnam: before he met my mother even. We've only really got together here. I couldn't believe it when I heard he was getting a tour here that overlapped with me."

Charlie found it difficult, too, remembering what David Halliday had briefly told him about Paula-Jane's father and wondering why the MI6 man hadn't mentioned the godfather connection. "Is this what you wanted to tell me?"

Paula-Jane laughed. "Heavens, no! I thought everyone knew about Bill and me. I'd even told London, fortunately, before Paul-Asshole-Robertson."

"Why fortunately?"

"Robertson described it as a conflict of interest, which is bullshit: we're both too professional to let work overlap. I think Robertson was made to look stupid by London already knowing about it. He's been made to look even more stupid after his run-ins with you, hasn't he?"

Their food arrived. Charlie shook his head against tasting the wine before they'd finished the vodka. "How'd you know about that?"

"He might be their division director but the guys monitoring your telephones think Robertson's an asshole, too."

If they'd gossiped about that they would have gossiped about the incoming calls, too. And that would have included Irena's. "An informant is hardly necessary in that damned embassy is he: the place is like a twenty-four-hour public address system."

Paula-Jane stopped with a gingered prawn between her chopsticks. "This is terrific! I'm glad I left the ordering to you." She became serious. "And our embassy leak is what I want to talk to you about."

"Talk then," encouraged Charlie.

"I don't believe Robertson is any closer to finding who it is now than he was on the day he first arrived here. I think he's casting around for a way out and you could be it."

"You want to spell that out a little more clearly?"

"He had me in front of his panel yesterday, for the second time since he got sent back. The questioning was concentrated on what I knew of you and Svetlana Modin and disinformation."

"What did you tell them?"

"There was nothing I *could* tell them, was there?" demanded Paula-Jane, rhetorically. "I didn't know—not until then at least—anything about you and Svetlana and disinformation. Which is what I told them and why Robertson pulled what he thought to be the ace from up his sleeve but which proved instead to be up his ass, about Bundy being my godfather."

"You didn't know until *then*, which was yesterday?" questioned Charlie, determined against any missed nuance.

"Yesterday was the first time it was put to me and I didn't understand what I was being questioned about," elaborated the woman. "I do today, completely, from all the other pissed-off people under Robertson's control. And I wasn't the only one called in, incidentally. They recalled Dave Halliday and put him through the same hoop about you and Svetlana."

"I got you called back the first time and as far as I can remember you called me a bastard for doing so," recalled Charlie. "Why are you warning me like this?"

Paula-Jane smiled, extending her wineglass to be filled. "I still think you're a bastard and I wouldn't trust you if the Pope gave you a personal reference. But you were being professional, putting me back in front of Robertson's people. I accept that now although I didn't at the time. What I don't accept is a colleague, even a bastard of a colleague, being set up as Robertson is trying to set you up to cover the fact he can't do the job he's been sent here to do."

"That's very altruistic."

"I'd like to think it's me being professional."

"*Can't* Robertson do his job?"

"He hasn't caught our spy, has he?"

"I don't know. Hasn't he?"

She frowned, pained. "We'd know, believe me!"

"Thank you, for the warning."

"You *are* a bastard, aren't you? I'm not trying to make you into a friend, just to get a free lunch," said the woman, retreating into her more usual shell.

"I didn't mean to sound as I just did."

"Don't you think you're treading a fine line, doing whatever it is you are with Svetlana Modin?" she demanded.

"Every end justifies its means."

"If that end's successful," she qualified. "You think it is being successful?"

"I'm still not yet sure what the end is going to be."

She came forward across the table, her glass cupped between both hands. "Don't you believe your dead man was a gangster, as the Russians are saying he was?"

"I'm still trying to work through their evidence."

"But you're not going back to London yet?"

"I haven't been recalled yet."

"You think you are a decoy—me, too, I guess—for a covert operation between the Americas and people we don't know about?"

"What's your godfather say about that?"

"I told you, we don't talk shop."

"You want me to believe you haven't asked him?"

"I mean he reminded me we don't talk shop when I *did* ask him. He's as ornery a bastard as you are."

"I've been used as a decoy before," accepted Charlie. "I didn't know it then, any more than I know if it's happening now."

"Maybe I should be thanking you after all, for keeping me at arm's length."

"I thought you already have," said Charlie.

"So now I'm thanking you again."

"Which makes us equally grateful, one to the other."

"What are you going to do about Robertson?"

"Watch my back, which as you know I always do," shrugged Charlie, gesturing for the bill.

Paula-Jane grimaced rather than smiled. "I can't tell you how much you remind me of Bill! And lunch was exceptional."

"I thought so, too," said Charlie, wondering if Paula-Jane meant it for the same reasons as he did.

The fuller smile came when Charlie picked up the briefcase as he straightened from the table. "Now that's one way you didn't remind me of Bill, until now. I never had you pegged as a brief-case man."

"It's the militia material I told you I was working through. I need to keep it secure and I don't have a proper office or an available safe."

"We've got an office safe that's as secure as Fort Knox, for Christ's sake!"

"Maybe I could use it when I've finished what I have to do," said Charlie.

★

"It's not looking hopeful," announced Aubrey Smith. "The Americans seem to be using at least three different ciphers, with no obvious linking connection even when they switch between them. Some code-breakers even likened it to ENIGMA, unbreakable without the key."

"I'd hoped we'd moved forward a long way since the Second World War!" criticized Charlie, disappointed.

"It was the best example they could think of to illustrate their difficulty without possessing the key," dismissed the Director-General. "The one advance is that we think AJAX is the CIA director."

"Which would explain the involvement of the KGB chairman," suggested Charlie, thinking back to his earlier uncertainty. "Like for like."

"Exactly, *if* we're right," agreed Smith. "Anything more from your end?"

Charlie shifted in the claustrophobic cubicle, unsure how far he could stretch his response. He still hadn't properly thought through the conversation with Paula-Jane, nor had he completely read Mikhail Guzov's invented murder case file. He said, "I've got to finish what the Russians claim to be their murder solution— the medical stuff particularly—to see if there's anything I can use to get Ivan's body."

"Copy it all to me here," ordered Smith. "You really think they'll surrender Oskin's body, even if you find enough to challenge them? *And* agree to it coming back here, for whatever supposed reason?"

"No," admitted Charlie, flatly. "Neither do I think Irena will cooperate anymore if we don't have some hope to offer her."

"She's already given us what Ivan stole from the archive."

"But that . . ." started Charlie, but was stopped by a sudden thought.

"What?" demanded the Director-General, when Charlie didn't continue.

"I wasn't thinking properly . . . it wasn't going to make sense," hurriedly improvised Charlie. "There doesn't seem to be much progress in the mole hunt here?"

"That's not your priority. Or your remit."

"Nor's it Robertson's to question how and with whom I'm trying to fulfil my function here," said Charlie. It wouldn't be an easy contention to defend if push came to shove. Quickly, to implant the innuendo in Aubrey Smith's mind, he added, "Unless Robertson was acting to your instructions."

"He certainly isn't following my instructions."

Which meant they were from Jeffrey Smale. Charlie decided he'd got everything he wanted out of the exchange and was anxious now to pursue the thought that had belatedly occurred to him. He made an additional copy of the Russian dossier on the murder he scanned in full to London and spent the rest of the afternoon toothcombing through it himself, impressed by how well the Russians had fictitiously woven the murder and dumping of Ivan Oskin's body into the drug-trafficking gang's arrest and claimed retribution killing of Sergei Pavel. Charlie believed he found four discrepancies in the Oskin medical evidence, but judged none sufficient to mount an effective, body-disposing challenge, particularly keeping in mind his conviction that the Russians could—and undoubtedly would—confront him in return with the blood fabrication.

He divided his growing bulk of material between his briefcase and the fortunately concertina-sided folder in which the murder files had been delivered, and after filling the briefcase, carefully rearranged its combination lock numerals, getting to Paula-Jane Venables's office just after five.

"I decided to use your safe for my briefcase," he told her.

"Cleared an entire shelf for you," said the woman, her back to him as she opened it. Over her shoulder, she said: "The combination is 61617E."

"I won't open it without your being present," promised Charlie.

"What about the folder?" she asked, nodding to what Charlie still had under his arm.

"Stuff I've still got to go through," said Charlie.

★

Irena answered on the second ring, the uncertainty obvious despite her usual hoarseness. He said, "I need to see you."

"I've just got in from work. Where are you?"

"In a call box. I've just left the embassy." He hadn't anticipated a Metro madrigal today, he remembered.

"Is everything arranged?"

"No."

"What is it then?"

"I have to see you," he repeated. A means justifying an end, Charlie thought again, reminded of his need to talk to Svetlana Modin.

"Where?"

"Your apartment."

"What if . . ."

"I'll be clear."

"I'm frightened."

"I'll be there in an hour," said Charlie, knowing that wasn't the reassurance she'd wanted. Knowing, too, that he should feel a shit, which he didn't.

31

IRENA NOVIKOV PERCHED ON THE VERY EDGE OF THE window-fronting couch like a frightened bird about to burst into flight, both hands gripped tightly in her lap but unable to stop the fear twitching through her, a nervous tic pulling at the corner of her mouth on the unmarked side of her face. Her eyes were fixed on the folder that Charlie left very visibly on his lap. "There is a problem?"

"A big one." Charlie was wedged on the straight-backed chair, its discomfort matching the ache from his protesting feet at the pursuit-dodging underground train ritual. He was sure he'd identi-fied two people—a man and a woman, working separately—who'd kept up with him for four route switches before he'd managed to lose them, convincing him that the surveillance manpower had been at least doubled to defeat his evasion.

"What?"

"We can't break the code. There's more than one, each of which needs separate unconnected ciphers. And there's obviously a further cipher—again, maybe even more than one—necessary to identify the participants. Without all the keys, we can't open any doors."

"Which proves how important it is: sensational, like Ivan said," insisted the woman. She lighted a cigarette.

"It isn't anything unless we can read it: understand it all."

"What about your code-breakers? They must have decoded *something*!"

"Ivan must have told you more?" coaxed Charlie, avoiding her question.

She hesitated, the nerve in her cheek tugging her mouth into an unintended smirk. "He said Cairo was involved."

"So he must also have told you a lot of the stuff was CIA traffic? That's where a lot of it came from, the CIA station in Cairo."

"He told me some of the early stuff was." She lit another cigarette from the butt of that she'd almost finished, coughing.

"*Told* you? Or *showed* you?"

"Told me . . . showed me some things." Her voice was almost inaudible now.

"He also told you it was sensational?"

"Yes."

"Why was it sensational?" pressed Charlie. "He must have told you why!"

Irena shook her head. "I told you. He said it was too dangerous for me to know."

"Irena, I don't think you're telling me the whole truth." Charlie very carefully kept his voice flat, hinting no irritation or annoyance.

She sat, avoiding his eyes, for several moments before her lips moved, as if forming words, but there was no sound.

"I didn't hear what you said, Irena?"

"People," she managed, in a hoarse whisper.

"What about people?"

"That's why it is sensational. Because of the people it is about."

"Who are they, these people it is all about? What are their names?"

The woman shook her head, the first forcefulness since she'd let him into the apartment. "No! He wouldn't tell me any names. That's what I couldn't know, to keep me safe. Any names."

"You read it all, didn't you?" Charlie openly accused. "Ivan didn't show you *some*; he showed you *all* of it, didn't he? And you looked at it all again, after he was murdered and you'd recognized he was the victim from the description at the press conference from which you got my number?"

The silence lasted much longer this time. At one point, Irena's shoulders started to heave and Charlie was frightened she was going to collapse, but she didn't, although when she looked up her eyes were red from the nearness of tears. "He showed me every-thing and I looked at it all again, when I knew it was Ivan who'd been killed. But I couldn't *read* it because I didn't have the ciphers to understand it!"

Charlie didn't speak immediately, either, knowing the impor-tance of every word in every phrase from now on. "Then there's no way forward. We're beaten."

"No!" Irena protested. "Your code-breakers and analysts haven't had it long enough! They've got computer systems that can do things, calculate things, in seconds. They'll break it, in time! They've got to!"

"In *time*, maybe," agreed Charlie, stressing the doubt.

"What have your people said in London? About me; about what I asked in return for giving you what I had?"

"Everything's possible, once they know what they're reward-ing you for. Which brings us back to time. You know how the Russians are trying to close everything down. Officially there's no reason for me to stay any longer in Moscow, if we publicly ac-cept their story. And I've got nothing with which to challenge their nonsense. And if I'm recalled, with me goes your contact . . . your only chance"—Charlie hesitated, in brief reluctance, before offering the folder across the narrow space between them—"which is why I've brought Ivan's material back to you."

For a moment Irena remained staring in astonishment. "You're not going to do anything? But—"

"London has a copy of everything, of course. And they'll go on trying but I don't know for how long . . . if they'll ever break it."

Irena hesitantly accepted the package, gazing disbelievingly down at it. "I thought your experts would work it out . . . that it was the way . . ."

"So did I," said Charlie, moving to get up from the uncom-fortable chair.

Irena finally burst into tears, hunched forward over the folder, rocking back and forth.

"I'm sorry," said Charlie, moving toward the door.

"Don't go," she pleaded, and stood up.

★

"Why didn't you tell me?" Charlie demanded, when he finished reading what she had brought from the bedroom two hours earlier.

Irena shrugged. "I thought you'd just take it. I don't want to be abandoned. I want to be helped."

There was nothing to be achieved by scolding her. He had it now. Everything. Not everything, he immediately corrected himself. "I'll buy you a ticket: a return, as if you're coming back. And get you a new passport, with a visa we can attach in London. I don't want you coming into the embassy. It's under media siege."

"No. I don't think I could do that."

"I'll need a photograph."

She began gnawing at her lip. "I don't have one."

"You must have something! We can enhance it in London if it's not very good."

She shook her head.

"There's photographs of you there," reminded Charlie, pointing to the shrine and its selection of pictures of her and Ivan together. "We'd have to cut Ivan out."

Irena hesitated. "All right. Then what?"

"I'll call. Give you flight numbers and tell you what to do."

"You won't abandon me, will you? Leave me here now that I've given you all I've got?"

"No, Irena. I promise I won't abandon you."

★

It was past midnight before Charlie finally got back to the Savoy, unencumbered any longer by the folder he had left with Irena, what little he now carried making no curious bulge inside his jacket pocket, glad in his initial moments of euphoria back at Irena's flat that he'd resisted the impulse to alert London instantly by going directly to the embassy. There was the customary hand-holding couple in the hotel lobby and Charlie was sure others watching the embassy would have inferred from such a late return that he had something so vital it had to be reported to London at once. To prevent such an assumption, Charlie sidestepped into the bar and ordered vodka that—unusually—he didn't want. Nothing could have improved his total exhilaration.

Which, unplanned though it was, made the bar stop a good idea: his first place and opportunity to sit and think beyond his almost unbelievable awareness. Ivan Oskin had been right—close to being terrifyingly right—in assessing as sensational what he'd found in KGB archives: could it, Charlie wondered, be *too* sensational? Not his question to consider. Or answer. His remit, the remit he'd insisted upon the Director-General acknowledging not that many hours earlier, was to solve the murder of Ivan Nikolaevich Oskin. Which, Charlie accepted, he hadn't done. Nor would he ever be able to solve it. What he had discovered was the *reason* for the poor, overconfident, desperate man's savage killing and doubtless prior, although unsuccessful, torture. Had Irena come close to guessing the unspeakable agonies Ivan Oskin must have endured without disclosing the whereabouts of what his captors would have been so frantically determined to recover?

Charlie resolved to make her understand: not the horror which would have been so bad that even Charlie didn't think himself capable of fully imagining it. What he'd try to make her understand was how much Ivan must have loved her to have resisted until he'd died rather than tell them where their secret was hidden.

And where it remained hidden, with Irena, because her unknown apartment was still the most secure place until he got her safely hidden away, beyond their reach and vengeance.

Charlie wished he was more confident of doing that. He'd studied her existing Russian passport and was sure that what he had, snug in his inside pocket, was sufficient for what he immediately had to do. His uncertainty was whether Irena could hang on as long as she had to for him to get her safely away from Moscow. His greatest uncertainty was whether he could satisfy everything she wanted, even after that.

The false lovers were still in the lobby when Charlie left the bar after the second vodka. It wasn't until he got to his suite that

Charlie abruptly remembered something else that Irena would insist upon, prompted, he supposed, by their charade. His painfully arduous and increasingly dangerous train hopping wasn't over after all. The familiar warning throb from his left instep told him that he'd overlooked something. And it was essential that he didn't overlook *anything*.

★

"What made you go back to her?" demanded the Director-General. For the first time ever, Charlie detected a quaver in Aubrey Smith's voice at what had taken him three hours the following morning to copy to London.

"A hunch," said Charlie, who wished another one would come as quickly. "It occurred to me when we were speaking yesterday."

"Why didn't you mention it then?"

"I could have been wrong about what she'd kept back."

"Let's hope you're not wrong and the deciphering experts confirm your analysis."

"I am and they will," predicted Charlie.

"If you are right, there won't be any more internal problems at this end."

"What about external? What will we do with it?"

"Not my decision. Our function begins and ends with us advising and protecting the government. Which this certainly does."

"Irena's desperate to get out."

"I'm hardly surprised. You think you've got everything?"

"For our immediate needs," qualified Charlie, deciding not to tell the man why he had to go back to Irena one more time. "A usable passport picture the most difficult. She always stands to hide the burn scars when she's being photographed. Will there be a problem with the copy of a Russian passport?"

"It won't be a copy: it's a genuine, forensically provable document. Which our visa entry and exit stamps will obviously be, as well."

"No problems there then?"

"You sure you don't want to copy everything to me electronically rather than use tonight's diplomatic bag?"

"The bag's safer in the porous circumstances here inside the embassy. And there might be other things I want to include."

"That's how it will come back to you, in the diplomatic bag. You sure she's capable of going through with it?"

"Her training was a long time ago," warned Charlie. "And she's very close to falling apart. The brush contact, to give her the passport, will be the most difficult part."

"You any idea how much surveillance you'll be under, leaving the country?"

"A hell of a lot," accepted Charlie. "And then some. I've tried to cover that."

"What are you going to tell the Russians?"

"That I'm being recalled for consultations. It would help if you could get that officially communicated through their ambassador to their Interior Ministry here."

"No problem," promised the Director-General. "Our forensic science people have picked up some discrepancies, particularly in the medical evidence. But I don't think there's enough for us to mount a serious objection: certainly not enough to get Oskin's body back here."

"I didn't imagine there would be."

"Does she suspect that?"

"No," said Charlie, bluntly.

"You're not to have any contact with her on the aircraft from Sheremetyevo," ordered the Director-General. "Or at Heathrow. You'll probably be under hostile surveillance on the plane and there'll almost certainly be more from the Russian embassy when you arrive here. We'll know her from the photograph you're sending. Warn her she'll be received by a man and two women, as if they're relatives or close friends. She'll be taken at once to a safe house. When it's judged she's really safe, she'll get a house of her own, wherever in England she chooses to live."

"Make sure that none of the three meeting her has any association, past or present, with anyone here at the embassy. Or with me. I don't want any recognition to link me with them and by association with Irena."

"Already ensured."

"What if Irena asks about money?"

"She'll have a tax-free income from an index-linked £500,000. Her eventual house or apartment will be paid for, as will all its services and utilities for the rest of her life. Plastic surgery—to alter her appearance, not essentially for the burn scarring, but that can be corrected if it's medically possible—will be available if she wants it. As well, obviously, as a new, untraceable identity."

"Apart from not having Ivan and his grave to grieve over, Irena should be happy enough with all that," acknowledged Charlie.

"You've done well, Charlie. Bloody well. And not just there. Here."

"There's still a lot—too much—that could go wrong," cautioned Charlie.

"Let's hope it doesn't."

"Let's," agreed Charlie, meaning it.

★

During the waking moments of a fitful night Charlie had mentally arranged his priorities, paramount among them successfully smuggling Irena out of the country but with other uncertainties still to resolve.

Paula-Jane Venables was already in her section of the intelligence *rezidentura*, designer demure in blue, smiling up as if in expectation of his arrival.

"You certainly like early mornings," she greeted, gesturing in invitation to the quietly hissing percolator.

"Coffee would be good," accepted Charlie. "I needed to speak to London early."

"Something come up?" she asked at once.

"I'm going back to London."

"When?"

"A day or two."

"Is it all over?"

"I'm not sure. I'm closing down the compound apartment: its use is over." He smiled up as she brought him the coffee.

"Did anything ever come out of it?"

"It was worth a try."

"What about the postponed Russian press briefing?"

"I've got to speak to the Russians about that. London doesn't seem to think I need to be here for it, even if they reschedule it."

"Doesn't seem to have worked out very well for you?"

"No."

"I'm sorry. Sorry that things weren't easier between us and sorry that it didn't go better for you. You going to have time for me to reciprocate that lunch?"

"There's rarely such a thing as a total success in what we do. And I'm not sure at this moment about the lunch. There might be a few more things to close down."

"It would have helped to have got this one right, though, in the current London climate, wouldn't it?"

"Would have helped a lot."

"You didn't bring your other stuff, to put in the safe?" said the woman, looking pointedly around Charlie as if she might have missed seeing the folder.

"Not quite finished with it all yet," avoided Charlie. "When I was stationed here permanently the diplomatic bag went around four thirty: is that still the departure time?"

"Four thirty on the button: you can set your watch by it." Paula-Jane made a vague gesture to the safe in the corner of her office. "What about your briefcase?"

"I'll pick it up later," said Charlie. "I'll let you know about the lunch."

There was an engaged sign displayed in the occupancy slot of Robertson's inquiry room door so Charlie continued on to the compound apartment. There were only four logged calls, three from Svetlana Modin and one from Mikhail Guzov. Charlie told the two monitoring technicians that he was closing the operation down but hadn't yet told Robertson.

"Everything wrapped up then?" suggested one of the men.

"Something like that," replied Charlie.

★

Charlie chose a public telephone kiosk at random on Deneznyj pereulok, ensuring he had sufficient coin before finally going into the box. The FSB general answered at once, the condescension very evident until Charlie announced he was being recalled to discuss what London considered a combination of anomalies and discrepancies in the Russian material.

"What anomalies and discrepancies?" demanded Guzov.

"I don't know—won't know—until I get back."

"I don't . . ." Guzov started, before correcting himself. "Neither my ministry nor the government expect this to become an unnecessary, possibly embarrassing dispute. As I am sure neither you nor your government wants, either."

"I won't know what my government wants or expects until I return to London," Charlie parried. "I thought it courteous—part of our continuing cooperation—to advise you. It would be unfortunate, for instance, if any more public statements—certainly a reconvened conference during my absence in London—were prematurely made."

"I had hoped you would have understood that there is not going to be a reconvened conference: that everything was going to be left to the court hearing."

"I also hope that will not prove to be a premature decision," matched Charlie.

"When can we speak again?"

"When I get back from London."

"When will that be?"

"I'll call from London, on this number, to tell you."

"Do that," demanded the Russian. "I fear there is a risk of some serious, even politically embarrassing, misunderstandings arising between us. Our forensic medical examiners found some inexplicable anomalies and discrepancies in some of your submitted material."

He couldn't have hoped for a better advantage, Charlie recognized. "Then it's fortunate that all the assembled evidence, particularly the embassy victim, remains for further examination."

Next he called Svetlana Modin, who also responded at once and with similar initial aggression. "We had a deal!"

"There was nothing for us to talk about."

"How did you know? Because I couldn't reach you we couldn't broadcast what I wanted."

Guzov couldn't possibly have reached her, to prompt the questions, Charlie knew. "What was it you were going to say?"

"You're not going to like it."

"Try me."

"That the combined murder dossier is complete, without any English input. And that the spy in your embassy has beaten you. What's your comment on that?"

"I don't have one."

"That's what I'm saying tonight!"

"What about the covert U.S. and British operation?"

"That it hasn't yet been stood down."

"It sounds like you have other, better, sources than me."

"We had a deal, remember?" Svetlana said for the second time.

"The embassy incident room has been closed down."

"Thank you," said the woman, in the belief that she was getting the confirmation she wanted.

"I can always reach you at this number?"

"I want you to."

"It might be difficult over the next couple of days. I'll call when I can."

Charlie's luck held for the third time with Natalia's immediate reply to his call. "I'm going back to London but only briefly. I want to see you, talk to you, before I go." Sure now that the car crash had only been a warning, Charlie was equally sure he hadn't put Natalia in any danger keeping their McDonald's rendezvous, any more than he would be doing now.

"I can't today."

She hadn't refused outright, he thought at once. "Tomorrow, the Botanical Gardens? One o'clock?"

"Not the Botanical Gardens," Natalia refused. "I don't like old memories."

Charlie frowned at the rejection. "Where?"

"The restaurant near the gardens."

"How's Sasha?"

"She's made you another picture. It's a tiger but it doesn't have any stripes. And it's blue."

"Can I buy her a present?"

"No!" refused Natalia. Seeming to realize her sharpness, she added more softly, "We'll talk about it tomorrow."

★

Irena was already in the apartment when Charlie got there promptly at twelve fifteen, opening the door at once to his knock. "It's all there," she said, nodding to the folder he'd left the previous night.

"I'll take that, too," said Charlie, nodding to the shrine. The Russians would never release Ivan's body but at least he could ensure she had her visible memories.

"Why?" she asked, frowning.

"You'll want it with you in England, won't you?"

"Yes, but—"

"I don't think it's a good idea for you to try to carry it out, do you?"

"I hadn't thought . . ." she groped, uncertainly.

"My way's guaranteed. We don't want anything to go wrong, do we?"

"What could go wrong? I don't really want to part with it."

"Luggage gets X-rayed as an antiterrorist precaution. Yours could be opened if the medals showed. Get removed. Trust me, Irena. Nothing will happen to any of it."

★

Charlie got back to the embassy just after three, with ample time to examine the briefcase retrieved from Paula-Jane's safe, together

with what he'd collected from Irena, and pack it into his specifically assigned and wax-sealed and stamped container inside that
night's untouchable diplomatic shipment to London.

"You're taking a lot of care," commented Paula-Jane.

"I always do, just like your godfather, remember?"

When he'd examined it earlier in his rabbit-hutch room, the
combination numerals on the briefcase were set as he'd arranged
them before it had gone into Paula-Jane's safe but the pages of the
Russian murder file were in a different order from how he'd assembled them and two sheets he'd intentionally inserted back to
front from their sequential order had been corrected. And the Savoy suite appeared to be untouched from how he'd left it but every
intrusion trap he'd set had been disturbed by intruders who had
conducted an otherwise very professional search.

Charlie poured himself the generous Islay single malt he
thought he might need and settled himself before his television
in good time for Svetlana's evening broadcast.

32

"IT WON'T WORK NOW!"

"It *will* work."

Irena was teetering on the very edge of hysteria, Charlie recognized. As he'd recognized, in his fury, how Svetlana had spun the broadcast totally to defeat his attempt to discover, from his carefully planted information, who was leaking from the British embassy. Guzov could have been the only source for Svetlana, actually using the words anomalies and inconsistencies in the official British Note to the Russian Interior Ministry, but Svetlana had talked of his being "recalled" to prove her insistence of further deteriorating relations between London and Moscow. She'd also used library film footage of him in a segment, suggesting that Charlie was taking new information back to London.

Charlie said, "It's all going to be as I promised."

"There's a permanent FSB watch at the airport. They'll just increase it: get the manifest naming everyone on board."

"I'm the only person they'll be interested in."

"We'll be associated—too close—when you pass me the passport and the ticket."

"The concentration will be *inside* the terminal," argued Charlie, the exchange that was necessary between them already formulated in his mind. "I will give you a precise time when I'll be arriving *outside*, to within minutes. You get there earlier so that as we go toward the entrance separately we get closer, bunching nearer the door; that's when I'll do the drop. You hesitate, as if you've forgotten something, so that you're nowhere near me when we get into the terminal. I'll do nothing to avoid attention if there is any—attract it, in fact—and you won't even be noticed: we'll *use* the attention, not suffer from it."

"None of this was how you promised it would be," complained Irena, although slightly less anxiously.

"Listen to the promises you are already guaranteed," insisted Charlie, taking his time to list the arrangements in place for Irena's arrival in London.

"You didn't say anything about Ivan's body," she isolated, the moment Charlie stopped talking.

"I didn't mention it because it hasn't been arranged yet."

"I want Ivan with me, in England. I want him buried there, properly; know the place where he'll be."

"He *will* be buried in England," stressed Charlie, hoping he sounded sincere.

"I won't go, leave here, until I know he's already there."

"It's got to be this way—you first, then Ivan."

"It *doesn't* have to be this way!"

"You know it does." He didn't need Irena anymore, Charlie thought, brutally. He'd got everything he wanted from her and there was no way the FSB could find her if she stayed in Moscow, so why was he bothering? Because she deserved better than the way in which she existed: because he *wanted* to. He'd abandoned too many innocent people in the past, but this time he'd do his best to at least get her somewhere better than where—and how—she was now. She'd hate him, he accepted, when she realized Ivan's body couldn't be brought to England—which he didn't think it could—but at least she'd get most of what she wanted. When there was no response from her end Charlie said, "Irena?"

"I don't think I can do it," she declared, sobs snatching at her words.

"You can. You must," insisted Charlie, knowing he had to force her. "Do everything I've told you. The moment you get to London there'll be people waiting at the airport, to look after you, as I've explained. From that moment you'll be safe, forever. It's got to be now, Irena. With me. No one will come back for you if you don't come now. There'll be no second chance."

"I know," she mumbled.

"So be there."

"I'll try."

"Be there."

Charlie was too early for his meeting with Natalia so he filled the time by going nostalgically into the Botanical Gardens that featured so much in their relationship. But wouldn't any longer. There was little more he could say or do to persuade her, all the promises and assurances used up. Could he quit the service, as he'd told her he could? He believed so, even if Natalia didn't. And he would resign. As well as keeping the personal vow never to lie to her again.

There'd be a lot he'd miss but a lot more than he wouldn't, assignments like this in particular. Not that he could genuinely recall any that were as similarly cluttered by what he now recognized clearly to be meticulously planned chaos, the reason for which he at last knew and now understood. What he still didn't know was precisely who those planners were and most important of all, what London would do with the sensation with which he'd presented them.

Charlie was already inside the restaurant, his chosen table so secluded in the corner farthest from the entrance that Natalia didn't immediately see him when she entered, fifteen minutes late.

"I was beginning to think you weren't coming," said Charlie, as she sat.

"I stopped at the gardens, for old times' sake."

"So did I."

She shook her head against an aperitif but Charlie held the waitress to get the ordering out of the way. Natalia appeared as disinterested in the food as Charlie, saying she'd have the same as him.

When the waitress left Natalia took a folded sheet of paper from her handbag and said, "Here's Sasha's tiger."

"You didn't tell me it had red ears." Sasha had strayed over the body outline again.

"They were an afterthought."

"Did you tell her we were meeting today?"

Natalia shook her head. "She wanted to give it to you herself if we bumped into you again."

Charlie held Natalia's eyes. "Does that mean we're not going to?"

"No, it doesn't mean that."

"What then?"

"A compromise."

"What compromise?"

"It said on television last night that you're being recalled. The inference was that you were in some kind of trouble." She raised her hand, a halting gesture, as Charlie moved to speak. "I don't want any details!"

The same fear as Irena of danger by association, thought Charlie. "I'm not in trouble. I expect to be back here in a few days."

"I'm glad . . . that you're okay."

They stopped talking at the arrival of borsch and the red wine.

Charlie said, "It's complicated, though."

"Things that we do always seem to be."

"You still haven't told me what you mean by compromise."

"How long's it going to be, before everything you're here for to be wrapped up?"

"I don't know. A few weeks, say three. A month at the most."

"There's not the difficulty there used to be, moving in and out of Russia," said Natalia. "I'm due leave and Sasha's school is breaking up for their summer recess. It would work perfectly if you'd completed everything in a month. Sasha and I could come to London for a vacation."

"Only for a vacation?"

"I'm not going to rush anything, Charlie. I want to see how I feel when I get there and I want to see how Sasha feels. We won't stay with you but we'll see you a lot and I want to be absolutely sure that it'll work before I make the final decision. If you don't think that's a good idea . . . that I'm not being fair and that it's not going to give me or you enough time, then I'll understand."

"I think—" tried Charlie, but Natalia cut him off.

"I've always been honest with you, but you haven't always been honest with me. So here's my honesty. I do love you, despite all the things that have happened in the past. But we're not starry-eyed teenagers. Love isn't enough. I'm thinking mostly about Sasha, the adjustments she's going to have to make. And we would have to make a lot of adjustments, too, both of us. That's my compromise: how I want us to go forward. As I hope we can."

"That's how I want us to go forward, too," accepted Charlie, at once.

Natalia sipped her wine, at last. "I'm glad that's over."

"So am I," said Charlie, meaning it.

"You're really not in trouble, are you, Charlie? That's what I'm really worried about: something happening that would ruin it all." She hesitated. "This is our last chance."

"It's complicated, as I told you." There wasn't a complication he couldn't overcome after this: literally everything was falling into place exactly as he wanted.

Which it continued to do, with minor exceptions, throughout the rest of the day.

Charlie was anxious to limit the time he spent that afternoon at the embassy. He sent a courtesy memo to Peter Maidment advising the acting ambassador of his return to London, carefully omitting departure and return dates and was glad that Paula-Jane Venables's absence from the *rezidentura* spared her assuming he was leaving the following day from his vagueness about her outstanding luncheon invitation. David Halliday wasn't in his section, either, but the newspapers were: Svetlana Modin's broadcast the previous night was yet again the basis for most of the print media coverage. His return to London—all using the word "recall"—confirmed an increasingly deepening disagreement between London and Moscow over the murder investigation. All reported the refusal of the Russian Interior Ministry to make any comment. Charlie didn't encounter Paul Robertson, either, and didn't try to locate the man.

Irena Novikov's passport arrived as promised in the diplomatic bag but separately from the preliminary forensic report Charlie had asked to be conducted on the briefcase and the Russian murder dossier it had contained. On both the dossier and the briefcase there were five different and fresh sets of fingerprints. There was also sufficient surviving residual finger sweat hopefully to provide DNA traces. One of the five sets was identified as Charlie's, from their being recorded on his personnel records. The other provable prints were Paula-Jane's.

On his way back to the Savoy, Charlie weighed the potential advantages against disadvantages of making contact with Svetlana Modin, and decided not to bother. There wasn't anything, either half true or totally invented, that might benefit him and he was determined not to risk anything that might further disorientate or unsettle Irena Novikov.

Would it take a month to conclude it all, as he'd told Natalia? Not everything, he accepted. To conclude everything, he'd have to identify Ivan Oskin's killers and he'd already acknowledged he'd never be able to do that. So it could even be as little as two weeks. He'd take leave directly afterward. He wanted to be free of any distraction or intrusion when Natalia and Sasha were in London. He'd have to get the right hotel: a suite, not a room, but not overwhelm them, as Natalia so often complained he did. Maybe not an hotel at all. Perhaps she'd prefer a short-term sublet apartment in which they could live more as they did in Moscow, and Natalia could get a better experience of what living in London would be like. They didn't necessarily have to live in London, not if Natalia didn't want to. That was another possible idea! Rent a car and drive around England, showing them the countryside and the beaches as well as the London tourist sites. They most certainly would never see the graffiti-daubed Vauxhall council isolation flat in which he lived during assignments.

David Halliday was already in the bar when Charlie entered, on the stool next to Charlie's accustomed corner seat, turning in greeting when he saw Charlie approaching in the bar's back-plate mirror.

"I was going to give you another ten minutes before calling up," said the MI6 officer, nodding to the waiting vodka. "Ordered for you when they told me at reception that you were here."

"Appreciate the forethought," thanked Charlie, as he sat.

"Thought I'd come to say good-bye. We didn't actually get together very much, did we? Pity. Moscow really has changed a lot since the last time you were here."

"There hasn't actually been much time for socializing," said Charlie. "Maybe when I get back."

"When will that be?"

"Nothing's fixed."

"I might not be here, which is why I came tonight," said Halliday. "Lvov's off on a triumphal tour before the inevitable: St. Petersburg, Odessa, south as far as the Black Sea. London's told me to tag along."

"Isn't that getting a little too close?" Charlie frowned.

"That's what I thought—and said—when I got the brief. Theory is that the media entourage will be so large we'll all be lost in the crowd. There's a rumor that the FSB have tried to bug the Lvov campaign headquarters after the conference hijack and that funeral business, and that they might try to derail the tour with staged agitators everywhere Lvov goes."

"*We'll?*" questioned Charlie.

"P-J's coming along as well and for the same reason. I'm to tell you good-bye and sorry about the lunch: maybe some other time and place."

"How'd she know I called by? I didn't go into her outer office to get picked up on her CCTV."

Halliday shrugged, unknowing. "You sure you're coming back?"

"That's the intention. Why shouldn't I be coming back?"

"You must have something a damned sight better than anomalies and discrepancies to face down Guzov!" insisted Halliday.

"We'll see," evaded Charlie.

"I'd hate to be in the wrong place at the wrong time," said the MI6 officer.

"Are you asking me something?" queried Charlie.

"Just a nod in the right direction," suggested Halliday. "Russia's a hell of a big place: takes days to get from one part to another. You think there's any reason for me to stay in Moscow instead of traipsing all over the country on a political ego trip?"

"No reason whatsoever," said Charlie.

"I appreciate the guidance," said Halliday. "And here's my offering, in return. I'm grateful for what you did but Gerald Monsford's as mad as hell you guys kept us out. He's making little wax effigies of you: you ever end up in the same room together, get out as fast as you can. He's a bastard."

"I'll remember that."

Halliday checked his watch. "I need to go; got a six A.M. start tomorrow. If we do overlap when we get back I'll definitely say thank you in a more tangible way. And Charlie . . ."

"What?"

"I'm sure as hell glad the embankment business was a coincidence, although I'm obviously sorry about Jack Hopkins."

"Thanks."

Svetlana made no mention whatsoever of the embassy murder on that night's program, which was entirely devoted to the possibility of staged FSB disruptions to the countrywide tour of the Federation by Stepan Lvov, indicating the present government's panic at Lvov's inevitable election.

The following morning Charlie walked the short distance from the hotel to use the telephone kiosk in Red Square.

"Ten o'clock," he told Irena, when she answered.

"I'll be there. I'm all right."

Charlie didn't think she was, from the tone of her voice.

33

BUT SHE WAS THERE.

Charlie saw Irena the moment his taxi joined the last ten vehicles in the final stop-start line to the departure terminal, and was as relieved as he was encouraged. Irena wasn't standing too obviously expectant or searching but fumbling with a baggage trolley, arranging and repositioning her single scuffed, camel-skin suitcase. Her handbag, which he'd examined and agreed perfect for their brush contact drop when he'd picked up the shrine objects, was exactly where he'd rehearsed her to put it, too, on the right of the trolley handle but at that moment with the top-opening zip only half undone.

Charlie abruptly ordered his cab to stop about five yards from where she had put herself, the sudden braking getting the horn blast he wanted. To give her further time to locate him, Charlie twice queried the charge, knowing that she had seen him and was walking in his direction when he turned toward the terminal with his single case in his right hand, his left hand inside his raincoat pocket, clutching the passport and her ticket in readiness for what he had to transfer to her. He let Irena pass and followed to within ten yards of the terminal entrance before closing the gap between them, able to see that she'd fully unzipped the handbag to gape open as he got level, shouldering into the bottlenecked crush directly outside the door. She showed no reaction to the slight tug she would have felt as he put the passport and ticket he'd bought the previous day into the bag, and in the brief seconds the drop took, he was physically aware there was no nervous shaking. Charlie continued straight on, hoping she'd remember to hold back the moment he entered to a possible ambush.

Which was exactly what he did.

The media frenzy was far more concentrated than he'd feared, a mob surging toward and around him, squawking an incomprehensible babble of questions. He recognized Svetlana Modin moments before the strobe and camera lights burst blindingly into his face, distinguishing her voice through the hubbub, although not what she was saying. Charlie forced his way on toward the check-in desk, shaking his head and repeating "nothing to say" and "no comment" before being brought up short by the check-in line he had to join. Blinking in the whitening lights, his lips opening and closing with his nothing-to-say mantra, Charlie guessed he'd look like a rare fish species landed from the deepest depths.

It would have been, he later decided, her recognition as the news-breaking leader that finally got Svetlana propelled into the demanding forefront of the media pack, which quietened in expectation of her informed questioning. To do so, she wedged herself directly in front of Charlie, physically cutting him off from the shuffling line. Despite the melee in which he was trapped Charlie conceded—and admired—the expertise with which she adjusted her questions for his "no comment" or "nothing to say" replies virtually to confirm what she was asking. Just as he did by remaining tight-lipped, head shaking, and mute, which was his initial reaction, as well as compounding the landed-fish impression. With which he had to live, Charlie accepted. The sole consideration had been to create a smokescreen into which Irena could safely and completely disappear, and Charlie was sure he'd done that.

His flight was actually being called when Charlie finally reached the check-in desk, breathing in like a drowning man coming up for air at the sudden release from the crush. Two plainclothesmen stood beside the counter clerk, the elder completely

bald, the other bespectacled and clearly subordinate. Both scruti-
nized Charlie's ticket and passport before passing each to the
clerk. When Charlie lifted his suitcase toward the loading chute,
the younger man gestured to a narrow gate beside the desk and
said, "Come through here with it, please."

There would be no problem if he missed the flight, Charlie
knew, meekly obeying. By now Irena had to be in the embarka-
tion lounge if not actually aboard the plane, and there were people
to receive her at Heathrow. There certainly wasn't anything to be
gained from protesting. There was a burst of light from behind,
from television cameras recording the latest episode of his personal soap opera. On the other side of the desk, he again followed
the gestures of the younger man into an awkwardly cluttered side
office. The main obstruction was a temporary bench, behind
which the two men positioned themselves, leaving Charlie on the
other side.

"A departure search is usual?" suggested Charlie, feeling that
some innocuous question would be expected.

"Security check," claimed the bald man. "Have you anything
to declare?"

"I'm not an Islamic terrorist but I'm glad you're taking the
risk seriously."

The men were meticulous, individually taking out and examining every item—separating each sock from its partner and
handkerchief from its layer—before feeling for anything a seam
or trouser turnup or lining might conceal. Each item was placed
beside the emptied case for it to be carried to another temporary
but smaller bench to be X-rayed, after which the younger man
repacked Charlie's suitcase with the meticulous care with which
he'd unpacked it.

"I hope I haven't missed my plane," said Charlie.

"You haven't," assured the older man.

Which was true. Everyone else was on board when Charlie
entered the plane, the door closing immediately behind him. To
further separate them on the flight Charlie had booked himself
in business class and as he turned toward it, Charlie saw Irena in

an aisle seat, halfway along the economy section. Charlie refused any food and limited himself to two whiskies, because it wasn't Islay single malt and he expected to be taken at once to see the Director-General.

Charlie hadn't anticipated a repeat of the euphoria at his finally understanding the significance of Oskin's material but he'd at least hoped for a feeling of satisfaction at getting Irena safely away. So why didn't he?

★

"There's a lot of traffic we're missing—a lot the Russians clearly failed to intercept—but enough for us to be sure that you got it right," congratulated the Director-General, the previous day's irritation gone. "It's definitely Stepan Grigorevich Lvov . . ."

"Who's going to become the next Russian president," Charlie broke in.

"Responding to whatever, whenever, and however Washington dictates," completed an interrupting Aubrey Smith. "It's the CIA coup of the century."

When he'd originally been admitted into this rarefied, top-floor sanctuary, the cream and green MI6 headquarters on the opposite side of the Thames at Vauxhall hadn't even been built, remembered Charlie. That visit had been to receive his first commendation: the one he had been promised today would bring his total up to eleven. "No doubt at all?"

"Absolutely none: Washington's confirmed it. And from our own archives we discovered that Oskin was in Cairo at the same time as Lvov. That must be how he picked up on the transmission: he would have known the ciphers of their CIA opposition there. There were three KGB officers on station in the Egyptian capital. The station chief was Valeri Voznoy. A Valeri Voznoy, officially listed as an army general, was killed in the same Afghan ambush in which Oskin lost his arm."

"Bill Bundy, who's been reassigned to Moscow, served in Cairo," said Charlie, recalling their Chinese lunch.

"I didn't know that. But everything fits, doesn't it?"

"No," refused Charlie. "Washington is aware that we know what's going on?"

"The majority decision was that we couldn't let an opportunity like this pass. It got to prime minister—to—president level. We've been cut in on the deal."

"We're going to handle Lvov jointly?" asked Charlie, wanting, as always, to know it all.

"That's the undertaking."

"The Americans wouldn't share anything of this magnitude," insisted Charlie. "They'll cheat and lie: give us just enough to make us think we're included and possibly use us for misinformation, to provide Lvov with extra cover."

"I agree and said so, at every meeting of the Cabinet and the Joint Intelligence Committee," said Smith. "I told you it was a majority decision. Mine was the minority, dissenting opinion."

"Who led the majority argument?"

"Jeffrey Smale, no longer the deputy Director-General. In a fortnight his promotion to director will be confirmed, after his return from Washington to sign and seal the deal."

"What about the embassy murder?" asked Charlie, resigned to the answer but building in time to think.

"We accept the Russian version, and let the frenzy die down and for everything to be forgotten."

"It's still an unsolved murder!" protested Charlie.

"He's a small-time, unimportant KGB clerk, whose mistress is going to live in luxury and safety for the rest of her life," corrected the soon-to-be former Director-General, unusually harsh.

"There's still a mole inside the Moscow embassy," reminded Charlie.

"To find who it is, Robertson will remain in Moscow and keep searching. And while he does, personnel replacement will be accelerated: a year from now those in any sensitive position will have been moved if Robertson fails."

"This isn't right," declared Charlie. "None of this is right."

"Too many things too often aren't," agreed Smith, with no way of properly understanding Charlie's outburst. Charlie didn't understand it himself at that moment: it was an involuntary re-mark to himself—a warning—he had to work out.

He needed a break; time to sift the uncertainties flooding in upon him. He wasn't uncertain about one thing Smith was tell-ing him, though. "What are you going to do?"

"Grow roses in Sussex," said the man, smiling wanly. "And you will definitely get the commendation, I promise you. It auto-matically guarantees your promotion to Grade IV, with an addi-tional £5,000 a year pension entitlement."

"Thank you," said Charlie. It was hardly a devastating end, he accepted philosophically. With Natalia and Sasha soon to be here with him, it was, rather, a decision made for him instead of having finally to make it for himself. This way he would leave the organization and finish up £5,000 a year better off. So why didn't he take the easy way out and let the inconsistencies go? Because it wasn't right. Believing America would keep its prom-ise wasn't right and a lot of what had happened in Moscow wasn't right, and how he'd thought he'd worked everything out wasn't right, and because he now didn't understand any of it anymore and he didn't know what to do to make it right.

"I'm sorry, Charlie," apologized Smith. "It'll look bad, pub-licly, because of all your exposure. But that same publicity would have made things operationally limiting for you, from now on."

"What about Irena?" Charlie asked, anxious to get some order into his confusion. "Does everything I agreed stay, as far as Irena is concerned?"

"Absolutely," guaranteed Smith. "That stuff you shipped back under the diplomatic seal is in the vault, by the way. Under your name and release authority."

"And Jack Hopkins?"

The Director-General looked blankly across his desk.

"The driver who was crippled instead of me, being driven off the embankment road?" prompted Charlie.

The other man's face cleared. "Full pension and medical sup-port, for life. An ex gratia payment of £25,000."

"I'm glad about that," said Charlie.

One of the several working condition improvements Charlie had enjoyed under Aubrey Smith's patronage was a single-occupancy, senior grade office, and Charlie had been there for only fifteen minutes, running all the thoughts and half thoughts through his mind when a call on the dedicated line from Aubrey Smith's office broke into his reflections.

"Seems there's a bit of a problem," announced Smith. "Irena seems satisfied enough with her safe house but she's refusing to undergo any debriefing until she's talked to you about what she gave you."

"That's not right," said Charlie, a man reciting a litany.

"I don't want anything to go wrong with the handover to Smale; give an impression of sour grapes," said Smith, ignoring Charlie's insistent interjection. "You're still officially her Control. Can you sort it out?"

"I intend to," said Charlie.

★

"Never expected—or wanted—to hear from you again," greeted Jack Smethwick, when Charlie identified himself on the telephone. "I submitted a disassociation report, like I told you I would after all that bullshit you had me set up."

"This is much easier," Charlie assured the forensic scientist.

"I'll protest again if it's not; I'm definitely not falsifying anything else."

"I'm not asking you to," said Charlie. "It shouldn't take you longer than an hour."

It didn't. Neither did the next telephone call Charlie made.

34

"I EXPECTED YOU YESTERDAY!" COMPLAINED IRENA, THE MO-
ment Charlie entered the room.

"I sent you a message that there were some things I had to sort
out," reminded Charlie, aware how cautious he had to be. "I'm
here now."

"I don't understand why I had to wait until tonight, either. Or
why I have been brought here," she continued, waving her hand
toward the obvious recording apparatus on the table separating
them. "This is a debriefing room, with the exception of that television, which I also don't understand. I've told you everything I
know; given you all I had."

"You know the bureaucracy of these things," said Charlie,
soothingly, spreading out his hands in apparent helplessness. "You
wanted to see me?"

"Ivan's things; all my memories and mementos. You said you'd
get them here for me but they weren't here when I arrived. I want
them with me, as I had them in Moscow."

"I've got them," promised Charlie.

Irena smiled, unexpectedly, her familiar tension lessening. "I
was frightened something might have happened to them when
they weren't here."

"They're all safe."

"I'm sorry I was rude, just then. But they're all I have . . . they're my life, what life I've got left, I suppose. Can I have them? I'd like to set everything up, as I had it all in Moscow."

"I first want you to see something that's very important," said Charlie, picking up the television control box. He estimated that he had an hour—ninety minutes tops—and the recording ran for ten minutes. Could he get it all, in that time? If he didn't he could, quite easily, be a dead man: he'd never gambled as desperately as this in his entire life and hoped it wasn't showing.

The room was filled with the familiar theme tune introducing ORT's nightly news, backing a montage of Svetlana Modin's recent exclusives before dissolving into a wide, outside broadcast shot of the anchorwoman with the British Houses of Parliament in her background, tightening down into a close-up of Svetlana's face.

"As you can see from the buildings behind me, I am broadcasting by satellite tonight from London, England, a country so recently the subject of so much mystery, intrigue, and speculation from Moscow, following the unexplained murder in its embassy grounds there. Tonight I can solve that mystery, identify the victim, and disclose the most sensational story in the history of modern—or even premodern—Russia. It is that Stepan Grigorevich Lvov, until tonight and until this revelation so confidently predicted to become the next president of the Russian Federation, is and has for almost two decades been an agent of America's Central Intelligence Agency. A spy against the very country he wanted to lead . . ."

Irena broke away from the hypnotism of the TV screen to look at Charlie, bulging eyed, the nervous tic pulling at her open mouth, which moved but from which no words came.

"Had Lvov attained that presidency then he—and the Russian Federation—would have become puppets performing in whatever way the strings were pulled by the president of the United States of America, reducing our great country to a vassal, jump-to-order client state . . ." Svetlana was saying.

The British picture dissolved into a compilation of library footage, dominated by film of Lvov at crowded rallies, at the hijacked

Russian press conference giving his undertaking of openness and cooperation with America, and at the funeral of Sergei Pavel, all the time with Svetlana's voice relayed over. She identified Ivan Oskin as a long-serving Russian intelligence agent and Afghan war hero, who discovered evidence of Lvov's treachery in KGB and FSB records but of his having been detected and murdered by an American assassination team as he tried to reach the sanctuary of the British embassy, believing as he had that it was impossible for Lvov to be working alone but supported by a major but unidentified cabal of suborned Russian spies deep within the Lubyanka. The outside broadcast returned to Svetlana, holding up to the camera a sheet of paper she claimed to be the evidence of secret CIA cables identifying Lvov's code name as ICON. Svetlana concluded that she was broadcasting from London because she'd feared the Lubyanka cabal would have prevented her transmitting from Moscow.

"She was right about that," remarked Charlie, conversationally, inwardly in turmoil at twenty-five minutes having passed since his entry into the room. "That was the full transcript. What was being shown in Moscow was blacked out after about four minutes, just enough time to identify Lvov as a CIA agent and to name Oskin. But the satellite feed came from London and went out worldwide, translated and uncensored to all the TV stations who'd bought the transmission—blind, before its broadcast—on the reputation of her previous exclusives. . . ."

"Do you realize . . . have any conception . . . the destruction . . ." Irena groped, no coherent thought held in her mind.

My destruction uppermost, thought Charlie, completing the woman's thought. "I think I do. I was close to missing it because like everyone else I missed the little things and as an actress you were phenomenal. If you hadn't been so anxious to get your phony shrine back, so that you could destroy it, you would probably have gotten away with it. The message I got was that you wanted the things you'd given me, meaning what I shipped here for you. But then I remembered you gave me the ciphers for the transmitted CIA cables. Which wouldn't have been in the KGB archives, so conveniently close to the cables themselves, would they? It would be unthinkable for them to be together even in an ongoing operation, precisely because it would make it all so easy to understand, as it was easy for me virtually to understand. . . ."

"You're talking in riddles . . . not making sense."

"I think I am making sense, Irena, although that isn't your real name, is it? That phony shrine, which totally fooled me, was your only danger, wasn't it? I'd missed your having the ciphers ready to convince me further and I really did think your shrine was genuine. . . ." Come on, Charlie thought, for Christ's sake, break! Forty minutes had already gone by.

"You're mad . . . gone mad," accused Irena, shaking her head.

"Our forensic people thought all the memorabilia was put together brilliantly," continued Charlie, as if she had not spoken. "Those superimposed photographs of you and Ivan together were fantastic. They really did look as if you and he were a genuine couple. Did you ever really know him? You weren't ever in Cairo together—that camel-skin case was a clever prop, by the way—because we named everyone who was there and they were all men. An oversight but again, one that would have been easily missed."

"Stop it!" demanded the woman.

"None of it would have amounted to a row of beans without your shrine, though. You totally convinced me it was your altar to the man you loved. But then I thought back to the picture I had to have for your passport. That wasn't your real apartment—I realize now it was an FSB operational nest—and you wouldn't have had any individual photographs of yourself there. But instead of promising to find one the following day, you let me cut up one supposedly of you and Ivan together, in happy times. That was your one mistake, although again I didn't realize it at the time, only when other things didn't knit together. Loving him as you convinced me you did, you'd never have let me destroy a picture of you and him together, but you were thinking more of how cutting it up would destroy the evidence of it having been doctored photographically to join you and him together. Which it did. It wasn't until all the other stuff was looked at scientifically that I worked it out." When the hell was she going to crack and fill in all the missing bits!

"I want help . . . someone to get me away from you."

"We'll send you back to Moscow, of course. We've got everything we can possibly get from you. There're no more flights tonight—I've checked—but there's plenty tomorrow."

"No!" she said, her tone audibly different.

He was getting there! Shouldn't rush. "Irena—it's easier to go on calling you that—now it's you who isn't making sense. Why should we keep you here . . . look after you here . . . knowing what we know now?"

"They'll think I told you, not that you worked it out; had the sense to have that fucking shrine forensically examined," blurted the woman.

He'd got her! "Not my problem. You've got nothing more to give me."

"Yes, I have. You haven't got the half of it. I've got all of it."

It took her thirty minutes, running right up to his longest time estimate, and throughout it Charlie remained coiled spring–tight, tensed for the interruption that might still have ruined everything but never came.

When she finished he got as far as, "You'll get everything I promised you. What I—" before the door burst open and the room was suddenly crowded with men.

To Charlie, the leading arresting officer said, "We've got you, you bastard!"

★

One of Charlie's many fears was that he'd be interrogated at the American embassy where he would probably have been denied any opportunity to speak. He wasn't, although there was little comfort in his being taken to an anonymous hut complex at the security-restricted RAF base at Northolt, on the outskirts of London, with the obvious threat of his being put aboard an always-denied CIA rendition flight to the United States or, worse, with

Islamic terror suspects to one of the torture destination flights to Romania or Albania.

But at least it appeared that Jeffrey Smale was chairing the panel of eight unidentified men confronting him. The deputy director was the only man Charlie recognized apart from the Director-General himself. Aubrey Smith was not part of the examining group but ostracized to one side, like a fellow defendant. From the way they were dressed, at least three of the men facing him were American. Charlie's reassurance came from the operator hunched at the recording apparatus on its separate table and that in their urgency to get him before a kangaroo court, his arresting officers had not searched him to discover the video he had extracted from its debriefing-room recording machine seconds before they had swept into the room in which he'd been with Irena.

"Normal formalities are being dispensed with," announced Smale, his usually red, blood-pressured face purple with unsuppressed fury. "You have knowingly wrecked an intelligence operation twenty years in its planning and execution, and caused incalculable harm and damage to the United States of America and to this country. Any recovery or salvation of that operation is impossible but you will provide, immediately, the names of all others with whom you are in contact for them to be detained as soon as possible. Is that clear to you?"

"Time isn't your problem," said Charlie. "You've been saved, all of you, from making the biggest intelligence mistake since the creation of the CIA and possibly in the modern history of either British security service."

There was at least a full minute of total silence before the man next to Smale exploded in an accent confirming Charlie's American recognition: "For Christ's sake, what's happening here?"

Aware of at least six of the arresting officers grouped in a semicircle behind him Charlie extended his arms fully in front of him and said, "In my right, inside jacket pocket is the recording of my debriefing of the woman known as Irena Novikov. If you will not allow me to take it out, to be played to you, I ask that someone does it for me."

"Stay as you are!" came the command behind him and a hand was thrust roughly into his jacket. The man who'd called Charlie a bastard came into view, examining the disc. To Smale, the security officer said, "It's a recording, not a weapon."

"Start it as eighty-four on the use register," Charlie told the recording technician, at Smale's nod of agreement.

Into the room came Charlie's voice: *You've got nothing more to give me.*

Then Irena's: *Yes I have. You haven't got the half of it. I've got it all.*

Charlie: *That's what it's got to be. All of it.*

Irena: *It's my only operation, ever. A lifetime's work, all gone.*

Charlie: *I'm waiting.*

There was no hint of the anxiousness he'd been feeling, decided Charlie, satisfied.

Irena: *The Americans were wrong, as they so often are, about my not having been in Cairo. They simply didn't identify me. Valeri Voznoy wasn't the KGB station chief. I was. My cover was a typist. It was my idea, all of it, after Vladimir Putin left the KGB and became the Russian president. Why can't we become president of the United States of America? I thought. That was my concept. And I chose Lvov, too. We were lovers even then. Bundy was the CIA's Cairo station chief*—a laugh—*That was our first success, making Bundy into the supposed Russian expert, feeding him whatever we wanted. It was genuine stuff, of course, but low level. Everywhere Lvov went, Bundy was transferred with him: the CIA was convinced Lvov was theirs and Bundy was his Control. Lvov fed him the idea of going into politics, using Putin as an example and the stupid bastards fell over themselves: over maybe ten years they've paid us over $20,000,000, all of which has gone into other operations against them*—another laugh—*Christ, they're so gullible and stupid.*

There was a visible shift of discomfort from five of the men facing him, finally identifying the entire American contingent.

Irena: *It couldn't stay perfect, of course. Cairo was the problem, from where it all began. I didn't bother about Oskin or Voznoy, after Cairo. It was only when everything started to go wrong, when it was too late, that I went back through their personnel files and discovered they'd been posted to Afghanistan together. We never found out who suspected anything, although it was no secret that Lvov and I were sleeping together but I suppose it must have been Voznoy: we couldn't interrogate him, because he died in the ambush in which Oskin lost his arm. It wasn't us who killed Oskin—although I would have done, if I'd known the blackmail he was trying to set up. He died under American interrogation and we don't know enough of what he told them, just scraps. Like he didn't go at first to the Americans but tried to speak to the British embassy . . .*

Charlie: *I've got to stop you there. How did the British embassy come into it? Why was Oskin's body dumped there, if he died under American interrogation?*

Irena: *If only we could have known it all, it wouldn't have ended like this: it would have ended with Lvov as the president of the Russian Federation appearing to work for the CIA, as far as they believed, with the American president unquestioningly reacting in whichever way we wanted, because Lvov had supplied them with genuine, low-grade material, for so long. The American president would have been dancing to our tune! I wouldn't have had to improvise so much, give away so much. What we do know is that before he died—of a heart attack, incidentally, not from the bullet to the back of his head that blew his face away—he said he had been to the British embassy. But not who he'd seen or what he said . . .*

Charlie: *Oskin was already dead. Why shoot a dead man?*

Irena: *Probert decided on a mystery: as much confusion and disinformation as possible, according to what Bundy told Lvov.*

Charlie: *How? How do you know this?*

There was a long silence.

Charlie: *Everything, Irena. I want it all.*

There was a further laugh from the woman.

Irena: *I'm not holding out on you. She's not our spy. Not anyone's spy, not properly, I suppose. Just a little gossip who can't keep her mouth shut.*

Charlie: *She?*

Irena: *Your colleague, Paula-Jane Venables.*

Charlie: *You're losing me.*

Irena: *She's been seduced, in every meaning of the word. It started out normally enough, like these things do: an affair—besotted on her part, according to Bundy who couldn't stop boasting to Lvov—between her and John Probert. She's drawn to all things American, her father having been one. She became more than a bed partner for Probert when Oskin talked of going to your embassy before trying to sell whatever he thought he knew to the Americans. She didn't know what it was; she hadn't seen Oskin. But Halliday might have. It was Probert's ridiculous idea to dump the body in your embassy grounds, which was stupid and wouldn't have happened if Bundy had already been in Moscow. But he wasn't, not for another five days by which time it was too late. Probert thought Paula-Jane would be able to get whatever it was from Halliday if the body was dumped literally on his doorstep—don't ask me the reasoning: I don't think there was one, just CIA stupidity—and that it would be an investigation handled by Russian police that would get nowhere because Bundy could get it fixed through Lvov, which he could have done; still tried to. Instead of which you came and refused to have anything to do with the Venables woman and started your own disinformation, which we had no way of stopping. And Halliday didn't have anything to tell her anyway, because it wasn't until Probert got back to the embassy after having the body dumped that he was properly able to read the pages he'd ripped from the gatehouse log of the day he knew Oskin had gone there that Oskin hadn't seen anybody. Neither Venables nor Halliday had been at the embassy. The log note was that Oskin had refused to give a name or a contact when he'd asked to see an intelligence officer, which is hardly surprising, but that he'd call back. Instead he went to the American embassy and told Probert what he knew, expecting to be paid off. But instead he got tortured to death.*

There was renewed and even more obvious discomfited movement from the Americans confronting Charlie.

Charlie: *I still don't understand how you know as much as you do.*

Irena: *Dumping Oskin's body in your embassy was disastrous for me. I didn't have control anymore. But we had an open line into the American embassy, through Lvov's constant contact with Bundy, who in turn milked the Venables woman as much as he could, because he really is her godfather, which he told her to report to your people to avoid any suspicion. But it still wasn't enough for me.*

Charlie: *Who put the bugs into the embassy?*

Irena: *The Americans. Probert could come and go as he liked to see Venables before you arrived: that's how he knew the embassy CCTV cameras were faulty and could dump the body after fixing the distraction for the gatehouse guards that night. Bundy told Probert to do it, with some Russian bugs they'd found in an earlier sweep of their Moscow embassy and electronically tweaked them to their receiver frequency. You found those we put in your Savoy suite, of course? You never talked as I hoped you would for me to get in front, not behind you. I guessed you'd found them and wanted to play against us.*

Charlie: *I never understood the different design, though. How did the bugs get into Stout's apartment?*

Irena: *I told you, Probert could come and go in your embassy, whenever he liked. More accurately he could come and go in the residential compound: your embassy under Sotley's ambassadorship and Stout's nonexistent security was a joke. We needed to cover ourselves against there being a sweep that found the other bugs Probert planted in Stout's apartment on his way from a sex session with the Venables girl. It was easy for Probert to get into Stout's apartment, which she'd pointed out to him and which Stout, of course, never bothered to lock. It was Bundy who persuaded Venables to finger Stout to your spy catchers, after we had Lvov suggest it to him.*

Charlie: *Paula-Jane beat the polygraph.*

Irena: *Bundy laughed about her to Lvov that she genuinely didn't believe she was doing anything wrong, so I suppose she didn't have any guilt taking the polygraph, which is a flawed test anyway.*

Charlie: *Who killed Pavel?*

Irena: *We did. He was a bad choice and I was wrong in not supervising the militia enough, which was how Svetlana Modin came to be arrested later and why we had to stage Lvov's big scene. Pavel was too ready to listen to whatever you suggested, like that ridiculous press conference of yours. Even too willing to go along with you instead of his own force and use public telephones. Our own monitoring at Petrovka fouled up and we were frightened he'd taken some calls we didn't know about. It was easier just to get him out of the way and for Guzov to take over, although he wasn't much better: I had to suggest that your phony blood samples be tested for DNA.*

Charlie: *And you decided to take me over?*

Irena: *Twenty years of planning was all going wrong! I had to get back in complete control. And I was, with a double bluff that would have worked if I hadn't had to let you take that fucking shrine to avoid your becoming suspicious.*

Charlie: *Tell me about the car crash on the embankment.*

Irena: *I was getting desperate, because I wasn't able to take you over. I thought your people would withdraw you if you didn't actually get killed; put in someone else less awkward. The Venables woman, hopefully.*

Charlie: *But I stayed and you were running out of options.*

Irena: *The only one left was for me to get personally involved.*

Charlie: *With your only weakness, the shrine. Which I brought here because I knew we'd never get Oskin's body here and wanted to leave you with something.*

Irena: *My last hope was that you might have packed it in your case. I arranged for it to be searched. If it had been there, the whole operation would still have worked. The shrine would have been seized and I, the grieving woman, couldn't have lived here in Britain without my memories, could I?*

Charlie: *But it wasn't in the case.*

Irena: *I still had one last fail-safe. You wouldn't have gotten Ivan's precious body back, even if you'd tried. I'd made sure of that. All I had to do was get that fucking shrine back, destroy it to stop your discovering it was a fake, and maintain the grieving-woman shit and demand to go back to Moscow to mourn.*

Charlie: *And from the Lubyanka, through Lvov, you'd have led Washington and London along whatever paths you wanted them to follow. You'd have ruled the world.*

Irena: *Not the entire world but America and England would have been enough.*

Charlie: *You'll get everything we agreed but I'd imagine you'll have to properly work for both Washington and London a lot more now.*

Irena: *I think I'd like the plastic surgery to fix the scarring.*

Charlie: *How were you burned?*

Irena: *It was Stepan with me in the restaurant that night. We were celebrating hooking Washington and looking forward to how it would all work out. We stayed lovers, all the time, right up to last week. Marina is a front to satisfy the American need for celebrity: all part of the game plan for a game that isn't ever going to be played.*

The recording clicked off. Charlie broke the following silence. "I'd like to go back to London now. I'm sure no one has any objection."

"You can come with me," offered the Director-General.

35

AUBREY SMITH APPEARED FAR MORE SUBDUED THAN HE'D been when Charlie left him the previous night after a celebration dinner at the Director-General's Pall Mall club that had included two bottles of vintage Margaux and four double-measure snifters of fifty-year old-brandy. Charlie knew the other man had been at Thames House by nine while he'd had an additional four hours to recover.

"It's been a very busy morning," said the Director-General.

"Everything resolved?"

"I don't imagine the Americans would describe it as that but at least they haven't suffered the public humiliation: the good people of Des Moines will still sleep soundly in their beds, believing they are protected by the best intelligence service in the world."

"What about our good people of Barnsley?"

"I've never believed the people of Barnsley have the country's intelligence services in the forefront of their mind."

"And Jeffrey Smale?"

"He's resigned, with immediate effect. His last official duty was to order Paula-Jane Venables's recall from Moscow. We won't bother with any Official Secrets Act nonsense with her: it wouldn't suit any practical purpose. Just the wrong person in the wrong job; should never have been employed in the first place, with her father's background and with a serving CIA officer as a godfather to boot. She was a Smale protégée, by the way. As were Fish and Robertson. They'll both be leaving the service, of course."

"I've never been involved in such an operation before but it all seems to have concluded successfully?" Charlie suggested.

"No, it hasn't," denied Smith. "You won't have heard yet, of course. It's not yet reached any of the wire services."

"What?'

"Svetlana Modin's car was shot up from three other vehicles on her way in from Sheremetyevo Airport this morning. She, a cameraman, and their driver all died instantly. Stepan Lvov's limousine blew up when its ignition was turned outside his hotel in Odessa, about the same time. His wife, campaign manager, and secretary were in the car with him."

"I gave Svetlana back the embarrassing film of her exposing herself, to thank her," said Charlie, reflectively.

"You realize the implications?"

"I think I do."

"Every resource is available to you. Safe house wherever you choose. Everything paid for, of course. And plastic surgery: that will be very necessary, after so much exposure."

"I've never fancied a protection program. I think I'd go mad, trying to be someone else. And whatever precautions there were, I'd still be recognizable from the way I walk with these awkward bloody feet of mine."

The other man didn't smile. "You need to think about it. Think hard. You certainly need to go directly to a safe house from here: totally abandon your apartment. We'll have anything you particularly want brought to you."

"For a few days," agreed Charlie.

"For the rest of your life," insisted the Director-General.

★

Charlie didn't expect Natalia to be at her Moscow apartment but she was, her voice lifting the moment she recognized Charlie's voice. "I've already taken leave and told Sasha. She's very excited;

already colored you another picture. I'm going to buy the tickets whenever you tell me."

"No," said Charlie. "You can't come, not now."

"What's happened?"

"You'll realize why, when you hear the news."

"How long, before we can come?"

Charlie couldn't immediately reply.

"Charlie?"

"Never," Charlie finally managed.